Nicole,
Listen to you
♡ *Amy Stephens*

Don't Turn Back

The Coming Home Series
Book one

Amy Stephens

Chapter 1

Jennifer

"COME ON, COME ON," I mumble then pound on the steering wheel of my car. I look over to see the time on the dash and realize that even if no one were in front of me, three minutes is hardly enough to make it to work on time. I continue riding the car's bumper until I'm able to see the turning lane leading to the hotel I work for.

"Geez, doesn't anyone know how to drive around here?"

Aggravated, I zip into the parking lot only to find that someone has already parked in my spot. *Dang it!* It's not like the employees actually have their own designated spaces, but with our staff being small, pretty much everyone has one they like to call their own.

I drive around the lot trying to find a spot closest to the hotel's front office. It's not that I mind the walk, but I always feel better when I'm able to look out and see my car. I've been working the overnight shift at the hotel for three years now, and you never know what could happen in the middle of the night. It's not the greatest job, but it pays the couple of bills I have, and it works for my college class schedule.

I squeeze in-between two cars, grab my lunch bag, jacket, and book from the front seat, and make my way to the office. As I pass by my "unofficial spot," I notice it's occupied with a rather run-down looking car. A couple of the hubcaps are missing and the paint has started to flake off on the trunk—a classic piece of junk. It's a wonder some cars are even allowed on the freeway these days. I shake my head at the site and walk on inside.

"Sorry I'm running late, Rebecca. I got hung up behind this ridiculously slow driver, and I could never get around them. Then, I get here, and someone's already parked in my spot." I throw my hands up in the air as I apologize. She can tell I'm flustered just from the way I'm tossing my things away in the drawer. "Looks like you've been busy though—the parking lot's full. Were there a lot of check-ins tonight?"

"It's no big deal. Seriously, don't worry about it. Just glad you made it. I was finishing up some paperwork." Rebecca grabs up the couple of pages laid out in front of her on the desk and shoves them into a folder. "Yeah, we're completely sold out for the night. I think there's a group in town that's working on the construction of the new mall. And, well, I might have checked in a couple hot guys, too." Rebecca winks and heartily laughs while sharing this bit of information with me. It doesn't help that she's constantly pointing out my single status, but I know it's all in fun, and she means well. I think she'd do just about anything to fix me up with someone.

"Well, I guess I'll be *checking them out* in the morning then." I giggle. "Literally. Unless they're staying here for a while."

"Come on, Jenn. You know good and well if there's a good-looking guy in this town, he sure wouldn't be trying to stay. He'd be asking for directions to leave," Rebecca adds jokingly.

I nod my head in agreement. She's right about that.

Rebecca and I both attended high school together in Morgantown and remained the best of friends after graduation. Now, it seemed that all the decent-looking guys had moved on to bigger and better things. I'd rarely dated in high school, and it was pretty much the same now. Rebecca, on the other hand, had continued her relationship with her high school sweetheart, Greg. After graduation, he decided to join the Army and is currently stationed in Georgia. She's hoping he'll be able to come home for Thanksgiving when he gets a few days' leave.

Now that we're both in college, not only have we shared a few classes together, but we also work for the same hotel. While she mostly works the late afternoon to evening shift, I work the overnight one five nights a week. We have a really generous boss, too.

We typically have Saturday nights off, so we pretty much hang out together. Rarely do we ever do anything special though. Sometimes we go down to the mall or go watch the latest movie that's playing. And, if we're both just feeling a little wild and crazy and need to unwind, we'll get all dressed up and go out to *Night Moves*, the local club for college kids located next door. It's always nice to hang out with my best friend, no matter what we decide to do.

Although the club mostly attracts garage-type bands trying to break out and get noticed, the owner always books a cover band we all know and love at least once a month, and everyone packs into the club. Greg doesn't mind us hanging out together and is glad to see her doing something rather than sitting at home all alone while he's away.

I pull up the guest registry on the computer and scroll through the list of names. Trying to make it a joke, even though it did irritate me, I ask, "Did you happen to see which guest came in driving that silver Honda that's parked in my spot?"

She's gathering up her things when she turns to look at me. "No, it's been pretty hectic up 'til now. I hadn't even noticed it until you pointed it out. You'll have to keep an eye open in the morning when you start doing checkouts. Maybe then you can politely inform them you didn't appreciate it one bit." She says this with a smirk on her face, then turns to walk towards the door. "Have a good night. Call me if you get bored. I'm going to finish up my report for history class before going to bed, so I'll be up for a while. And I'm crossing my fingers I'll have an email from Greg."

"See you later, chick. Drive safely," I tell her as the door closes behind her. I know Rebecca misses him and I don't envy their separation. Thank goodness he's able to send her emails regularly, and he's remained here in the States. She'd go crazy if he ended up getting deployed overseas.

I walk around the office and straighten a few things. Not that there's really anything out of place, but I'm kind of anal about stuff like that. Rebecca's done most of the paperwork already, so the night's going to pass slowly not having much to do.

I glance out the door and look over again at the car parked in my spot. From what I can see of the tag, it doesn't appear to be anyone local. Not sure why it really concerns me, but I find myself staring out at it several more times throughout the night. The four-door sedan definitely is an eyesore and probably belongs to some old, fat guy. Even from this far away, I can tell how dilapidated it is.

Around two o'clock in the morning, while engrossed in the book I'm reading, I'm startled when a man walks in the door and asks if there're any rooms available.

"I'm sorry, sir, we're full for the night. You can always check with the next hotel over. It's just a few blocks down the street," I tell him, and he nods his head to leave. I always hate having to turn down guests, especially when I know they're tired from being out on the road. But having no vacancy is actually good for the hotel.

Before the door shuts, I hear loud music playing. No doubt, it's coming from *Night Moves*. I'm surprised to hear someone's still playing at this time of morning. By now, they've usually shut down.

There've been a couple of times when a few patrons who've had a little too much to drink have ventured over to the hotel looking for a room. I'm always glad to help someone who realizes they don't need to be out on the road driving. The ones I hate to see, though, are the one's who're just looking for a room for a couple hours because they think they're going to score with some hot chick or random guy they happen to have picked up.

Regardless, I hate turning someone away.

I finish up the chapter of the book I'm reading, then nibble on some chips I'd tossed in my lunch bag—my comfort food to get me through the night.

Finally, the clock overhead reads five o'clock. I'm thankful to see Sylvia, another hotel employee, pull into the parking lot. It's been a long night and I've struggled to stay awake. You'd think after working this shift for so many years I'd be used to it.

Sylvia works the early morning shift, preparing the continental breakfast and the clean-up afterwards. She's married with grown kids and enjoys the extra hours the job allows her to have outside the house. Despite our age difference, Sylvia and I have a great work relationship, and I often look to her as a mother figure since my own family has moved away.

My father recently retired as a college professor. With his announcement, my mom decided she'd retire from her job as a loan officer at one of our local banks as well. They bought a pull-behind camper and a heavy duty pickup truck, sold our family home, and set out to travel the country. Why not? They had worked hard and had successful careers, so they should be allowed to enjoy their time together doing what they'd both dreamed of. The only thing they left behind, though, was me.

I find myself missing them from time to time, but it's also nice not having them constantly looking over my shoulder. I receive emails from them regularly letting me know their latest expeditions along with some photographs of a few campsites. They both seem to be enjoying each other's company—I hope one day I'll meet my soul mate and share the same happiness my parents have had all these years. No doubt, growing up, we were the perfect role-model family.

Finding a soul mate might also keep them from worrying so much about me, too. Both my brothers live close by and are only a phone call away, but with me being the baby, I have a special place in their hearts. You know the old saying, daddy's little girl. They've not been back for six months now, and it's been over a week since I've spoken to them on the phone.

Before they left, as a going away gift to me, they paid a year's worth of rent on a one-bedroom apartment downtown. I know this was a generous gift from them, but I hated knowing they still felt they needed to support me. After all, I do work full-time, and my scholarship covers most of my school expenses.

It's not uncommon to find a little "gift" in the mail from them either. It's usually no more than twenty or thirty bucks, and I always like to do something special with it, like treating myself to a manicure or pedicure. I do pretty good budgeting my expenses, and I've even started my own savings account. You just never know when you might get in a bind. Plus, I don't always want to have to depend on them to bail me out.

"Good morning, Jennifer!" Sylvia calls to me as she walks in the door. This lady always has a smile on her face. She reminds me so much of my mother.

"Morning, Sylvia."

A well-dressed gentleman walks in behind her. He's tall and slender, probably in his late thirties. He passes his room keycard over to me, and I know he's there to check out.

"Did you enjoy your stay, sir?" I try to be warm and friendly to all the guests, despite it being so early in the morning.

"Everything was very nice. Thank you," he replies.

After getting his room number, I hand his receipt over to him and remind him of the complimentary continental breakfast.

"No, thanks. Got to get an early start."

I watch as he walks outside in the direction of the silver clunker that I'd almost forgotten about needing to pay attention to, and climbs into a red pickup truck parked two spots down from it. I should've known from his neat appearance he wasn't the driver of that piece of junk.

I busy myself helping Sylvia with the breakfast and checking out more guests. My office replacement arrives, so I gather up my things to leave. I say goodbye to everyone then walk out the door towards my car. Not that I really would've said anything, but I was a little disappointed knowing I wouldn't get to see the car's owner.

Chapter 2
Brian

I SIT UP AND RUB my eyes. For a moment, I have trouble remembering where I am. I must have slept really hard despite my uncomfortable sleeping arrangement—the front seat of my car.

It'd been after nine o'clock last night when I'd looked down at my gas gauge. I realized if I wanted to drive much farther, I was going to have to stop and get gas or else I'd be stuck on the side of the road. Or, I could pull over for a nap and worry about the gas situation when I woke up. I opted for some sleep since I still had a lot on my mind, right along with a pounding headache.

My girlfriend–I guess I should be referring to her as my ex-girlfriend now—Macy, decided she no longer wanted to be in a relationship with me. We'd had a few words and, basically, she'd told me to hit the road.

I'd been feeling the tension building between us for the last several days, especially because I still hadn't found a job. Sure, I hated having to borrow money from her from time to time when I was between them, but I promised her I'd make it up to her soon. Sadly, what started out as a promising relationship turned sour simply because nothing I did was ever good enough anymore.

Okay, so maybe there is a little more to the story, but who cares about the details? I don't.

Fine, if that's the way she wanted to be, she could have her way. Looking back, our breakup was inevitable. Her constant complaining and whining had begun to get on my nerves. While I really wanted to blame her for our problems, I knew, deep inside, everything had been my fault—just like it'd been with all the others.

We'd been planning a nice dinner with a few friends when the evening had imploded. Macy had discovered a slight oversight on my part and, basically, ended our relationship right there on the spot.

I knew I'd been in the wrong when I'd decided to keep the rent money instead of paying it like she'd asked. I was going to pay it back. Honestly, I was. She hadn't wanted to hear any of my excuses. What was a few days going to hurt? I'd pay the damn late fee for her.

Instead, she kicked me out without so much as a chance to explain. There was so much animosity between us, she'd told me I needed to come back later to get my things because she couldn't stand to look at me for another minute.

The next morning, following our episode, I'd parked just off to the side of the parking lot in the apartment complex and watched as she got into her car to head to work. When I felt it was safe, I pulled up closer and used my key to get in. I guess she forgot I still had it. *Serves her right, that crazy bitch!*

I entered the apartment and pulled a duffel bag from the closet. I grabbed my clothes, even throwing in a few extra things that belonged to her—a blanket, a towel, a pillow, and some junk food from the pantry. I went ahead and grabbed something for breakfast too while I was at it.

I reached on top of the refrigerator for the bread container and popped a few pieces into the toaster hoping it'd be enough to hold me over 'til lunch. I glanced through the pantry for the peanut butter and stumbled across a container with something unusual-looking inside. Laughing to myself, I couldn't believe my eyes. How had I never noticed this before?

I pulled out the folded bills and started to count. It was only four hundred dollars, but since I'd come to the conclusion it'd be best for everyone if I left town, and even though I had no idea where I was headed yet, it was just what I needed to get me started.

Sure, she'd be pissed when she realized her stash was gone, but let's face it, concealing it in the Tupperware container in the back of the pantry wasn't exactly the best hiding spot on her part. Besides, I looked at it as payment for me to get away from her. I tucked the money in my front jean's pocket and didn't feel the least bit guilty about it. By now, I was over it, and her too.

If the fighting with Macy got to be too much, sometimes I'd sleep over at my brother, Jake's, house. One night he'd told me, "Man, just grow up, will you? Get a job, take on some responsibilities, and just please stop being an embarrassment to the family." Yeah, that hadn't felt too good hearing.

Jake had worked hard and saved up enough money to buy himself a fancy new truck. Feeling sorry for his little brother, he passed down his old silver Honda to me. The car had so many miles on it, I'm surprised it still ran, but each time I got behind the wheel, I'd always cross my fingers it'd hold up and get me where I needed to go. So far, the car was still hanging in there, and I was thankful.

Anxious to get away in case someone happened to see me, I threw everything in the backseat, and backed out of the parking spot quickly, causing the tires to squeal on the pavement.

I had no idea where I was going yet, so I figured I'd drive as far as I could until I got tired. I needed to get away from everyone and everything that had turned against me lately. The money wouldn't last long, but it was more than I had before I'd found it. Yeah, she'd regret ever hiding it there.

So I drove. I traveled from one end of the state to the other. I figured it was about as far away as I needed to be to start fresh—away from a whining ex-girlfriend, away from my old life and bad habits, away from anyone who knew me. No one was going to tell me how to live my life. Never again would I suffer through another bad relationship.

Hours later, the red light had come on, a sign the gas was running low. I was tired and had been battling a massive headache for a while now. I was also mentally exhausted. Despite having no set plans, I pulled off the interstate at the last exit before crossing the Alabama/Tennessee state line.

I drove through a couple intersections and pulled into a hotel parking lot. The last thing I wanted to do was draw attention to myself, preferring to park farther out towards the highway, but the only available spot was up front, close to the entrance. A bar or club of some type was next door, so I assumed the full lot was probably from those patrons.

Not wanting to waste any money on a hotel room, especially since I'd already used over a hundred dollars just on fuel alone throughout the course of the day, I figured the parking lot was as good as anywhere for a quick nap. If I could grab a couple hours sleep, I'd be good to go. Who knows, I might even like it here and decide to stay.

As soon as I closed my eyes, I fell fast asleep.

****

It's still dark in the early morning hours. I get out of the car and stretch my legs, my muscles tired and stiff from the drive yesterday and from being in the front seat for such a long time.

I walk across the street to the gas station and into the bathroom. Looking at myself in the mirror, I see just how tired I still look. My eyes have dark circles underneath, and my hair is looking pretty ragged, sticking out in all directions. Good thing I put my baseball cap on before I left the car. My clothes are badly wrinkled, too. I'm pretty sure I could use a shower as well--the last thing I need is to start smelling. Too bad I hadn't thought about stopping at one of those truck stops. I could have gotten a shower there.

After leaving the restroom, I walk over to the beverage section and grab a Coke. I glance at some other snacks displayed, and decide on a bag of chips. Hopefully the caffeine will kick in and help ease the dull pain from my headache that's still lingering from the previous night.

I grab a travel size package of ibuprofen and place everything on the counter. I pull out the wad of cash that's still in my front pocket, oblivious as one of the bills falls to the floor. I hand the guy behind the counter a crumpled twenty. As he's giving me the change, I nod and thank him, never glancing down.

"You must be new 'round here. Never seen you before," the guy says to me.

"Yeah, you could say I'm new here. Looks like a pretty nice place," I reply and grab the bag off the counter. *How the hell am I supposed to know if this is a nice place or not?* At the moment, I'm not particularly in the mood for small talk.

I get back into my car and adjust the pillow before laying the seat back again. It's still got a distinctive smell that reminds me of Macy. I quickly push the thought of her from my mind and drift off to sleep again. Right now, I just want to get rid of this stubborn headache.

I'm jolted awake from the sound, I assume, of a car door being slammed. Rubbing my eyes, I sit up and look around. For a moment, I don't remember where I am. The sun is now brightly shining, and I really wish I could remember where I tossed my sunglasses last night. I glance up at the visor and pat the seat beside me. Nothing.

I notice a couple getting into the car parked beside me and glance in my rearview mirror, pretending to look for something.

While I'm doing so, I notice a young girl, maybe in her early twenties, walk out from the hotel entrance, and is headed straight at me. *She must work here*, I think to myself noticing her uniform top. I follow her in the mirror, then see her shake her head at my car as she passes behind it. I slide down hoping she doesn't see me. The last thing I need is someone asking me questions.

After a few seconds, when I feel it's safe, I sit back up again. I watch as the car she got into pulls out3 and disappears into the flow of traffic.

It's kind of nice not having to be anywhere at any certain time or answering to anyone. With nothing better to do, I get out of the car and lock it up behind me. Might as well start checking the place out.

Chapter 3

Jennifer

I WAKE UP SOME TIME in the middle of the afternoon. At first, I think it's later in the day than what it actually is because the room is dark. Then, I hear rain drops falling outside. This definitely makes for a great afternoon to stay indoors and watch some television. It's Friday, and I don't have any classes today, so I just decide to take it easy. Working nights sometimes throws me off, and I often have to check the calendar just to know what day it is.

I glance over at my phone for any missed calls or texts while I was sleeping and find nothing. I fix myself a bite to eat and grab the remote from the coffee table. After an hour of flipping channels and finding nothing to hold my interest, I get started on my laundry. I'm very fortunate to have my own washer and dryer—it's so much more convenient being able to do it at my leisure, instead of having to haul everything down to a laundromat.

Between loads, I give Rebecca a call at work to see how things are going. Although we work different shifts, I'm glad we're able to spend a few minutes together before she heads home at night.

"Please tell me that car has finally moved from my parking spot," I say while laughing. It's funny that the car became somewhat of a joke between us last night.

"Actually, Jenn, it's still here. It's too bad we don't require the customers to list their tag numbers anymore, or I'd be able to find out who it belongs to."

"You've got to be kidding me," I reply.

"Well, from the looks of it, you're right, it's a piece of junk. I don't know how that clunker made it here in the first place," Rebecca adds.

"Well, make sure it's gone by the time I come in tonight. I want to be able to park up close like always. I'll see you in a little while," I tell her before hanging up the phone.

I run a tub full of hot water, adding a little bubble bath, and soak for a few minutes. As the water starts to cool, I turn on the shower to rinse out my hair. Just one more shift to go before I'm off for a few days.

I put on my typical work attire: red polo shirt with the hotel logo on the front pocket and khaki pants. I allow myself plenty of time to get there should I get stuck behind another slow driver again tonight. Also, with it being the start of the weekend, it's likely traffic will be heavier than usual. Punctuality was a valuable lesson I learned from my parents.

I turn into the hotel parking lot and, sure enough, there it is—the silver Honda. By the looks of it, it doesn't appear to have been moved at all. *Grrr*, I think to myself as I pull into the vacant spot beside it.

I grab all my things and head inside.

"Jeez, girl, I thought you were going to make sure that thing was gone," I tell Rebecca while putting my things away. We both laugh.

"I checked our guest registry and couldn't find any that were staying multiple nights. So maybe someone's just passing through and decided to leave their car here."

"Oh well, I'm sure it'll be gone soon enough. If it isn't, we can always report it to the cops as being abandoned. Heck, maybe it was intentionally left here."

"There's no telling. You'll probably look up later on and see it's gone and never get the opportunity to tell the driver how you feel about them taking your spot. Maybe I should get you a sign with your name on it to put out front just in case this happens again. Instead of one that says "Employee Parking," it'd say "Jennifer's Spot," Rebecca jokes as she gathers her things, ready to call it a night.

"Looks like *Night Moves* is rockin' again tonight," I mention as we both reach the door. The music is blaring loudly and the parking lot is overflowing with cars yet again. There's even a line at the entrance for people waiting to get in.

"Yeah, a big bus pulled in earlier. Must be a well-known group playing tonight. You know, maybe we should plan on going there tomorrow night. It's been a while since we've done anything like that," she adds.

I look over at her with a smile on my face. "Sure. Let's do it. We need a night out."

She walks out the door just as a few cars pull underneath the covered entryway.

****

"Your room number is 311." I smile and pass the room key over to an older gentleman and his wife after getting them all signed in. "If there's anything else you need, be sure to let us know. Our breakfast hours are from six to nine. Enjoy your stay."

I check in quite a few more people and realize the time has definitely gone by faster than it did the night before. Keeping busy sure makes a difference.

I stop what I'm doing when I spot a police car out in the parking lot. It's not unusual for one to ride through, even if it's just a routine patrol to check on things. With *Night Moves* being next door, there've been a time or two when fights have broken out. Usually, though, the owner tries to handle this with his own security staff so the cops don't have to get involved.

The patrol car's lights come on, so I get up and walk quickly to the door. I'm curious to know what's going on. Much to my surprise, it stops right behind the silver Honda. The sliding front doors open, and I step further out onto the portico, curious to see what's going on especially since my own car is parked beside it. Two officers circle the Honda, shining their lights inside.

I knew there was something about that car that made me uneasy.

A few minutes go by, and I see one of the policemen talking to someone—someone *inside* the car!

What the heck? Someone's in there?

Suddenly, chills run through my body. I typically don't get too worked up or scared being here at night, especially since there's a security guard who patrols the grounds, as well as the convenience store directly across the street. He's usually quick to investigate anything that appears abnormal. While I'm watching, I notice one of the officers escorting a young man my way. I remain out front while the other officer pulls the patrol control car up. I recognize him, not just from his patrols here, but from knowing my parents as well.

"Hey, Mr. Benson. What's going on?" I ask before the others are within earshot.

"Evening, Jennifer. Nothing to worry about here. Someone just called in saying they noticed movement in a car in the parking lot. Thought maybe someone had gone into the club and left their kids out in the car," he explains to me. "Turns out, this guy's just passing through. He got low on gas and couldn't get his credit card to work at the pump. He tried to get ahold of someone earlier tonight to wire him some cash, but hasn't been able to reach anyone yet. Thought he could crash out in his car until morning then try to call someone again."

"Oh, okay. Well, that would explain things," I tell him. "I did notice the car here earlier."

"We ran his plates and the car's not registered to him, but to someone he claims is his brother. He's got no proof of insurance but says he can get the information once he talks to him. I'm going to cut him some slack, but he's got 'til then to have the car moved before we have to tow it. Can't just have him hanging out around here."

"Thanks, Mr. Benson, for checking on things," I add, although I don't want to share with him this is the second night in a row the car's been parked here.

The other officer, whom I don't recognize, speaks up and asks if the guy with him can use our phone.

"Sure, let me go behind the desk, and I'll put it on the counter," I tell him.

I make eye contact with the car's owner almost immediately then quickly look away. Much to my surprise, he's actually not bad looking. Not bad looking at all. While he's not what I pictured the owner to look like, he's definitely got potential. His clothes look a little sloppy, but considering he's supposedly been asleep in them, it would explain why they're all crumpled. I'd say he's about my age with dark, almost black hair, and gorgeous, piercing blue eyes. He looks over at me with a slightly crooked smile on his face. He's got a thin build and is probably a good six feet tall. Nope, not at all what I thought.

"Hey, do you mind if I use your phone?" he asks, and quickly looks away. I can sense he feels awkward being in the company of police officers.

"Here, go right ahead." I slide the phone over and walk back to the officers, allowing him some privacy.

I glance back at him a time or two and see him punching numbers into the phone. Although I never see him actually say anything, I start to feel bad for him. Apparently, he's not having much luck reaching anyone.

After several minutes, Officer Benson turns towards him and asks if he's finished yet.

"It's the same thing. No one's answering," he says. "I'm sure I'll be able to reach my brother first thing in the morning though. He and his wife are probably just out for the night."

"Son, I need your word you're going to have this car moved by morning."

I can tell by Officer Benson's tone he's getting a little aggravated with the situation.

"Just give me 'til morning. I promise, it'll be gone."

I decide to speak up. "If it's okay with everyone, I can spare a couple of bucks. I don't mind helping out if he needs gas to get somewhere."

The guy looks over at me, then turns to the cops. I can see what appears to be relief on his face just from hearing my offer. I walk back behind the counter and pull my purse out from the drawer. Luckily, I've got a twenty-dollar bill on me — another gift from my parents.

"Here, it's on me," I say and hand the money to him.

"Thanks, I really appreciate it. More than you know," he tells me, and our gazes lock for a brief moment.

Hoping this settles the ordeal, the officers escort him outside. I hate that he wasn't able to speak to anyone on the phone, but at least he'll be able to move his car. No one wants a run-in with the authorities. I continue to watch until he climbs inside his car. When I see the lights come on, I let out a sigh.

I'm glad the mystery of the car is solved, although I wish I'd had more time to talk to him. If nothing else but to catch his name. The more I think about it, he *was* pretty cute. Oh well, I doubt I'll ever see him again, or my money either. It's okay though. I'm glad I could help him out.

It's been an interesting night to say the least, and I can't wait to share it all with Rebecca.

Chapter 4
Brian

DAMN, I THINK TO MYSELF as I pull out of the hotel parking lot. Those officers were being complete dicks.

I'm thankful they believed my credit card story, especially since no one in their right mind would give me one, but I feel kind of bad taking money from the girl at the hotel. Even though I don't have a whole lot of my own money left, I'm glad she spoke up to help me out. It was bad enough I pretended to be calling someone, but I sure as hell didn't need any more trouble from those cops, especially in front of her. I'm pretty sure she was the same girl I'd noticed watching me earlier, the one who'd walked behind my car and shook her head.

Not wanting to really go anywhere in the middle of the night, I drive around for a little while, taking notice of certain places. Lightning fills the sky off in the distance, a sign that a rainstorm is fast approaching. I pull into a fast food place—one of those that serves a full menu twenty-four hours a day—and park my car in the back. I don't want to draw any more attention to myself, and I figure I'll be safe here amongst the other employees' cars.

Within seconds, drops of rain start to fall. The car windows fog up quickly, so I lay the seat back and get more comfortable. I don't think anyone walking by would be able to see inside now, so I reach for the pillow from the backseat. Tucking it behind my head, I listen to the raindrops landing on the car. Their soothing sound sends me into a deep, relaxing sleep.

The next morning, I drive back to the convenience store—the one across the street from the hotel. I'm not sure why I come back, unless, of course, it has something to do with seeing that hotel attendant again. She appeared friendly enough and was kind of cute. It was hard to tell much about her with her work outfit on, but from what I could see, she kept up with her girlish figure. I'm just thankful she came to my rescue.

It's no longer raining, but there's still a dreariness looming in the sky. Either the sun is slow coming up today, or there's more rain in the forecast.

Before getting out of the car, I look back towards the hotel. There doesn't appear to be too much activity going on yet. If I'm not mistaken, the car she got into was a small black sedan style. I turn to get a better view but still there's nothing. Oh well, she's probably off by now anyways.

Inside the gas station, I pick up a small tube of toothpaste and a foldable toothbrush. I can't believe I forgot mine when I was grabbing things to take with me. The clerk rings up my purchase, and I walk towards the bathroom in the far back corner.

I splash my face with water from the sink. It's icy cold, but just what I need to wake me up. I brush my teeth, then comb my fingers through my hair, noting how long and shabby it looks, before quickly putting my cap back on. It's past time for a haircut.

I grab an orange juice and a snack cake and head toward the front again. Not exactly the breakfast of champions, but it's cheap and should curb my hunger pains, at least for a little while.

"Mornin'." I tell the clerk. Not that my appearance is any better now, but at least I feel somewhat better about myself having brushed my teeth.

She smiles. "You find everything you need this time?"

I nod my head. "I think so."

I pay for my food and twist open the juice's cap, drinking over half the bottle with just one swallow. I contemplate buying another one but figure it's probably best to save the money.

"You new around here?" she asks.

Funny, but the clerk from last night asked me the same thing. "Yeah, you could say that. Got into town a couple days ago. By the way, my name's Brian," I tell her.

"As you can see by my name tag here, I'm Maggie. Welcome, Brian." She says and extends her hand.

"It's nice to meet you."

One thing's for certain, while the cops might not be friendly here, there's at least two people I've met so far who seem genuine—Maggie here, and the girl at the hotel.

I finish up with my so-called breakfast and toss the trash away.

I look over at my car before getting back in and notice how run-down and ragged it looks. Even now, I can still hear my ex harping on me about the way it looks. It embarrassed her so bad that any time we'd go somewhere together, she'd insist we always take her car—mine wasn't good enough. *Spoiled bitch*. The more I think back on our relationship, the more I wonder what I ever saw in her in the first place.

I pull out a fresh t-shirt from my bag and change into it. I check the pockets of my jeans and pull out the money, figuring it's a good idea to know how much I still have. I pat my pockets again, front and back, this time digging a little deeper.

"Shit," I say out loud. "What the hell!"

I count it over and over, coming up with much less than what I thought I should have. I do the math in my head and add in the twenty from the girl at the hotel last night. That can't be right. I'm short a hundred dollars.

"Fuck!" I say, a little louder this time, and pound my fist on the steering wheel.

I kick open the car door and look around on the ground, thinking maybe I dropped it before getting in.

Nothing.

Next, I rummage through the trash that I've collected in the floorboard but come up empty-handed. *How the fuck did I manage to lose a hundred dollars? I need that money.* I slam the car door shut and hurry back into the gas station again. Just maybe...

A little bell chimes on the door alerting Maggie that someone's entered. She looks up from what appears to be a crossword puzzle book.

"Hey, Maggie. Did anyone by chance turn in any money? I think I might've dropped some when I was in earlier."

She looks at me with a sorrowful expression on her face and says, "Sorry, *hun*, haven't seen anything. I'll keep my eyes open though, and if someone finds any, I'll be sure to keep it at the counter for ya. You can check back later on if you'd like."

"Thanks, Maggie. I'm going to check in the bathroom real quick." I nod, still hopeful of finding it.

Sadly, my search comes up empty-handed. I hope this isn't an indication of how the rest of the day will be. I'm so mad at myself for being careless, knowing I should've paid better attention. I needed that money.

Disgusted, I throw my hands up in the air and storm out the door. "Have a good day." I call out to her somewhat rudely, knowing good and well it's not her fault for my carelessness.

****

After spending the good part of the day browsing through several stores in a shopping center I found, I decide to treat myself to something to eat from a hamburger place out by the road. I spot a newspaper on a nearby table, so I pick it up and look through it while I eat.

I come across all kinds of jobs listed in the classifieds: fast food workers at every place imaginable, delivery help at a local newspaper stand, security and custodial help at a hospital, maintenance workers at a hotel. You name it, the same typical jobs that are available everywhere. This town isn't any better than where I came from.

To humor myself, I also glance at the listings for apartments. I'm almost in shock to discover what they're going for here. One thing's for certain, I either need to find a really good paying job, or figure out how to manage two part-time jobs if I'm actually going to be able to afford one on my own. It's tough trying to make a fresh start with absolutely nothing.

I hate not having anything to do. I pull across the road and spend the next couple hours browsing in an electronics store. I've never spent so much time randomly walking and having nothing to buy.

I've gotten some suspicious stares from the store personnel—probably thinking I'm trying to steal something—so I finally leave. The clouds have started to move in, threatening rain again. With no access to a television or a phone, I'm not sure what the weather calls for. But, with the look of the clouds and the swift wind that's suddenly whipping around, it's obvious another nasty thunderstorm is near.

I make it to my car just as the raindrops start to fall. The longer I sit here, the more difficult it gets to see anything outside. I crack the window because it's getting a little stuffy, but the wind blows the rain inside. I roll it back up again and deal with the humidity as best I can. A loud clap of thunder rumbles loudly, causing me to jump. The lightning is sharp and

I see one bolt after the other light up the sky. I grab my pillow, shut my eyes, and listen to the rain as it pelts against my car.

Bang, bang, bang. I jump abruptly, startled from the noise.

"You okay in there?" I hear a voice call out.

It's nighttime now and someone is standing just outside the car's window, trying to get my attention.

I roll it down, and a flashlight beam shines on me, square in the face. "What the...?" I call out, perturbed, and bring my arm up to shield my face. The light's so bright, I can't see a thing.

"You alright in there?" the voice asks again.

The beam shifts and I'm able to make out a security patrolman. *I'm like a magnet to these people.*

"Sir, can you please step out of the car?" he asks, this time a little more gruffly.

I unlock the door and do as the gentleman requests. I stumble slightly, but only because my legs are numb from being sound asleep and in the same position for so long.

"Is there a problem, sir?" I ask him irritably, pissed that he's now using his flashlight to look around inside my car. First, the two cops from last night, now this jerk? What could they think I'd have hiding in there?

"You got some identification on you? I've noticed your car's been parked here all afternoon."

"My wallet's inside, so is it okay to get it?" My voice is clipped.

I'm trying to control my temper to prevent from causing a scene, but *damn*, it's ridiculous how a stupid security cop can question me like I'm guilty of something.

I lift my wallet from the center console and shove my driver's license at him. "Here."

He picks up on my tone. "Long way from home, aren't you?" he asks after checking out my information.

"Look, I just recently moved here and haven't had a chance to get anything updated. I'm picking my roommate up from work, and I guess I dozed. He should've been off by now but he's not, so he must be working over." I'm getting pretty good with these made-up stories.

The officer looks at me again, and I can tell by the expression on his face that he actually believes me. He actually fell for my made-up story! "Alright, son, I don't see any reason to question you further. Have a good night."

Good thing it *is* night, because if it'd still been light out, he may have seen right through me. I don't like being questioned by anyone, especially cops, and I sure as hell don't like being told what to do. Thank God he didn't ask me who I was waiting for. That would've really put me on the spot.

I have absolutely no idea what to do now. It's a given that anywhere I go, someone's going to spot me. I really hate being in this predicament, but I guess I should've made better plans before leaving my hometown so abruptly.

I wait until I can no longer see the security car, then pull out of the parking lot. I'm willing to bet it's only a matter of time before he circles back around to see if I'm still here.

Suddenly, a thought occurs to me. I make a U-turn at the next light and head in the direction of the hotel. I'm crossing my fingers the girl who gave me the money is working again. And if she's not, well, I'm back at square one again.

I pull in and look towards the front office. I'm able to make out someone standing behind the counter who resembles her, but I'm not a hundred percent sure. I take my chances, find a parking spot, and walk inside. What've I got to lose?

The doors slide open, and she turns around. Yes, it's her.

I clear my throat, hoping my words don't come out jumbled. "Hi. I'm, uh, Brian. I was here last night. You gave me some money for gas."

If I didn't know any better I'd say, judging by the expression on her face, she was happy to see me again. "Yes, I remember you. Never expected to see you again though."

I notice she's got a nice smile and a friendly disposition about her. She's kind of pretty—not some drop-dead gorgeous babe, but she's nice looking. Her light colored hair is pulled back in a ponytail and she's wearing the same red top again. I can't help but notice her radiant blue eyes and how they're staring straight at me.

"I wanted to thank you again for the money last night." I hesitate before continuing. "You see, I sort of wasn't being *completely* honest with you, or the cops last night."

"Oh?" I see a worried look immediately replace her smile, and she takes a few steps back from her position behind the counter. "Look, I don't need any kind of trouble, or an explanation, for that matter. I did all I could last night to help you. I should've known the cops were after you for a reason."

"Whoa. Wait, let me explain," I quickly interject. "I *was* low on gas, just like I told you and the cops last night, but I didn't have any plans to meet up with my brother to get any money. And I sort of didn't call him either."

"Okay, I'm not sure I'm following you."

"It's kind of a long story. You see, I got into a situation back home and, rather than cause any more problems, I decided to leave. I guess you could say I sort of ran away. It was kind of sudden so I didn't have time to do much planning."

She seems intrigued now, so I tell her a little more. I bring up Macy, the dispute we had, and how she kicked me out. And to add to it, how I couldn't go back home or to my brother's house, purposely leaving out certain parts—some things are just better left unsaid.

She just stares at me without saying a word. I'm not sure if she's sympathetic or just having trouble believing everything, especially when I brought up my ex. You know how women are, taking up for one another when it comes to something a man has screwed up. "I'm very sorry about your situation, but I'm not sure what you want me to do. And please don't think you need to repay me. It's not necessary"

"I know this is probably a long shot and I'm crazy for asking, but do you think there's any way you might be able to get me a room tonight? I've slept the last two nights in my car, and I really don't want any more run-ins with the cops. They don't like me sleeping just anywhere even though I'm not hurting anyone." I lay it on thick. "Just earlier tonight, I took a nap while it was raining. Next thing I know, a security cop comes by banging on my window. Said I couldn't stay there. I'm just running out of options." I drop my head down even though I know I'll have a better chance of her feeling sorry for me if I make eye contact with her.

"And you think I can help you? I don't even know you."

I can see she's starting to withdraw. Maybe I went a little farther than I should have.

"Wait. You were very generous last night, and I thought maybe you could be again. I just don't know where to go." I give her a shame-faced look.

"Shouldn't you have thought this through before you decided to run away? I would've at least saved a little bit of money and had a better plan."

"You're right. I should've put more thought into it, but it all happened so suddenly." I turn and step toward the exit. "I'm sorry for bothering you again."

"Wait," she says. "Maybe there is something I can do."

I look back at her, knowing I've weakened her resolve. I just may be getting somewhere with her now. Yes, there may be some hope, after all.

"I could really get in trouble for this, you know." She stares at me for a long moment as though she's reconsidering.

"But here's what I can do. You can have a standard room on the house, but you've got to be gone first thing in the morning."

"Are you serious?" I'm really playing this up good. "You'd really do that for me?"

"My shift's over at seven, so I'll need you to be gone by then. Gone, like out of here and off the premises. I'll take care of the paperwork part, but I don't want my co-workers questioning anything."

"Look. You tell me how I can make it up to you, and I will. I owe you big time." I can hardly believe I'm going to have a nice bed to sleep in tonight as well as a hot shower in the morning. My plan worked. She completely fell for it.

"Like I said, I need you gone by seven," she repeats. "Don't bother bringing the key card to the front desk. Just throw it away after you leave. And just so you know, the keys don't work anymore after check-out time so don't go getting any bright ideas about sneaking back in later on."

"Thank you. Thank you so much..." I suddenly stop. I've just spent the last few minutes talking to her, and I never bothered to get her name. I stick my hand out to shake hers. "I didn't catch your name."

"Jennifer."

"I'm Brian."

"It's nice to meet you." A smile forms on her lips, her doubts about me slowly slipping away.

"I'm just going to grab my stuff from the car. I'll be right back." I get to the door then turn to look back at her. "Thank you, Jennifer. It's really nice of you to do this for me."

Out at my car, it's hard for me to hide the grin on my face. I did it. I played the "poor guy" part and she bought it.

I head back inside with my things to find she's already got the room key ready for me.

"Here. You're at the end of the hall, down there on the left." She points in the direction for the room, and our fingers lightly touch during the key exchange.

I take it from her and toss my bag over my shoulder. Sensing there's something else she wants to say, I hang back.

"Wait, hold on a minute." *I knew it.* "Have you had anything to eat tonight?"

Not wanting to sound even more desperate, I reply, "I'll be okay. I had something earlier."

Actually, I'd not had anything since the burger at lunch, but I didn't want to overdo it. My stomach had been rumbling for the last several hours and I figured, since I'd made it this far, I'd just grab some chips or a candy bar from the vending machine.

"Are you sure? 'Cause I can grab you something from the kitchen. We don't have a whole lot, but I don't mind."

"Well, if you insist. I could use a Coke." I really was thirsty. Truth be known, I was sick of junk food, but that's all Macy had in the apartment at the time. I'd had no way of keeping anything cold, so bringing along anything perishable hadn't been an option.

"Why don't you put your bag down over there, and I'll be back in a second." She points to a sofa in the lobby and walks into a closed-off room, just off the side of the main check-in counter.

While I wait for her to return, I walk to the front window and peer out at the parking lot. It's shortly after midnight and everything appears quiet outside. Peaceful. The rain obviously long gone now.

When she returns, she's carrying a tray loaded down with several items. She sets it down on the table and I take in the items she brought back: a can of Coke, a couple of assorted fruit Danishes, and a packaged muffin. There's also some packages of instant grits inside a Styrofoam bowl. She even remembered plastic silverware.

"You didn't have to do all that," I tell her. This time, feeling genuinely appreciative.

"It's no problem. Sorry I don't have anything hot. We won't have coffee or tea 'til in the morning. We always keep plenty of these on hand, though." She points down to the assorted items on the tray. "There's a microwave in your room though."

"No, this is plenty. Really." I open the Coke and take a swallow. *Damn, it tastes good.*

I get the feeling she's enjoying my company and doesn't want me to leave just yet. So, we make small talk between the two of us as I tear into one of the Danishes.

Before long, I open up even more. We talk about where I'm from, how I hated school, and the couple of jobs I've had since graduating. Then, it's her turn and she opens up to me as well, about herself, about her parents selling their home and their plans to travel full-time. She brings up her best friend, Rebecca, the classes she's taking in college, and her desire to become a teacher. There's very little she doesn't talk about, and I'm amazed how much she's elaborated on so soon. I mean, I'm still a total stranger to her. Surprisingly, we've hit it off quite well, despite my bit of troubles that really don't seem to faze her.

Then, she tells me about the apartment she has by herself and how she sometimes gets lonely living all alone.

Before we know it, an hour has passed.

Coincidentally, we discover we both have two brothers each, and we like some of the same music and television shows. She tells me about her favorite band that she likes to listen to at *Night Moves*, the club that's next door. She says I'd really enjoy their music and if I'm still in the area Saturday night, I should stop by to hear them. She and Rebecca have plans to be there around ten o'clock. *Where else did she think I'd be and could she be any more obvious about wanting to see me again?*

"I'll, um, definitely think about it. They sound like a band I'd be interested in," I tell her. "And I'm sure I'd enjoy meeting your friend, too."

I realize just how tired I really am when I'm unable to hold back a yawn. If I'm going to get some rest, I probably should be heading to my room.

I stand to dump the trash from the tray.

"Here let me have that." She reaches for it, and I pick up the still-wrapped muffin and the throw-away bowl with the packaged grits.

"If you don't mind, I think I'll save these for in the morning."

"Sure. If you want some more I can get them for you."

I realize from her abundance of kindness, I could probably get her to do just about anything for me. In a sense, she's almost too nice.

"I'll be okay. By the way, I've really enjoyed talking with you, and I can't thank you enough for everything. I promise you, I'll make it up to you some way, Jennifer." I'm doing it again—making subtle suggestions to see her again.

"Okay. And don't forget, if you don't have any plans, we'll be next door tomorrow night if you'd like to join us."

"I'll definitely consider it," I tell her, not wanting to hurt her feelings.

"Goodnight, Brian. Hope you can get some rest."

I wave goodbye to her and walk down the hall to find my room.

Chapter 5

Jennifer

MY SHIFT IS ALMOST OVER, and for the last hour I've watched the hallway leading to Brian's room constantly. I thought of him nonstop and kept replaying in my head everything he'd shared with me. I can't imagine leaving everything behind and starting over someplace new, not knowing a single soul. How do you even choose where to go? How do things get so bad to the point you need to escape from it all and start fresh?

I keep thinking I'll see him leave, especially since I reiterated he needed to be gone by seven. I go to the back for a moment and grab my things before stopping by the time clock. I have to admit, Brian did seem appreciative for the room. I just hope he doesn't make a habit of it.

I can't recall if I told him the nights I'm off, but I'm glad I hinted around about going to *Night Moves* tonight. Will he show up? Given his money situation, I seriously doubt it, but a girl can hope right?

I say my goodbyes, excited to be off for the next couple days.

I can't wait to call Rebecca and tell her about everything that's happened—she's going to flip! She barely believed my story from the night before. *Brian, oh Brian, why must you cloud my mind?*

When I get outside, I'm surprised to see his car is already gone. I wonder how I missed him since I'd hardly taken my eyes away from the hallway. I know I kept reminding him about being gone, but I'm saddened he didn't say goodbye.

As soon as I'm inside my car, I make the call to Rebecca. I don't even care that it's early morning either. It goes straight to her voicemail which typically means she's got it turned off. *Nooooo, I want to tell her about Brian.*

I try my best to fall asleep as soon as I get home, but I can't seem to get him off my mind. Strangely, there was just something about him, something I can't let go of. After he'd gone to his room, I couldn't help but feel sorry for him. The things he shared with me lingered in my mind. Sometimes in life, some people are just dealt a bad hand. Everyone deserves a second chance, though. I'm appalled by his ex-girlfriend's behavior, but I remind myself there's always two sides to every story. I'm sure he was probably leaving out a few details to save face, too.

I finally lie down on the couch and wrap up in my blanket. It's no use. I toss and turn constantly. I try watching television, hoping it'll help. Any other time, I wouldn't be able to keep my eyes open.

Later that evening, after finally getting in a few hours, I wake, only to discover it's already dark outside. I panic and grab my phone from the side table. Sure enough, I've missed a few texts from Rebecca.

Rebecca: Hey girl. Saw where you'd tried to call. We still on for tonight?
Rebecca: Jenn, you up yet?
Rebecca: Call me.

I must've been sleeping hard not to hear the message alerts. I immediately text her back.

Jennifer: Sorry, I'm just now getting up. Yes, still going out tonight.

Rebecca: Starting to get worried about you.

Jennifer: I'm fine. Had hard time falling asleep.

Rebecca: Pick you up at 8:45?

Jennifer: Sounds good. See you then.

I manage to pry myself up off the couch and walk into the kitchen. Standing in front of the refrigerator, I realize there's not much here to eat. I really hate that I slept most of the day away, but the night's just getting started. I've got the next two days to catch up on everything. I pop a frozen dinner in the microwave and head back to my bedroom. I need to pick out something really cute to wear tonight just in case, you know, someone happens to show.

So far, not a single thing looks right. Normally, I'd wear something comfortable, yet trendy. Tonight, though, I'm looking for something a little more eye-catching, a little slinky, and sexy. After all, you only get one chance to make a good first impression and tonight could be it.

Out of all the clothes I own, finally, I see something that might just be what I'm looking for. From the very back, I pull out a silver, sparkling spaghetti strap top and hold it up. *This will definitely do.* I decide to pair it with my favorite jeans and wedges, then add a little curl to my hair for an added touch to make me feel special.

Yes, I think to myself. This will most definitely catch his eye. The microwave beeps, and I'm returned to the present, but not before I question whether I'm getting just a wee bit overboard with this whole Brian thing. We are, after all, just getting to know each other. If this were a real date, my behavior would totally make sense, but I shouldn't rule out the possibility of meeting someone else either. I know it's too soon to be getting all excited.

I quickly eat my food and jump in the shower and am finishing with my hair and makeup just as the doorbell rings. I head to answer it, always happy to see Rebecca.

"Dang, girl," she squeals, taking in my appearance. "Since when did you start dressing like this? And your hair! It looks amazing." She reaches up to touch one of my springy curls.

I feel my cheeks blush. "I just decided to do a little extra tonight. You never know who we might run into."

I can't wait for the right opportunity to tell her more about Brian, and I'm going crazy trying to hide it right now. If she knew he was the reason for my added efforts tonight, she'd think I was a tad bit insane. And who knows, I may actually be investing more into it than what it's worth. There's always the chance he won't show. The butterflies I'm feeling right now indicate otherwise, so I take it as a sign.

"Sure you don't have a secret date lined up?" she jokes. "I thought I was your date for the evening."

Rebecca and I have a rule about going out—we arrive together, and we leave together. Simple as that. She's always fun to hang out with, and we have a great time together. Greg trusts her completely and encourages the two of us to go out often.

If we drink any alcohol, we limit ourselves to two apiece, and nothing after midnight. Though we consider ourselves regulars and not ones to get out of control, we do know how to have a good time.

I take one last look at myself in the mirror. *Yes, I look pretty damn good tonight.*

"I'll drive if that's okay with you." Rebecca says on our way out to the parking lot.

"I'm good with that." I loop my arm through hers, something girls can get by doing.

In the car, I scan through a couple different radio stations trying to find the right music to get us pumped up.

"What's up with you tonight? You've got this glow about you," Rebecca comments, noticing my cheerfulness.

"Oh, nothing. It's just that it's been a long week and I'm ready to unwind." If she only knew just what she'd missed.

"You sure you haven't already had a drink or two?"

"No, I'm just in a good mood. I can't help it." I look over at her and smile.

When we get there, a long line has already formed at the door. It moves rather quickly, but while we're waiting, I catch myself looking around for any sign of Brian.

"Let's grab a table and order something to eat. I'm starving," Rebecca says once we're inside. I'm not all that hungry, since I ate before we left, but I agree to share a little something with her. This will also give me the chance to check out who's here.

"I don't know why I even bother looking at this thing," Rebecca adds, holding the menu in her hands. "I think we've tried just about everything here."

A waitress walks up to our table, introduces herself, and takes our drink orders.

"I think I'll have a margarita on the rocks please," I tell her. "With salt."

Rebecca nods. "And I'll have the same."

Tonight, I'm going to relax and have fun regardless if he shows up or not.

"How about the chicken tender basket? That sound okay to you?" she asks.

"That's fine by me," I tell her. "Get whatever you want though."

Rebecca orders her food when the waitress returns with our drinks. Just from the looks of the people already here, it's going to be a packed house tonight.

"Damn, that's good," she tells me after taking her first sip. "Okay, are you going to tell me why you keep looking around? Are you looking for someone? Every time I look over at you, your head is turned towards the door."

I am so busted! I instantly feel my cheeks flush.

"Huh? What are you talking about?" I try to play dumb and pretend I don't know what she's talking about. "Just seeing who's here tonight."

"Yeah, right. Girl, you can't fool me!" She giggles, knowing she's on to something.

The food arrives, thank goodness, and I'm able to quickly change the subject. There's literally enough food here for several people. Rebecca doesn't waste any time digging in and I nibble on a few of her fries. The waitress comes back to check on us, and I go ahead and place another order of margaritas for both of us.

"These are sooo good tonight." I hold my drink up— what's left of it—and she agrees. At the rate we're going, we may have to break our limit tonight. My body is already feeling warm and relaxed after the first one. We can always call for a cab to take us home if we have to.

Rebecca reaches over and grabs my arm to get my attention. "Don't look yet, but I swear there's a really cute guy over at the bar that keeps checking you out."

Of course I turn around to see. Who doesn't when they're told this?

Sure enough, it's him and I start to get all giddy inside. Brian's leaned up against the bar holding a beer in his hand. A huge smile comes over my face and I wave at him.

"Wait, you *know* him?" she asks, suddenly confused from my gesture.

"Eh, not exactly," I manage to get out, just as he walks over to our table.

"Brian, hey, I see you made it." I grin from ear to ear. "This is my best friend, Rebecca. Rebecca, this is Brian."

He extends his hand to her, and she replies with a "Nice to meet ya."

Then, she looks over at me and asks, "So, Jenn, you going to tell me how you two know each other?"

"Well, we, um, we met at the hotel." I stumble over the words, suddenly embarrassed. "Brian's new in town, so I extended an invitation for him to join us. You know, so he can see what we do for fun."

All of a sudden, Rebecca shoots me a concerned look. "Uh, Brian, will you please excuse us for a moment. Jenn and I need to go to the ladies room. Please help yourself to some food while we're away." She grabs my hand and literally drags me down the hallway towards the bathrooms before I can get in another word edgewise.

"Okay, lady. Spill it," she demands as soon as the door shuts behind us. "Please tell me how you've managed to meet someone but not shared the details with me."

"No, he just moved here. You know I tell you everything..." Laughing at her sudden overprotectiveness, I proceed cautiously. "Eventually. Remember that piece of junk car that was parked in my spot at work for those few days?" I stop long enough to let it all sink in. "Well, you're never going to believe this, but that's him. That's his car."

Worry is clearly evident on her face. "Come on, Jennifer. You're kidding me, right? Surely, you can find someone better than that! Even you were cracking jokes about the condition of *that* car." She quickly throws this back at me.

Okay, maybe she's right but I don't' exactly like how she's pre-judged him without giving him a chance yet.

"I know, I know. I had a few choice words to say about it, too. And, honestly, I shouldn't have without knowing who it belonged to."

"Okay, but you still haven't told me how you know him. So the car is his, but how did you find that out?"

"Well, it's a weird story, but the other night, the cops happened to be patrolling through the parking lot, just checking on things. Apparently, someone had reported a vehicle with kids left in it and they thought his was the car."

"Okay, so how does this involve you?" She is still staring at me with concern.

"Brian had pulled over for the night, short on gas and cash. When the cops discovered him sleeping in the car, they woke him. Once they realized everything was okay and it wasn't the car they were looking for, they sort of gave him a hard time about parking there. They brought him up to the hotel so he could use the phone to see about getting some help. He came back last night to thank me and to see about getting a room. We talked and talked forever. In fact, we probably could have talked all night had he not needed to get some sleep." By this point, I hope she's a little more understanding. I leave out the part about my giving him money though. It wasn't much, but I don't need to raise any more red flags where's she concerned.

The look on her face is still skeptical. "You know I love you like my own flesh and blood. I just want you to be careful since you don't really *know* anything about him. I believe what you're saying, but if he's not from around here, then suddenly shows up out of nowhere? Well, he could be trouble." She reaches out to give me a sisterly hug.

As I pull away from her, I quickly add, "I know you mean well. It's not like I invited him home or anything. My God, this is a public place. Isn't this much safer than anywhere else? We just talked. He's new here, and I was being nice. And besides, he can't help that he's also very attractive. Did you notice those piercing blue eyes of his?" I try lightening the tone of the conversation and steering it in a different direction.

"Come on, Jenn. He probably thinks we got lost in here. And you're right. No harm in being friendly." I see a smile return to her face and hope we're both right about him.

While we were gone, Brian ordered himself another beer, judging from the extra bottle left on the table.

"Sorry we took so long. Girl talk, you know." I grin and climb up on the stool next to him.

"That's okay. Hope you girls didn't mind me finishing off your food. I didn't realize how hungry I was."

Damn, he's got a killer smile, too.

Being the awesome friend that she is, Rebecca speaks up. "Welcome to town, Brian. I'm glad you could join us tonight."

She's going to give him a chance, I hope.

"Well, if I'm fortunate enough to find a job, I plan on hanging around here. I sort of had to leave my last place unexpectedly, so I don't exactly have a lot of money. I've got some buddies over in the next town, but I kind of like the feel of it here." He doesn't really speak directly to either of us, and just sort of stares straight ahead. Until he says, "Not to mention, I've met some nice people, too." I feel his gaze on me.

Funny, but I don't recall him mentioning before about having friends close by. It's not really a big deal, I suppose, but it is a little strange he didn't mention it before.

"I'm not sure what kind of work you're looking for, but the fast food places are always hiring. Then there's the grocery stores, too, and the new mall being built down the road. Surely someone can give you a job."

Looking from Rebecca to Brian, it seems they could both go on and on, just like it'd been between me and him. I grab them both by the hand and pull them toward the dance floor.

"Come on, guys, let's go have some fun. Brian, you can worry about a job tomorrow."

The band takes the stage and runs through a few notes. Suddenly, the lights darken and the crowd goes wild when a trendy tune starts blasting from the speakers. Everyone is swaying to the music, hands in the air, and pelting the words to the song. Not wasting any time, the band continues with several more hit songs in rapid succession.

Both my friends seem to be having a really good time, and Brian doesn't mind having the two of us to dance with. In fact, he takes turns dancing with Rebecca first, then turns to face me for the next song. When the band slows the beat for a slow ballad, we all take a break from the earlier energy and head back to our table. I'm a little uncertain how the three of us would've danced to that one.

I've lost the buzz I had earlier, but that's okay. I'm hot and sweaty and could actually go for another drink, even though I've already reached my limit.

Glancing down at my watch, I notice it's almost two o'clock in the morning. *Where did the time go?* The band continues to play, but I realize just how tired I am when I reach up to cover a yawn. I've had a great night, but as the saying goes, all good things must come to an end.

"Did you all see what time it is?" I throw in.

Rebecca's the first to speak up. "Dang, I didn't realize how late it was getting. I don't know about you guys, but I've had a blast tonight."

"Me, too," Brian quickly adds. "Thanks, ladies, for letting me hang out with you. Maybe we can do this again sometime."

Then Rebecca clearly ruins the moment without even knowing it. "Brian, where are you staying tonight? Did you drive or can we give you a ride somewhere?"

I could kick her right about now.

I notice his gaze fall to the floor. "Well, my car's in the lot by the hotel, so I'm good as far as a ride goes. I haven't exactly decided where I'm staying though. Maybe I'll see if there's a room still available."

He looks over at me, knowing full well I'm aware he doesn't have any money. I never thought to ask how he paid for his beers earlier, and I would hate to put him on the spot now if I brought it up. Of course, it's really none of my business. I don't want to mention any of this in front of Rebecca, so I keep walking towards the exit.

I tell Rebecca I'm going to walk Brian to his car and I'll meet her in a few minutes.

"Thanks for coming tonight, Brian. I had a lot of fun." I'm trying to be as friendly and cordial as I can, keeping the door open for him to suggest possibly seeing each other again.

"Both of you were a blast. Thank you, Jennifer, for inviting me." He reaches over and gives me a hug. "Hopefully, we can do it again real soon. It's been a long time since I've been able to let loose and not worry about things."

I don't mention his lack of set plans for the rest of the night, and he doesn't volunteer it, either. It's best, for both out sakes, to leave it alone.

He gets into his clunker of a car, and Rebecca pulls up behind it to pick me up. We both wave back to him as she drives away.

Chapter 6
Brian

I GET INTO THE CAR and hope the girls don't wait for me to leave first. I have no idea where I'll go or where I'm even going to sleep tonight, but I don't want to take the chance of them following me. Jennifer's friend, Rebecca...Well, let's just say, she didn't mind getting a little too personal with all her questions. Frankly, my life is none of her business.

I use both hands to rub my face and eyes, tired from the night's events. Surprisingly, I actually had fun. I pull out of the parking lot and up beside them at the red light. I figure if they're going one way, I'll go the other.

"Hey, you okay?" Jennifer yells over to me.

"Yeah, I'm fine." I give her the thumbs up. "One too many beers tonight." I hold my hand up to my head and pretend to pound it hoping she gets the gist of what I'm saying.

She motions to the gas station across the way and points. "Pull over there. I've got something you can take."

This wasn't at all what I had in mind doing, but I go ahead and turn in behind them. Before I'm able to shut off my car, she's already gotten out and is running over to me. I'm so embarrassed for her to see my car up close.

"I'm sorry you're feeling bad. Here," she says and shakes a bottle of pain reliever at me. "Just keep them. I've got more at home."

My hand briefly touches hers as I take the bottle from her. I look over to Rebecca in the driver's seat, but she's focused on her phone. "Thanks, Jennifer. I appreciate it. I'm just going to run inside and grab something to wash these down with Thanks again for a great time tonight." To be honest, I don't want her to leave yet. I know it's for the best that she doesn't hang around though.

Her face lights up. "I did too. Maybe we can do it again sometime."

One thing's for sure, this girl is way too nice for me. I'd really like to ask her if I could see her again, but given the circumstances, I'm not really sure that's a good idea.

"Well, goodnight."

"Goodnight, Brian." I see her eyes twinkle as she turns to get back in the car again. I hope I didn't just disappoint her.

Judging by the expression on her face, it looks like I'm already having an effect on her and with very little effort on my part. If I didn't know any better, I'd say she's already getting one of those premature crushes. Lord knows that wasn't my intention.

Sadly, though, if I don't figure out some kind of plan soon, I may have no other choice than to seek her help. Not necessarily for another room again, but she did say she had her own place. Maybe she'd consider having me for a roommate.

I really don't have a headache, but something cold to drink does sound pretty good right about now. I hadn't planned on spending money on the few beers I had earlier tonight, but I didn't want to look like a lightweight, either. I was glad the girls let me finish off their plate of food though. It sure saved me from having to figure out something to eat since my junk food supply is almost down to nothing. The chicken was pretty darn good, too.

Walking out of the bathroom, I notice the same lady from the previous night working. Maggie. I place my drink up on the counter and can tell by her expression she recognizes me, too.

"Hey, Maggie. So, by chance, did anyone turn in the money I lost?" I ask her, hoping by some miracle she's holding it for me.

"No, but I didn't really expect anyone would, either. Not in this day and time. It's hard to find a good soul anymore. I've seen my fair share of people come through here, and way too many are looking for handouts." I'm not sure why she's volunteered this much information, but I nod in agreement, pay for my drink, and walk back out to the car.

I don't have a clue where to go this time in the morning. I drive out towards the fast food places again, knowing there's bound to be some place I can park my car where it'll go unnoticed.

I see a flashing "open 24 hours" sign underneath the name of a place I'm not familiar with, so I pull in. Sure enough, there are a couple of cars out back. I park amongst them and figure I'm good for a few hours at least—long enough to grab some sleep.

I close my eyes and sleep takes over quickly. A loud noise suddenly wakes me and I jump, sitting straight up in my seat. For a moment, I swear, I thought my car was being towed. It was just that loud! I look off to the corner of the lot and see a garbage dumpster being emptied. The big truck is unusually loud and takes a few moments before it returns the dumpster back to its spot, just inside a wooden fence. I see someone shut the door on the fence and the truck pulls away. So much for getting any sleep now.

****

I wake later on in the morning with the sun beating down on the windshield. I run my fingers through my hair and let out a yawn. I'd give anything for a nice, comfortable bed to sleep in. Right now, though, I'd settle for just a bathroom!

I really enjoyed the couple of hours I'd gotten the previous night at the hotel. The bed was a little firm for my liking, but I wasn't complaining. The hot shower had been even better. I hadn't wanted to say anything in front of her friend, but yeah, I must remember to thank Jennifer again.

I look down in the front floorboard and see all the empty junk food wrappers I've not bothered to throw away. I know I should do a better job cleaning them up. My stomach growls loudly just thinking about food. What I wouldn't give for a nice, hot breakfast!

I step out of the car and look around. I hadn't noticed it when I'd pulled in early this morning because it was dark, but right next door is a McDonald's. It's not the hot breakfast I had in mind, but it'll work. I walk inside, and I'm met with the aroma of coffee and maple syrup. I'm in heaven.

I smile at the lady behind the counter and look up at the menu above her. "Good morning. What can I get for you?"

"I'll have a large coffee and a sausage biscuit." I figure it's probably the least expensive of anything they serve. I count out a couple bills and hand them over to her. "I'll be right back for my tray," I tell her and immediately take off for the bathroom.

Staring at my reflection in the mirror, I look an absolute mess. My clothes are all wrinkled from my unfortunate sleeping arrangements and my hair, well, we won't talk about. Thank God for ball caps. I'm going to have to find a laundromat soon, too. Almost all the clean clothes I packed are now dirty and scattered in my backseat.

Figuring my food is probably ready, I head back up front. Sure enough, there's a tray waiting on the counter. The nice lady slides it over towards me, a bright smile on her face. "Here you go, son."

To my surprise, there's an extra biscuit and an order of hash browns.

"I think this must be someone else's. I only ordered a biscuit and coffee," I politely inform her.

"It's yours, hun. You look like you could use a little something extra this morning. Enjoy."

Well damn. How about that?

She reminds me a lot of my grandmother, and it makes me wonder if I'll ever see her or my family again. At this point, it's too early to tell.

I take a seat in a booth near the window. There's yet another newspaper left out on the table. I try not to eat too quickly, wanting to savor every bite, but everything tastes so good. I flip through the pages, looking for the classified section. Sadly, the help wanted ads look the same as they did the day before.

I look up just as the lady from the counter walks by with cleaner and a rag in her hand. "Can I get you anything else?" she asks.

"I'm fine. Thank you, ma'am."

"Here, let me take your tray if you're finished. Would you like a refill on your coffee?"

"Sure. That's very generous of you to offer." When she returns, I ask if she knows of anyone hiring.

"What kind of work ya looking for?"

"Right now, I'll do just about anything. I've got lots of experience, and I can start right away."

"You know what? You just might be in luck. If you go to the oil change place down there a few blocks in front of the Target, ask for Jared. Tell him I sent you. He's looking for someone to wash cars. It might not be what you're looking for, but it's a job." She pats me on the shoulder. "It's worth a shot, maybe. Good luck."

I thank her then stand up to leave.

Since its Sunday, I know the place she told me about won't be open. So there's no need to inquire about the job today.

I count out the money I have left and it depresses me. Tomorrow, I must get that job.

I'm tired of riding around burning gas, so I pull into the movie theater to see what's playing. No, I don't need to spend money on an over-priced movie ticket, but what else am I supposed to do? The one good thing about going to the movies during the day, though, is that the matinees are usually cheaper.

Inside the theater, the smell of buttered popcorn fills my nostrils. I can't resist and end up ordering some as well as a Coke. I walk inside the darkened room just as the movie starts playing. About halfway through, I nod off to sleep. I wake up just as the credits are rolling across the screen.

I'm angry at myself for missing it, especially since I had to buy the damn ticket. *What the hell!* Instead of leaving, I move up to the last row of seats at the top and sit back down. I wait to see if anyone comes in to clean up. When the credits finally end and the previews start playing all over again for the next showing, I figure it's safe to stick around.

My friends and I used to do this all the time back home and never once got caught. In fact, it's almost too easy not to do it. New patrons start filling in the seats for the next showing and the lights eventually dim again. This time, I manage to stay awake the entire movie.

When it's over, I walk out in the hallway. The evening crowd is coming in and people are walking in and out of different theater doors with no one paying any attention. It's almost like everyone is on the honor system. I know it's wrong, but I walk inside another theater and wait for the next movie to start.

When it's over, I'm pretty tired of sitting and so I walk outside to an almost empty parking lot. I crank up the car and, according to the time on the dash, it's much later than I thought it was. One thing's for certain, watching multiple movies sure helped to pass the day.

And just like last night and the night before that, I start racking my brain, trying to figure out yet another spot to park for the evening.

I turn down a highway that looks to be leaving out of town. I don't want to venture too far away, especially with it being late. I notice a roadside sign indicating a hospital up ahead. Bingo! Relief overcomes me since this is the sort of place I need. People stay overnight at hospitals all the time, although most generally stay inside. I'm pretty certain I can park there without any trouble.

****

The next morning, after having several hours of halfway decent sleep, I walk into the hospital carrying my stuff. Not a single person pays me any attention. Even with my bag, I don't look any different from other people that are coming and going. I take my time in the bathroom, wiping down with paper towels dipped in warm water from the sink. I rinse my hair then use the hand dryer to dry it as best I can before walking out. I want to look somewhat presentable before attempting to find a job today.

I return to my car and drive back the way I came last night. When I get to the main highway, I turn in the direction of the oil lube shop. I hope the lady from McDonald's is right about the job because I'm desperate for anything at this point.

It doesn't take long to find the place, and I pull in, parking in the first available spot.

As I walk up to the door, I notice cars are lined up two and three deep waiting for service. All the attendants are busy assisting customers. Finally, a guy dressed in a blue uniform approaches me. According to the stitching on his shirt, his name is "Jared."

"Can I help you with something?" he asks. "If you're needing your car serviced, it'll be after lunch before I can get to ya. We're kind of slammed right now."

"Actually, I'm here for something else. I was told you were hiring. The lady down at the McDonald's said for me to see you," I tell him.

"Ahh, you must've met my mom." There's a slight bit of humor to his voice. "She's such a sweetheart, always looking out for me. What kind of job you looking for?"

"Well, I've never done this kind of work before," —I point over to the service area— "but she said you were looking for someone to wash cars and I'm pretty good at that. I'm new here in town and really desperate for a job."

Jared nods his head. "Well, here's what I got. I run a reputable business here and have lots of repeat customers. As an added service, I always like to provide a complimentary car wash to my customers, since so many of them refer my business. It's just a basic wash and vacuum. Some customers like to tip, but it's not mandatory, nor is it expected of them, either. Since I don't know you and really don't have time to do much of an interview, if you're willing, I can let you try it out to see if you'd like it. It's minimum wage to start out, but you'll be able to split the tips with the other guy, Clint."

"Are you serious? You're offering me the job? Just like that?"

"Yep, the job is yours if you're interested."

I reach out to shake his hand and thank him for the opportunity. "Man, I really appreciate it. Looks like you got yourself a new employee." I already like Jared and I haven't even started yet.

"Be here in the morning, promptly at eight. If you've got time to fill out some paperwork today, you can see the lady at the front counter and she can get you started. Oh, and be sure to pick up a uniform, too. Thanks, uh...I'm sorry, I didn't get your name."

"It's Brian. Brian Collins. Thanks a lot, Jared. I'll see you first thing in the morning." I nod my head to him as he turns and walks back into the building.

I figure I might as well go ahead and see about tending to the paperwork today since I've got nothing better to do. Before leaving, I'm issued two sets of basic light blue uniform shirts, without my name of course, and two pairs of shorts. As I walk back outside to my car, I throw my hand up and wave to Jared. Thank goodness I have a job. It's not exactly what I wanted and I know I'm not going to get rich from it, but it'll be a paycheck until something better comes along.

Chapter 7

Jennifer

I ROLL OVER IN BED and pull the covers over my head. Not wanting to get up, I peep out from underneath my cozy spot and look at the clock on the table. It's almost one in the afternoon.

You've got to be kidding me!

Thoughts of last night and Brian fill my mind again as I head into the bathroom and step into the shower.

I wonder whatever happened to him.

After I finish with my shower and I'm drying off, my phone dings, indicating a missed call. I grab it off my bedside table and see it was Rebecca. For a brief moment, I wish it were from Brian, but then realize I never gave him my number. Sadly, he hadn't asked for it, either.

I call Rebecca back and sense her chattiness coming from the other end. "'Bout time you decided to get up. I've only sent you a dozen texts."

"Sorry, I was in the shower. What are you up to?" I feel as though I'm still half asleep.

"I thought maybe you'd want to grab a bite to eat tomorrow before class."

"Sure, I can do that. Does two sound okay? That'll give me plenty of time before I have to be there. What'd you have in mind?" I ask.

"Why don't we hit up that new burger place, right off campus? Sound good to you?"

We both agree on trying it out then end the call. I put on a pair of yoga pants, pull my damp hair back into a ponytail, and slip on some running shoes. There's nothing better than a nice stroll through the park. Hopefully, the fresh air will do me some good.

****

The next morning, I tidy up my apartment and finish putting away the laundry left from the day before. When I got back yesterday, I decided to be lazy and called it an early evening. I do a little bit of studying before packing up to meet with Rebecca.

On my way there, I pass by the hotel parking lot, just in case someone's car happens to be there. I know it's a long shot, but when Brian drove away Saturday night, I couldn't help but wonder where he's been since.

For some reason I can't explain, I'm drawn to him. I realize, though, that it might not be a good thing. From what little bit he's told me about himself, he hasn't exactly had the best track record. I just feel that I could inspire him, that I could help him be a better person. It's sad he's had this run of bad luck, and I know the warning signs are there: new guy in town, sketchy background, no job, sudden breakup. So why do I feel that he was put in my life for a reason then?

Oh well. I may never see him again, so there's no sense in getting all worked up over it.

I pull into the parking lot at the restaurant and see Rebecca already seated at a table on the patio.

"I didn't know what you wanted, so I held off on placing our order," she tells me when I take the seat across from her.

"This is a really cool looking place," I add, looking around at the setup. A notice a stage over in the far corner and wonder if it's used for live performances. Strings of lights are draped through the trees and a covered bar extends from the main building. No doubt, it looks very pretty at night. Since it's so close to campus, I bet it's a lively place to hang out.

We flip through the menus trying to decide what to eat. I've never seen so many different combinations of items to put on burgers. I pick up a printed advertisement that's next to the napkin dispenser and read through the day's special.

"I think I'll have this." I point at it, figuring it's a safe choice. "The quarter pound burger served with fries and a soft drink."

"Sounds good to me." Rebecca is so easy to please. I don't think I've ever met someone so carefree and laid back. It's part of the reason we get along so well.

We place our orders with the waitress, and I know from the look on Rebecca's face she's ready to start asking me questions about Saturday night.

"What?" I ask, pretending not to know where our conversation is headed.

She slides to the edge of her seat and places her elbows on the table. Then, looking at me with a mischievous grin, she asks, "So, did he ask you out?"

"No, he didn't," I quickly reply. "Was he supposed to?" Although I try to act nonchalant, I'm sure the expression on my face shows differently.

"Well, I figured maybe you'd dropped the hint that you were single *and* available. You have to let guys know these things sometimes. They don't always read between the lines."

She had a point there.

"It's still too early yet. Maybe when he finds a place to stay and can get a job." Again, I wonder where he's been sleeping. Surely he's come up with an arrangement by now. "Poor guy. I kind of feel sorry for him. First, he gets dumped by the girl he was seeing, who was difficult to get along with in the first place. Then, she kicks him out without having a place to go to."

"Who knows? But if he's got baggage, you need to tread carefully."

"I know. I shouldn't get my hopes up too much. Besides, if he's coming right out of one relationship, he's certainly not ready for a new one. More than anything, sounds like he just needs a friend."

"I have to say you're probably right. But I loved seeing your face light up when he walked over to our table the other night. By the way, why didn't you tell me you'd invited him?"

"I didn't want to get myself all worked up in case he didn't show. I didn't want you thinking I was crazy." It's easier to admit this now. "I did tell him when I'd be working again though, so maybe he'll stop by and see me." *I can only hope, right?*

"Well, just be careful and don't do anything I wouldn't do."

I can't help but laugh at her comment. As if she's never done anything off-the-wall before.

The waitress brings our food and our conversation shifts to other things. We talk about Greg, my family, and work. Before we know it, time has gotten away from us. As we finish up, we both agree to come back again. The hamburgers were the best, almost as good as the ones my dad used to make for us. Just thinking about him for that brief moment makes me miss my parents so much.

****

After class, I stop back by my apartment and change into my uniform. For once, I'm actually eager to go to work. I check my reflection in the mirror one last time before heading out. Just in case, you know, someone decided to stop by.

I pull in and, just like every other night since we met, I take a quick look around the parking lot. There's no sign of his ragged car. My usual spot is waiting for me, empty. I hope the look of disappointment doesn't show on my face when I make it inside.

"Just to warn you, it's been a slow night," Rebecca says as soon as I walk through the sliding front doors. "Hope you brought a good book with you."

"You know me, I always carry one with me wherever I go. Besides, I could use the time to work on my paper for American Lit. I can focus better here than I can at home."

"Oh, I know the feeling. I'm always so busy checking in guests though, that by the time I get started on my schoolwork, it's usually right before you get here."

"I'm just always so exhausted by the time I get off, I never feel like doing anything. All I want to do at that point is go straight to bed. If I can get it done here, I'm doing myself a favor," I tell her. "Anything I need to know before you head out?" She knows what I'm hinting at, I hope.

Him. She's got to know I'm curious if she's seen him tonight.

"No, like I said, it's been slow. Not much foot traffic tonight. I did get an email from Greg though. He's hoping he'll get leave time the week of Thanksgiving. It's been months since I've been able to wrap my arms around that man."

I know how much she misses him, and right now her expression shows it. In some ways, I'm envious of their relationship. She's very lucky to have a man who trusts her and is willing to have a long-distance relationship. So far, she's been able to deal with his absence fairly well, but I know his frequent emails and phone calls are what keep her smiling.

I can't help but hope that one day he will pop the question to her. She's been in love with Greg since we were all in grade school together, and they deserve nothing but a happily ever after.

"I got a card in the mail from my parents," I tell her when I see she's still not going to bring up the subject of Brian. "Looks like they aren't coming home for Thanksgiving. I called Mom to thank her for the money they sent me and to talk about their plans. She offered to fly me to the closest town near where they're staying and have Dad pick me up at the airport, but since I'll have finals the following week, I told her I'd pass. Besides, I know they're planning to be here for Christmas. What's a few more weeks, huh?"

Surprisingly, I've dealt with their being gone quite well. The time alone has taught me a lot about responsibility.

"You know you're always welcome at my family's," she adds. "You're the other daughter they never had."

I follow her towards the door, hoping she won't call me out on how I'm steadily looking towards the parking lot.

"Girl, you got it bad don't you?" She giggles at me.

I'm busted.

"What?" I play dumb, but she knows me all too well.

"I saw you looking around. You're looking for his car, aren't you?"

"Well, you never know when he might show up again," I tell her, the front doors sliding closed behind us.

"If he does, please be careful. Call me if you have to. I can come back in no time." The way she says this makes me think she doesn't feel comfortable about me being alone with him. I've never gotten that kind of vibe from him and I wonder why she felt the need to imply it.

I watch as she climbs into her car. I may have been caught looking, but one thing's for sure. There's no sign of him out there tonight. I've combed over the entire lot, and nothing.

Instead of staying behind the desk, I sit out in the lobby in one of the comfortable chairs and prop my feet up. With my literature book positioned in my lap, I get started on my homework. Every now and then I look up, but there's nothing for me to see. Maybe it's time to accept he's never coming back.

Chapter 8
Brian

SEVERAL DAYS HAVE PASSED SINCE I started working at the oil lube shop. I won't lie and tell you I love my new job, but right now I'm earning money towards a paycheck. Money I've not had in a long time.

As long as the weather stays pleasant, I think I'll be able to tolerate it. But the closer we get to the holidays, the cooler it will get, making it more of a challenge.

I'm really shocked how steady Jared's business is. Everyone knows him by name and he always makes time to stop and talk to every single one of them. The guy has done pretty darn well for himself, and I'm impressed. So far, he's a very likable boss and has insisted on paying for my lunch every day. Can't complain about that.

I've gotten into the routine of stopping by to see his mom and to grab a bite to eat before going in. She was so happy to learn I'd gotten the job working for her son.

I've also started using the restaurant's bathroom facilities to freshen up. The handicap stall has its own sink, so no one pays much attention to what I'm doing. Wiping down this way has gotten old pretty quick. I'm surprised Jared's mom hasn't caught on to what I'm doing, since I always have a change of clothes with me. And if she has, I just hope she keeps it to herself.

On Friday, I ask Jared if he knows of a laundromat close by. I have the weekend off and I'm desperate to get my clothes cleaned. When I punch out at the end of my shift, he approaches me with an envelope in his hand.

"Here, man, I know things are hard for you right now, and since you're not getting paid until next week, I wanted to give you a little advance."

I glance down at the envelope in my hand, and I much as I could use it, I push it back toward him. "I can't take this."

"I insist. You've worked hard this week," he continues.

"Man, you really don't have to. I was able to make a little bit in tips so it'll hold me over."

"No, take it. Treat yourself to a nice, hot meal. See 'ya Monday morning." He pats me on the shoulder and heads back inside the shop.

He's never questioned me about where I'm staying and I've not talked about it either. When I filled out the application with the lady, I told her I wasn't certain of the address yet, so she said I could get back with her. I'm sure I'll have to come up with something by the time paychecks are cut since they'll need it for tax purposes.

I don't open the envelope until I'm in the car. When I do, I find a hundred dollars. I'm so excited, and still can't believe Jared did it. First Jennifer, and now Jared. Pulling out from the parking lot, I roll down the window and sing the lyrics to the song that's playing on the radio. The week has, no doubt, ended well. I pull up at the red light and look over to the car beside me only to see the driver staring right at me. Well, I never was one for carrying a tune.

I don't have anything special planned for the night, but I pull into the first gas station I come to and quickly change out of my work clothes. There's nothing pretty about them but they've saved me from running out of clothes to wear this week. I locate the laundromat, but it's already closed for the day. It's just as well since I've got the whole weekend to get them done.

I take Jared's advice and grab a bite to eat at a sport's bar I remembered seeing. There, I'm able to watch a football game on the big screen and it only reminds me how much I've missed out on seeing them. I finally settle my tab when it's over. I know I shouldn't have spent so much money on food but I felt I deserved it.

I've thought about Jennifer several times this week. Many nights I wanted to stop by and see her, but I talked myself out of it at the last minute since I don't really have anything to offer her other than my friendship. She was nice and all, but why would she want anything to do with me? After all, we come from two totally different worlds. Tonight, I figure what the hell. What do I have to lose? Yeah, I'd love to talk to her. After all, it's been lonely this week hanging out in my car every night.

I pull into the hotel parking lot and into a spot that allows me a direct view inside. She's busy with a few people checking in, so I decide to wait until the lobby has cleared out. I'm relaxed from the couple beers I had earlier, so I close my eyes for a few moments.

I jump all of a sudden from a loud knocking noise. Realizing where I'm at, I look over and see Jennifer standing outside my car. Shit, the sun is coming up. No doubt it's early in the morning. *How the heck did that happen?*

I'm so mad at myself right now. I can't believe I fell asleep and never made it inside to see her.

"Hey, stranger," she says as I roll down my window.

"Hey, yourself. Are you always this cheerful so early in the morning?" I hope that doesn't come across as rude but for someone who's been up all night, she's clearly either glad to see me or isn't the least bit tired.

"Not exactly. I thought you were long gone from here, but what a pleasant surprise. How long have you been out here?" she throws in. It's my understanding she thinks I've only been here for a little while and not the entire night. "You up for some coffee this morning?"

"Sure. Where's the nearest Starbucks?" I ask, knowing it's supposed to be a great place for coffee. I really can't afford Starbucks, but how can I turn down an invitation from her? Yes, I'd say she's happy to see me.

I decide to fess up in case she asks again. "I actually pulled in late last night and had plans to come inside. You had several customers you were waiting on, and I guess I dozed off. I hadn't realized how tired I was."

"*Awww.* Well, I hate you slept out here, but I'm glad I got to see you this morning. If you don't mind, before we go for that coffee, could we stop by my apartment so I can change clothes? I sort of spilled some juice on myself when I was refilling the machine earlier." She points at a big stain on the front of her shirt. "Or, I could just fix us some coffee there and we can sit out on my patio. It's totally up to you."

"Sounds good to me. That is, if you're okay with me coming to your place." Now, it's my turn to be excited. She's invited me over instead of going to some overpriced coffee shop. I like the way she's thinking. If I play my cards right, I might even be able to grab a shower while I'm there, something I sorely need. "You want me to follow you?"

"Okay. It's about a ten-minute drive from here. When we get there, just park beside me, okay?" She runs over to get in her car and I go ahead and crank mine. I follow closely behind, paying special attention on how to get there in case I'm invited over again.

I'm completely blown away at the complex we pull into. These apartments are very nice and probably costs a fortune. I help gather her things from her car, then walk down the breezeway behind her. Her unit is on the lower level all the way in the back. I look around noticing that, being on the backside, she has privacy that other don't. We walk in together, and the first thing I notice is how clean it is. Everything's so neat and orderly, and there doesn't appear to be a single thing out of place. It's not as large as the one Macy and I shared, but it's still spacious enough. For an apartment, it's been maintained very well.

"Can you go ahead and turn on the coffee pot? It's over there on the counter. I always get it ready before I have to leave. Make yourself comfortable while I run back and change." She takes off down the narrow hallway then turns into what I assume must be her bedroom.

"Sure, no problem." I flip the switch and almost instantly smell the aroma of the coffee brewing.

Minutes later, she walks into the kitchen wearing a pair of pajama-like pants and a t-shirt. She looks very relaxed and comfortable, to say the least.

"Mind if I use your restroom?" I ask her. The few beers I'd had the night before are straining my bladder. She doesn't seem to be the least bit concerned that I'm here alone with her, someone who's still a total stranger.

"Not at all. It's down the hallway to the right."

I swear the girl does nothing but smile, probably even in her sleep. She just has one of those radiating personalities, and I'd be willing to bet she never gets angry about a thing. Sometimes "sickly sweet" can be a little too much though.

I make my way to the bathroom and notice that it, too, is completely spotless. The countertop is clear of any lotions, hairsprays, or perfumes. The only thing I see is a cute little bottle of hand soap from one of those specialty shops. Everything else, I'm sure, is neatly tucked away in one of the drawers underneath the sink.

I always hated having to help Macy clean the apartment back when I lived with her. I'd usually try to come up with some excuse of something I needed to do just to get out of cleaning. But, I guess if you maintain everything, it doesn't take much to stay on top of it. Macy had a bad habit of letting everything go during the week, then expected me to help her on the weekends. Looking back, I know I probably should've done more to help, especially when I was between jobs and home most of the time, but housework just really isn't my thing.

When I'm done, I walk back to the kitchen and notice she has two coffee cups sitting out on the counter.

"How do you like yours?"

"Um, sugar and cream please." I'll never admit it, especially now, but I'm not a big coffee drinker. I'll have a cup every now and then, but I wasn't going to turn down the opportunity to spend some time with her.

There goes that damn smile again.

"Oh, wow, that's the same way I like mine. Is liquid creamer okay?" She prepares our cups then passes one to me.

Yes, the smiling is a little overpowering.

I'm careful not to spill any and walk over to the sliding glass doors that overlook her patio. I spot a small grill over in one corner, as well as a swing that hangs from the rafters. "Nice swing you got there," I tell her. The view isn't the greatest since there's nothing but trees and woods to look at, but the swing is pretty awesome. I bet I'd spend lots of time out here on it if this were my place.

"Yeah, it belonged to my parents. They didn't want to get rid of it when they sold the house, but there wasn't room to take it with them in the RV. My dad got the maintenance man to hang it for me."

"I bet you spend a lot of time sitting out there."

"Sometimes I like to go out there when I get home in the mornings. Working the overnight shift really does a number to your body and I find it a great way to unwind. There're times I still have studying to do or homework to finish, but I try to do all that while I'm at work. All of my classes are in the evenings this semester, so I try to discipline myself to go to sleep as soon as possible or else I'm pretty grumpy when I get up."

Yeah, I'd like to see that. Her? Grumpy? I just don't see that side of her. Not at all.

She opens the sliding doors and we both walk out. The morning air is slightly chilly, a sure sign that fall is approaching. Otherwise, it's a perfect morning.

"I found a job this week," I announce as we both take a seat on the swing. I leave just enough room between us so it's not awkward.

"Oh, wow. That's awesome. I knew you'd find something. It's not too hard to find a job around here with all the new places being built. It may not be the kind of job you really want, but it'll be some money coming in until you're able to find something else."

"That's sort of the way I see it, too. It's a job. I'm not planning on making it permanent, that's for sure." I sort of lower my head, embarrassed to tell her what I'm actually doing. "I'm washing cars down at the local oil change place. The one in front of Target."

"Oh, yeah. I've been there plenty of times. The owner is super nice. My dad actually feels safe with me using them if he's not in town to service my car for me. My parents are a little overprotective," she throws in, then sets her empty coffee cup down on the ground between her feet.

"That was a pretty good cup of coffee," I tell her. "Thanks for inviting me over this morning. Would you like another cup?" I bend over to pick up her cup but she beats me to it.

"Sure. I'll make us one."

"No, let me. You sit back down." I just hope I can make them as good as she did.

"So, what have you got planned for the day?" she asks me when I return.

"Well, I need to stop by the laundromat. I'm completely out of clean clothes to wear." For a moment, I wonder if there's a laundry facility here at her complex. The one I shared with Macy had a small facility with several washers and dryers for the tenants to use. I'm sure it'd be less crowded if there was one.

"Why don't you just use mine?" she quickly suggests. "I have my own washer and dryer. Besides, it'd be saving you money if you just do it here."

Now it's my turn to feel a little awkward. Not only would I feel like it's imposing on her, but wouldn't that be a little strange bringing my stuff inside? I'm not sure I want her to see the little bit of clothing I actually own.

"But I don't have any detergent and stuff. I've not bought any yet and I wouldn't want to use all yours." Just listening to myself, I wonder what happened to the *real* Brian. When did he start turning down handouts?

"I insist," she tells me again. "I won't take no for an answer."

Not wanting to offend her, I say, "Okay, but just this once. Hopefully, I'll have my own place soon and I can do it there."

I'm not exactly sure that'll be the case, judging by the some of the prices I saw in the newspaper, but she doesn't have to know that. Hell, I haven't even started saving any money yet. It's going to take at least a month's worth of paychecks, if not more, just to have enough for a deposit and the first month's rent. I supposed a guy can dream, right?

I don't really want to tell her I've actually never had a place of my own before. From the time I left my parent's home,

I either lived with my brother, stayed with a few friends, or moved in with whoever I'd been seeing at the time. It's not the greatest track record, I know, but being independent has never been my thing or within my budget.

"Have you started narrowing down a place yet?" she asks me, concern showing on her face. "Every now and then, a unit becomes available here. You should stop by the front office and see if anything's vacant."

Me? Narrow a place down yet? Please, my biggest concern has been staying out of sight from the cops in this town. Just because they frown upon my temporary living arrangements, it doesn't make me a bad person.

"I'm sure a place like this is way more than what I can afford. I'd hate to tie up every dollar I make just on rent. I still need to eat, you know." I try to make some humor out of it. "The oil change place doesn't pay *that* good. Your place is really nice though. Maybe I just need to find a roommate and split the expenses until I can afford something of my own."

She looks over at me. "Yeah, you're probably right. Well, good luck with your search. I'm sure you'll come up with something soon. Now, let's get your laundry going. You grab your clothes, and I'll get the washer started."

There's no sense in arguing with her about it. I walk out to my car and retrieve my duffel bag from the back seat. It takes me a few moments to shove everything inside since they're tossed haphazardly everywhere.

"I'm pretty sure I can get them all done in one load," I tell her when I walk back inside.

"Don't be silly. You don't want to overload the washer and you surely don't want to mix your whites with colors," she says with a smirk. "Here, let me." She reaches out to take them from me, but I manage to pull back. Our hands briefly touch and I glance into her eyes. They're so mesmerizing.

"No, they're my dirty clothes."

"You act like I've never seen dirty clothes before. Remember, I grew up with two older brothers. I had to pitch in and help Mom around the house."

I can tell she was raised right just by the way she always mentions her family and helping out. I'm sure she misses them a great deal, too. I've said very little to her about my own, not so sure how she'd take to the troubles I've had.

I really hate to ask, but I do it anyway. "Do you think while my clothes are washing I could maybe take a hot shower?"

Before she even says yes, she's already walking down the hallway towards the bathroom. "Please, by all means. The towels are under the sink. If you need anything, there're plenty of body washes and shampoos. I'll just be here in the kitchen putting together a shopping list. Maybe you'd like to join me for a little shopping after lunch. That is, if you don't have anything else planned."

I laugh to myself. Hmm. *What kind of plans could I possibly have?*

I already like the direction this is heading.

Chapter 9

Jennifer

I LIKE BEING FRIENDLY and accommodating for Brian, but is it really safe having this guy who I've only known for a short period of time in my apartment? And, using my shower?

It's a little too late to be thinking about that now. I push the thought away and try to convince myself I'm helping someone out who's had a run of bad luck. Besides, he's done nothing so far to warrant any insecurities. So far, he's been fun and I already think of him as a friend.

He's still in the shower when the washer cuts off. Rather than have his clothes sit, I go ahead and toss them in the dryer. The sooner they're all done, the sooner we'll be able to head out.

I try not to notice, but some of his things are quite shabby and worn. I'm not judging him by their quality but, poor guy. He could stand to have a couple nice new outfits.

Minutes later, Brian emerges from the bathroom. I look up and see him standing in the hallway, leaned against the door frame with a towel wrapped around him. My jaw drops.

Sweet Baby Jesus, what do I have standing in front of me? Wow! Who knew he looked like that underneath his clothes.

His cheeks instantly turn red, no doubt, from the look on my face. He stands there for a couple moments, letting me take *all* of him in. Finally, he speaks, breaking my stare.

"Man, that was one of *the* best showers I think I've ever had." He looks refreshed, and oh, so damn sexy.

What I wouldn't give for that towel to slip and fall to the floor right about now.

I turn away from him and face the dryer to hide my embarrassment. "I went ahead and put your clothes in the dryer for you. Hope you don't mind."

"Oh, thanks. I, uh, sort of forgot to leave out anything to change into. I'm, uh, going to use your towel until they're done."

Surely he knows he's driving me crazy. I'm barely able to look up without being flushed and flustered.

"Why don't you hang out in the living room and see what you can find to watch on television?" I suggest. "While we wait, I've got some homework I can work on. Maybe then we can go and grab a bite to eat."

"Sure, if you don't mind the company. I've got the weekend off, so I'm free to do whatever."

Yes! He said yes!

And with that, I head down the hallway towards my bedroom. On a normal Saturday, I'd be crawling into bed, too tired to keep my head up. Now, I'm wide awake and it's got nothing to do with the two cups of coffee I had earlier. I just hope I can concentrate long enough to finish my assignment.

I pull out my Biology Lab book and study guide and spread everything across my desk. I can hear the TV playing from the other room, tuned in to a sports channel. Each time a commercial comes on, Brian changes the channels to another game. Typical male, that's for sure.

I've been stuck on the same question for the last ten minutes now. I've flipped through the chapter repeatedly, looking for the answer, but my concentration is completely shot. My mind keeps drifting back to images of Brian standing in my hallway, wearing only my towel.

I hear the bathroom door shut and figure his clothes must be dried now. I swear, I don't think I could've sat in the same room with him, towel and all.

Could I see myself dating him? Maybe. My parents repeatedly drop hints to me about meeting someone. I've had guy friends, but nothing ever too serious. But, I enjoy hanging out with Rebecca while Greg's away, too. I figure when the right one comes along, I'll know and, well, it's still too early to tell about Brian. One thing's for certain, since being around him, I've definitely noticed some different emotions being stirred up inside me. Emotions I've certainly never felt before.

I finally give up on studying and close my books. I put on a cute outfit, suitable for hanging out, and we both end up in the hallway at the same time.

"I don't know about you, but I'm starving," I tell him, almost at a loss for words. He looks nice in his jeans and t-shirt "How about I treat us to lunch to celebrate your new job?"

"Sure, sounds good to me."

I grab my phone and step into a pair of flip-flops. We walk outside and I immediately pull out my sunglasses. It's such a beautiful day to be stuck indoors. I unlock the doors to my car and we both get in. As soon as I crank the engine, music blares from the radio.

"Sorry about that!" I say and reach over to turn it down. I'd completely forgotten I had it so loud when I came home earlier this morning.

"Not a problem. I actually like that song." He turns it up again and starts singing the words. He doesn't sound too bad either.

I pull out of the apartment complex into traffic and ask Brian for suggestions of what he'd like for lunch.

"I'm open for pretty much anything. What do you recommend?"

"I know of a really good pizza place if you're in the mood," I suggest, thinking pizza's a pretty safe choice.

"Okay. Let's do it." He looks over, smiles, and I almost melt. "By the way, thanks for inviting me to lunch."

"You're welcome."

The remainder of the drive, we're silent. I use the time to think about the words to the song that's playing. It's something about falling in love, and I wonder if it's meant to be a sign of the future.

When we get to the pizza place, Brian opens the door for me. He places his hand at the small of my back and guides me in. I'm not expecting it, so I'm not sure how to react. Anyone seeing this would think we're a couple. It's hard not to think of this as a date.

Desi's is one of my favorites, and Rebecca and I come here quite often. The hostess takes us to a booth in the back corner and I slide in first. To my surprise, Brian takes the spot next to me. I'm shocked, but no less giddy with happiness. *Isn't this what couples do?* I'm not trying to read more into this, but I certainly like the feel of things right now. I'm really curious to know what *he's* thinking.

We both order sweat teas, and he passes me a menu. When the waitress returns with our drinks, she tells us the day's special, but we agree on a hand-tossed pepperoni pizza. I should be nervous about eating in front of him, but I'm not.

Neither of us knows what to say next, but that's okay. Brian glances towards one of the big screen televisions and zeroes in on it. Men and their sports! Geez. I pretend to be interested, too, even though neither of the teams sound familiar. The waitress interrupts with our food and it smells divine. I'm glad I suggested coming here.

We both reach for the same slice, and I immediately pull my hand back as it brushes against his.

"Here, it's hot," he says, pretending the moment didn't happen. He slides the pizza onto my plate and I seriously hope I don't make a mess with all the runny cheese.

We continue to make small talk about the things we like and dislike, and soon realize we have more things in common than either of us ever imagined. I've thoroughly enjoyed this time together, especially in a more relaxed atmosphere. I look up and notice he's got a little bit of cheese stuck to his chin.

I suppress a giggle and reach for my napkin to wipe it off. "I hope you've enjoyed lunch."

"This is the best pizza I think I've ever had," he quickly adds. "Thanks for suggesting it."

I don't want our lunch date to end, but I know the waitress needs the table for other customers. She leaves the ticket on the table and Brian reaches for it.

"No, I invited you. It's my treat." I hold my hand out, hoping he'll pass the check to me.

"Let me take care of it. You've already been generous enough this morning."

"How about next time? You can pick the place and I'll let you buy," I suggest, hoping he's good with my offer of a next time.

"Sounds like a plan to me."

For a brief moment, our eyes meet and we both smile. I leave enough money on the table to cover our food and tip, then excuse myself to the bathroom before leaving. I need a moment to regain my composure.

I find Brian waiting for me outside. He's leaned up against a pole with his foot propped up. *Damn, I can't believe anyone in their right mind would kick this guy out.* There's something magnetic about him, and I quickly look away when he sees me taking him in.

I ask Brian if he minds accompanying me to the grocery store before heading back to the apartment. I know I talked about it earlier, but I just want to confirm he's still good with it. I'd like to spend as much time as I can with him, but I don't want to overdo our first outing, either.

"Hey, I'm cool with that. I've got no other plans for the afternoon, especially now that you've helped me out with my laundry."

"It won't take long. I just need to pick up a few things to get me through the upcoming week."

Upon entering the store, Brian grabs a cart while I scan through my list. He casually points out a few things he likes while we look around, and I'm quite surprised we have the same tastes in many of these items, too. As discretely as possible, I toss a couple items into the cart and wonder if he notices.

We stop at the butcher counter next, and I immediately entertain the idea of picking up a few steaks for the grill. Is it too soon to ask him to stay for dinner tonight?

"It's been so long since I've had a nice, juicy steak," he mentions. "Maybe when I get my own place, I can fix us a couple of these." I like his mention of seeing me again.

"You know I've got the grill at home," I point out. "Why don't you pick us out a few? We can grab some beer and enjoy the evening out on the porch." As soon as I say this, I realize it could sound like I'm being a bit pushy.

"Are you sure you haven't had enough of me already? First lunch, now dinner?"

"I've actually enjoyed spending the day with you." And I really have. I reach over and nudge him on the arm.

"It's a deal then, but I'm buying these. My treat," he says while looking over at me. He leans down, picks out two of the best looking steaks, and places them in the cart.

I nod my head and reply, "Okay, if you insist. But everything else is on me."

I grab a couple more items for our meal, including a twelve pack of beer. I'm still stuffed from lunch, but I'm already looking forward to tonight.

Chapter 10
Brian

WHEN WE GET BACK TO Jennifer's place, I help her unload the groceries. I'm not sure where she likes the items arranged in her cabinets, so I stick with putting away the cold stuff. I figure I can't go wrong there. She saves the empty plastic bags and shoves them inside a larger bag in the bottom of the pantry. This is the same thing my mother used to do.

"Would you like a beer?" she asks after closing the pantry door.

It's still a little early in the day for a drink, but who am I to argue if she wants one now.

"Sure." I pull two from the cardboard carrier inside the refrigerator and take a seat next to her on the couch. We're back at that awkward stage again, something all new relationships experience in the beginning. Wait. Did I just say relationship? Is this what we're in? A relationship?

She turns the television on and lowers the volume. I steal a glance at the screen, curious to know if my team won earlier. Football. Oh, how I miss the days when I used to play.

Growing up, I'd always wanted to be a running back. My father told me I wasn't built for the position and I was too slow, but I worked hard to prove him wrong. It was at the end of my junior year when things started getting bad at home. My grades had slipped, and football became a thing of my past. I was devastated. Not only did I disappoint myself, but the coaches didn't seem to understand why I couldn't just unload my frustrations on the field instead of taking them out on my dad. That was easier said than done. If they'd only known.

I was probably good enough to earn a scholarship, too, but without the support of my family, nothing mattered anymore. It got so bad, there were many nights I just stopped going home. I'd crash at a friend's house for days at a time. My parents never showed much concern as to my whereabouts.

By the time I graduated, with just barely passing grades, I was out of the house completely. I'd stop by to see my mom, often staying a couple nights, but then my dad would start in on me. My visits back home became less and less.

I probably stayed at my brother's house the longest. Jake was always busy with work, putting in long hours and coming home late. He never seemed concerned that I'd come home in the middle of the night or the following morning or just not at all. I'm not saying I was proud of that lifestyle, but I was getting by without anyone telling me how to live my life.

By that point, the piece of junk car I'd been driving since I'd had my license was nothing but an eyesore. There was always something going wrong with it or I was having to repair it myself. One night, I'd had a few too many drinks with a buddy, and I somehow ran it off into a ditch. Nothing about the car was worth saving, and I often wondered why my life was spared following the accident. I realized then that I needed to get my shit together if I was ever going to make something of myself.

It sucked not having a way to go. Jake bought himself a new truck he'd been saving for, and I ended up with his silver Honda. It'd been his first car, the one he'd bought all on his own while still in high school, and he didn't want it to go to just anyone.

At the time, I was in and out of relationships, nothing ever getting too serious. After all, no one wanted to date a loser. Jake threatened to kick me out if I didn't get my shit together. One night in particular, when he'd gotten in late, we shared a few words. I realized then I needed to find another place to stay before we both said something we'd regret later.

Shortly after that, I met Macy and we all know how *that* ended.

I hadn't realized I was lost in my own thoughts until Jennifer waved her hand in front of my face several times trying to get my attention.

"Earth to Brian."

"Sorry, I was just thinking about something." I didn't want to divulge too much of my past for fear she might look at me differently. We were headed in a positive direction and I wanted to keep it that way.

One beer led to another. And another. It wasn't long before there were only a few bottles left in the refrigerator. We'd almost killed the twelve-pack.

We laughed and carried on with each other, and I soon realized how easy she was to talk to. What I can't figure out, though, is how the poor thing is still awake. She worked all night and hasn't slept any today. With all the beer she's consumed, she ought to sleep good tonight.

I notice it's getting dark outside. With wobbly legs, Jennifer stands up and walks over to open the patio doors. The fresh air feels good against my skin. I know I should probably limit my intake, but instead, I do just the opposite and grab one more. I walk up behind her and touch the cold bottle to her leg. She screams playfully and runs around the room trying to chase me, nearly falling over onto the couch. She makes several attempts to tag me with her own beer, but I'm much too quick for her. She sets her bottle down on the end table, and I give in. Moments later, she's tackling me on the couch.

We take turns tickling each other like kids, and at one point, she's close enough to my face, I can feel her warm breath against my cheek. For a brief moment, I look her in the eyes and probably hold my gaze longer than I should. I believe she feels the connection, too, because she suddenly jumps up, taken aback by our closeness.

"Wait." I reach for her hand before she walks away. "Come here."

I pull her towards me and wrap my arms around her. No longer laughing and giggling, I stare deep into her eyes then place a gentle kiss on her lips. She tastes of beer, but I'm sure I do, too. It's a soft, tender kiss, and one I don't want to end anytime soon. Just when I think she's enjoying the moment and we might be going somewhere with it, she pulls back again.

"Why don't you go ahead and get the grill fired up. The charcoal and lighter are in the box on the porch," she manages to say before heading down the hallway towards the bathroom.

I'm not sure if I embarrassed her, or if maybe she was afraid of what the kiss might lead to, but it was actually fun to let loose, laugh, and have a good time with her. I can tell through some of her actions that she's not very confident with flirting, but I can quickly remedy that if she allows me to.

I walk outside and begin prepping the grill. Jennifer joins me several minutes later with each of us another beer. I try to read the expression on her face, but she won't look me directly.

"Babe, you better slow down on that beer. At the rate you're going, I'm going to have to cut you off before the food's ready."

She pokes me in the arm and winks at me. "I'll be okay. It's not often I get to do this." She points her beer up at me. "Thanks for allowing me." She stands up close to me and brings her arm up around my waist. Her actions surprise me, but I know the beer is working on her big time.

I'm not sure how to respond, so I wrap my arm behind her as well. She loses her balance and leans into me. I catch her stumble and hold her upright.

"Oops, sorry 'bout that." She giggles and casually kisses me on the cheek.

"It's alright," I tell her as she regains her balance. Maybe the kiss from earlier wasn't a setback after all.

I flip the steaks with my free arm, and the aroma drives me crazy. "Shouldn't be too much longer," I tell her, noticing the glassy look in her eyes. One more beer, and she's a goner. The only thing that might save her is if she gets some food in her. It just might help to sober her up some. It's funny to listen to her talk. If I could record it and play it back for her later, she'd really be embarrassed.

She's right about one thing—kicking back and taking it easy sounds like a good idea tonight. I've been through a lot these last few weeks and if anyone needs a break, it's me.

We sit on the swing again and wait for the steaks to finish cooking. I lay my arm across the back of her shoulder and she leans into me, dropping one hand down on my leg while the other holds onto her beer. I've been keeping an eye on it and she's yet to take a swallow. She lays her head back to rest in the crook my arm, and I notice how she fits perfectly there. *Focus, Brian. Focus. Don't let the effects of the beer get to your head, too.*

She gets quiet, and for a moment I wonder if she's fallen asleep. I nudge her slightly, afraid she's going to spill her beer if that's the case, and she sits up.

"What?" she asks.

"You tired?"

"Umm, yeah, a little bit."

"If you're ready to eat, I'll pull the steaks off."

"I'll get the table ready inside, okay?"

I watch her stumble to the door and wonder if she'll even make it to the kitchen without passing out.

When we sit down at the table, Jennifer selects the smaller of the two steaks then lifts her beer bottle to clink it with mine.

"Cheers. Here's to new friendship, great company, and a damn good-looking meal. Hope it tastes as good as it smells." She surprises me with her choice of words.

"Cheers," I echo. We both dig in, and I must admit, I did do a darn good job on them. The pre-packaged potato salad isn't bad, either.

"We did a fabulous job tonight, huh?" I ask, making sure to include her. I stand up to clear the table when we're finished but she remains seated. I look over at her and can't help but laugh. "What's the matter, baby? You have a little too much to drink?"

She rolls her eyes at me, but in a playful sort of way. The look on her face says it all—she's done for the night.

Chapter 11
Jennifer

BRIAN STARTS TO CLEAR AWAY our dishes, but sadly, I feel if I attempt to move from the table to help, I just might drop to the floor. He looks over at me and laughs, not in a mean way but because of the condition I'm in. I drank entirely too much and my body is letting me know it.

He brings me a glass of water to drink in hopes the affects from the alcohol will subside some. I feel helpless right in my own kitchen. The room slowly stops spinning and I stand up, taking a couple steps towards the hallway. I'm in desperate need of the bathroom, not because I feel sick, but because I've exceeded how much my bladder can hold.

Once in the bathroom, I slip out of my jeans and pull on a pair of cotton pajama shorts. It's too much of a struggle to change shirts, so I leave on the one I'm wearing. A knock on the bathroom door startles me.

"You okay in there?" Brian calls from the other side.

I didn't think I'd been in here *that* long.

I open the door and find him leaning against the doorframe. His crooked smile is the first thing I see, and I'm immediately ashamed at myself. I should never have gotten this carried away. My cheeks instantly heat up, and I suddenly break out in a nervous sweat.

"Yeah, I'm fine," I tell him slowly, bringing my gaze up to meet his. Then, I notice something that looks like a change of clothes rolled up under his arm. "You going to change, too?"

"Yeah, I got the kitchen done. You might find some things out of place, but I wasn't sure where you kept everything."

"That's okay. You know you could've left those for later."

"Well, I didn't mind."

How was he able to function just fine when we both drank the same number of beers? At least, I think we had the same amount. I could've lost count.

"You up for watching a movie?" I ask, uncertain how far I'll actually make it without going to sleep.

"Sure, but only if you are. I don't want to overstay my welcome."

"I don't mind. Not at all," I manage to say. I realize I'm flirting, maybe even a little too much, but it sure feels good.

A few minutes later, Brian joins me on the couch. I'm pretty sure my mouth falls open, and I'm uncertain if it's my eyes or the effects of the alcohol that are playing tricks on me.

Oh. My. God.

When Brian said he was going to change, too, I had no idea he meant into this. He's… nearly naked. Okay, so he's wearing some loose fitting shorts, but that's it. It's the same body I saw earlier today, right here in this very apartment, but now it looks so much more mouth-watering and inviting. *What the heck is he trying to do to me?* Yes, it's got to be the alcohol.

I wonder why he decided not to put on a shirt. He knows I'm a bit out of it and not my normal self. Surely he knew me seeing him like that would have an effect on me. I'd love to slide my hands over his taught muscles…*Stop, Jenn. Just stop it!*

"I'd offer to make us some popcorn, but I'm still stuffed from that delicious steak you made," I tell him.

"It was pretty darn good, if I do say so myself. But, I agree. I don't think I could eat anything else right now, even if I wanted to." It doesn't help that he puts his hand against his stomach, indicating he's full.

Yes, I see the damn thing and it's driving me freaking crazy.

For some crazy reason, I lean over and switch off the lamp. I can't take seeing him bare-chested anymore. The previews begin to play and I scoot over, as close as I can get, beside him. I'm slightly chilled and his skin is warm and feels good against mine. He brings his arm down and pulls me close.

"You cold?" he asks.

"Just a little." I feel my hardened nipples against the fabric of my shirt. Thank goodness the room is dark. I pull the blanket off the back of the couch and spread it over my lap.

He gives me a funny look, then asks, "Are you going to hog that blanket all for yourself, or are you going to share it with me?"

I cuddle into his chest and pull it up around both of us. I've been out with other guys and spent time with them alone, but the feeling I get from Brian right now is totally different. I still can't believe that I met him only days ago.

"Mind if I lay my head down?" I ask after a while.

"If you're comfortable with that, go right ahead."

I lower my head to his lap, and he readjusts the blanket. He trails his fingers over my shoulder and down my back.

Suddenly, my eyelids get heavy and I drift off.

****

I feel Brian shift behind me on the couch and realize we must have fallen asleep. I'm uncertain what time it is but I know it's late.

"Come on," he whispers into my ear. "Let me help you get into bed." We both stand and, although I'm still a little unsteady on my feet, I hold onto his hand while he walks me back to my bedroom.

I lean down and pull back the covers.

"I'll make sure you're comfy before I leave."

"What? Where are you going?" I ask, suddenly sensing he's about to leave.

"Baby, I'm putting you to bed. Then, I'm going to head on out." They're words I really don't want to hear.

"No, please stay," I beg, afraid that if he leaves, I might not see him again. "Please stay with me tonight."

"I don't know." I hear the concern in his voice. "Are you sure about this? I don't want to make you uncomfortable or anything."

I tap the spot next to me and slide over. "Come here."

Brian climbs in next to me, and I make sure there's plenty of room. He snuggles up behind me and rests his arm against my waist. I've never shared a bed with a guy before—I just hope I'm making the right choice.

Suddenly, I'm wide awake. It hits me how very little I know about him. I know what he's told me, but I have to ask myself if this is too soon. Am I making a huge mistake?

He slowly traces his fingers along my arm. His touch is soft and gentle, and I'm loving the feeling that courses through my body. I'm having a hard time lying still, and I press my backside against him, as close as I can possibly get. He slides his hand down my hip, and I can feel him pushing against me. Suddenly, he becomes erect and I feel it through my shorts. I'm instantly turned on and not at all frightened, although I'm uncertain what I should do. My body's instinct is to grind against him more, but I don't want to appear too desperate, too fast.

"Mmm, you feel nice," he whispers. The softness of his lips so close to my ear ignites my desire even more. It's as if he knows just the right areas to touch me to make me lose all self-control. "You like this?"

He kisses the sensitive area behind my ear, then works his way downward. I'm losing myself with this man. I lean my head back against his shoulder and he casually places his hand atop my left breast, gauging my reaction, before gently massaging it through my shirt. Uncertain what to do, I just lay here enjoying this moment. His fingertips grace my nipple, and he alternates rubbing his thumb and forefinger over it, round and round, before he gently tugs it. He kisses me again on the back of my neck, and I begin to wonder where this is headed.

When I'm unable to handle this torture anymore, I roll over to face him. The alcohol is no longer an issue—its effects are long gone. At least, I think so. Everything is so real now, my focus completely on him.

I draw my face close to his, and together, our lips meet for a light, tender kiss. It becomes deeper, yet passionate, and before long, we're wrapped tightly around each other.

The slight moan that escapes his mouth turns me on even more. I know, without a doubt, my panties are soaked. Wanting to feel every bit of his hardness against me, I run my hands down his back and stop just above the band of his shorts. *Should I?* With my fingers just inside the band, I slide my hand around until it brushes against his erection. I love teasing him this way since it seems he likes it, too. It's all new for me so I hope I'm doing everything correctly and in a way that's pleasing to him. It would be embarrassing if I had to reveal my innocence to him.

He takes my hand and guides it inside his underwear. His manhood is well-endowed and completely fills my hand. I feel a hint of moisture at the tip.

Lost in the moment, Brian slips his fingers inside my panties. "Damn, baby, you're soaking wet."

His words are like magic to my ears, my body producing even more juices. The moisture makes it easy for him to slide his fingers in and out.

I kick the covers back from the rise in my body temperature, and he asks, "Is something wrong?"

I kiss him again. "Mmm, no, baby. Nothing at all."

With no effort at all, my body responds to him. We're merely responding to the feelings and emotions that are overtaking us both.

Then, without questioning our actions, we simply finish removing our clothes. It feels like the natural thing to do.

Brian climbs on top of me, and I position my hands on his upper back. His is muscles tighten beneath my fingertips and the sweat makes it easy for them to slide up and down. I close my eyes and imagine how it would feel to make love to him.

"I'm......I'm not sure if we're ready for this," he whispers, as if reading my mind and drawing me out of the trance I'm in, "but I'm damn sure enjoying this moment."

I sort of choke up, reality kicking in, and I have to take a moment before I can respond.

"I've never felt this before. About anyone. Ever," I share.

Using my hand, I guide him towards my exposed entrance. I hold my breath, wondering if what everyone says is true about the first time. *Is it going to hurt?* Will he know I'm still a virgin? Am I going to bleed? As these questions run through my mind, I take the initiative and lift my hips off the bed.

He enters me slowly, then teases me with short, careful thrusts. Each motion allows him inside me a little deeper each time. Suddenly, he pulls almost completely out as though he suddenly realizes it's my first time, but then he pushes back inside. This time going even deeper. I won't lie, it's slightly painful, but it's nothing like I feared. In fact, it's starting to feel...good.

"You ..." I let slip. "Incredible."

"Shhh." He places a finger to my lips. "Just let it take you away."

I'm in heaven.

Unexpectedly, a different sensation takes over my body, and I'm immediately unable to breathe. The feeling is so intense. He knows I'm close, so he thrusts deeper and deeper, until I hear a moan escape from my own mouth. Together we rock back and forth, the feeling beyond just pleasure and, almost as fast as it all began, it ends. We both lay there silently in each other's arms. Together.

Chapter 12
Brian

WHAT THE HELL? SUDDENLY, I'm wide awake and sit straight up. Where am I? Then, it hits me. I'm not in the front seat of my car. I'm lying in bed. In a bed next to her. Jennifer. The girl I met not all that long ago. *How in the world did this happen?*

Looking over at her in the pre-dawn, early morning light, she's sound asleep on her stomach with the covers pulled up to her neck. Her lips are curved with slight smile. She looks happy, peaceful.

Hours ago, I took something from her that she'll never have again.

Innocence.

How was I supposed to know she was still pure in that sense? And the worst part is, neither of us mentioned using protection. Have I lost my mind? I know nothing about her personal protection. Is she on birth control? Is she able to get pregnant?

Yes, I'm in shock. How could we be so careless?

I think back to when Macy and I were still together. We were extremely sexually active, but she made it clear to me upfront about her being on birth control. There were times when we'd both be so drunk, wearing a condom was the last thing on my mind. But I knew she was protected by the Pill. But Jennifer…we never discussed it.

I slowly ease off of the bed, careful not to wake her. I wonder if she'll think about the same thing when she wakes up. Will she be angry at herself? Better yet, will she blame me?

As quietly as I can, I go to the bathroom, carefully feeling my way around in the faint light. I manage to find a bath cloth from underneath the sink. I don't wait for the water to heat and quickly wet it. I wipe myself off, the cold water sending chills through my body, then throw on some clothes when I'm done and retrieve my duffel bag full of clean laundry from the kitchen. I don't even bother to lace up my shoes. I just hope I'm not making a terrible mistake. I stop for a moment, my hand on the door latch, and ask myself one last time if it's really what I want to do? *Do I want to walk out of her life this way?*

Without giving it anymore thought, I close the door behind me and walk out to my car. I toss my bag into the backseat and do nothing for several minutes. I keep staring at her apartment, wondering if she's going to come running out after me. Did she even sense me leaving? I crank my car and slowly put it in reverse. I have to do this, for my sake and hers.

I drive around for a while, trying to figure out some place to go and settle for the parking lot at the mall. With it being Sunday, there'll be enough cars out that my own will blend in.

I sit here staring blankly ahead, frustrated with myself. *Why am I so drawn to her? Why did I just suddenly leave without telling her goodbye?* While I'm not exactly ashamed of what we did, I simply can't stand to see her pretty face upset.

By now, the inexpensive breakfast I picked up on the way here is cold, and I've lost my appetite. I toss the bag down to the floor, disgusted with myself.

****

Thankfully, the next few days go by rather quickly, but there's not a day that passes that I don't think of her. Thanksgiving is next week, so the shop's been busy with people getting their cars serviced before heading out of town to be with friends and family.

Clint, the other guy I work with, and I are racking up tips. People do seem to be more generous during the holidays and for that, I'm thankful. It's not like we're getting rich, but right now every penny matters to me.

I just hope I can somehow manage to find a permanent place to stay soon. I'm so tired of sleeping in my car and it's near impossible to actually rest. One thing's for sure, I can't keep doing it much longer, especially with winter fast approaching.

Desperate to see her, I come up with a plan. Since she told me her classes were in the evening, as soon as I get off work, I drive across town to the campus. I don't know a thing about any of the buildings, nor do I even know what her classes are or which ones are on which nights, so I do the next best thing. I ride through all the parking lots until I'm able to locate her car. It's not like I have anything better to do.

It doesn't take long for me to spot it. I park a couple rows over but still close enough to keep an eye out for her without being seen. Fortunately, the lot's well lit, too.

My breath hitches in my throat the minute I see her walking to her car. Although I'm not the jealous type, it is a relief to see her walking by herself.

She's wearing jeans and a hooded sweatshirt with a backpack slung over her shoulder. Even from my car, she looks sad and hangs her head low. She doesn't even look up until she's almost at her car. I just hope I'm not the reason for her sullenness.

I'm tempted to follow her, just to make sure she gets home okay, but I don't. If she should happen to see me or even suspect she was being followed, I'd have some explaining to do. It's hard watching her pull away, but I'm glad I got to see her, even if it was only from a distance.

I end up doing the same thing the next night, only this time it's raining, making it harder to see. I almost miss her when she rushes out to her car. Poor thing, she doesn't have an umbrella and isn't wearing a jacket.

She sits for a while before leaving. I strain to see if she's okay or in some kind of trouble. The rain lightens a bit, and what I see next almost breaks my heart. Both hands come up to cover her face. No doubt, she's upset. Finally, she turns on her headlights and pulls out.

****

On Friday evening, I pull off at the drugstore. All day I kept thinking of ways to reach out to her, some way to apologize for walking out on her.

I find the greeting card rack and browse through what seems likes hundreds of them before find the perfect one. I ask to borrow a pen from the lady who checks me out, and run back out to my car. It's time to apologize for being a jerk.

When I'm done, I drive over to the hotel. I still have some time before Jennifer is due in. Rebecca looks up as soon as I walk inside. The expression on her face isn't a pleasant one. Without giving me a chance to speak first, she blurts out, "If you're looking for Jennifer, she's not here yet. But, if I were you, I'd stay away from her. She's...uh, she's...not too happy with you right now."

I sense the anger in her tone and I can't say I blame her for being upset with me.

Rather than start an argument since, apparently, I was pretty good at doing that with Macy, I hand Rebecca the sealed envelope.

"Would you please see that she gets this when she comes in?" I turn and walk towards the door but not before Rebecca has a few choice words of her own to say.

"Why can't you give it to her yourself? Or are you too afraid of what she might say to you?"

"Look, I'm sorry. I know she's probably wondering what happened and she has every right to be angry with me. Just please give her the card."

Chapter 13

Jennifer

IT'S BEEN THE LONGEST WEEK of my life and I thought Friday would never get here. I don't have any plans for the weekend, but since I've had trouble sleeping, the only thing I want to do is crawl into my bed. Just a few more hours before sleep is all mine.

The more I think about Brian, the worse I feel. Why? Why did he leave me without so much as a goodbye? I thought we'd shared a really intimate moment. Now, I have to ask myself *was I that bad?*

With Thanksgiving next week and knowing my parents won't make it, I only feel even sadder. Rebecca invited me to spend the day with her family, but I politely declined her offer. At first, she seemed hurt, uncertain why I'd want to be alone, but then I told her I really needed to cram for finals. I think she knew I was lying since I'm always on top of my schoolwork, but she didn't push any further. Truth be known, I really want to spend the day with him.

Earlier in the week, she and I had lunch together, and I unloaded everything on her. What had started out as a fun, eventful weekend, had ended with me feeling sad and confused, uncertain about myself.

"Look, sweetie, some guys are just assholes," she told me.

"But, Bec, something was there between us. We'd had such a great afternoon and we'd clicked. Yes, I probably had a little too much to drink, but Brian was drinking, too. We were laughing and carrying on like we'd known each other forever." It was so painful to talk about it.

"I know it hurts. It was your first time, and he took something special from you that you'll never get back again. It doesn't mean *you* did anything wrong. Please, just don't keep blaming yourself." Her words of encouragement were sincere, but it still hurt nonetheless.

****

On Tuesday morning, I drove by the oil lube shop before going home after work. I caught a glimpse of Brian off to the side of the building. He and another guy were wiping down a small, compact car. I didn't have the courage to stop or much less honk the horn. A single tear had made its way down my cheek, but I forced myself to keep on driving.

It occurred to me that maybe Brian had only been leading me on. Maybe the stories he'd been telling me weren't true at all. It's possible he's married or has a girlfriend which would explain his frequent disappearances. I let that thought leave my head just as quickly as it had entered, refusing to believe either to be true. Neither of us had felt it important to mention our current relationship status, so I'm pretty sure since his previous relationship with that girl Macy had been so disastrous, there's been no one since.

Still, I keep looking for reasons to blame myself. Maybe I'd embarrassed him when he'd discovered I was still a virgin. They say guys know when it's a girl's first time. Luckily for me, it hadn't been the very painful experience I'd always been told and read about. We hadn't even made that much of a mess, either.

What bothers me even more, though, is that we'd both been so caught up in the moment, neither of us had bothered using any protection. I've always had regular periods, and because I've never been sexually active before, there wasn't a need for birth control. I honestly don't think either of us had anticipated it happening. It was one more thing I didn't need to worry about, but unfortunately, I'd have to now.

I pull into the parking lot at work and glance around. It's simply out of habit now. I might not know where he's staying, but at least I do know he's working. That part of his story I do know he was telling me the truth about.

Rebecca looks up from the counter as I walk in the door. "Hey, you. How's it going?"

One look at my face explains everything. "Same as usual."

"I've got to figure out a way to cheer my girl up. I don't like seeing you so sad." She comes over and gives me a hug.

"It just hurts," I mumble and keep my head down. I don't need the flow of tears all over again.

"I know, honey. I know." She does her best to comfort me. "I've pretty much gotten everything done, so it should be a fairly easy night."

"Gee, thanks." I attempt a smile. I know she means well and has me in her best interest. "Having nothing to do only gives my mind more time to ponder everything."

We walk outside together and I note the drop in temperature already. *What if he doesn't have a warm place to stay?* We talk just a few more moments before I rush back inside.

I stop just inside the door and look back out again. No, he's just not here.

I hear my cell phone ringing as I walk back to the desk, and I run back behind it. I see Rebecca's name lit up on the screen. "Hello?" I answer sounding winded.

"Hey, I forgot to tell you. There's an envelope for you inside the desk drawer." She hangs up before I have a chance to ask her who it's from.

I snatch open the desk drawer and see a pale pink envelope with my name written on the outside. At first, I think it's from her, just a little something to cheer me up, but the handwriting doesn't belong to her. *Could it be?*

I'm suddenly scared to open it, fearful of who it's from and what it might say.

I sit down in the chair and stare at it a few moments. Finally, I peel open the back flap that's tucked inside and pull out a card. On the front is a young boy bent down on one knee handing a little girl a bouquet of daisies. The image is black and white but the bundle of flowers is in color, adding more depth to the card's simplistic cover.

I'm overwhelmed with emotion and slowly open it. Printed inside are the words "I'm sorry. Will you please forgive me?" and right below it, in very neat handwriting, is a message from Brian.

There are no words to explain why I left that morning. I hope you'll find it in your heart to forgive me. I'm truly sorry. I'd really like to get to know you and see where our newfound friendship takes us. Please say you'll give me another chance.

Brian

I choke back a sob and suddenly get the feeling I'm not alone. I look up, and there, standing in front of the counter, is Brian.

At first, I pretend I'm angry because this entire week I've blamed myself, thinking I'd done something wrong. He walks around behind the desk, and I ball both my fists, wanting to pound his chest. But when he puts his arms around me and pulls me close, I lay my head on his shoulder and choke back a sob.

"Baby, I'm so sorry." He releases me, then reaches down and firmly holds both my hands in his. "Will you please forgive me?"

"I just didn't know what happened. I thought everything was going so good, then ...." I'm not able to finish before he pulls me to him again, this time, putting his lips to my forehead.

I could stand here and let him embrace me all night. I can't get over the impact he's had on me in such a short period of time.

We quickly pull apart when we hear someone clear their throat.

"I'm sorry to interrupt you both, but I just need to see about getting a room," says a gentleman standing a few feet away from us.

"Oh, I'm so sorry about that, sir." I wipe my eyes as I walk back behind the counter, slightly embarrassed.

While I take care of the guest, I watch Brian from the corner of my eye. He goes down the hallway towards the bathroom—I'm almost afraid to loose site of him. I apologize again to the guest and patiently wait for him to return.

We spend the next several hours reconnecting. It's just like before, when we'd first started talking. He tells me he's still sleeping in his car and I feel so bad for him because it doesn't have to be that way. For a moment, I play with the idea of offering my place to him, like a roommate kind of thing. I'm not sure how my parents or Rebecca would take to that idea, though. After all, I'm still getting to know him, so I just allow the thought to linger in the back of my head.

"I'm not going to get you in trouble hanging around here am I?" he asks and looks down at his watch. It's almost five o'clock in the morning.

"No, you're fine," I tell him, afraid if he leaves again, it could be just like last time. "It's actually been nice to have someone to talk to, even more so because it's you. It gets really lonely being here. Unfortunately, I didn't get much studying done, but that's okay. I've still got time to cram before finals." I can't hide the happiness he brings out in me. I just hope it doesn't come across as being too much.

A few minutes later, Sylvia walks in the front entrance. I can tell Brian feels uncomfortable being here now that my co-worker has shown up. I make introductions between them—referring to Brian as a close friend of mine—then walk behind the counter and retrieve my keys from my purse.

"Brian, why don't you go ahead and head on over to my place. I'm going to help Sylvia get everything ready, then I'll be on my way. It shouldn't take too long."

He looks surprised at my offer. I even surprised myself by suggesting such a thing.

"Are you sure?" he asks.

"Only if you're okay with it. I mean, unless you've got some other place you have to be."

"No, not at all," he adds quickly. "So, I'll see you in about an hour?"

I nod, then walk him to the door and he pulls me in for a hug before walking out.

Chapter 14

Brian

I PULL UP TO JENNIFER'S apartment and look around. As I sit here reminiscing about last night's events and how well everything played out, a subtle smile comes across my face. Honestly, I never anticipated getting involved in a relationship again so quickly after my sudden breakup with Macy. It's even got me wondering if maybe Jennifer and I are more than "just friends."

There's something about her that I'm attracted to. Not only is she sweet and considerate, but she's smart and has a pretty good head on her shoulders. She's ambitious and I'm proud to see her going to school while working and living on her own. Okay, so her parents are helping her out, but she's got goals and that's more than I can say for myself right now. Oh, and she was fun to hang out with, too. Now I don't think her friend is too crazy about me, but I'm sure in time she'll be more accepting of me. Since they're best friends, then Rebecca should like me just because Jennifer does, right? Surely she wouldn't want to disappoint her.

I get out of my car and walk up to the front door. This place has such a good feel to it. Inside, I notice some of her books spread out on the coffee table. I'm a little nervous being here alone, but I know she'll be here soon enough. I open the curtain covering the sliding glass doors and allow the growing sunlight to penetrate the room.

Hoping she won't mind, I go ahead and jump in the shower. Even though I've wiped myself down every day this week, nothing beats a nice, hot shower. Talk about refreshing. There's no better feeling than the hot water beating down on me.

When I'm done, I grab the towel hanging on the back of the door to dry myself. It smells like the lotion Jennifer uses and I breathe in its aroma before hanging it back up to dry.

I take a few minutes to shave, one of my least favorite things to do, and take in the dark circles under my eyes. It's the first time I've noticed them and I wonder if they're evident to anyone else. I'm pretty sure they're from lack of rest since I only manage to get in a couple hours each night.

I scan the contents of the kitchen cabinets to see if I can find something to fix us for breakfast. I'm not an expert when it comes to cooking, even though I did prepare us a pretty good steak last weekend. I get the coffee started and settle on making us some blueberry muffins from one of those pouch envelopes that only needs milk. It's simple and surely I can't screw that up.

Since I received my first paycheck yesterday, I'd like to take her out to eat later today to make up for my absence. It was about what I expected to bring home, nothing to get excited about, but the money is burning a hole in my pocket. Besides, she deserves a special evening.

I should probably see about getting my own bank account. If I keep cash on me, I'll be tempted to spend it more freely. Hopefully, a bank account will help me be more responsible with my money since I've not been too frugal with it in the past. Something else I need to see about—if Jennifer will let me use her address. Just temporarily so I can give it to

Jared. The lady doing payroll reminded me I hadn't turned it in to her yet.

A knock sounds on the door and I figure it's Jennifer needing me to let her in since I have her key. Sure enough, I look through the peep hole and see it's her.

"*Mmmmm*, something smells delicious," she says, walking in and taking her shoes off by the door.

The timer on the oven beeps at the same time I'm about to embrace her in a hug. The muffins are ready so I set them on top of the stove to cool. I fix both of us coffee, since I remember from last weekend how she likes hers, and bring everything into the living room.

"Aww, you made my favorite. I love blueberry muffins," she says and lifts the plate to her nose.

I look over at her and see the sparkle is back in her eyes once again. "Jennifer, I just want to tell you again how sorry I am for bailing on you last weekend. The more I look back on it, I realize I was a complete jerk."

"I know we weren't planning on what happened between us, but I was crushed thinking I'd done something terribly wrong. Or, even worse…" –she pauses for a moment– "that I'd been a terrible lover."

I'm not sure how to respond. There was nothing terrible about our love-making, nothing at all, other than it wasn't planned. And we'd failed to use protection.

She takes a bite of her muffin then looks over at me. "It's been a while since I've been in a relationship, especially a serious one. I'm not exactly sure if you're looking for anything right now, given your recent situation back home. I hope you do decide to stick around and make your home here, though." She hesitates before continuing. "I am curious what's in it for us, but please don't feel like I'm forcing anything on you."

Wow, talk about throwing everything out in the open. Being honest and upfront is one thing, but she's laying everything out for the taking. Wow. I finish my cup of coffee and lean towards her, planting a light kiss to her cheek. "Thank you for allowing me into your life. I'm a firm believer that everything happens for a reason. I'd —I'd like to see what's in it for us, too."

She yawns, and I know how tired she must be. "I'm sorry," she says and covers her mouth.

I gather up our mugs and plate and take them to the kitchen. When I return, I find her lying on the couch.

"Mind if I join you?" I ask.

"No, not at all. Will you grab another blanket from the hall closet?"

I crawl in behind her and drape my arm over her side. Within minutes, we're both sound asleep.

I wake up hours later to an empty couch. Not sure of the time or how long I've been asleep, but the television is on, no sound coming from it. I sit up and look around. I hear running water coming from the bathroom and assume Jennifer must be taking a shower. I go into her bedroom and pull out the nicest pair of jeans and shirt I own from my bag. I could stand to buy a couple new things to wear, especially if I'm going to start taking her out.

I zip up my pants just as she walks into the bedroom.

"You decide to finally wake up?" she asks, smiling at me. "I hope I didn't disturb you."

"No, actually I needed to get up. I'd hate knowing I slept this beautiful day away. What do you say we get out of here? Maybe let me treat you to dinner this evening?" I cross my fingers hoping she's up for it.

"Sure, sounds like a plan. I'm off for a few days and could stand to get out for a bit as well." She winks at me and I'm surprised she's so enthusiastic. "I'm all yours."

I just hope I don't disappoint her.

Time freezes for a moment as I stare into her beautiful brown eyes. I reach over and pull her to me, our lips quickly meeting in a passionate kiss. I almost don't want to let her go. She's definitely doing a number on me.

"I'll wait for you in the living room so you can finish getting ready," I tell her. She extends her arm out while I still have my fingers entwined with hers. She doesn't want to let go either.

Several minutes later, she walks into the room. Her hair is down and I can't help but notice how pretty it looks. I'm so used to seeing it in a ponytail, yet this look is very becoming of her.

"You ready to get out of here?"

"Damn, baby, you're looking pretty hot," I flirt, causing her cheeks to blush. "What would you like to get into this afternoon?"

"Come on, let's go." She grabs ahold of my arm as though she's got a plan of her own, and I follow her out the door.

We take her car, for obvious reasons. She hasn't said very much about the condition of mine, but I know she's more comfortable in hers, as would anyone for that matter. I admit my car is embarrassing, but right now it's all I have.

"Where're we headed?" I ask after we've been on the highway for about fifteen minutes.

"You'll see," she tells me, still not eager to reveal our destination.

Minutes later, she pulls into a place that has miniature golf and what looks to be go-carts and an arcade. "You up for a game of putt-putt?"

"You bet I am. It's been years since I've played. How 'bout I challenge you to a game?"

"You're on, buddy. Loser has to buy the winner ice cream. Deal?"

I look at her and grin. I lightly punch her on the arm, in a friendly way. "Deal."

We take turns putting the ball into several of the holes lined up throughout the course. We're laughing and teasing each other, having a really good time. I don't think I ever had this much fun with Macy, or anyone else for that matter. She was always so bossy, and everything had to be done just so.

We get to the last hole with our scores tied. It's all or nothing. I let her go first and, unbelievably, she makes it in with one shot. I know there's no way I can do it, too, but I'm willing to give it my best try. I take aim, and at the same time I'm ready to swing, she reaches over and tickles me. Naturally, I miss the ball. She jumps up and down, then embraces me in a hug.

"I beat you. I beat you," she teases, then loops her arm through mine while we walk back to return our putters.

"You so cheated. You know that's not fair," I tell her, pretending to have my feelings hurt, even though I'd do it all over again just to see that smile on her face. It's priceless.

"Ha. You just don't like losing."

"You just wait. I'll get you back when you least expect it."

Next, we stop at the ticket booth, and I purchase enough so we each can have our own go-cart. I'm barely buckled in mine before she takes off.

I catch up with her rather quickly, and we take turns passing and cutting the other off. After several laps around, the attendant motions our race is over. I extend my hand to help her out, and she doesn't let it go. Together, we walk towards the arcade, hand in hand.

Kids of all ages are running around, having a blast. I stick a couple of bills into the money changer and pass a few of the tokens to her. I'm not much into video games, but I've been known to rack up a pretty high score playing ski ball. She puts her tokens in the game beside mine, and we take turns aiming the ball up the ramp. I ring the middle hole several times, causing my score to quickly add up, while she barely gets her ball across the bottom ring.

A handful of tickets shoot out from my game, and I pass them over to her so she can count them. "You only need a couple thousand more to win me that big stuffed animal up there," she says, pointing up to the ceiling at the huge teddy bear that's probably been hanging there for years.

"There's no way anyone has ever won enough tickets for that thing. I'd be better off buying you a brand new one."

"You're probably right. But he's still cute."

"He's not as cute as you." I brush my hand along the side of her cheek. She steps up on her toes and plants a kiss on my lips. I return one of my own, and before we know it, we're both standing in the middle of the arcade with our lips locked. Such a needy kiss could be considered X-rated by some standards. We break apart, realizing it may not be appropriate in a public setting to show this much affection. After all, there are kids here.

Damn, I truly like this girl!

I reach for her hand again and we walk towards the exit. "I've had such a good time this afternoon," I tell her as we climb into her car again.

"Me too. I'm glad we were able to go."

"So what's next?" I don't want tonight to end any time soon.

"You hungry? I could go for some food myself," she tells me.

"I'm starving. I thought you'd never ask. You did pretty good picking out that pizza place, so any suggestions for now?"

"Let's see." She pauses for a minute. "How does seafood sound? It's been a long time since I've had some fresh shrimp. Or we could do Mexican and maybe a margarita."

"I can't remember the last time I had shrimp, either. That sounds pretty good to me." I really want to treat her right, and taking her out to a nice meal is a start in the right direction. Besides, I owe it to her. Even though Mexican food is somewhat less expensive, I don't want to risk something bad happening should either of us have one too many margaritas.

Chapter 15

Jennifer

I'M SO HAPPY THAT EVERYTHING is going well tonight. Brian has really been a lot of fun. I can feel my heart pulling me closer already. I just don't want to rush things. Again. Yes, I truly believe this could be the start of something.

When we get to the restaurant, the waitress seats us in a booth, and this time it's my turn to take the seat next to him. He seems pleased and we order an appetizer and a pitcher of beer.

"Look, I promise I won't get carried away this time," I tell him as soon as the waitress is out of earshot. I don't think I can emotionally deal with the events of *that* night all over again.

"Don't worry, if you get too carried away, I promise I'll make sure it's with me." Brian teases me.

The waitress returns with our pitcher and Brian pours our beer into the icy mugs. We spend the time waiting for our food to arrive talking about all the fun we had earlier. We can't afford to have weekends like this all the time, but it's a promising start to our relationship.

"This sure is a lot of food," I mention once our food arrives. I wish now I'd considered sharing a plate with him. There's no way I can eat everything in front of me.

"Whatever we don't eat, I'm sure we can take home with us," Brian suggests. "Heck, I'll even take it to work with me. This beats fast-food any day."

"You like working there?" I ask him, eager to hear more about his job.

"It's a job. Don't get me wrong, Jared's got a pretty good business going, but I know it's just temporary. Besides, with the weather turning colder, I'm not sure I want to be outside washing cars all day."

"I don't blame you there. I'm not much for the colder temperature either…"

We finish eating, and the waitress drops off our check. Brian scoops it up before I can get to it. I know he's trying to save his money, but he insists it's his treat. I offer to pay my half, but he still refuses.

"Consider this our first real date," he tells me.

My heart pounds, and I'm once again filled with emotion just by hearing him say those words.

On the drive home, he reaches over and places his hand on my leg. I put my own on top of his, enjoying the feel of it.

"You know, Brian, I've been doing some thinking. Since you still don't have a place yet, would you maybe consider staying with me?" *Please don't let me be making a huge mistake.* "I'd hate asking you for rent, but you could just help with the food and the power bill, maybe." I let out a deep breath.

I pull up to the red light and look over at him. The look on his faces shows my offer has taken him by complete surprise. I've actually surprised myself, to be honest, but it's something I feel inclined to suggest.

"Are you sure about this? What would your parents think, especially since we just met and all?" he asks.

"Well, I've thought about that, and since they're not coming into town next week, I've got some time to figure it all out. I'm sure they won't be thrilled about it, but I'll smooth things over with them. Besides, I work nights and you'll be working days. With our schedules being opposite, it's not like we'll really be there at the same time anyways."

He wastes no time deciding what to do. "Jennifer, you just made my night complete. How can I ever thank you?"

I don't know how he's been doing it, sleeping in his car, night after night. I've heard stories of entire families being homeless and having to live in their vehicles, but this is my first time personally knowing someone who's had the experience first-hand. Working at the hotel, I've had to help out several guests who didn't have enough money to pay but that was only for one night. The hotel allows us the flexibility to help from time to time if we feel the need is legitimate. But to stay in your car for weeks at a time, with no place to call home, is so sad. For sure, everyone has unique circumstances.

"I don't know about you, but I'm really tired and full. What do you say we call it an early night?" I suggest as we near the entrance to the apartment.

"Yeah, I'm pretty beat myself. Someone kept me awake all last night," he teases, even though I know I wouldn't change last night if I had to.

Thinking back to the previous evening, I don't think I'll ever forget looking up and seeing him standing there in the doorway. My heart had melted.

I tell myself that tonight will be different. I'm not going to worry about waking up to an empty bed in the morning. Not now since he's agreed to move in.

We stand at the food of the bed waiting to crawl in. "Is there a certain side you prefer?" he asks.

"I'm kind of partial to that side," I tell him, pointing to the right. I keep my alarm and cell phone charger on that little side table.

"That's fine. Come here and let me hold you." He crawls in and motions for me to join him.

I snuggle up to him, and he drapes his arm across my stomach. I admit to myself how comfortable this feels. *Yes, this feels nice.* "Goodnight."

"Night," he says so softly that I think he's nearly asleep already.

A few minutes later, he shifts a little bit, getting more settled. "Jenn? You still awake?"

"Yeah."

"I just want to thank you. I can't tell you how much it means to me for you to let me stay here. I tell you, I was really starting to wonder if I'd made the right decision coming here. It's a scary feeling having to sleep in your car every night. And..." –he pauses for a moment– "it's embarrassing. "

"Look, Brian, it's going to be okay now. I couldn't continue to let you sleep out there."

He pulls me even closer to him, and we both drift off into a deep, peaceful sleep.

****

The next morning, I wake first and reach over just to make sure he's still here. Relief fills my body, and I relax. I trusted him when he told me he wouldn't leave, but the possibility otherwise remained in the back of my mind all night.

I fix us a light breakfast, and hear him moving around in the bathroom before too long.

From the hallway, he calls out, "What smells so good in there?"

I turn to see him leaning against the doorway. He's wearing nothing but his boxers. I quickly turn my head so he doesn't see my cheeks redden. *Damn, he's hot. Why does he do this to me?* He walks up behind me and kisses me softly on the neck. I want to melt right here on the kitchen floor.

"You sleep well?" I ask, trying to allow my cheeks to cool.

"Mm hmm."

I want to reach out and run my hands over his chest. How can someone be so hot first thing in the morning? My mouth waters, and suddenly I feel dampness down below.

I can't let that happen so suddenly again.

"Anything special you want to do today?" Other than preparing for my finals, I don't have anything going on.

"Do you think we could stop by the mall or somewhere so I can pick up a few things? I could use a new shirt and a pair of jeans."

"Okay, we can definitely do that. Then, on the way back, I need to pick up some things from the grocery store for this coming week."

Since it's Sunday, and the mall doesn't open as early as it does during the week, we spend the next couple hours hanging around my apartment watching television. I swear he could watch *Sports Center* all day if I'd let him.

Surprisingly, Brian is almost as fun as Rebecca when it comes to shopping. Most guys don't like to shop, but he is having a blast trying on clothes and coming out to model them for me. *I'm loving this!*

The afternoon passes too quickly, and as we walk back out to the car, the sun has already started to set. Brian settled on a couple of outfits, and I hope it makes him feel better now. He also picked out a warm jacket that was on sale.

We stop by the grocery store, and Brian pushes the shopping cart again. I convince him to pick out a few things he'd like to eat this week. I don't want to appear too pushy, but he knows more about his likes and dislikes than I do.

Before we head to the checkout, I notice him observing the aisle signs as though he's looking for something in particular. Not sure where he's headed, I follow behind. I almost die when I see what he stops to look at. The family planning section. We're both amazed at the variety of condoms available. There're so many different choices—pleasure for her, pleasure for him, ribbed for stimulation, sizes, colors, flavors... I could go on and on.

"I'd—I'd just like to be prepared for next time. If, you know, there is a next time. Is there a certain one you would like to try?" he asks, and it's taking all he's got not to burst out laughing.

This moment is so embarrassing, but I know it happens to everyone. *Why can't there be just one option?* Instead of reading each box to see what they offer, I pick up a purple one and toss it in the cart. "Let's just try this one."

As I unload the groceries, I still feel funny about the condoms. I try hiding them underneath the bread, but the clerk doesn't even hesitate as he scans the box across the monitor.

Brian bags everything and offers to help pay for our purchase once the clerk tells us our total. "Just give me twenty," I tell him, knowing it's nowhere near half the amount we've spent, but I simply can't allow him to contribute more right now. He just got his first paycheck, and with the new clothes he just bought, I'd feel bad for taking the little bit he has left.

"Are you sure?"

"Maybe next time, okay?" I hand him the keys and let him drive us back to the apartment. It's amazing how we've gotten so comfortable with each other over the weekend, like we're meant to be.

Chapter 16
Brian

SHE SLEEPS SOUNDLY, PEACEFULLY. WITH her head in my lap, I try to sit as still as possible so as not to disturb her. I had no idea I'd be moving in with a girl, but it has all happened again, just like it did with Macy. I promise myself, this time I'll be a better person. I can't go through another bad relationship like I did with Macy. I just can't. Besides, Jennifer and Macy are complete opposites.

Macy never suspected I was having the guys over during the day while she worked. Or, if she did, she never let on. There came a point where I really didn't care to even look for a job anymore. I know it wasn't right, but she continued to take care of everything. She hadn't seemed to mind whether I contributed or not, so maybe it was her own fault that our relationship blew up in her face. At some point, she should've put her foot down instead of letting me continue on like that.

Jennifer is different though. She's such a good-hearted person. I knew this about her from the first night I met her at the hotel when she gave me money. She never even gave it a second thought. I'm going to try my hardest to be as good to her as I can.

****

The next morning, Jennifer packs my lunch and surprises me with it as I'm getting ready to walk out the door.

"What's this?" I ask as she hands over the bag.

"Just a little something I made for you since you mentioned there was a microwave at work." She reaches up to kiss me on the cheek, and I return one to her forehead. It saddens me that I couldn't remember my own mother ever doing anything like that for me, a simple gesture so small, yet so meaningful.

I get to work in plenty of time and in a great mood. Jared comes out to check on me mid-morning, and I greet him with a handshake. "Hey, man. How's it going?"

"Not bad. Not bad at all."

We make small talk for a moment while the cars continue to line up for service. I start to wonder if there's even going to be a chance for a lunch break today.

It's nearing one in the afternoon when Jared finally lets me stop long enough to eat. I grab my lunch bag from the car and head inside, eager to see what Jennifer packed for me. Inside the bag, I find a sandwich and a plastic container of soup. Near the bottom, I uncover a yellow post-it that says: *Thinking of you. Hope you're having a good day.* My heart swells with pride. It feels so good to know I'm not alone in the world anymore.

I eat quickly and return back to my work.

The afternoon goes by so quickly, I don't even realize it's time to get off. *Wouldn't it be nice if every day went by this fast?*

I get home from work to find dinner waiting on me. *Now this is nice!*

When we're done, I help her get everything cleaned and put away, and we both relax in the living room. I'm dreading her having to leave for work in a couple hours. It still feels funny calling this place my home now. It's too bad I can't just pop in and surprise her at work like I've done in the past but not only do I need my rest now, I can't keep showing up at the hotel, either.

It sucks, though, not having any way to get in touch with her. Jennifer has her cell phone, but a lot of good that does me. I know it's not an expense I can afford to have, but everyone has cell phones these days. Surely there's got to be some way of getting one, even if it's one of those pre-paid deals. Maybe when I get my next paycheck I'll check into it.

Jennifer gathers everything she needs for work and stops at the door. "I'm going to miss you tonight." I see the sadness clearly on her face.

"I'm going to miss you too, babe." I embrace her, lightly kissing the tip of her nose.

"If I don't see you in the morning before you have to head out, maybe I can meet you for lunch."

"That'd be awesome. I'd really enjoy that." I don't want to let her go, but I know I have to. I might as well get used to it. "Be careful tonight."

Once she's gone, I relax in front of the TV, but it's not the same without her here. I fix myself a glass of water and rifle through the kitchen cabinets. I'm not hungry, but I feel like munching on something might help me relax. Finally, after one in the morning, sleep takes over and I'm out for the night.

****

The next morning, I wake up and make a pot of coffee, drinking two cups before heading out the door. I'm running late since I had such trouble falling asleep, so I don't bother to grab anything for breakfast.

Clint shows up a few minutes after me, and we immediately get busy washing cars. Once again, the customers are tipping generously. The way it works, Clint and I place our tips together in one container. Then, at the end of our shift, one of us turns it in to the desk manager. On Friday, we each get half of what was collected. I feel that's fair, and last week I made an extra hundred bucks. Clint was a little perturbed he'd be splitting them again now that I'm on board, but we're washing twice as many vehicles. It's too bad he doesn't see it this way. I've overheard him making a few comments to some of the other guys.

Whatever.

It's the way Jared runs his business, whether Clint likes it or not. This week, we'll be getting our tips paid out on Wednesday, and my plans are to take Jennifer out for a nice Thanksgiving meal since she won't be having one with her family.

She's mentioned more than once how she'll miss spending the day with them, so I figure it's the least I can do for her. Even Rebecca extended her invitation to include me in her family's celebrations, but I told Jennifer I was still a little uncomfortable since I don't know her very well. I'd go if she insisted, but I was leaving the decision up to her. She was a little sad at first, but I think she understood the way I felt. I then told her my plans to take her out to eat, and she said that would be even better.

Shortly before noon, I look up and see Clint watching someone that's walking across the parking lot. "Check out that hot, pretty momma. *Mmmm, mmmm.*"

It's Jennifer, and I don't like his comment one bit. I make introductions between them both, Clint not seeming to care at all about his previous remarks. *What an asshole!* It's certainly altered my mood, and I don't bother waiting for Jared to tell me to take lunch, I just go.

The more I think about it, the more pissed I get. What would she think if she'd heard him? She'd have been so embarrassed.

Jennifer suggests we grab a burger at one of the nearby places in the shopping center. "What was up with your friend?" she asks me after we sit down to eat. "He sort of looked at me funny. Made me feel a little uneasy."

"That's the first time I've seen that side of him. He's usually pretty quiet." It's taking all I can to swallow my food.

"I kind of felt funny about it," she continues. "Oh well, some guys are just jerks."

"Yes, the world is full of them." I bite my tongue, not wanting to lose my cool in front of her.

We finish up our meal, and I'm sad she has to go. Hopefully, that punk Clint will be on break when I get back and it'll give me some time to cool off.

I walk Jennifer over to her car, and she kisses me goodbye. I look over and see Clint sitting in his car, staring us down.

What the fuck?

Chapter 17
Jennifer

DESPITE THE WEIRD WAY HIS co-worker made me feel, I really enjoyed having lunch with Brian. With all the time we've spent together, he's really growing on me. I'm still not fond of our opposite schedules, but hopefully it'll make our relationship stronger in the end.

Relationship.

I suppose that's what we have. We've just sort of fallen into it. It feels like a relationship, and he treats me like I'm his girlfriend and not a roommate.

Rather than studying when I get back to the apartment, I crash on the couch. Sleep is long overdue for me.

I wake up when Brian comes home from work. "Hey, baby, you okay?" He leans over, a worried look on his face.

"Yeah, I guess I was more tired than I thought." I rub my eyes and push my hair out of my face.

I certainly feel better after my nap, but dang, it only leaves a few hours before I have to leave. Rather than fixing a meal, I suggest we order pizza. It'll be quicker, plus it won't dirty up the kitchen. Brian agrees and quickly changes out of his work clothes before joining me on the couch.

"I missed you today." He leans over and pulls me to him for a big hug.

"I missed you more." *He's making it so easy to fall for him. He's almost too good.*

I feel the sudden urge to lean over and kiss him. We start making out pretty hot and heavy, only to be interrupted by a knock on the door. I readjust my clothes and glance at myself in the mirror just inside the doorway. Just a couple more minutes and ... No, we can't do *that* tonight. I'll never want to leave.

I grab my purse off the kitchen table and take care of the pizza delivery guy.

****

On Thanksgiving morning, my parents call to check on me. I tell them I have dinner plans with "a friend" instead of spending the day with Rebecca, like I'd considered at one time. My father is pleased I'm not staying home alone to study, but after speaking with my mother, I get the impression they're not too sure of this sudden friendship they knew nothing about. I'm cautious with what I say about Brian, not wanting them to know a whole lot about his past. I know he's not proud of it and I'm not either, but that's something that doesn't need to be discussed over the phone, if at all. My mother, always the worrier, is suspicious of Brian's intentions, and I guess I can't really blame her. I end the call before we say something we'll regret later.

I take my time getting ready for our dinner tonight. It's a special occasion and one I hope we'll remember for a long time. Brian wears one of his new outfits and looks so happy with himself. I allow him to take care of everything at the restaurant, giving him a feeling of self-worth and an ego boost. The meal is exceptional, and I commend him in selecting the restaurant on his own.

I'm so full and by the time we get home, I don't even want to think about going in to work. Normally, I would've had the holiday off, but before Brian came along, I'd already volunteered to work.

He walks up behind me in the bathroom while I'm changing into my work attire, and I look up to see our reflection in the mirror. I never expected to see myself with someone as attractive as Brian. I wonder, though, if we'd met a few years ago would things have turned out differently for him. Would he have such baggage?

I turn around to face him, and immediately get swept into a breathtaking kiss. I pull away after a few moments, needing a minute to slow down my racing heart.

"Wow! Where did that come from?" I manage to speak while trying to even out my breathing.

"You have no idea how bad I want you right now, baby." I see the intense desire in his eyes.

I bring my lips to his and challenge his kiss with one of my own. Brian lifts me up and sets me down on the bathroom counter. I break the kiss long enough to take a few breaths, then run my fingers through his hair while I bring his face closer to mine.

I wrap my legs around his waist, and he places his hands underneath me, pulling me closer to him. I hang on tight while he manages to walk us backwards towards the bedroom. Dropping me down on the edge of the bed, I raise my arms while he lifts my shirt up, eventually dropping it down on the floor. I'm not used to being this nearly naked around anyone, so I pull my arms in front of me to cover myself.

Brian senses my uneasiness, and not that it really helps me out any, he takes off his own shirt. Starting at my forehead, he plants light, gentle kisses before working his way down the side of my neck. He stops at the area just above my cleavage.

Next, he fumbles with the clasp on my bra, testing to see if it's really what I want him to do. We know there's not much time before I need to leave. When my breasts are exposed and both nipples are hard as tiny rocks, I watch as his tongue carefully grazes the dark pink area that surrounds each one. He shows them both equal attention, sending uncontrollable sensations throughout my body. I'm on fire.

I'm also not sure what I'm supposed to do.

I listen to the sucking noises he makes and I'm unable to speak, much less breathe. Slowly, he kisses a trail down towards my stomach, stopping just above the waistline of my pants. I lift up just enough for him to unfasten and slide them down. Using his fingers, he traces the lace of my panties, which are now completely soaked.

I'm unsure if I should be embarrassed or if it's a completely normal reaction, especially since he was the one to make them that way. He slides my panties over to the side, then inserts two fingers vary carefully. I let out a soft moan, enjoying the sensation that's started to heighten. At the rate we're going, I won't last long. I already feel my inner muscles gripping his fingers tightly and he's just barely sliding them in and out.

I'm just about to come when he suddenly pulls his fingers out. I'm sure he knows I was close, but I sure wish he'd kept them there. At least so I could find pleasure. Brian crawls up on the bed, on top of me, and I don't waste any time pulling him to me.

I reach down between us and rub his dick up and down, hoping it's providing some kind of pleasurable feeling for him. He's so big and firm.

"Hang on a minute," he whispers and eases off the bed.

I watch him leave the room, then hear the sound of the drawer in the bathroom slide open. It's where we left the box of condoms. He struggles to open the plastic wrapper, then I hear another unusual sound that, I'm sure, is the foil ripping open.

He walks back, and I use my hand to feel that the condom is already in place. He's ready for me. Slowly, he runs his fingers back and forth, spreading my own moisture and heat all around. I love the feel of his fingers massaging me, but I'm even more eager to feel him inside of me again.

He places the tip of his dick at my entrance and barely enters. *Ahhh, I love the way he's teasing me.* All at once, he pushes inside, deep. At first, my breath hitches, then I exhale slowly as I relax around him. The feeling is shocking. When he feels me get more comfortable around his size, he slides in and out again, slowly, then increasing to a pace that leaves us both panting. He feels amazing. We're … we're …making love? Or are we just having sex? I'm not sure I know the difference between the two just yet.

All at once, Brian slows down. "Baby, I'm about to … come."

Using my hands, I grab ahold of his ass. I pull him to me, forcing him to go deeper and deeper until I can't push him inside any more. The muscles in his butt tighten and relax with each thrust.

The feeling is building in me, and I'm ready to go with him.

"*Please…*" I manage to say before I'm forcefully grabbing him, pushing him further inside. I'm lifting my hips from the bed trying to get as much of him inside as I can.

"That's it, baby. Let go."

"You… feel…so… good. Don't…stop, yet!" I'm barely able to speak between each pant.

All at once, he collapses on top of me. We're both silent for the longest time. Moments later, he reaches for my hand and entwines his fingers with mine. We lie this way, holding hands, until I hear his breathing return to normal.

My phone rings off in the distance, and I'm instantly startled. *Shit, I fell asleep.* I ease out from underneath his arm and run to grab my phone from my purse.

"Hello?" I say into it, still sounding half asleep.

"Jenn, are you okay?" Rebecca asks on the other end, and suddenly I'm wide awake.

"Oh my God. I'm so freaking sorry." I've never been late before. "I must've fallen asleep. I'm on my way."

"Hey, take your time." Her voice is calm, reassuring. "I'll cover 'til you get here. It's no big deal. I'm just glad you're okay."

"Thanks, I'll be right there." *How did I manage to fall asleep, knowing I had to be at work?* I run to the bathroom to get cleaned up.

It's hard for me to stay mad at myself when I look over to my bedroom and see Brian, sound asleep in my bed. The sheet is pulled up just over his butt, leaving the rest of his naked body exposed.

Chapter 18
Brian

I WAKE UP IN THE middle of the night to an empty bed. I sit up and look around, but the apartment is dark and dead silent. Once my eyes completely focus, I'm able to see the nightlight shining from the kitchen. The first night I stayed over, Jennifer told me how she felt more comfortable leaving a nightlight on even when she wasn't here. She said she wasn't scared or anything when she was here on her off nights, but she just felt better having the faint glow throughout the apartment all the time. I think it's more for comfort than anything.

I walk to the kitchen and flip on the main light. It's bright and hurts my eyes. I look around and see a note left on the table.

"Sorry, babe. I overslept and I'm late for work. See you in the morning. –J"

Since Jared figured business would be slow the next few days with everyone out doing their Black Friday shopping, I have the next couple days off. Although I need the money, Clint has seniority over me and is going to work a few hours each day, for as long as the business needs it.

Here it is, the middle of the night, and I'm wide awake now.

I find the bath cloth Jennifer must have used to clean herself up draped over the side of the sink and run it through the hot water. I'm not all that sticky, thanks to the condom, but I don't want to put on a pair of clean boxers without wiping off.

I'm physically drawn to her, but I just need to keep my shit together with no screw ups. I've got something good going on with her and I don't need to lose it.

****

The next couple of days seem to fly by, and before long, it's time to head back to work again. Jennifer has her finals this week, and I can tell by her actions she's nervous about them. I know she's going to do well, but she takes her schooling so seriously.

On Friday afternoon, Jared calls me to his office. Since I'm the closer, I finish getting all the cleaners and hoses put away before heading inside to see what he wants. I throw my jacket across the front counter and see Clint leaving from Jared's office.

"Have a good weekend, man," I tell him. I've tried hard to be civil with him, but he's a tough nut to crack. Ever since the day he made the comment about Jennifer, he's been very short and standoffish with me. We never spoke about the incident, but he knew I wasn't pleased with his remarks.

He looks over at me and forces his words, a shit-eating grin on his face. "Yeah, man, you too."

I can't stand the cockiness in his tone and it really rubs me the wrong way.

I knock on Jared's door, even though it's open, and he invites me to come in.

"Hey, what's up?" I take a seat in one of the chairs across from him. "Sorry it took me a minute. I wanted to pick up outside first."

Jared looks up at me, but he doesn't have his usual cheerfulness about him now.

I'm suddenly concerned. "Everything okay?"

As he stares at me so severely, I get the feeling this is not going to be good, that something's happened.

"Brian, when I first hired you, I explained to you how I run a very reputable business here, and how I have a lot of repeat customers. Do you remember that conversation?" It doesn't take me long to realize the shit's about to hit the fan. Something's going on.

"Yes, sir. I'm not sure I'm following you though," I tell him, trying not to immediately get defensive. "So far, all the customers I've met have been friendly. They've spoken so highly of you."

"Last week…" He hesitates before continuing. "I had a gentleman tell me some money went missing from his car. He swears it was in his glove box before he got here, then, when he got home and placed his service paperwork in the glove box, it was gone. At first, he thought maybe he'd just misplaced it, but then he found the envelope under the seat. The envelope he'd used to hold the money."

"Well, that's a relief that he found it." I let out a deep breath still uncertain where the conversation is going.

"Empty."

"What?"

I stared at him coldly, not sure I heard him correctly.

"That's right. Empty. The envelope was empty."

"So, what are you saying then? Are you implying I took it? Because you're wrong, if that's the case. Jared, I didn't take anyone's money." I'm completely shocked he'd think that…that I had anything to do with that man's money. I struggle to stay focused on what Jared's telling me. It just can't be.

"I really want to believe you, Brian. I honestly do. I spoke with Clint about this first, and he said you were the one that washed the gentleman's car that day. He said it was during his lunch break."

Disappointment shows all over his face.

"Jared, I swear to you, man. I didn't take anyone's money. Yes, I'm still trying to save up for my own place, but now that I'm staying with Jennifer, I'm doing okay." I know my face must still show shock, but I'm starting to get angry that I'm being accused of something I really don't know anything about. I can't help but feel I've been set up. Would Clint do this to me? Is this his way of getting back at me?

The knot in my stomach tightens. I can already tell Jared's about to give me some bad news—news I'm not going to like.

"Brian, I really like you, but I'm going to have to let you go. I can't afford to have negative things said about my business, or customers distrustful of my employees. This is my livelihood, and I have to make sure my employees are absolutely trustworthy if they're going to represent me. My business takes care of me and my family."

I drop my head. "Come on, Jared. Why can't you believe me? I promise you, I did not take that money!"

"Brian, my decision is firm. Since this is my personal business, I feel the need to repay the customer for his missing money. I've also refunded him for the service he received that day. I don't feel it's necessary to take all of it from your check, but as you'll see, I did deduct half. I'm sorry to do this to you, but it's my final word on this matter. Now, if you will, please leave." He hands me a sealed envelope I assume to be my final check. I'm too scared to even open it right now.

I don't even remember leaving and driving to the apartment. I don't know what the hell just happened.

I sit outside in the car for a few minutes trying to figure out how I'm going to explain this whole mess to Jennifer. I bang my hands on the steering wheel. *How the fuck did this happen? How? How did I lose my God damned job? Did Clint set me up? That damn fucker. I'll get him!*

I tear open the envelope and see just how much I'm left with. "Shit!" I say pretty loud, although no one can hear me since I'm still in the car. Here is it, almost fucking Christmas, and I'm without a job. And left with this. I flip the check down into the floorboard of the car. It's hardly enough to even call a paycheck.

I want to scream.

I want to punch something, anything, to deal with the frustration I'm going through at the moment. What did I do to deserve this? For once, it wasn't me. It. Wasn't. Me. I didn't do what I'm being accused of.

I somehow manage to pull myself together before going inside. I can't drop this bomb on Jennifer now. What will she think of me?

I take my time getting out of the car. When I get to the door, I count to ten before opening it. *Stay strong, Brian,* I tell myself. Surely there's been a misunderstanding.

"Hey, babe. I got good news." Looking at me, she sees I'm clearly not myself and her happiness quickly fades.

"What's that?" I force a fake smile in her direction.

"Are you okay? You look like you don't feel well."

"Yeah, I've got a slight headache," I lie. Now's not the time to give her my bad news. "What's your news, baby?"

"I aced all my exams! I did it!" She's so excited it's almost sickening. "And I received straight A's for my final grades this term."

"Babe, that's wonderful. I knew you would." I try my best to be happy for her, including the fake smile I'm wearing. It's not her fault I'm having a rough time right now. I give her a hug and hold her for a few seconds, long enough to reassure her I'm proud of her, before giving her a congratulatory kiss on the cheek.

"You don't look so hot. Why don't I get you some Tylenol, and you can relax on the couch—take a load off. I'm sure you had your hands full today."

If she only knew.

I hear her rummaging through bottles in the bathroom cabinet, and she meets me in the bedroom where I'm changing out of my work clothes. *Stupid Jared, he's not getting these son of a bitches back. I'll...I'll....* I chuck the clothes on the floor.

"Here you go." I take two pills from her and swallow them down with the glass of water she's holding. It's lukewarm and quite disgusting. Now I really do feel sick.

I have no idea how I'm going to break the news to her. Everything had been going so great in my life, until now. Now, it's totally fucked up and I'm not much better than when I first met her. In fact, I'm probably worse off now.

"Thanks. You're too sweet." She's too damn good for me. I gently rub the smooth skin on her hand, back and forth. It's comforting, but not enough for me to tell her everything. Not yet.

"Try to get some rest," she says while I walk back out to the living room. Taking a seat on the couch, she bends down to kiss me on the forehead. "I hope you're not coming down with something."

She walks to the kitchen, immersing herself with cooking something to eat. Food is the absolute *last* thing on my mind right now.

I toss and turn, even switching ends on the couch. I'm miserable, to say the least. Nothing on the TV even holds my attention.

I try closing my eyes, but images of Jared accusing me of taking the money fill my mind. The more I dwell on it, the angrier I get. I can't believe the stupid fucker would blame me, then turn around and fire me without so much as giving me a chance to offer my own conclusion. And to take some from my paycheck. *Grrr.*

A couple hours pass, even though it feels like I've been laying here forever. Jennifer's pretty much left me alone, honestly believing I'm ill. And I am ill, just not the ill that she's thinking. I hear the bathroom door shut and figure it's time for her to get ready for work. I lay as still as I possibly can, hoping she'll think I'm asleep and will leave without saying anything. I just want to be alone. Is that too much to ask right now?

****

Morning finally comes, and I'm still in a pissed-off mood. I can't believe I slept on the couch all night long. My body is stiff and sore, just like the way it used to feel after a night of sleeping in my car. Jennifer should be coming home any minute now, and I've got two choices: I can fess up and tell her about being falsely accused, or I can pretend to hide my bad mood until later. How much later, I'm not sure.

I settle for later, although I know it's not the right thing to do. Who knows, if I'm lucky, maybe I'll find another job, something that's even better. It's sure to make the story of leaving the lube shop less painful.

I jump in the shower and just as I'm toweling off, I hear her walk in. It's now or never.

The apartment is quiet, then suddenly, the bathroom door opens.

"You scared the crap out of me."

"I'm sorry, I didn't mean to. Are you feeling any better this morning?" She pulls the towel from my hand and dries a couple spots I missed.

"Thank you," I tell her and hang it up to dry when she's done. I follow her out, slightly disappointed she didn't attempt anything with me not having any clothes on. The moment could've turned into something intimate.

I throw on some clothes and meet her in the kitchen. She's brought home muffins from a local bakery. "Thought I'd surprise you this morning." She places one on a plate and passes it to me.

"This looks delicious." I bring the muffin to my nose, and it truly does smell heavenly. She hands me a cup of coffee, and we sit down together at the small kitchen table.

I try not to look at her directly, but I don't want to call any attention to my behavior, either. Somehow, I feel like she is going to see it all written on my face. *Focus, Brian*. I must focus and keep myself together, for her.

Surprisingly, I have never been this bothered and emotional before about losing a job. Not that I was all that proud of the job itself, but I feel like I have let her down, as well as myself. I told her so much about my previous bad luck with jobs, I can only imagine what she's going to think of me now. After all, coming here is supposed to be a fresh start for me.

We eat in silence until I can stand it anymore. "How was work last night?"

"It was okay. Rebecca hung around for a little while after she got off and updated me about her plans to spend Christmas with Greg. He's scheduled to be home for a few weeks and has planned a trip for them. He's not telling her where they're going, and the suspense is killing her. Personally, I think he's going to propose." She sounds so excited for her best friend.

"Do you think she'll say yes if he does?"

"They've been together for so long, I know she will. I don't know how much longer he's got in the military though. I hope it won't mean she'll have to move, if that's what he does. I don't know what I'd do if I didn't have her close by all the time."

She gets up to put away our plates. I run my fingers through my hair, still feeling a little dampness from the shower. I desperately need a haircut, even more so now that I'm going to be looking for a new job again. I don't even want to think about it right now. I've got two days to come up with a plan.

"You up for doing anything today?" she turns to ask me.

"Sure. What'd you have in mind?" I can't pretend to have another headache today, I just can't.

"How about, I've got my own little surprise planned for you," she teases, her face suddenly lighting up with excitement.

"Oh yeah?"

"First, I need a nap, so you're going to have to wait a little while. But when I get up, you better be ready."

"Aww, babe, you're killing me. I can't have one little hint?"

"Nope. I'm going to test your patience," she teases.

"You know that's not fair, but I know you're tired. You're not leaving me much of a choice though, huh?" I offer her a wink, but she's already walking back towards the bedroom.

I don't think she gets nearly enough rest, because she always wants to spend as much time with me as she can. Now that her classes are over with for the semester, it'll help some, but not so much for me. We've just got to see how this all plays out.

With nothing to do, I end up falling asleep again myself. That's something I can say I never get too much of.

****

"You ready to head out?" she calls out, waking me from my nap. She's already changed into a nice outfit and sits down on the couch to put her shoes on.

I rub my eyes, trying to adjust to the daylight that now pours in through the opened blinds.

"Sure, just let me change really quick, then we can go." I run to the bedroom and throw on a pair of jeans and a sweatshirt. "You going to tell me where we're going now, or are you still going to make me wait?"

"Nope, not 'til we get there."

Truth be known, I'm not a fan of surprises. I've simply had one surprise too many throughout my lifetime, but I pretend to look excited for her sake. I just hope this is something good.

Chapter 19
Jennifer

BRIAN STARES OUT THE WINDOW, not saying a word, the entire drive. I noticed earlier that he seemed distant, as if he had something important on his mind. But I figured if he needed to talk about whatever was bothering him, he'd have mentioned it. I just hope he loves the surprise I've planned.

"We're here," I announce, and pull into the parking lot of the cellular phone store.

He looks around, and an unusual expression clouds his face. "Okay. I'm still not sure what this surprise is that you're referring to," he says.

"Think of it as an early Christmas present for you. You're getting your very own cell phone." I think I'm more excited about this than he is. "I know you mentioned getting one of those pay-as-you-go phones, but I hear they don't have very good reception. So, I checked into it, and I can add you on to my plan for a few dollars extra each month. There's a couple phones we can pick from so, hopefully, you'll find one you like."

"Are you for real?" Brian asks, suddenly sitting up straighter in the seat. "You know you don't have to do this, right?"

Talk about being shocked. Whatever troubled him earlier is obviously forgotten now. It makes me wonder if I'm the only one who's ever done anything nice for him before.

"I want to," I assure him. "Besides, I hate not being able to talk to you when I get lonely at night or if you're running late getting off from work. And I need some way to get ahold of you in case of an emergency. This way, we'll always be just a phone call away."

Entwining our hands, we walk in together. A salesman immediately greets us and leads us to an area with the new phones. He makes a couple recommendations, discusses the changes I'll see on my bill, and answers all our questions. Within an hour, we're done and Brian is now the proud, new owner of a cell phone.

"Here, let me see it for a minute," I ask once we're outside.

Since the phone is similar to my own, I'm familiar with its features. I click on the camera button and snap a picture of the both of us. Making a few clicks, I add the photo to his home screen, then turn it around to show him. A smile appears across his face, and I'm glad to see he's no longer showing signs of the weird mood I detected earlier. Whatever it was must be gone now.

We climb back in the car, and Brian plays around with the phone. "Thank you, Jennifer. I never expected this at all."

I reach over and cover his hand with mine. "You're very welcome. I just figured it'd be better in the long run to do it this way. Plus, cheaper, too. With those pre-paid deals, you'd constantly be adding minutes or data on there." I pause a moment before adding, "Don't get mad, but I sort of have another surprise, too."

"Wait what? You've been generous enough already. You're making me feel bad."

"Yeah, well, this *is* our first Christmas together, you know. Besides, there's nothing wrong with a couple surprises. Keeps you guessing." I'm hardly able to contain my excitement. Christmas is my absolute favorite holiday.

"Well, you going to tell me or are you going to keep me waiting again?"

"You're no fun," I tease. "If it's okay with you, I'd like to get our very own tree."

I know it may seem like I'm rushing into this relationship, and things do appear to be progressing rather quickly, but it just feels so right. Besides, even if Brian and I were not together, I'd still planned to get my own tree. Being able to share this with him is just an added bonus.

I drive us to Target and, like a little kid, I head straight for the seasonal section, taking in all the pretty decorations. There're so many trees to pick from, I'm having a hard time selecting the right one. Brian makes the final decision for us, and he props the oversized tree box across the cart. We continue shopping, looking at all the decorations, and together we pick out lights, garland, and ornaments that will make our tree beautiful.

Now, more than ever, I'm so eager to get home to get started.

We make it back to the apartment in record time. Brian unloads the tree from the back while I grab all the bags of decorations. Placing everything in the middle of the living room floor, we sit down and discuss the best place to put it.

"I think it'd look nice in front of the patio door," I suggest first. "That way, we can open the blinds and see it from the outside."

"Or do you think it would look good over in that corner?" He points to a spot over near the television. "Being on the bottom floor, are you sure you're okay with having the blinds open where anyone could walk by and see inside?"

I agree with what he's saying, so we go with the spot he recommended.

We spend the next several hours assembling the tree and trimming it with all the decorations. The only thing left to do is to place the angel on top. Brian's gotten quiet again, but I don't say anything. Maybe this holiday stuff is a little much for him. He hasn't mentioned going back to see his family and I wonder when the last time he spoke to them was. He takes the trash outside to the dumpster, and when he comes back inside, I meet him at the door.

"What do you think?" I ask, grabbing hold of his hand and walking him to the tree. "We did a pretty good job, huh?" I'm pleased with it and hope he likes it, too.

"It's beautiful. The last time I can recall helping decorate, I think I was still in grade school. Guys kind of outgrow that sort of thing, but it's still nice to have the house ready for the holiday. You know, the real meaning behind Christmas." He shares this personal memory with me. "My mom popped the popcorn and I helped to pull the string through it. My dad would fuss at her, saying it would attract bugs, but it was something she did as a little girl. Do people even put that on their trees anymore?"

Suddenly, I'm full of emotion. Christmas is supposed to be joyful and spent with loved ones. I want this year to have a special meaning in his heart—our first one, together.

I turn out the overhead light, and I'm in awe at the way the lights twinkle. Brian sits down on the couch, and I crawl in his lap.

I turn towards him, inhaling his scent. Our gaze locks for a moment and it doesn't take long before his hands are roaming all over me, removing my clothes one piece at a time. I allow him to explore, slowly at first. I become impatient for his touch, so I slide over on top of him and strip him down to nothing. We make love in front of the tree that night, and I never want to forget this memory I've just created with him.

****

The next few weeks, we fall into a simple routine--he goes to work each morning around the same time I come home from the hotel, and in the evening I make sure to have dinner fixed for us as soon as he walks in. Every now and then he's gone before I get home, but I don't think much of it. We still get a few hours together before I have to leave for work, and that's enough for me. It's nice having this bit of extra time together since school is out.

I still feel that something's bothering him though. He doesn't discuss work very much anymore, if at all, and I don't dare bring it up. Maybe it's that guy Clint. Maybe they've exchanged words again. He's not asked me to have lunch with him, either. Once the holidays are over, and everything's back to normal, I'll have to stop by and see him.

Finally, it's the week before Christmas. My parents are due back in town today and we've made plans to go out to dinner tonight. It's time for Brian to meet them as well as my two brothers. I have to admit, having him around has definitely kept my mind off of missing them so much.

This evening, standing in the bedroom wearing nothing but his jeans, he asks for my opinion on which shirt to wear. Appearing nervous, he wants to make a good impression, I'm sure. I'd be the same way if I were meeting his family for the first time, too. I help him select one, and he looks very nice once he puts on his belt and shoes. "Don't worry, they're going to love you," I reassure him and straighten his collar.

"I hope you're right. I've never been any good when it comes to meeting the parents."

"Oh, my parents are harmless," I quickly add. "You and my dad will start talking sports, and you'll never get him to shut up, I promise you." I don't want him to feel awkward, but I must admit, I'm trying to reassure myself, too.

We arrive at the restaurant, and I see my mom and dad are already here, sitting at a large table in the back. They stand up to give me a hug, and I make the introductions. My dad shakes Brian's hand while my mom nods her head and says she's glad to meet him. We finally sit down again, and I feel like my parents are eying him up and down, which I guess is to be expected for their little girl. I just want everyone to feel comfortable, if that's even possible. Everyone is unusually quiet except for the sound of the forks scraping against our plates. It's the complete opposite of what I was expecting for the evening.

I finally break the silence. "Where's Mark and Dale?" I ask, referring to my brothers.

My mom is the first to speak. "They should both be here any minute. Mark helped us earlier setting the RV up in the driveway. He was waiting on Tiffany to finish getting ready as we were leaving. And Dale. Well, you know him—always late."

"It's sad that they both live here, yet I hardly ever see them. I guess if I worked normal daytime hours, we could work something out," I tell my parents, trying to make conversation.

"How's work going?" my dad asks me.

"It's the same, except we seem to be having more check-ins now than we've ever had before. In fact, most nights are already full by the time I come in. Doesn't leave much for me to do though."

Every time I look up at my mom, she's staring at Brian, and I get the feeling she's not pleased with something about him. So he needs a haircut, but that's not a big deal and surely doesn't warrant being watched like a thief. I try to steer the conversation in a different direction and ask about their travels. "Sometime this week, I'd like to come over so you can show me all the pictures you've taken."

It'd be much easier if they had Facebook and they could upload all their photos there, but I'm just happy my dad finally learned to text. It's progress. I'll work on Facebook later.

My brothers and their wives finally arrive, and I make introductions again. Brian attempts to talk with Mark and Dale, mostly about football and who's in the playoffs. Surprisingly, my dad contributes very little to the conversation. I just knew he and Brian would connect since they both enjoy sports so much.

I'm thankful when the food arrives because the night is quickly going downhill. Brian, much to my dismay, is pretty much left out of all the conversations and the look on his face shows his discomfort. It's not like my parents not to include a guest. I regret not ordering a drink to settle my nerves, but now I just want to finish eating and leave.

The waitress returns to collect our empty plates and to offer dessert, but I politely decline. "No thanks. We're, uh…we're going to pass." Brian doesn't even bother to look up.

My dad takes care of the bill, and we walk outside together. We finalize the plans for Christmas day, agreeing to meet at Mark's house at noon. It'll be easier on my parents with the RV parked there.

"Brian, will you be joining us or do you have plans with your own family?" my mother questions, and I don't know if I should be happy that she finally acknowledged him or not.

"I'd love to join you all. Thank you for inviting me." It's evident from the look on Brian's face that he wasn't expecting that at all.

My mother, on the other hand, sounded forced, but at least she asked nonetheless. Maybe she didn't think he'd accept and was only trying to be nice.

I'm beyond ready for the evening to be over. I give everyone a hug, and Brian and I make our way across the parking lot to the car. I'm appalled at my family's behavior tonight and I can't get away quick enough.

I'm hesitant to say anything on our drive back to the apartment. When the silence becomes more than I can stand, I tell him, "I'm so sorry for my parents' behavior."

"You don't have to apologize for them. I'm sure a lot of it has to do with our living arrangement and how quickly we've progressed. It's probably a little much for them don't you think?" he reasons actually coming to their defense.

"I know, but still, they acted rude. They usually aren't that way." I wonder if it's going to be any better when we're all together again on Christmas day.

I pull out my phone and discover a missed call from Rebecca. I listen to her voicemail, inviting me to accompany her Christmas shopping tomorrow.

I mention it to Brian, and he says he's fine with it. He tells me there're some games on TV he'd like to see and to have a good time. It'll also give me the chance to look for a gift for him, something I've not been able to do yet.

We stop and pick out a rental movie before heading home. I realize I'm more tired than what I thought, and tell him I'm going to call it an early night. We can always watch the movie in the morning. I hear one of our phones chirp, indicating a message. I glance at mine expecting it to be a response from Rebecca on the time she wants to meet, but there's nothing there.

"Was that your phone?" I ask. I hadn't realized he'd given his number out so soon.

He grabs it off the table and slides it open. He quickly turns it back off without saying anything.

"Well…?" I'm being nosy, I know, but I'm curious to know who'd be sending him a text.

"Well what?" He looks at me, trying to focus on the TV remote. "I don't know who it is. Must be the wrong number."

I'm not sure if it's my imagination or what, *but did his mood suddenly change following the text?*

I change into my pajamas and fall sound asleep as soon as my head hits the pillow.

Sometime in the early morning hours, I feel Brian crawl in the bed with me. I figure he must've fallen asleep on the couch, something I do all the time. I roll over and put my arm around him. I really love having him here with me, regardless of what my parents think.

The next morning, I leave Brian asleep while I get ready to meet with Rebecca. She texts me letting me know she'll be by within the hour. I think about the text that come through on his phone last night and consider checking it. Maybe it was the wrong number, just like he said. After all, who'd be sending him a message that time of the night? What if it wasn't though? What if it's…It's none of my business and he's given me no reason to doubt him.

I grab my stuff and walk outside to meet her. I don't want to risk waking Brian when she gets here. I'm about to close the door behind me when I hear his phone beep again.

Chapter 20
Brian

I FINALLY WAKE UP ONLY to discover it's well into the afternoon. I hadn't realized just how tired I was. I've been so worried about the stupid job issue, then the way Jennifer's parents acted last night, and now with Christmas being days away—I guess it all just finally caught up with me.

I go into the kitchen and grab a glass of water. It dawns on me that Jennifer's out with Rebecca, which explains why the apartment's so quiet. I look over at my phone on the kitchen table and notice the light flashing, indicating I have messages.

There they are again. Those stupid texts from someone I don't even know.

Unknown: I really enjoyed talking to you last night.

Unknown: Call me when you're alone.

What the hell? I don't even know who the heck this person is so why would I call them?

Jennifer: Out with Rebecca. Hope you got plenty of rest. Be home later tonight. Luv you.

What? Did she just tell me she loves me? I'm not sure what to think about those little words. And dang it, there's more of those texts from the number I don't know—more than likely from the person who previously had this phone number. Even though they don't mean anything to me, it's still aggravating. I just wish that whoever keeps sending them would stop. I think about how Jennifer would react if she found them. Of course, she'd see I didn't reply back.

Jennifer's stays out pretty late and I find myself actually getting a little lonely without her here.

To my surprise, I hear a noise outside the door, and Jennifer walks in, arms loaded down with shopping bags.

"What did you buy? The entire store?" I can't help but laugh at the way she looks.

"I couldn't help it. I got some really good deals. I hereby declare I'm officially finished with everything. At least I hope I am." She looks exhausted, as if shopping is such hard work.

We haven't really discussed buying gifts for each other, so I hope her purchases are for her family and not for me. I know she said the cell phone was her gift to me, but I have, since then, seen a few small packages with my name on them appear under the tree. I don't have much money left anymore, so I need to figure out something for her and quick. Christmas is in a few days, and time is running out.

****

The next morning, I get up, just like I've done for the past few weeks, and pretend to get ready for work. I dress in my work uniform and cringe at my reflection in the mirror. I hate knowing I have to wear this damn thing out because I don't have the guts to just tell her the truth. How much longer can I keep this up?

I kiss her goodbye and walk out to my car. Just like I did when I first moved here, I've taken in a few matinee movies, rode over to the next town, and taken lots of naps. Which would explain why I've had such a hard time falling asleep at night. I've even gone as far as rubbing dirt on my clothes to give them a "hard working" appearance. But mostly, I play games on my phone until I can take no more or my battery runs too low. I'm a sad situation, no doubt.

I'm running out of options, and as each day passes, it's only getting worse. My conscience is eating me alive. All I'm doing is wasting gas, money on junk food, and time that I should be using to look for a new job. But that's part of the problem—if only I could find one.

I did ask around at a few places, but everyone is fully staffed right now. Most of the seasonal workers will become unemployed just like me immediately following the holidays. Temporary work sucks.

Figuring it's probably safe, I drive down to the mall. It wouldn't hurt to walk into a few stores just to get an idea of what I want to get Jennifer for Christmas. I pass one of the many the jewelry stores, and glance at one of their display cases up near the entrance. I know there's no way I could afford anything here, but it doesn't hurt to look. I spot a really pretty bracelet that I'm sure she'd love. It's white gold with a unique, elegant style. What I wouldn't do to be able to give her something like this.

A sales lady walks over to see if I need any assistance. I ask to see the bracelet, and it's even more beautiful out of the glass case. I take a quick glance at the price ticket, shocked it costs so much. I pass it back, explaining it's a little more than I can afford right now. *Okay, it's a great deal more, but I don't want to sound like a smartass to her.*

"Is there something else I can show you, sir?" I'm sure she's probably used to customers like me—those that have a hard time making up their minds or just don't know at all what they want.

"Do you have anything similar, just maybe a little cheaper? I love the design, but it's more than I'd planned on spending."

I follow her over to another case, and she points out a few more styles that might be of interest. "This bracelet here is very similar to the one up front, except it's sterling silver, and the stones are simulated. Would you like to see it?"

I figure why not. After all, I'm just getting an idea.

She hands it over, and I hold it up, letting the light capture each stone. "The stones really do look real," I tell her.

"It certainly is a nice piece, and I can give you a really good deal on it today." She looks over at me and smiles, hoping to convince me to make the purchase. *Well, of course she can. I'm sure she tells everyone that today is their lucky day.*

She does some figuring on her calculator that happens to be close by on the counter and turns it around to show me her offer. It's definitely a better deal than the first bracelet, but I'm still left a little shy of having enough to cover the cost.

She notices my hesitation. "It's very pretty, and I think she'd really like it. Is there any way you can hold it for me? Maybe 'til tomorrow?" I'm not sure why I ask that. I don't think one day is going to make much of a difference for me financially.

"I'll tell you what I can do. I'll take off another ten percent. Will that put it more in your price range?" The sales lady is really trying to make this sale.

I stare at the bracelet a little longer. I know it would look very pretty on Jennifer's arm, and I want to get it for her so bad. I just simply don't have that kind of money.

"Can you give me a few minutes to make a phone call?" I ask, an idea suddenly coming to mind.

"Sure, I'll put it back at the register. Just let me know what you decide."

I walk to the entrance and stop right outside the doorway. *What am I going to do?*

I pull out my cell phone and look through the numbers that Jennifer programmed for me. There're only a few names, and I tap my finger on Rebecca's.

It rings a few times before a male voice answers. At first I think I've gotten the wrong number. "Hello?" I hear the person on the other end say again.

"Uh, yeah, hi. I'm trying to get in touch with Rebecca. Must've made a mistake. Sorry…" I'm about to hang up when I hear him tell me to hang on.

"Brian?" I hear Rebecca on the other end. "Is everything okay?"

I totally forgot about her boyfriend coming into town, which would explain why he answered.

Jennifer must have given her my number too since she knew it was me.

"Yes. Hey, sorry to bother you. I completely forgot you'd be with Greg today."

"That's okay. We got back from the airport around noon. What's going on?"

I'm a little hesitant at first, but then decide I might as well ask her since I've got her on the phone. *At this point, what do I have to lose?* Plus, she's being nice to me. "I'm down at the mall, trying to find Jennifer a Christmas present. I actually found a bracelet I think she'll love."

"*Ohhh.* Going to surprise her, huh?"

Rebecca has no idea.

"Well, I'd love to, but you see, I don't quite have enough to cover all of it. I really hate to ask you this, but do you think you could loan me a little bit, and we can work out a payment arrangement? The sales lady has dropped it to a really good price, and I'm afraid if I don't get it now, it'll more than likely be gone later on today."

The phone goes silent for a few seconds, and I start to think we've been disconnected. Then I hear her make a slight coughing sound, like she's trying to clear her throat. "How much are we talking about?"

I give her an amount, making sure to add a little bit to it just so I'll still have some spending money left over.

"You know, I'm really not into loaning anyone money. It...it's just not something I'm comfortable doing. I feel like it's a set up for something to go wrong in the future." She pauses again, and I'm about to give up hope. "But because I love Jennifer like a sister, I'm going to go against my better judgment. I'll loan you the money."

"Rebecca, you're the best. I can never thank you enough." I'm grateful she's agreeing to help me out and I'm struggling to hide my excitement.

"I'll need to run by the ATM, so meet me out in front of the mall in about fifteen minutes."

****

The sales lady wraps the bracelet for me, and I can't wait to see the look on Jennifer's face when she opens it on Christmas morning. I know it isn't much when it comes to value, but I've never given anyone jewelry before. This is a big step for me.

When I get back to the apartment, I decide to leave the bracelet in the car underneath the seat until she leaves for work tonight. Then I'll sneak it inside and place it under the tree. I'm curious how long it'll take her to find it.

I walk in and the smell of something delicious meets my nose. This awful feeling suddenly overwhelms me, knowing I've got to, once again, pretend that I've been at work all day. I don't know how much longer I can keep it up. Each day it gets harder and harder and it's driving me crazy.

I change into something more comfortable and meet her in the kitchen. She gives me a hug, keeping her arms wrapped around my neck longer than normal. "I missed you today."

"I missed you too, baby."

"I met up with Mom today and helped her with some last-minute Christmas plans. Looks like everything is coming together nicely. We just have to finish wrapping the gifts."

Just the mention of gifts puts a sparkle in her eye. I swear, she reminds me of a little kid that can barely contain her excitement Christmas morning, while waiting for the rest of the family to wake up.

I think back to the bracelet and hope she likes it.

****

Christmas Day is finally here. It's been such a relief not to have to pretend going to work these last few days. I explained to Jennifer that Jared's shop would be closed through New Year's and that I'd be off. I mention the lack of work, as well as a paycheck, during this time off and how something else would sure be nice. It's the wrong time of the year to go without a paycheck. Unfortunately, she doesn't comment one way or the other, so I'm no better off than I was previously.

It's early, yet we're still lying in bed. I roll over and place my arm around her, pulling her close. "Have I told you lately how much I really appreciate everything you've done for me? I...I don't know where I'd be right now if you hadn't come into my life."

She turns to face me and traces her finger along my jawline. "How about you let me show you just how much I love you being here with me."

I slide her t-shirt off, and she tosses it to the floor. I reach down to grab her ass and feel nothing but nakedness. Somehow, she removed her panties without my knowing it.

"Merry Christmas, baby," she whispers and slips her hand down to the waistband of my boxers.

I'm instantly hard, ready for her to grab something else. I thrust my hips towards her, indicating I'd like her to explore more.

She picks up on my subtle hint and together, we slide my underwear down. I slip my hand down between her legs, and she opens them further for me, completely exposing herself. She's dripping wet for me already. I'm amazed how easily she's turned on.

Rubbing back and forth over her mound, I insert two fingers, and she lets a pleasurable moan escape her mouth. I know she's ready for more just from the way her hips lift up off the bed. Without wasting any time, I climb on top of her, and within seconds, I'm sliding in and out of her. Suddenly, I stop, realizing I forgot to put on a condom. *Damn it, I can't believe I keep forgetting.*

"Baby, hold on a second. I need to get something from the bathroom." I try to pull out, but she holds onto my butt cheeks and pulls me in deeper.

"Please, don't stop. I'm so close already," she pleads.

She's into this, hot and heavy, and before I have a chance to mention the condom again, she's panting and meeting me thrust for thrust. It doesn't take long before I'm coming, too, and I swear she climaxes again before we're finished. She may be new at this, but sex with her is out of this world.

I lower my head down between both her breasts and listen to her heart beat. It gradually slows until she's breathing steady and even again. We lie there for a few moments not saying anything. She runs her fingers through my hair, applying light pressure with her fingertips on my scalp. It's such an incredible feeling and I don't want her to stop. It's as if she's putting me under her spell.

I'm just about to doze off when she shifts underneath me. "I need to use the bathroom," she whispers.

"Are you sure?" I ask, not wanting to move from our comfortable position. "You feel so damn good right here in my arms."

She squirms and I know she wouldn't have mentioned it if she wasn't serious about needing to go.

I slide over and she slowly stands up. It truly is nice knowing today is only the first of the next several we'll have together. Jennifer decided to take some vacation time so she could spend it with her family before they leave again. As for me, I plan to take advantage of every chance I can to be alone with her. The connection is there for us, no doubt. Even if her parents don't care much for me.

I hear the water to the shower turn on and I'm still for a moment while my mind wanders. Then I get up and walk to the bathroom door. Rather than knocking, I test the door knob. Just like I suspected, she didn't bother to lock it behind her. Quietly, I push it open, and take in her reflection through the sliding shower doors.

"Mind if I join you?" I slide the door back just enough to peek inside, startling her. She turns to face me and my eyes immediately zero in on the trail of water running between her breasts. I harden again just from the sight.

She opens the door the rest of the way, inviting me to join her, and I accept her invitation without any hesitation.

We take turns pleasuring one another in multiple ways. I even cause her to orgasm again, once with my fingers, the other with my cock. I stroked myself to the point I had to have her, again and again. I yearned for her that much. Yes, I have to say, sex first thing in the morning is very enjoyable. The water begins to turn cold, and unfortunately, our playtime ceases.

Neither of us want to eat too much since we're planning a big Christmas meal later on, so I fix us something light—toast with jelly and scrambled eggs. Jennifer joins me in the kitchen, her hair still damp from the shower. She looks amazing and so refreshed following our morning escapade. That 'just been fucked' look sure looks good on her.

"What?" I ask, with mock innocence. "Why are you so happy?"

"Oh nothing. Just thought maybe you'd like to open one of your presents early?" The grin on her face is huge.

Just to add to the moment, I tease her. "I don't know. You know I've been a bad boy this year and bad boys aren't supposed to get presents. Unless, of course, we're talking about some other kind of present." I immediately shift back to the subject of sex again but she doesn't take the bait.

"You don't have a mean bone in that body of yours," she quickly replies. "You don't know how to be bad."

"*Ahh*, is that what you think?" *If she'd only known me a few months or even a year ago, she'd think differently about that.*

She pulls a small, wrapped box out from behind her back and hands it over to me.

I feel bad because I only have the one gift for her. I'm not sure if I should give it to her now or wait until this afternoon when we're with her family. Would it change their perception of me?

"Happy first Christmas together," I tell her. I place the package on the table and pull her to me, kissing her intimately. When we break apart, I add, "I hope to have plenty more Christmases to share with you."

"*Awww*, Brian. That's so sweet. Here, open it." She hands me the box again.

I carefully pull back the paper and discover a new pair of jeans. "Thank you, baby. I really need these."

"I figured you'd be happy with some new clothes. Besides, you can't wear shorts all the time. You'll freeze to death at work, being out in the cold."

Why did she have to mention my job again? Everything was going so good until now.

Chapter 21
Jennifer

CHRISTMAS MORNING WAS CERTAINLY EVENTFUL, to say the least. If only every morning started out this way. Well, it'd be nice but neither of us would be able to walk we'd be so worn out.

Brian tries on the jeans I gave him and walks around the kitchen modeling them for me. He's got them positioned low around his hips, and if he doesn't stop with his fancy moves, I can't promise what I might end up doing to him. Let's just say, we'd probably be late for dinner and that wouldn't sit well with my parents. It seems I'm already treading thin ice with my choices lately, and I'd hate to cause any more tension with them. If he only had on a shirt, I could stop fantasizing about all the dirty things I want to do to him.

He walks over to the tree and pulls a small box out from underneath it. *How have I not noticed it before?* Either he's just recently put it there, or he carefully covered it up amongst the gifts for my family. It's neatly wrapped in gold paper with a glittery gold bow on top. I'm impressed.

He hands it over to me, a concerned look on his face. "I know it's not much." He pauses before continuing. "I really wanted to get you something more, but since I haven't had time to save a whole lot, I hope you'll consider this just the beginning of many more gifts to come. I hope you like it."

I pull off the bow and carefully slip my finger underneath the tape. Inside is a white box with a jewelry store's named embossed in gold on the top. I recognize the name as one of the ones down at the mall. That little sneak somehow managed to slip down there without my knowing it. "Brian, you shouldn't have." I look up, surprised he'd buy me jewelry so soon in our relationship.

I'm almost afraid to lift the lid to see what's inside. I slowly lift it and find a beautiful, silver bracelet. I bring my hand up to cover my mouth, surprised by such an elegant gift.

"Do you like it?" he asks.

"Brian, it's gorgeous." I remove it from the box and hold it in my hands. I can't help but wonder if he had help picking it out. "Will you help me put it on?"

He fastens the clasp, and I hold my arm out for both of us to admire. "I hope you like the colored stones. They aren't genuine, but someday I'll replace them with the real thing."

"I love it. I wish I could show it to Rebecca." I know she's been on pins and needles lately with Greg coming home which would explain why she's been a little standoffish. I grab my phone from the table and turn on the camera.

"Come here. Be in the picture with me." I pull him close to me and hold the bracelet up so it's visible in the photo. With a few clicks, the image of us is on its way to her along with this message: "Check out my Christmas present from Brian. I love it."

I truly never expected anything from him, especially something so nice. How could he afford it?

A few minutes pass before I hear the text alert. I'm impatient to know what she thinks but when I turn my phone back on, there's nothing there.

"Hmm, that's funny. I thought I heard my phone. Is it yours?" I ask, setting mine back down on the table.

"I doubt it," he quickly replies. "Who'd be texting me?"

162 · Amy Stephens

I think back to the other texts he received a few days ago, the ones he said weren't meant for him but for someone else who'd probably had his number. Was he telling me the truth?

"Well, was it yours?" I ask again.

"Wrong number, again," he says after glancing at it.

"Oh. I still think it's strange, don't you?" About that time, I hear another alert, only this time it's from mine, and I instantly forget all about his mysterious text.

Rebecca: Very, very pretty. From Brian?

Me: Oh, yes. He did good picking it out don't you think?

Rebecca: Yes, it's very nice.

Me: Merry Christmas to you and Greg. I'm dying to know what he got you.

Rebecca: It's official! We're engaged!

Suddenly, I'm bouncing around the kitchen, jumping up and down. "Brian, Rebecca and Greg got engaged. He proposed!" Even though it was almost imminent, I'm so happy for my best friend.

Me: OMG! What an awesome gift for you.

Rebecca: I was truly shocked.

Me: Can't wait to see your ring. Maybe tonight we'll stop by.

We end our texts and I walk into the living room to find Brian playing around with his phone. The mysterious texts come to mind again, although fleetingly.

"This has got to be the best Christmas ever," I tell him as I sit down on his lap. He quickly turns off the phone and tucks it in his pocket. He puts his arms around me and squeezes. I tell myself not to worry about the texts—I'm sure there's nothing to them. Somehow, though, I can't shake his sudden attachment to his phone.

****

We spend the afternoon with my family and, thank goodness, everything goes smoother this time. I'm grateful they included Brian, despite their mixed feelings about him in the beginning. I truly feel like they treated him like one of their own because when we left, both of us had our arms loaded down with packages, him having just as many as me. Hopefully, he felt that way, too.

I'm so tired when we get back home, the only thing I want to do is fall asleep. Brian tells me to go ahead and he'll come to bed shortly. He wants to catch the second half of the game that he'd been watching over at my brother's house. I shut the door to the bedroom, blocking out the noise. As soon as my head hits the pillow, I'm out.

Not sure how long I've been sleeping, but I wake to an empty bed. I'm not surprised to find Brian fast asleep on the couch, covered with one of my blankets. He's looks content, happy. I stand there for a moment in complete awe. I'm so in love with him. Yeah, I honestly think I love him. So he's got a rocky past—who doesn't have baggage at some point in their life? There's a part of me that wants to know it all, the good and the bad, but I also realize dredging up painful memories may not sit well with me or him. I also need to consider that my lack of relationship experience might not be able to handle his previous complications and frustrations. He warned me some of it wasn't pretty.

I see his cell phone on the coffee table, and I'm tempted to take a peek. I'm just a little concerned about those text messages. I ponder the thought, but decide against it. No, it's just not right. If he tells me he doesn't know who they're from, then I have no other choice than to believe him. I've got to trust him.

What if his ex-girlfriend has contacted him and they're from her? Wait, wouldn't that mean he'd had to of reached out to her first, to give her his number?

I pull the blanket up closer to his neck, not bothering to wake him. It's been a wonderful day; one I plan to remember for a very long time. Our very first Christmas together. I look down at my bracelet for a moment. It's very pretty, even if it's not the real thing. It was the thought that mattered. I grab a book off the table and head back to my bedroom not wanting the light to disturb him.

****

It's New Year's Eve and I'm so excited to be celebrating the night with my two favorite people, Rebecca and Brian. I just hope they can tolerate each other long enough to make it through the champagne toast that *Night Moves* has planned at midnight. Not to mention, our favorite band is playing.

Rebecca's a little sad since her fiancé—it seems so funny calling him that now—had to leave early this morning. Brian and I promised her an evening out, one that'll take her mind completely off Greg.

She gets to our apartment just shy of ten o'clock. When I open the door, she's standing there with her overnight bag in her hand and the most pitiful look on her face.

"You look gorgeous." I wrap my arms around her for a big hug, hoping it'll make her feel better. "I love those shoes." She looks stunning in a strapless, silver mini-dress with matching silver glittery heels. There's no way I could handle the dance floor wearing them, but they're fabulous with her outfit. The only thing missing is the familiar sparkle in her eyes, but I plan to work on that soon enough.

"Thanks. You know you can always borrow them." We've traded clothes and shoes so much over the years, sometimes it hard to remember which one of us was the original owner.

She looks over at Brian and says, "Hope you're able to handle us tonight. I'm in serious need of a drink."

Since we all plan to drink tonight, it's a good thing we decided to call a cab. Earlier, I made margaritas in the blender and Brian and I have already been sipping on them. Normally he'd prefer beer but he says my concoction isn't half bad. When Rebecca sees the pitcher on the counter, she grabs a cup and immediately pours herself one.

"This," she takes a swallow, "is just what I need."

"I'll do my damnedest to take care of you pretty ladies." He winks at me then takes a sip of his own.

I look down at my watch and notice it's nearing a quarter after the hour. "Our cab should be here any second now," I say and empty what's left of the margaritas into cups we can take with us. "Here's to a fun night. Cheers!" I hold my cup up to both of theirs, and we bring them together for a toast, except mine sort of misses. I let out a little giggle, embarrassed to be to be feeling warm and fuzzy already.

I hand Brian my driver's license and keys since I don't want to be bothered with a purse tonight. I also give him some money, enough to cover drinks for us both, and to take care of the cab fare home. We walk outside just as the cab pulls up. Brian opens the door, and we all climb in the back seat together, laughing a bit too loudly, trying to make the most of the time we have left of this year.

The cab driver drops us off at the front door. The moment we step out, we can already hear the loud music. I'm looking forward to a night of letting loose and having fun. Brian loops his arm through mine and Rebecca's and proudly escorts us inside.

The dance floor is packed, with barely enough room to walk around the perimeter. Eventually, we work our way to the back, and I order a round of margaritas, figuring we might as well stick with what we've already been drinking. The band is pumping out the tunes, one continuous song after the other. It's almost impossible *not* to be having a good time here.

I lean over and ask Brian if he's ready to dance. He shrugs his shoulders, and I'm not sure if he understood what I asked with the noise level so high, but I take it to mean he is. We disappear into the churning crowd. Rebecca remains off to the side, laughing at the both of us. I'm not the best dancer, but right now, no one cares or pays any attention to us.

Brian and I move to the beat and, thanks to the particular song, it doesn't take long before we're grinding against one another. I catch Rebecca staring and motion for her to join us. She weaves her way through and hands a much needed drink to each of us. With the three of us dancing together, it doesn't take long before we're hot and sticky. After several more songs, the band calls for a break. It's a good thing, because the moment I stop moving, I feel dizzy and lightheaded.

I excuse myself to go to the ladies room, telling Rebecca and Brian to keep our spot up front on the dance floor. We worked too hard to get this close to the stage. As I weave my way to the back, I tune out the lewd remarks made from drunk guys. I feel several hands reach out to touch my breasts and my butt, but I push them away, knowing most of the people aren't even aware of their own actions tonight.

I'm one of them.

I'm so intoxicated, it's a wonder I even make it to the back without stumbling and falling flat on my ass. It's too late now, but maybe I should've had one of them accompany me after all.

Inside the bathroom, it's quiet and just what I need to get a grip on myself. I relax for a minute in the stall, closing my eyes and placing my head against the cool metal wall. My ears ring and I can't stop the feeling that I'm floating. It wouldn't take much for me to go to sleep right now.

Suddenly, I'm jolted back to reality from the sound of someone knocking on the stall door. *How long have I been in here?* I stand up much too quickly and bring my hand up against the door to steady myself. I pull my clothes up and walk out to wash my hands. My eyes struggle to focus on the reflection staring back at me in the mirror. I readjust my top, making my cleavage appear deeper, and then pull open the door. Sadly, I miss the door handle the first time and have to reach for it again. *Yep, I'm definitely drunk.*

I grab us another round of drinks—as if we really need them if the others are feeling anything like me—and I do my best to carry them in my hands without spilling any. The band has already started back up again and I have trouble working my way back through the crowd. Finally, I see Brian off in the distance, lewdly dancing with Rebecca. Yes, lewdly. If I didn't know any better, I'd think they were together. There's hardly any space separating the two. A pinch of jealousy sweeps through me, and I blame it on the alcohol. I quickly push all negative thoughts away. *They're just having fun.* Tonight is not the time for any of that. Brian looks up, sees me struggling, and comes to my rescue.

"Thanks, babe," he tells me, and takes a sip. "You must've been reading my mind."

"We thought you got lost." I'm barely able to hear Rebecca above all the noise.

"It's so hot in here, I figured we could use another round." I use my free hand to fan my face while holding my drink with the other. Maybe I don't need one after all. I haven't been this intoxicated in a long time. Well, not since the night Brian and I got a little carried away.

We dance together in our little circle again, and Brian, no doubt, appears to be enjoying his spot in the middle. He takes turns facing me first, then her. I glide my hands over his ass, shocked at some of the moves I'm making here in a public place. Even though no one notices or even cares, I'm usually a little more conservative.

Rebecca seems to have put her concerns about Brian to the side. No doubt the alcohol has eased her mind; I just hope she still acts the same towards him tomorrow. I knew that if she'd only just give him a chance, she'd come to like him just as I did.

The band announces one final call for drinks before midnight. Brian looks at the two of us and I shrug my shoulders, uncertain if I should be having another one. I'm pretty toasted as it is. He hurries toward the back knowing the lines will be long. What's one more going to hurt? Rebecca and I don't say much, but I blame it on the noise and how hard it is to hear. The place is almost out of control.

Brian makes it back just in time for the countdown.

"Ten." The crowd shouts.

"Nine."

He turns towards me and places a sloppy, salty kiss to my lips. It's safe to say, he's had a little too much as well.

"Five."

"Four."

He faces forward again and the three of us lift our drinks towards the ceiling and scream as loud as we can.

"One. Happy New Year!"

The crowd roars and I almost want to drop to my knees and wrap my arms around my head, just to stop the pounding. The room is so loud I can't even hear myself think.

I notice just how glassy and bloodshot Brian's eyes are when he turns to face me. My gaze follows his lips until they're inches from my own. I brace myself, ready for his kiss. His tongue enters my mouth, and for once, it's not pleasant. He's messy and I can taste the tequila on his breath. I pull away, needing fresh air.

I reach over to give my friend a hug so she doesn't feel excluded, but not before he plants a kiss on her cheek. I suppose it's okay considering we're here together. It's not like it meant anything.

Brian turns his cup up, draining the last of his margarita. "Damn, these are so good," he tells both of us again. I've lost count how many times he's already said it.

I look towards him and let out a little giggle. I'm afraid to move. "If I have one more of these," I lift my drink slightly, "someone's going to be picking me up from the floor." One thing's for sure, tomorrow isn't going to be pretty.

We leave our spot up front, making our way off to the side. No doubt, we all need a break from dancing *and* drinking. For sure, we've had our fair share of fun tonight. Some of us a little too much.

Rebecca looks tired as she leans against the wall, rubbing the calves of her legs. "I really love these shoes, but they're killing my feet. They're certainly not made for dancing."

"I don't know how you've lasted this long in them," I tell her, knowing I'd already have pulled them off long ago.

"Are you ladies about ready to call it a night? I hate to be a party pooper, but I'm going downhill, fast." Brian's words are slurred, making it almost impossible to understand what he's saying. He's draping his arms over both of us and it's not helping the way I'm feeling at all. He's sloppy drunk, and I'm not sure how I feel about it. Of course, I'm a fine one to talk.

At the side door, he holds it open for us to walk out. Cabs are already lined up alongside the curb as far as I can see. Rebecca says something I think is so funny, and suddenly we both burst out laughing uncontrollably. Brian puts an arm around both of us and guides us to one of the waiting cars. It's time for tonight to come to a close.

Inside the car, I rest my head against the headrest. I close my eyes for a moment and let out a deep breath. Actually, it's the wrong thing to do once the car pulls away from the curb. With the movement, everything starts spinning and my stomach begins to churn. I breathe deeper, praying the feeling will subside. *I will not get sick. I will not get sick,* I keep repeating to myself.

Once the queasiness eases off some—or so I think it does—I open my eyes and look over at Brian. He's deep in conversation with Rebecca about something and she's giggling hysterically. I'm not sure what's so funny, but my pounding head simply can't take any more. It's as though she's flirting with him, doing her best to put herself out there for him. *No, no. I must be imagining it. She wouldn't do such a thing.*

I can't hide the jealousy that quickly overcomes me. *I'll show her. How dare she flirt with my boyfriend!* I place my hand on the top of his leg and begin to rub, slowly working my way towards his crotch area. I couldn't care less if she notices or not. I'll show her who he belongs to. Just because I'm drunk, it doesn't give her the right to put the moves on Brian. What would Greg think of her behavior?

I move my hand up a little higher, finally feeling the swell in his pants. Brian reaches down to shift himself. Then, he places my hand directly where he wants it so I can continue with my torture. If my distraction's done one thing, it's put an end to their conversation. I close my eyes again, thinking all is okay again, while I continue to massage him. He appears to have more control than me, although all three of us are wasted.

I feel his breath on my cheek, just before feeling the tenderness of his lips on mine. We engage in a messy kiss that turns into a full blown make out session, our hands groping and rubbing each other. When we pull apart, I force open my eyes and look over to Rebecca. Suddenly…

No, no it can't be. That can't be her hand up on his pants. Surely my eyes are playing tricks on me. I tell myself it's nothing, that this is all a big mistake. None of us are aware of what we're doing. She'll realize she's gone too far and stop.

I crave another kiss, even though there's nothing passionate about it, so I lean towards him, doing my best to claim what's mine. I think about what it would be like to take him on right now, here in the backseat of the taxi. Just to prove...what? That he's mine? Oh, I'm pathetic.

Quickly, I pull away for air. Struggling to find the button to lower the window, I finally find it and let the fresh night air engulf me. The coolness eases the nausea that I'm suddenly feeling again. Brian notices something's not right with me.

"You okay, babe?" he slurs in my ear.

"Yeah, I'm just feeling a little queasy. I'll be okay."

I muster up the courage to look down at Brian's leg again, and this time, I definitely see Rebecca's hand on him. The cab's dash lights illuminate just enough for me to see more than I ever cared to. I pretend my eyes are deceiving me and quickly look away, but I know I saw her hand moving up and down.

Tears sting my eyes so I shut them tight, figuring if I can't see it happening, then surely it's not. I don't want to see my drunk best friend fondling my boyfriend.

Damn stupid alcohol!

Damn stupid bitch! It's just...it's just not her, not something she'd do in a million years. I know her better than this.

If I can just make it home, I promise I'll never drink this much again. Ever.

Funny, everyone seems to make this promise at one point or another.

The cab stops in the parking lot just outside my apartment. I fumble for the door handle but Rebecca is already getting out on the other side. *Yeah, she better get out that way because I'll, I'll...*

When I finally make it out, I see her holding her shoes high above her head and swinging them back and forth. Drunk. She laughs loudly and dances around the parking lot without a care in the world. She's completely drunk off her ass.

Brian holds onto my arm and guides me to the front door. He attempts to grab ahold of Rebecca as well, but I pull away. Then, it suddenly hits me—the urge to throw up. I'm going to be sick. I lean over, and Brian pulls my hair back just in time. All the alcohol I consumed tonight comes right back up. It stings the back of my throat, making me feel even worse. I absolutely hate getting sick, especially in front of anyone, but this time I can't help it.

Brian assures me everything's going to be okay. "When you think you're able, let's try to get you inside. You definitely need to lay down." He rubs my back as I hold on to the porch railing.

I cough and spit, the burning sensation in my throat almost more than I can bare.

Rebecca approaches me, and even in my inebriated state, I feel myself pulling away from her. "Jenn, come on, sweetie. Let's get inside."

"Just leave me alone," I hiss. I know it's harsh, but now is not the time to make me more upset than what I already am. Does she not realize what she was doing to *my* boyfriend? I just want to lie down and go to sleep so this nightmare will go away. I don't know her anymore.

"Jenn, I'm just trying to help. What's gotten into you?"

"I said, get the hell away from me. Now!"

Brian just stands there, his hand on my back, dumbfounded.

Chapter 22
Brian

I GET THE FEELING JENNIFER is slightly embarrassed getting sick in front of Rebecca and me. It's happened to all of us at some point, but what's up with the attitude? It's a side of her I've definitely never seen before. Can we please just take this inside before something gets said?

Rebecca offers to help me, but then she snaps again. Wow! *It's so unlike her.* Did I miss something somewhere?

"Just leave me alone," Jennifer spits out. She's irate.

I cannot believe what I'm hearing between those two. It's got to be the alcohol, and tomorrow everything is going to be better for everyone, myself included. I feel like shit.

I unlock the door and force Jennifer inside. It's for her own good. Rebecca locks up behind us, and I tell her I'll be just a moment while I get Jennifer changed and ready for bed. I really feel bad for the way they've both acted towards one another, and I'm sure whatever is going on will work itself out. Best friends just don't get drunk then suddenly get bitter with each other for no apparent reason.

Jennifer flops down on the bed, then falls back onto her pillow. She's limp and carefree, almost like a ragdoll. I manage to get the bedding turned down and slip her legs underneath them.

"I'm going to bring the trashcan in here just in case you need it. I'll also get you a wet washcloth." The sooner she falls asleep, the better off she'll be. She needs sleep and lots of it. I bend over and kiss her on the cheek. "I'll be back to check on you."

"I just…I just want to… go to sleep," she mumbles. I'm not sure if she heard anything I just told her. "Just make it all go away."

There's no hope getting her to change from her clothes, so I just let her sleep in the ones she wore out tonight. Right now, the less she moves around, the less chance she'll have of getting sick again.

I make my way to the bathroom and turn on the water to the sink. Before dampening the cloth for her, I splash some of the cool water on my face. It feels good, shaking me from the alcohol stupor I've been in myself. *Why did I have to drink so much? Couldn't I have had just as much fun sober?*

I grab everything I need and walk back out to the bedroom. There's nothing worse than cleaning up someone else's vomit, so I spread a couple towels down on the floor around the trashcan just in case. I look over at her and she's sound asleep.

Back out in the living room, Rebecca is sitting on the couch, a beer in her hand. Yes, a damn beer. Like any of us need anything more to drink. The TV's on, but I'm not familiar with the show that's playing. The volume is turned down low, so low I'm not sure how she's even able to hear it. When she sees me, she reaches over to hand me a beer I hadn't noticed was there.

"What's this?" I point to the beer. "Haven't you had enough already?" I pretend not to notice the way she's slightly pulled up the bottom of her dress, revealing just a little more of her leg than I'm comfortable seeing. If this were a different situation altogether, and it wasn't Jennifer's best friend, I might feel compelled to act on her behavior, but I can't shake the fact it's my girlfriend's best friend. Not to mention, she just recently got engaged. I sit down on the opposite end of the couch from her. Going against my better judgment, I pop open the beer even though I honestly don't want it.

"Oh, I'm definitely buzzed." She looks down and rubs her temples. I catch her looking over at me just to see if I'm paying her any attention. "I just can't stop thinking about Greg. I want to call him, but I know he's not allowed phone calls in the middle of the night unless it's an absolute emergency."

I'm uncertain if she's truly sad or if she's just trying to get my sympathy. I hate doubting her in case she really is in need of some support. We seem to have overcome some of our previous qualms with one another. At least I think we have. So, I try to comfort her by saying the right thing. "You'll be amazed how fast time flies. Before you know it, he'll be home for good, and you'll never have to be apart again." The last thing I need to deal with right now is Rebecca drunk-calling her boyfriend. If I can talk her out of her misery right now, she'll thank me for it later.

"I know. I just miss him so much. I hate that we couldn't celebrate the New Year together." She looks down at her finger, staring at her engagement ring. "We...we just got engaged."

"Your ring is very pretty. He did a good job picking it out." I know this isn't a typical guy response, so I quickly say something else, not giving her a chance to comment more about it. "I want to thank you again for helping me with Jennifer's bracelet. I don't know what I would've done without you."

"You owe me, big time," she quickly adds. "You're lucky I'm starting to like you. You just better be good to her." She takes a long swallow of her beer before finishing it off.

Not wanting to waste my own, I take a swig hoping it doesn't disagree with all the tequila that's already in my system. She stands up and almost loses her balance.

"*Whoa*. Hang on." I jump up from the couch to help her regain her stance, unsure of where she's trying to go.

"Care for another one?" she splutters and stumbles into the kitchen. *Like she really needs something more to drink! I can't believe she would ask me that.*

"I'm good," I call back to her. I almost forget to keep my voice down. The last thing I want is to wake Jennifer.

When she comes back to the living room, I notice the moisture on her cheeks. Using the back of her hand, she wipes the side of her face. *What now? Drunk women! Laughing one minute, squalling the next.* She sits rather close to me, but I play it off, not wanting to embarrass her or me by saying the wrong thing.

"Oh, Greg. Why did you have to leave me again?" she says, then takes a swallow of her beer. She's so wasted, yet she continues to drink like it's nothing. I'm ready to call it a night myself, but she keeps talking and drinking.

It's really sad how alcohol can alter your actions in such a short period of time. I place my arm across the back of her shoulders and pull her to me for a friendly hug. I don't mean anything by it and I hope she doesn't read more into it. "I know you miss him. You need to think about getting some rest though, and then you can call him in the morning. I'm sure he'll want to know all about the fun you had tonight."

I bring my arm back and try to stand up, but she stops me and rests her head against my shoulder. "Don't go just yet. Stay here for a minute, please."

I hear the sadness in her voice, but I know she needs to sleep more than anything. And for God's sake, she doesn't need anything more to drink. Jennifer's the one to provide comfort for her friend, and that's going to have to wait 'til later. Now

I'm starting to feel awkward. This is getting to be a little too much for me.

I think back to the cab ride earlier tonight. I was so buzzed, but for a moment, I could've sworn she'd had her hand on my leg. Was it her or Jennifer? I honestly don't know. Nothing came from it, so I played it off.

"You need some sleep. I do, too," I try to convince her again.

I'm finally able to pull away, but Rebecca reaches up to stroke my cheek. She slowly pulls my face close to hers. I know what I should do is to pull away from her immediately, whether she likes it or not. But stupidly, I don't.

I bring my hand up, wiping the single tear that slips down her face. *No. No, you've got to stop this.* I keep hearing the words repeated in my head, but my hand pulls her face to mine. For one simple moment, I lose control of my own actions.

I part my lips and the tip of her tongue gently glides over them teasingly. I pull back long enough to moisten them, and we touch again. Only this time, it's a little deeper than just on the surface.

Rebecca and Jennifer are like sisters, so why is this happening? Why am I letting this go on? Jennifer would kill me.

Suddenly, I detect movement out of the corner of my eye, and I quickly pull away.

"What the hell is going on in here?" Sure enough, Jennifer stands in the doorway watching the scene unfold in front of her. I freeze, unsure how to respond to being caught. *No, it's not what it seems. Please tell me I didn't just kiss her best friend.*

Rebecca simply sits there, stunned. I stand up and walk towards Jennifer, but she turns to go back to the bedroom, slamming the door right in my face. I hear the lock click, and I know I'm in a serious bit of trouble. It's not going to be good. How do I explain this one?

"It's not what it looks like." I bang on the door. "Just let me explain." *But what exactly is there to explain?* I've screwed up big time. And not just me, but Rebecca, too.

I hear her throwing things around in the bedroom and it doesn't sound good. I pray she doesn't disturb any of the neighbors.

I slip down to the floor and lean back against the wall just outside the bathroom. If she opens the door, she'll have no choice but to face me. If I have to wait here all night, it's exactly what I'll do.

I wake up with my cheek pressed against the bathroom door. I'm still on the floor and wearing my same clothes. I have no idea what time it is. I slowly try to stand and grab ahold of my throbbing head. I look around but the apartment is much too quiet

Jennifer's bedroom door is now open, so I peep around the door frame. I'm not surprised to see her still sleeping. The trashcan and towel are no longer next to her where I left them, and she has on different clothes now. After a closer look, I spot the trashcan on its side over in the corner along with several pairs of shoes and her clock. Her throwing frenzy must have landed everything there.

I walk to the living room but there's no sign of Rebecca. I'm not certain if that's good or bad. I think back to everything, hoping it was just a bad dream and not something that really happened. I know there's no way I could've kissed my girlfriend's best friend. It's just not something I'd do. *Would I?*

I grab a bottled water from the refrigerator and chug a good bit of it. My mouth is parched, yet it hardly soothes my dry, scratchy throat. I open the cabinet door and look around for pain reliever, something to kill the dull ache in my head.

"What are you looking for?"

I turn around, startled to see Jennifer standing just a few feet from me. The look on her face is not a pleasant one.

I take another swallow before answering. "I'm just looking for something to take for my headache."

I really don't know what else to say to her, if anything at all.

I begin to walk towards her, thinking maybe if I could hold her hand or embrace her, it'll mean everything is alright. *It was all just a bad dream, right?*

"Don't touch me!" Her words are sharp, bitter.

"Look, I'm sorry. Can we at least talk about this?" I suppose that response was nothing more than an admission of guilt. I'm nothing more than a piece of shit.

"I don't want to hear your pathetic excuses, or hers either for that matter. The two people I care for the most have completely betrayed me."

"Please..." I beg. "Please give me a chance to explain."

"Just get out. I don't want you here."

She turns to walk away, and I'm left standing alone. She slams the bedroom door behind her and I'm almost certain I hear her sobbing on the other side. *How could I have been so freaking stupid?*

I really don't care about the way that I look right now. I just need fresh air to clear my head. I grab the keys off the table and head out the front door. I figure the best thing for me to do right now is give her some time to calm down. I need to leave, just like she told me to do.

Chapter 23
Jennifer

THE ROOM IS DARK WHEN I finally wake up. I feel like I've been run over by a bus as I rub my eyes with the palms of my hands. I glance over at the clock but it's not where it should be. I spot it on the floor over in the corner. The red glow shows it's almost nine o'clock. I've literally slept the entire day.

"Shit!"

I've got less than an hour to shower and get ready for work. I think about calling in sick, but not only is that not in my nature, I've already taken a fair amount of time off in the last two weeks. It wouldn't be right this late at night to try to find someone to cover my shift.

Brian is nowhere to be found in the apartment. *Good. I'm not in the mood to see or deal with him.* There's no doubt he knows how pissed I am with him and Rebecca. Maybe pissed isn't the correct word. Disgusted is more like it.

There's simply not enough time to do everything I need to do to get ready, so I don't bother washing my hair. It'll have to wait until later. I pull it back in a ponytail and dab on just enough make-up to make me look presentable. If I'm lucky, no one will come in tonight to witness my weak attempt at looking decent.

I leave the lamp on like always and walk out to my car. The parking space next to mine, Brian's spot, is empty, just like the space in my heart right now.

It dawns on me that I haven't eaten all day, so I pull through the drive-thru at McDonald's. I don't think my stomach can handle much of anything so I order something light.

I pull into the hotel parking lot and see Rebecca standing at the front door, her purse already on her shoulder, ready to leave. I'm not sure what to say to her, if anything. It's definitely an awkward situation and one that I'm not ready to discuss. Right now, I just want to be left alone. I'll most likely say something I'll regret later if she pushes the subject. I suddenly see a flashback of her and Brian engaged in their kiss, and it ignites my anger all over again.

Neither of us say a word and she storms past me. I put my things away, hardly believing she left like she did. Hopefully, there's nothing I needed to know pertaining to work. *I wonder, is she even sorry, or is she proud of what I walked in on? And just who initiated the kiss first? How far would things have gone between the two of them had I not caught them?* Just thinking about it sickens me more. Just goes to show you can't trust anyone anymore, not even your best friend.

I try to eat some of my food, but end up tossing it in the trash. It's going to be a very long night.

****

I am so relieved to see Sylvia the next morning.

"Sweetie, you feeling okay?" she asks me, noticing the bags under my eyes. Mirrors don't lie—I still look like I've been through hell.

"Not really, but I'll be fine. I just need some rest." How's that even possible when I slept the whole damn day? The alcohol sure did a number on me and my body is slow to recover. I don't feel like sharing any more information with her, even though I'm sure she'd have some good advice for me. She's the closest thing to a mother that I have right now.

"Why don't you go ahead and head out? I'll manage the front until someone else gets here."

"Oh, Sylvia, you're an angel. I owe you." I walk over and give her a hug, all the while holding back my sobs.

I'm barely able to keep my eyes open as I drive home. It's early but I won't lie—I glanced through a couple parking lots on the way. Brian has to be somewhere. At least I know he's not with *her*, since she still lives at home with her parents. *God, what would Greg think about her if he knew?*

I finally make it to my apartment and breathe in a sigh of relief—his car's still not here. Right now, neither Brian nor Rebecca are worth the worry.

I walk inside and get the strangest feeling someone's been here. Sure enough, when I walk into the bathroom, I see water droplets on the shower door. *Yep, I knew it!*

Brian, knowing I'd be at work, must've come by to shower before heading to work. That and to get his work clothes. He knew how much time he had before I'd get home. For all I know, he could've come in just as soon as I left last night and stayed the whole time. Maybe he was even in the parking lot watching. I can't lie—I miss seeing him, but my heart can't take the pain right now. I'm just not ready to face him or listen to his lame excuses.

****

The next few days go by in a haze. It's the same routine: I go to work and replace Rebecca each night, yet she still won't look at or speak to me. It's killing me, this awkward behavior that exists between us, but it's the way it has to be right now. I know we can't go on like this forever, but she betrayed me. My best friend totally betrayed me.

I still haven't seen or heard from Brian, either. I wonder if he's found somewhere to stay and if he's been in touch with her. He hasn't been back to the apartment anymore, at least not from what I can tell. Yeah, I'd be willing to bet she knows of his whereabouts, but I'll be damned if I ask her about it.

I think back to the text messages that were mysteriously coming through Brian's phone and wonder if they were from her and not some unknown person like he led me to believe. Maybe they'd been going behind my back the whole time.

On Friday morning, my dad calls just as I'm getting home from work. It's comforting to hear his voice since I've had such a hellish week, but I don't bother to tell him of my troubles. He and my mother would never let me hear the end of it.

We chat for a few minutes, then he tells me about the appointment he's made for me to have my car serviced. My dad is always on top of things like that for me. I just wish he'd got with me before he scheduled it. I've tried to explain to him I'm more than able to do these sorts of things on my own, and when it's convenient for me, but he always insists.

Right now, I'd rather crawl under a rock than face Brian on his job. Looks like I've got no other choice than to visit Jared's shop. I think about taking my car somewhere else, just to avoid him, but I know my dad wouldn't be happy if he found out. He's loyal to Jared whether I like it or not.

I bite the bullet and get ready to go. I'm just thankful that after tonight's shift I'll have the next two nights off. My anger and pent-up frustration has really been unbearable this week.

I pull into the parking lot at the oil lube shop and look for Brian's car first thing. Funny, but I don't see it. It's not like him to be off on Fridays, but something could've happened this week and I wouldn't know it. Jared recognizes my car and walks out to meet me.

"Hi, Jennifer. Haven't seen you in a while. How were your holidays?"

"Everything was very nice, thank you. I got to spend some time with Mom and Dad before they pulled out again. You know them, always traveling now." I hope Jared doesn't notice my eyes roaming around the shop.

"I sure miss having your dad stop by on a regular basis. He's always so meticulous about things, but that's what I like about him. Maybe next time they're passing through, you could ask him to stop by. Talking to him on the phone just isn't the same."

"I'll definitely send him by to see you. He was so persistent about my coming here today, even though I just got off work. You know him; he follows every service reminder like clockwork. By the way, I didn't see Brian's car. Is he off today?" I try to keep a calm expression on my face, not wanting Jared to know there's tension between the two of us.

Jared looks startled, like I've suddenly put him on the spot. "Um, Jennifer, Brian doesn't work here anymore."

"What?" I am taken off-guard.

"He didn't tell you?"

Suddenly, a burning sensation occurs in my gut, and I think I may be sick.

"What are you talking about?" I swallow back my tears, sickened something must have happened these last few days since I'd told him to leave. Everything had been fine through the holidays. *Hadn't they?*

"He's been gone since right after Thanksgiving." Jared hesitates before continuing. "We had an incident happen here at the shop and, well, I had to let him go. It's a shame because I really liked the guy, too."

"I had no idea, Jared. He didn't bother to tell me." I'm fighting everything within me not to throw up. "Jared, can you point me in the direction of the bathroom please? I'm suddenly not feeling very well."

"Sure. It's just right through there, on your right. I'll get your car right on in so you won't have to wait long."

I run inside to the courtesy area, barely making it in time. Thankfully, no one is occupying the single bathroom. I lock the door behind me and drop down to my knees. Holding on to the toilet, I reach over to turn on the water from the sink. I'm embarrassed for anyone in the waiting area to hear me straining and heaving. I've already had a nervous stomach this week, and now this.

When I feel I have nothing left to come back up, I stand up to look in the mirror. The person staring back at me looks unrecognizable. My face is pale, void of any color, and my eyes are puffy and swollen, thanks to the strain from all the vomiting. I splash cold water on my face and pat it dry with a paper towel.

When it's safe to walk out, I breathe a sigh of relief at the empty waiting area. *Thank goodness.* Just off to the side sits a vending machine and I fumble in my purse for some loose change. A carbonated beverage just might sooth my stomach long enough for my car to get finished.

Jared walks in, and obviously judging by my appearance, asks if I'm going to be okay.

"I think so. Must be a bug or something," I tell him, struggling to hold my head up. "Do you mind if I come back next week sometime? I just don't think I can wait."

"Of course, that won't be a problem at all. Can I call someone to come and get you?" Jared offers.

"No, I think I can make it. My apartment's not too far from here. I appreciate you for asking though."

"Sure thing. Be careful driving, and get yourself some rest. Oh, and tell Brian I asked about him, will 'ya." Jared slaps his hand down on the counter in a friendly kind of way, then points at me. "Take care, sweetie."

Right now, I just want to get home. Brian and his lies are the last thing I want to worry about. How much more can I take? He's turned out not to be the person I thought he was. First Rebecca, now his job? What else has he lied to me about? Just knowing he lost his job before Christmas, yet he's still been getting dressed and pretending to go in, just sickens me more. What kind of a fool does he think I am?

Oh, Lord. Just please make all this go away.

I make it home just in time to get sick again. My hands are trembling so bad I can barely prop myself up on the side of the toilet. *Please, I just want to feel better.*

It's times like this I wish I had someone here with me. Rebecca, Brian, or even my mother. Yes, just someone to make it go away so I don't have to be alone. First the alcohol, now this. I can't take much more.

I manage to crawl into bed, but it's no use. The cramping and nausea are so severe, there's no way I can relax enough to get any sleep. I force myself to nibble on some crackers, but I'm scared they're just going to come right back up. I've been sick plenty of times, but I can't recall ever feeling this way. And for it to hit so suddenly.

Around the time I should be getting ready for work, I realize I'm simply too weak to even get up to take a shower. The pain has eased off, but I sincerely doubt I'll be able to make it through the night. What if it hits me again and I've got customers to wait on? Or worse, what if no one's around and it gets so severe I can't stand it?

I place the call to my boss and apologize for the late notice. He suggests I drink lots of liquids, since I could very well be getting dehydrated from all of the vomiting. He's very sympathetic and for that, I'm thankful. For a brief moment, I think about messaging Rebecca just to let her know what's going on. But on second thought, I'll let her find out when my replacement walks in. I don't owe her anything.

I try to relax on the couch and get comfy by propping the pillow up behind me. I look over at my phone, and I'm reminded how quiet it's been all week. Other than the phone call from my dad, no one has called or texted.

I can't keep going on like this. I...I miss him so much.

I pull the blanket up to help with the chill I'm feeling, and I'm met with the smell of Brian. Suddenly, I grab my stomach, the pain so sharp it takes my breath away. It hurts so bad...

Chapter 24

Brian

IT'S TAKEN FOREVER FOR FRIDAY to get here. The week has been long and very lonely. Thank goodness I remembered to grab my phone charger when I stopped by the apartment for a shower earlier in the week. I knew Jennifer would be at work, so I made sure to pick up behind myself, just so she wouldn't notice.

My phone's been eerily quiet all week. No texts, no calls—not one word from her. I just knew she'd call, letting me have it about the mess that happened over the weekend. I'm still unclear what all took place. I just know I had entirely too much to drink, as did the others.

With nothing better to do, I pull into the movie theater parking lot. Just like old times again. I've seen every release that's come out in the past few weeks, even catching a few of them twice. Rather than sneak inside, which I've gotten pretty good at thanks to saving my ticket stubs, I lay my seat back for a nap. I just can't take another movie tonight. Parking here for a little while should give me a couple hours of uninterrupted sleep.

All week, I've filled up on other people's leftover popcorn and drinks. I know it sounds gross, but when you're hungry, you'll take whatever you can find. A few times, I got lucky and took the empty containers to the concession area for free refills. My concern was not letting the same person wait on me each time. If they'd picked up on what I was doing, I'd probably be kicked out.

I'm down to counting loose change now. All of it's going towards gas, getting me back and forth across town. I know it was a bad thing to do, but I did scoop out a handful from the jar Jennifer keeps in her bedroom. I couldn't bear to take the whole thing because, at some point, I hope to have the chance to win her over again. She's got to understand, I didn't realize what was happening with Rebecca. The last thing I want to do is go back home and deal with my family. I've come too far to turn back now. With a little begging and a little pleading, she's got to give me a second chance. She just has to. Besides, it was Rebecca who initiated the whole thing and that's who she should be mad at.

The nine o'clock movie lets out, and I'm awakened by the variety of noises outside my car. For a brief moment I think I'm back at her apartment on the couch and the noise is coming from the TV. Once I realize where I am, my mood dampens.

All around me, hordes of teenagers are walking through the parking lot to meet their parents, as well as couples holding hands and literally hanging all over each other. It's almost too much to watch.

Right now, I'm really missing her. If I called her, would she talk to me?

I charged my phone earlier today when I was at the library, a place I never realized I could spend hours at. No one seemed to mind that my phone was plugged into the socket on the wall behind me while I browsed through an endless number of magazines. I stayed there as long as I could, but on Friday's they closed up at five, so I had no choice but to leave.

Looking down at my phone, the battery is still showing a nearly full charge. *Damn it!* Even an angry text or hang-up call, just some kind of communication from her, is better than nothing.

And just like some kind of magic, my phone lights up alerting me I have a text. I hold my breath, scared to open it to see who it's from. I even look down at it twice thinking maybe my eyes are playing a trick on me.

I slide my finger over the mailbox symbol and her name and number appear on the screen. It's a message from her!

Jennifer: Are you able to help me?

Well, that surely wasn't what I was expecting to read. I figured something more along the lines of 'I'm sorry' or 'can we talk.' Puzzled, I sit up and move around in the seat. Is she in some kind of trouble? Is it a joke? I reread it again, making sure I read it correctly the first time. Something's doesn't feel right about it.

Brian: Are you in trouble? Do I need to come to the hotel?

Almost instantly, she replies back.

Jennifer: Very sick. Throwing up all day. Hurt so badly. Need dr.
Brian: Home? Hotel?
Jennifer: Home
Brian: Be right there.

I watch the "E" on my gas gauge, praying the whole way that I make it to her place. Now's not the time to run out of gas. When I get there, I pull into the first available spot, not caring if it's one of the ones designated for her unit or not. She needs me right now, and that's all that matters.

I shut the car off and quickly jump out. I stop when I get to her door and wonder if I should use the key she gave me or if I should knock first. I put my hand on the doorknob and give it a turn. It's unlocked. Before barging in, I knock softly just so she knows it's me.

I don't know what to expect, but the sight of Jennifer curled up in a fetal position on the couch alarms me. I kneel down next to her and touch the back of my hand to her forehead. Her body is on fire.

"Baby, are you okay? What's going on?" I gently brush her hair back that's stuck to the side of her face.

"I don't know," she mumbles, and I'm barely able to hear what she says. "It just hurts."

"How long have you been this way?" It pains me to see her grip her midsection, obviously in excruciating pain.

"I've not felt right all week, but today I started throwing up. I thought it was getting better..." She reaches for the cloth on the edge of the couch and her face contorts from the pain.

Please don't let her get sick, not in front of me.

I offer her my hand to help her sit up. Whether she wants to or not, we're going to the ER. She can't continue this way. Surprisingly, she takes it. I hate that these are the circumstances that brought us together again, but I'm just thankful I'm the one she called and not Rebecca.

"Can you grab my purse? All my insurance information is inside." She sounds so pitiful. "Thank you."

I put my arm around her middle and guide her toward the door. She's so weak, she can barely put one foot in front of the other. I help her into the front seat of her car, and she hands me the keys to drive.

In a few moments, I turn into the emergency room entrance and pull up as close as I can to the door. I get out and run around to open the car door for her. She's so frail looking, I almost want to pick her up and carry her, but I don't.

We walk to the front admittance desk, and I sign her name on the clipboard. A female nurse looks up from her computer monitor and immediately instructs us to take the first room on the right.

"Do you want me to go with you?" I ask, not wanting to upset her if she doesn't want my assistance.

"Please."

Inside the room, she struggles to climb up on the table, then carefully lowers her head down on the thin, paper-like pillow. She's trembling, not only from the cold but I'm sure from being nervous and scared, too. There's no sense in asking for a blanket, so I hold on to her hand, hoping the warmth helps some. The nurse starts out asking her a series questions—first personal, then about her symptoms. I wish she'd contacted me sooner. We could've already seen to whatever is ailing her

"The doctor will be with you in a few moments." The nurse leaves, taking her ID and insurance card.

"Baby, they're going to find out what's wrong, okay?" I notice the tears that have pooled in the corner of her eyes. "They're going to help you feel better." I rub her hand and try to reassure her as best I can. I also never leave her side, not even to sit down for a moment.

Just when she closes her eyes, the pain somewhat easing off, the nurse knocks on the door and walks in carrying a small plastic bottle used to collect a urine specimen.

"Are you able to do this by yourself, or do you need some assistance?" she asks.

"I think I can do it." Jennifer slides off the table and follows her out to the restroom designated for patients. Instead of waiting for her to finish, the nurse walks back in and questions what my relation is to Jennifer. Without hesitation, I tell her I'm her boyfriend, omitting our recent separation.

She finally returns, and the nurse passes her a paper gown. "Go ahead and get changed into this. You'll be fine to leave your socks on. I'll grab your specimen and get it on over to the lab." She turns to leave and I see the look of skepticism on Jennifer's face.

"I'm just going to step out in the hallway, unless, of course, you need my help," I tell her, not wanting to make her feel awkward or pressured.

"Thank you."

I give her several moments then knock on the door before entering. She's in the bed now, her legs curled up beside her.

"I'm so sorry you're sick. You did the right thing by calling me. They'll find out what's wrong and get you well again."

She closes her eyes, despite her awkward position in the bed, and for a moment I think she's drifted off to sleep. Several minutes pass and I begin to wonder if the doctor is ever going to come check on her. I pull out my phone, silencing the volume, and play one of my games again. I've got nothing better to do. I can't just stare at the walls; it'll drive me crazy.

Almost an hour later, a light knock sounds on the door. An older, silver-haired man wearing a white coat with a stethoscope draped across his shoulders, walks in. Jennifer awakens and attempts to sit up. As he approaches her bed, he extends his hand. "Hi, Ms. Davis. I'm Dr. Porter. What seems to be troubling you tonight?"

I listen as she retells the same story over again. The doctor glances over some notations made on her chart, asks her a few more questions, then pushes on her abdominal area. "We have the results from the lab and your white cell count in your bloodwork appears normal—they're right where they should be. If I had to guess, I'd say you've probably gotten a virus. Have you had this trouble with morning sickness for long?"

Uhh, what? What the hell did he just say? Morning sickness? Is there something going on I don't know about? How could she not have told me?

Almost like a slap to my face, I think back to the few nights we had sex and neither of us had bothered to use protection. *How could we have been so careless?* Yes, we did discuss it afterwards, but I never expected *this* to happen. *When was she planning to tell me? And what about all the alcohol she consumed last weekend. It wasn't smart on her part. Even I know that.*

I look over to her, so helpless on the hospital bed. She's silent. Shocked? Yes, she looks shocked out of her mind, even more than me. Does this mean she didn't know?

"Ms. Davis? Are you okay?" the doctor questions her when she's unable to answer.

"Did you say… morning sickness?" Her face looks even paler now than when we first arrived here, if that's even possible.

She turns to face me, then quickly looks away, as though she's embarrassed. We've hardly spoken since I brought her here, but this isn't really the place to talk about our troubles or what led up to her calling me for help tonight.

"I'm going to give you something to help with the nausea. If this is a stomach bug, it should help with your throwing up, too. You're borderline dehydrated, so please make sure to drink plenty of fluids, especially those containing electrolytes. When you're able, I suggest something light for your stomach, maybe some clear broth and crackers. It'll help to regain your strength.

"I'm judging by your expression the pregnancy is news to you. If you need a recommendation for an obstetrician, my nurse can help with that, but you do need to see one as soon as possible. If anything changes in the next twenty-four hours, you experience any spotting or your symptoms get worse, come back as quickly as possible. Our nurses are also just a phone call away." The doctor stands and shakes both of our hands. He's mostly spoken to her while I've just sat off to the side, but I move around in the chair, reminding them both that I'm here as well.

"Thank you, doctor. We appreciate everything," I speak up for the both of us.

"If you don't have any questions, I'll send my nurse in with your shot and you can be on your way."

The doctor closes the door behind him, the sound echoing in the silence that has taken over the room. I don't know what to say or do at the moment.

Suddenly, Jennifer reaches to cover her face with her hands. I stand up to walk to her side, but she brings her hand up to stop me.

"No. Don't," she manages to say between her sobs.

I hate this strain between us. "Baby, I ...."

"I said stop. I can't believe this is happening."

My first reaction is to punch the wall. Yes, I'm mad at myself for being so irresponsible, but I do my best to remain calm, for her sake and mine. I don't need to cause a scene, especially here at the hospital, or to upset her more. If she only knew the temper I had prior to meeting her, she'd know I was trying.

Through her sobs, she manages to say, "Just go. Just get away from me."

I stand there, helpless. I can't just walk away from her, not now. I may have walked away from all my other problems in the past, but this is different. This is a baby we're talking about.

A baby. How am I going to take care of a baby?

A knock sounds on the door, and a nurse enters with a shot in one hand and release papers in the other.

"Here you go," she says in a sickly sweet voice. "This will sting a little, but you should start to feel a little better real soon. Make sure you get plenty of rest and drink lots of fluids. By the way, congratulations to you both." It's obvious she's mistaken Jennifer's tears for those of joy instead of sadness and hurt.

I step out behind the nurse so Jennifer can change into her regular clothes again, and to have a moment to herself. I walk out to the lobby, and it feels like everyone is staring at me, as if they somehow all know how careless I've been. I turn just as Jennifer walks through the doorway.

I hand over her coat and tell her I'll pull the car up to the door. Since she didn't ask for her keys back, I assume her earlier remark telling me to leave was just said out of anger and frustration. She has to know we'll deal with this together. I'm not going to leave her alone. We'll get through this somehow.

Neither of us say anything the entire ride back to her apartment. She stares blankly out the window, no tears and certainly no excitement. She appears to be feeling better physically, but otherwise, emotionally, it's safe to say she's in a state of shock. After I park the car, I walk around to open the car door for her without any resistance.

So far, so good.

Once we're inside, I hang up her coat in the hall closet and place her purse on the counter. Again, she seems okay with me being here. I've missed this place and wonder if there's some way I can convince her to let me stay and help her.

"Here, I'll get those out of your way." She slides off her shoes and I move them off to the side. I've never so willingly wanted to help someone until now. I reach for the blanket, spreading it over her, and adjust the pillow behind her until she looks comfortable.

"Thank you," she says in the softest voice.

I look through the refrigerator only to discover how very little she has to drink. I pour a glass of water and set it down on the coffee table across from her.

I go out on a limb and ask, "Jennifer, can I run down to the store and pick up a few things for you?"

"I don't want to put you through any trouble. You were kind enough already to take me to the hospital, and for that, I thank you." It pains me to hear her distant, emotionless tone.

"I want to help you. Please, just let me do this for you," I plead with her.

"Fine, if it'll make you feel better."

"Jenn, I know you're upset with me and I can't blame you."

"Just get me my purse will you," she says, finally giving in to me.

I don't want to upset her but I feel if I'm persistent, it'll show her I'm willing to do whatever it takes.

I quickly grab her purse and hand it over. She pulls a few bills from her wallet and passes them to me. At first, I'm hesitant to take them. It's embarrassing enough as it is that I don't have money to take care of the things she needs. But if I don't take it, I'm even more screwed because I won't have any way of paying.

"I know you're broke, so you might as well just take it," she says.

I don't know how to respond, so I just stand there, a dumbfounded look on my face.

Chapter 25
Jennifer

I MAY BE TIRED AND weak at the moment, but I've got Brian in a corner now. The only choice he has is to come clean. He turns to face me from his spot over by the patio door.

"I guess you know, huh?" He ducks his head, unable to look me in the eyes.

"Yeah, I know about your job. Or should I say, your lack of one. Look at me, Brian." I pull all my strength from deep within and hold my own with him. "How could you? How could you lie to me?"

"I didn't exactly... lie."

"I'm tired of the bullshit, Brian. You didn't exactly tell the truth, either."

"I didn't want to disappoint you." He looks at me for only a brief moment before turning his head again. "It's been this way my whole life. I've told you, it happens every time I think I've got a good thing going."

"What happened? Jared wouldn't go into details with me, but I know whatever it was, he was disappointed." It's taking all I've got to remain calm much less just to speak to him. Thank goodness the medicine has eased my nausea, or else I'm not sure I'd be able to take him on. "Brian, I'm waiting. If you won't talk to me, then there's the door."

After a few moments of dead silence, he walks over to sit beside me on the couch. "I'm sorry. It's...it's just... some money went missing from a customer's car, and I got blamed for it. I swear to you, I didn't take it. I don't know who did, but I swear, it wasn't me."

This was not what I was expecting to hear and it leaves me being the one that's speechless. I never in my wildest imagination would've thought this. I was expecting to hear that he broke something or maybe he'd gone in late a couple times. But this? Being accused of stealing is serious.

"Jared caught me off-guard, and I had no way to defend myself. I was backed into a corner with no way out."

"Did you tell him the truth?" I ask.

"Yes, I told him. I told him that I had nothing to do with it, but he'd already made up his mind. I guess he talked to that jerk, Clint, first, and took his side. I don't know. Maybe Clint set me up."

"Was he that bad of a person?"

"Ever since that day I confronted him about his remarks towards you, he's been an ass. Jennifer, you've got to believe me."

If he's lying, then he's doing a damn good job of it. Judging by the look on his face, I sincerely want to believe him. I truly do believe he's telling me the truth.

"Brian..."

He cuts me off to say more. "The worst part about it all, it had to happen right at Christmas."

I want to be angry with him because, first of all, he lied to me. He got up every single morning and pretended to go into work. He'd come home and talk about how tired he was. He. Lied. To. Me. He fucking lied to me! If he'd just told me when it happened... it might not be so hard to talk about now.

So now, we're not only dealing with his lack of a job, but the fact that I'm pregnant, too.

"Have you been able to find something else?" I can try to be somewhat understanding if I at least know he's making an attempt to find another job.

He runs his hands through his hair and looks down at the floor. His expression speaks for itself. I'm not sure I want to know the answer.

"I've checked around, but it's not looking good. There were so many people working temporarily during the holidays that they're desperate for something now, too. You've got to believe me when I tell you I want to do better. I want to be able to provide for you, for us. Especially us, now that ......" His words break off and he stands like he's about to do something rash.

"Brian! Wait." It's too late. He storms out the door, letting it slam shut behind him.

How could everything that felt so right a month ago be so wrong now? Everything had been so...it'd been so perfect. Maybe it'd never been right at all and I was just living in a fantasy world.

I try to relax and take a couple deep breaths, but everything floods my mind. I simply don't need this stress in my life right now. For once, I'm thankful my parents are on the road instead of here. How would I be able to explain everything to them?

I close my eyes to fight the tears that have started to form. Can my life get any more complicated?

****

Sometime later, I awaken. My mouth is parched, my tongue sticking to the roof of my mouth. *Water.* I need water to drink. I attempt to sit up but my body tells me differently. The muscles in my abdominal area scream. I'm no longer nauseous, but the tightness from all the straining earlier is almost more than I can stand.

I look over towards the TV that's now playing. Funny, but I don't remember it being on before. The sound is muted, preventing me from being disturbed. It only tells me one thing—Brian's back.

I listen carefully and detect the sound of water coming from the direction of the bathroom. He must be in the shower.

I manage to stand and slowly walk to the kitchen. Inside the refrigerator, I see a variety of beverages—juices, sports drinks, and bottled water. *At least he did pick those up for me.* I twist off the cap and take a swallow. I lean back against the counter when I glimpse something out of the corner of my eye.

"Oh!" I jump, not expecting him to walk in on me. The bottle slips from my hand and quickly empties out onto the floor.

"I didn't mean to scare you. Here, let me get that up." Brian reaches for the kitchen towel and blots up the spill.

In the meantime, I take a seat in one of the dining room chairs, too weak to stand any longer.

"I hope I didn't wake you." He looks up from his spot on the floor.

"No, I woke up on my own. I see you made it to the store. Thanks. You ran out so quickly, I didn't know if you would go or not."

"I apologize for earlier. I'm just shocked and not sure what to make of everything. It's not easy, you know."

"You're telling me." For a moment, our gaze locks and I can't look away. Is it crazy that I still feel something for him, even after everything we've just gone through?

"I wasn't sure what flavors you would like, so I grabbed a couple of each."

"Huh? Oh, I don't mind. I'm just thankful you got them for me."

"Are you up for something to eat yet? I also picked you up some soup and crackers. I wasn't sure if you'd have some already here and, well, since I stormed out of here so quickly, I didn't have time to check."

My sick heart and body could really stand a hug from him right about now. I'm almost willing to give in to him, to have him embrace me and just hold me. I'm so close to giving in, but I put up my walls again. No matter how nice he's trying to be now, I'm still not ready to push everything aside yet knowing there is still another situation we've yet to discuss— him and Rebecca.

"Mmm. That sounds good. I can't tell you the last time I ate something." He helps me back to the couch and I try to get comfortable again. As he warms the soup, I can't help but smell its delicious aroma. Maybe, just maybe, it's what I need to feel better again.

He brings over a soup mug for each of us and places a tray of crackers beside me. I'm so weak, my hands tremble from the weight. He notices my struggle and offers to pull out one of the fold-up trays I keep stored away in the hall closet. I have to admit, he *is* trying.

Instead of unmuting the sound on the TV, he reaches over to the remote and turns it completely off. The silence is a little awkward, but I let it go.

"Jenn, I'm trying. You've got to give me time. I need that second chance to make things right with you again. Please. I'm begging you. I don't like being lonely, and I don't like being away from you."

In all my life, I don't think I've ever had someone beg for my forgiveness like Brian's doing now. I have to wonder how sincere he is.

"First, can we talk about what happened with Rebecca?" I pause before saying more. I also want to judge his reaction just by my saying her name. As much as it pains me to bring it up, I know it's something we've got to come to terms with. "I'm willing to be more understanding about losing the job, but I'm not so sure I can easily move past what I walked in on last weekend. Talk about having your heart ripped to shreds."

"Have you spoken with her since then?" he asks curiously.

"No, not at all, so if you're wondering if I've heard her side of the story, the answer is no. I have not. It hurts me tremendously, but I need answers." I try not to get upset and bite my lip for the distraction. "We've practically ignored each other at work, to the point you'd think we were enemies."

"I'm… I'm sorry. I…"

I put my hand up, signaling him not to say more. "And to make matters worse," I struggle to remain calm, "I get sick on top of everything else. It's not been my week at all."

Brian just stares at me, probably afraid that anything he says right now will make me snap. He may have made progress a few moments ago, but now, we're back to square one. Surely he can't think I'd forgive him for everything that quickly.

"Can you just tell me why I walked in the room to see you and my best friend making out? Just tell me!" I plead with him.

"Jennifer, you know we all had way too much to drink that night, and we weren't making out. It was barely one kiss," Brian says. "You were completely wasted and I wasn't much better."

"It still doesn't excuse anything, Brian."

"I know that. When we got back here, she kept talking about her boyfriend and how much she missed him. She even talked about calling him. I knew that wasn't the right thing to do, especially with the condition she was in. She wouldn't stop drinking, either. I knew I was well beyond my limit and I tried to get her to stop. She said she didn't want to drink alone."

He had a point—the condition she was in. It wasn't like her at all to drink that much, but I knew just from what I'd seen of them dancing and in the cab ride home, that she was out of control. Brian had his hands full for sure. So if she had continued to drink more... I didn't even want to think about it.

She was supposed to be my best friend and true friends don't do shit like that. Unless, of course, they're wasted. As for him, he could've pushed her away. It wasn't his place to console her. No matter how persistent she may have been, he failed. Now the question is, can I forgive him? If I could go back and change that night, I would in a heartbeat, starting with how much alcohol I'd consumed.

"I admit, I did have another beer with her. I could tell she was getting upset the more she talked about Greg, so I gave her a hug and things just went to hell from there. I swear, I thought it would help, not make it worse. Jennifer, I'm so sorry."

I stare at him blankly, trying so hard to believe that my best friend and boyfriend would not betray me on purpose. Tears sting my eyes, but I force them away. I will not show weakness in front of him.

"Please, I never saw it coming. I swear to you," he begs. "I can promise you it will never happen again."

I want to believe him. I want to believe him more than anything in the world.

"How am I supposed to trust you again?" I ask, a slight edge to my tone. "Now that I've heard your side, how do I know that neither of you will be tempted to try something again, only next time, behind my back? And what about all those text messages you kept getting? How do I know they're not from her?"

"My God, Jennifer. How many times do I have to tell you? Those texts are from someone I don't even know. They're not for me!" His voice rises and for a moment, it's a side of him I'm not sure I like. I realize I'm putting him on the spot, but this is my life, too. "Here, look at my phone. See for yourself." He pulls the phone out of his pocket and tosses it over on the couch.

Instead of losing my cool or making this any worse, I let it all drop. I also don't look at his phone.

Trust.

That's the issue here. Trust. At what point can I trust anyone again?

Brian gets up to put away our dishes while I lie back on the couch again. The tension is thick, but that's to be expected. I really want to accept his apology because my heart yearns for his touch. I need to feel his embrace and his love in my life again.

Minutes later, I sense his presence in the room and glance towards the door to see him standing there. His eyes are focused on something on the small table next to the couch. "I'm going to give you some time, okay? As bad as I want to be near you right now, I know you've got to search your heart for what you feel is right. I just ask that you please consider giving me a second chance."

I push myself up to see him better and whatever he's staring at. My bracelet is sitting there, right where I left it when I took it off earlier in the week. I had planned to put it away in my jewelry box when I'd told him to leave, but I'd forgotten to. It was much too painful to wear it, knowing how much it meant to him when he'd given it to me.

All of a sudden, I freeze. If he got my bracelet right before Christmas, but he'd already lost his job, then... I'm not dumb, nor am I naïve. I can sense something's not right about it.

"Brian, where did you get the money for my bracelet?" I ask as straightforward with him as possible without sounding accusatory.

He immediately senses where I'm going with this. "No, you can't be thinking that. I swear to you, I had nothing to do with that money going missing at work. Please, you've got to believe me."

"I'll ask you again. Where did you get the money?" It's a good thing I'm not feeling well or I'd come unglued on him. How dare he try to pull a fast one over on me.

"I really can't say." He hesitates before saying more. "I had a friend help me out."

Surely he knows this answer is not good enough for me.

Not wanting to deal with this any longer, I throw my hands up in the air. *I give up.* "Get out! Just leave right now. When you think you can be truthful with me about it instead of beating around the bush, then maybe we can talk. But until then, I have nothing further to say."

Brian simply stares at me, his mouth wide open, almost like he can't believe I'd tell him to leave again.

"What part do you not understand?" At this point, I'm pretty angry. The last thing I need is to get upset. I've been through enough. "I said get out. I can't be with someone who's dishonest, and you obviously have a problem with telling the truth."

Instead of putting up a fight, he turns to walk away. Minutes later, I hear the door shut behind him.

I can't believe Brian. One minute, he's begging for my forgiveness. The next minute, he's running from his own lies. *Why do I continue to allow him to rip my heart apart?*

Chapter 26

Brian

I CAN'T BELIEVE THIS IS happening all over again. I thought we were getting somewhere. We were finally at an understanding. I thought we'd made progress. Now, all my efforts tonight were a complete waste.

I walk outside and sit on the steps in the breezeway. I have no money, no gas in my car, and I'm no further along in getting back with Jennifer than I was yesterday. I might even be worse off now. The sun is shining brightly for a winter day, but everything in my world is cloudy and lifeless. I swear, from the day I was born, I was doomed to be a failure.

I pull my phone from my pocket and look back to the text message she first sent asking for help. Yeah, she did text me instead of her crazy, drunk-ass friend, but it's too late. Where's her damn friend now?

I walk out towards the parking lot, unsure what to do next. It's the weekend and there are several people out and about today. I decide to take a walk around the block to clear my head and hopefully come up with a plan.

A couple hours pass when I decide to turn back and head towards the apartment again. I just knew she'd text me asking me to come back. She proved me wrong though. Not one word from her. I stop when I reach my car. This is it—time for me to make a decision. Do I make one last attempt at reconciliation or do I give up and walk away?

Someone walking through the neighborhood catches my attention. The mailman is going door to door dropping off mail in each of the units' slots. I wonder the likelihood Jennifer is getting mail today?

I sit back down on the stairway leading to the next level of apartments and wait. Sure enough, the postman turns and heads my way. I notice the bag he has draped across his chest is loaded down and he's got several items already in his hand, ready to drop them off in her slot.

"Good morning."

"Morning to you, too," he replies and comes to a halt. He wipes the sweat across his brow.

"Might can save you a couple steps. You have anything for Davis? Jennifer Davis, apartment 308. I'm just about to head inside."

Wow. This is easier than I thought.

"Let's see. Here you go," he says and hands over a few things. "Have a nice day."

"Thanks, man, and yeah, you too." I take a few steps towards the door then stop. I turn around and see if he's out of sight before I glance through what he gave me. It's mostly junk except for one item—one very important item. An envelope from her parents.

No, Brian. No, you can't even be thinking this. I hold it up towards the sun and sure enough, I can easily make out the contents—money.

Jennifer had mentioned to me before how her parents liked to send her a little something from time to time. Nothing too much, usually twenty dollars or so. Just enough to pick up a little treat for herself. Twenty dollars in gas could get me down the road a good way, but what would I do then? And what about my clothes? All of my belongings are inside the apartment and I sure as heck don't want to leave them behind, especially now that I've acquired a couple nicer things. I can't just leave with what I'm wearing and nothing else. I might be crazy, but I'm not that stupid.

I sit back down again and try to think rationally. Is it possible she's expecting something from them or is this one of those times they're sending her their little "gift?" I hold the envelope back up again but it's no use. I want to know how much is inside so bad it's killing me.

Without any further hesitation, I slip my finger underneath the flap and peel it back. Inside is a white, folded piece of paper. I pull it out and before I'm able to unfold it, several bills fall out. Are people really stupid enough to send this much cash in the mail? I count out five twenty dollar bills. One hundred dollars. Not twenty like I'd anticipated.

My stomach quickly knots. What if she's expecting this? What if they were sending it to her for a specific reason? *I can't do this. I can't do this to her. But...I do.*

I shove the money and piece of paper back inside the envelope then fold it in half. I cram it in the back pocket of my jeans and pull my shirt down to cover it.

Think, Brian. Think. What are you going to do now?

Suddenly, I have an idea that just might work. I really don't want to leave, but if I'm going to get anywhere with her, I've got to be firm. I've got to show her I'm willing to do whatever it takes to win her back. I want to earn her trust again. I pull out my phone and send her a text.

Me: Rebecca. She loaned me the money for the bracelet.

A few minutes go by, and I start to wonder if maybe she's not going to reply. It's possible she's asleep now and doesn't hear her phone's alert. Just as I'm about to give up, thinking that my plan backfired on me, I see the message box light up. I heave a sigh of relief, even though I don't know what her response is yet.

Jennifer: Rebecca? I should have known. Thank you for telling me.
Me: Didn't want you to know. Wanted to keep a secret. Embarrassed I had no $$. Sorry to let you down.
Jennifer: Please come back. Let's talk.

The words are like magic leaping from the screen. *Please come back. Let's talk.*

I stand up and just as I get ready to walk back down the breezeway to her door, I notice something on the ground underneath the bottom of the steps where I'd been sitting. I bend over and see it's a small, hand-written message on a yellow sticky note.

Here's a little something to take care of your car service. Wish we were there to handle it for you.

Love, Mom and Dad

Shit! This money was supposed to pay for her car service at Jared's shop the day she discovered I was no longer there. Thank God I found this note. It must've slipped out when I removed the money from the envelope. I simply can't win! Unless, she didn't know her parents were sending it to her, then she won't be expecting it. On the other hand, if her dad calls just to make sure the service was fine, then he'll most likely bring up the money he sent, too. Well, goes to show, only an idiot would send that much cash in the mail.

I decide to walk out to the dumpster and dispose of the envelope and sticky note before going inside. Better to be safe than sorry. I can't risk her finding it in my jeans pocket. I'm already treading on thin ice and don't need anything else to go wrong. I fold up the hundred dollars and stick it inside my car.

Not the safest place to hide it, but it should be safer there than in my wallet or inside the apartment. And since most people cringe when they see my car anyway, it should be fine.

I turn the knob and push the door open. Jennifer is standing in the hallway, her eyes red and puffy. Neither of us makes any attempt to approach the other. I realize someone has to make the first move, so I slowly walk towards her with my arms outstretched. When she's close enough to me, I embrace her and promise not to let her go.

Chapter 27

Jennifer

I WAKE FROM MY NAP on the couch feeling refreshed, the best I've felt all weekend long. I attempt to move but realize Brian is behind me, his arm draped across my midsection.

He stirs. "Hey, baby. Did you sleep well?"

"I feel so much better. That shot helped tremendously and maybe your soup, too," I tease, thankful I was able to keep it down. I'm amazed how horrible I felt just hours ago. Maybe the doctor was right and it was just a virus I'd had. With everything I'd had going on all at once, it's sure taken its toll on me.

He helps me sit up and I stretch my arms and legs out in front of me. I'm still a little sore but nothing like I was earlier.

"What time is it?" he asks.

"It's late. The sun's already gone down." My words are muffled as I bring my hand up to cover a yawn. I finally stand, my knees wobbly, and head towards the bathroom.

"Where're you going?" He reaches his arm out pull me back, but I'm too quick.

"Bathroom. Gotta go. I'll be right back." I'm sure my appearance is a sight to behold by now. Looking down, I've got the same clothes on that I wore to the emergency room. Yep, I'd say it's time for a shower.

I grab a change of clothes from the bedroom then close the bathroom door behind me. I don't bother locking it in case he needs to come in for something. I adjust the water temperature just right and strip down before stepping inside.

I turn to look at my reflection in the mirror and stop almost immediately. My coloring is slowly returning to normal, but I can't help not noticing my lower stomach area. It's still nice and flat as I slide both my hands down, stopping right about where the baby should be growing. For a moment, time stands still. A baby. I'm carrying a real life baby inside me. Brian and I have created a beautiful life that's so pure and innocent. I couldn't imagine being a mother and having to do it all on my own. Please, just let things work out for us. I need him in my life and this baby needs *us* in its life.

My eyes glaze over with tears. It's still too early to know if I'm happy about this change in my life, or if I'm sad that everything about my future will be altered now. One thing's for certain, my life is never going to be the same again.

I slide the shower door shut behind me and close my eyes as the warm water flows over my naked body. This is definitely what I needed. I'm not sure how long I stand underneath the steady spray, but it's relaxing and soothing. I hear a faint noise and it startles me from the daydream I've been lost in.

"Would you like some company?" I hear Brian ask from the other side of the shower door.

"Umm, sure. I guess so." I'm not sure where my response came from, but I slide the door back, just enough for him to step inside and water not go everywhere on the floor. I can't help it as my gaze drifts down to his naked parts. I'm immediately embarrassed. I watch as his eyes travel over my nakedness, too.

He steps closer to me, and I bring my hands up to his smooth, hard chest, keeping our bodies not even an inch apart.

I feel his erection graze my leg, sending electric currents all through my body. He leans down and kisses my mouth, our first kiss in over a week. *Oh, how I've missed this.*

His tongue slips between my lips, his breath hot and inviting. I open my mouth further, allowing him to explore more. He gently sucks my top lip while bringing his hands up to cover my breasts. My nipples harden instantly from his touch, and a feeling of desire runs all the way down to my toes. I begin to twitch and throb between my legs. Who knew such excitement could occur in the shower.

"*Mmm.*" I plant small kisses all over his face. I'm not sure if the heat I feel is from the shower or from the closeness of his body against mine. Taking his dick in my hands, I stroke it up and down, careful with the amount of force I use. I want to feel it inside me, but only when we're ready.

He wraps his own hands around mine, and together we slide them in a way that's pleasing to him. He lets out a moan, the sound so desirable to my ears. When I'm comfortable with the rhythm, he slips his hands between my legs and rubs the area that's now swollen. He rubs his thumbs over my clit, back and forth until I raise up on my tip-toes. I'm about to burst and he hasn't even entered me yet. I feel my stomach flutter, knowing I won't be able to hold off much longer.

A grin forms across his face, no doubt proud of what he's doing to me. Suddenly, he drops down on his knees and spreads my folds apart. I take in a deep breath as he inserts two fingers inside me. I've never had anyone go near this area before with their mouth. His tongue rapidly flicks my clit and there's nothing I can do to stop the sensation that's now coursing its way throughout my body. I push my hips up towards his face, needing him to do more. Faster, faster. I grip onto his hair, burying his face deeper in my pussy.

"This... I... need more. Oh... Brian, don't...stop." I never realized how vocal I could be. The water continues to beat down on his face and I look down to watch his tongue and fingers performing their magic on my body.

And just like that, I push his face away. His lips *pop!* as they loosen their grip. My skin tingles but in a good way. Neither of us speaks, the look in both our eyes saying all that needs to be said.

We stand underneath the spray holding each other. Words can't describe how this feels. Brian brings his hands down to my belly and rubs it gently. I grab onto the shower bar as my knees go weak and I get lightheaded. *He's touching my stomach. He's feeling for our baby.*

"I want to make you all mine, baby. No one has ever been as understanding and forgiving as you. I want to be more with you."

I hear what he's whispering, but I'm not sure I understand exactly what he's implying when he says he wants to be more. Then, he completely catches me off-guard.

"Baby, marry me." He looks me straight in the eyes, his voice as sincere as it can be. "I need you to help me be a better person. For you, for me, for all of us. You make me whole."

"Brian, I…I don't know what to say." I'm so taken aback; I can't even think straight.

"You don't have to answer me right now. Just think about it. I need to get some things lined up for myself first, and then I want to make you mine. I want to do what's right, for the baby's sake."

I feel myself tense and I pull away. I never expected to hear the words 'marry me' from someone I met just a few months ago. I suddenly can't think straight, and I can't breathe. I need fresh air.

The steam from the hot shower feels like its strangling me, cutting off my airflow. I reach down to turn off the shower and quickly grab the towel hanging from the bar, throwing it around myself. I step out and lean down, my arms resting against the vanity counter.

I simply don't have any words to say. As I try to catch my breath, Brian opens the bathroom door and a burst of cool air rushes inside. When my heartrate returns to normal, I walk to the bedroom and take a seat on the edge of the bed. He gives me a moment to myself and tidies up the water I'd left all on the floor.

After a few minutes, I look up to find him leaned against the doorway. "Can I help you find something to change into?" he asks, pointing out that I'm still wrapped in my towel. "I didn't mean to upset you."

"I'll be okay. You just—you just shocked me is all."

"I... I kind of shocked myself."

"Please don't take this the wrong way, but I don't know what I want at this point."

"I know it's a lot to drop on you all at once. I realize we've both been through hell, but we're the only ones in control of our destination. No one else. We're the only ones who can make things go the way we want them."

"I guess I'm still having trouble with it sinking in. I'm pregnant, Brian. I'm going to have a baby. It's hard enough thinking about being a mother, much less someone's wife," I plead, desperately needing him to understand.

"Will you at least think about it?" The expression on his face is frantic, as though his life depends on my response.

"Brian, I told you I would, but you don't even have a job right now. We can't make it on just my salary, especially when I go on maternity leave. Who'll pay the bills then? We just have a lot to think about." I feel myself getting upset, so I push my way past him and leave him standing in the doorway. As far as I'm concerned, this conversation is over for now.

He follows me to the kitchen and traps me between his body and the countertop. He lifts me up to sit on the counter, and I have no other choice than to meet his pleading stare. Suddenly, I'm not able to look away. I know he's for real and not just saying this to me.

"I'm going to find a job first thing in the morning. You'll see. I want this for us. I am going to prove to you that this is what's best. I want you to be my wife, Jennifer." His voice is confident, very loud and clear.

"I know you mean well. Let's just take it one day at a time. There's no need to rush into something just yet." As hard as I try, I don't think anything I say is going to convince him otherwise. He's determined to win me over.

"You still don't trust me, do you?"

"Of course I do, Brian. If you didn't care for me, I don't think you would have bothered taking me to the hospital or bringing me home to take care of me."

"I love you, Jennifer."

"Oh, Brian, you can't possibly mean that."

"Yes, baby, I truly love you."

Chapter 28

Brian

DID I JUST TELL HER that I loved her and that I was crazy about her?

What the hell has gotten into me? Yes, I do have feelings for her. Are they as strong as I'm hoping to convince her? I'm not sure. I do know if she gives me a second chance to make things right, I won't screw up again. Just like I promised, I'll find a job. First thing in the morning, I'll start looking for something. I'll put everything I've got into making this relationship work. I just know I can't take another night of sleeping in the front seat of my car. I need to be home, caring for the woman I... the woman I… I think I love.

I sit on the couch, flipping the television from one channel to the next, my mind reeling from everything that happened earlier. Jennifer didn't want to overdo it, so she laid back down for a nap. I think she mostly wanted some time alone—time away from me—and I was okay with that. Besides, I didn't want her to do too much too quickly since she's finally starting to feel like her old self again. I promised her I wouldn't bring up the marriage question again until she could have some time to think about it, and by time, I meant more than just a few hours.

When I feel like I can finally close my eyes for some rest of my own, I turn off the television and all the lights. I make my way quietly to the bedroom, trying not to wake her when I strip down to my boxers and crawl into bed beside her. My days and nights are so mixed up now, but if I can get a couple hours of sleep in, I should be fine for tomorrow. I'll admit I'm not looking forward to the job search, but I promised her I would.

When I awake the next morning, the bed is empty. I glance at the clock that's back on the nightstand again and see it's barely seven o'clock. *Where is she? It's too early for her to be up.*

I walk into the living room and find her sitting on the couch reading.

She notices me standing in the doorway. "Morning," she says, closing her book. "Did you sleep okay?"

"Yeah, actually I did. I really did."

"I've slept so much these last few days, I don't think I can possibly sleep anymore. I figured I could catch up on some reading before I have to leave."

"Have you got plans for today?" She hasn't mentioned anything about having a previous engagement and I wonder if she's physically up for whatever it is she's planning to do.

"I've got to stop by school and pick up my new schedule for this term. Then I need to go by the bookstore and spend a ridiculous amount of money on books. And while I'm out, I might as well stop by work and let them know I'll be back tonight."

"Tonight? You're going back so soon?"

"I think I'm up for it. Besides, I need the money to pay for my ER visit. Who knows how much that's going to be."

"Don't you have insurance though? You gave them your card." *What do I know about that kind of stuff?*

"It's a good thing I do have insurance, but there's always doctor bills involved. And now with the baby coming… I don't even want to think about how much that's going to cost."

I cringe hearing her talk about the expense of having a baby. Will we be able to afford it?

"Have you thought about trying to go to school? I know you mentioned it once. You might not think it's a good idea now, but I'm sure it'd pay off when you got out. It could help you get a better job."

"Nah, I'm just not sure I'm cut out for it. Maybe my old man's right. I've not been too successful finding anything I'm good at." I'm not asking her for pity but just taking a look at my life in general. My track record hasn't been too promising.

I quickly try to divert our conversation since I'm not up for talking about my dad. "Are you sure you have to work tonight? Can't I convince you to stay home with me one more night?" I realize my asking her not to go into work goes against everything she's trying to help me with It's something the old Brian would do without having a second thought. Used to be, if whoever I was seeing at the time wanted me to stay home and spend some time with them, I'd think nothing of it. I called in sick so many times at different places. Looking back, it didn't say much about the person I was seeing either since they were okay with it.

That was the old me. Starting now, it's going to be a little different.

"Did you want to take your shower first?" She sits up and puts her book down on the table.

"I guess I do need to get going. I've got a big day ahead of me." Big day? Hell, I don't even know where to start. If I had my choice, I'd just crawl back into bed, watch a little television...

Speaking of showers, I wonder if I could talk her into joining me. Maybe we could pick up where we left off yesterday? Nah, I better not push my luck.

When I'm done showering, I pull on a pair of jeans and walk into the kitchen. "Hey, babe. Which shirt should I wear today? I want to wear something nice that'll make a good impression."

She follows me back to the bedroom and rifles through the few shirts I have hanging in the closet. "I think this one will do." She pulls out a navy blue polo and hands it over to me. "It'll bring out the blue in your eyes. You know, you won me over with them." Her cheeks redden from sharing this little bit of information. I had no idea she'd even paid my eye color any attention. Just goes to show you what I know.

"Oh, you think so, huh?" I offer her a flirty smile and a quick wink. She quickly looks away, embarrassed. "I'm just picking at you."

"You'll do fine today. Besides, how can anyone say no to you?"

"I hope you're right."

"Maybe we can meet up for lunch later?" She peeps her head out of the bathroom door.

"Sure, I'd like that." *Except for the part where someone has to pay for it.* Yeah, I've got the money hidden out in my car, but if I pull that out, even if it's just a twenty, I'm only setting myself up for questioning. She knows I'm broke, but the less I have to discuss money with her, the better off I am. "Shoot me a text later. Maybe I'll have some good news to report."

"I will and good luck," she says before closing the door. As soon as I hear the water turn on, I heave a sigh of relief. *Well, here goes nothing.*

Outside, I take a long, hard stare at my car before getting in. The sight of it is appalling. There's no way I'll ever get Jennifer to go anywhere in it with me. Honestly, I can't blame her, but it's not fair we're always using her car to go places.

If the job search is successful, I can hopefully put some money aside for a new one. Or, maybe I could talk her into co-signing a loan with me. *That'd be the day!* Just wait though, I'm going to show her I'm dedicated to this relationship.

I pull out onto the highway and head in the direction of the mall. There's bound to be somebody hiring. Even if it's only part-time, I'd be happy with that for now. I just don't want to get stuck working the weekends all the time. And if I can get something where I'm working inside instead of out in the cold, it'll be even better.

For a Monday, the mall is dead. Very few people are out and about, which isn't a good sign. You'd think shoppers would be out taking advantage of the after-holiday sales.

I walk by a sporting goods store and glance inside. There's a guy up on a ladder stocking footballs on an overhead shelf. I decide to give them a try. It can't hurt, right? I love sports, I'm fairly knowledgeable about them, and that's a plus in my favor.

"Hi, can I help you with something?" The guy appears to be in his early thirties and has on a striped black and white shirt, similar to that of what a referee would wear. Yeah, I could see myself wearing one of those.

"Uh, yeah. I was wondering, are you all doing any hiring?" I try to sound confident, as though I'm seriously interested in working there.

"You looking for something part-time?" The guy is perfectly content talking to me from his spot on the ladder and doesn't make any attempt to climb down.

"I'd prefer full-time but, if you've got something available, I might could consider it."

"Well, that's all we hire is part-time. I've got a spot though. It'd be for a couple hours a week."

My eyes light up when he says he's got something but then my mood shifts when he mentions the hours. "How many hours we talking about?"

"Eight to ten maybe."

"Oh, that's all?" Why is this guy wasting my time and his too for that matter? Who wants to work ten hours a week? "I'll think about it and get back with you."

I don't even bother to thank him for his time. Screw this place. That didn't take long to dampen my spirits.

Sadly, the next few places deliver similar results. I'm amazed how many places won't even talk to you until you've filled out an application online or you've taken their assessment test. I just want a simple job. It's not like I'm applying for a CEO position somewhere.

The day isn't going as I'd planned but I'm remaining hopeful. I walk towards another wing of the mall—the stores this way are similar to what I've already seen. On the other side of the food court, I notice a couple more stores and figure I might as well try them, too. What's it going to hurt?

I stop just outside a shoe store, one of those bargain places where nothing is over a certain price. A sign posted in the front glass catches my eye.

"Assistant Manager needed. Inquire within."

These aren't my type of shoes, but who cares. They need an assistant manager and I need a job.

I walk inside and see piles and piles of boxes everywhere. They're surrounding the check-out counter, down the aisles, and in any available area to be found. The store's appearance is so overwhelming from the immense assortment of shoes, I don't know how anyone could possibly shop. It's literally that bad. From the looks of things, this place definitely could use some help.

I stand at the counter, uncertain what I should do. When no one shows after several minutes, I wonder if there's even anyone working here. I walk down one of the rows, careful not to trip over anything. When I reach the back, I finally spot someone rummaging around.

"Excuse me," I call out, hoping whoever it is behind the stack of boxes hears me.

A young woman, not much older than myself, with long, straight blonde hair moves out from behind the tower of shoes but still doesn't see me. I notice earbuds stuck in her ears and she's humming a few tunes. It's no wonder she's unaware of my presence or anyone else's. Does she not know someone could be toting shoes out the front door and she'd never even know it?

"Um, excuse me." I must catch her by surprise because she turns around with a startled look to her face.

"I'm sorry, I didn't realize anyone was in here. Can I help you with something?" She comes across as friendly but not the least bit concerned about the store's operations. I can't imagine what her boss would think if they walked in and saw the mess.

"I saw your sign in the window about needing help. Are you still looking for someone?"

"Are we ever!" She looks up to me, as though she could hug my neck. As if I've just saved her life or something. "We ran into a few problems right after Christmas and had to fire almost the entire crew. I'm running the day shift and John, another associate, does the evenings. We've both been working every day since way before Christmas, and we'd both just love to have a day off."

She failed to mention who the manager is, unless, of course, it's her. I cringe, thinking she could be the very one in charge of this… fiasco. Even I know something needs to be done to improve the store's appearance.

"What kind of paperwork do I need to fill out to apply? Or do I have to do it online?" I hope she doesn't hear the clipped tone in my voice as I mention the online part. It's just crazy that no one wants to do a simple interview anymore.

"Do you have any prior retail experience?" she asks me.

I don't want to mention about getting fired from the oil shop, so instead I tell her, "I was working a service job that ended not long ago. I tried to find something else, but with all the temporary workers looking for work as well, I haven't had much luck."

"How soon can you start?"

"Are you serious?" *Did she just ask me when I could start?*

"I'm dead serious. The sooner I can get you trained, the sooner I can have a day off."

I swear, her responses make me want to laugh out loud. I have to wonder if I honestly want to work here. I look around at the mess. *Yes, this place.*

"Actually, I can start right now. If you can just let me make a quick phone call, I'll be right back, and I'll be all yours for as long as you need me today. Oh, by the way, I'm Brian. Brian Collins."

I'm not sure if I'm relieved I finally have a job or if I'm crazy for accepting the position. Either way, I've got my work cut out for me. I just hope the pay is worthwhile. It should be, being that it's for an assistant manager, but then again, it could be one of those salaried ones where I'll be working sixty or seventy hours a week. Doing the math, anyone working that many hours, regardless of the pay, ends up making less than the minimum wage rate. On the other hand, if it's an hourly job, I just might have an opportunity to rack up some overtime. Looking around at the mess, yes, this could take a while.

She extends her hand to me. "Welcome aboard. I'm Melissa. What you have on is good enough. We don't have any special uniform requirement, just something like what you're wearing. I'll get you a name badge printed while you make your phone call." Judging by the look on her face, I think I just made her day.

I step out into the mall area and call Jennifer. I just hope she's not disappointed I won't be able to have lunch.

"Hello?"

"Hey, babe. I've got good news. I found a job, and they need me to start work right away," I blurt out, not giving her a chance to get in a word edgewise.

"Do what? That sure was fast." I can already detect the happiness in her voice and I've not told her anything about it yet. "See, I told you you'd find something. I'm so happy for you."

"You're talking to the new assistant manager for that shoe store that's close to the food court at the mall." I turn around and look up at the name of the store above the entrance. It's pretty bad I didn't even know the name of the place yet.

"Get out of here! You're kidding me. An assistant manager position. Wow!"

"I'm serious."

"So can you still meet for lunch?"

"Actually, that's why I'm calling. You see, they need me to start immediately, and I sort of told them I could. The store's in pretty bad shape."

"Well, that's okay, I guess." Her voice falls, no doubt disappointed. "I can swing by and bring you something if you'd like."

"Why don't I text you later on. Maybe then I'll have some idea of how long they want me to work today. If I'm going to be here for a while, I'll definitely take you up on the food offer for later on. I love you, baby."

"Okay then. Well, I'll miss you."

I know I'm doing the right thing. Having her stop by on my first day on the job probably isn't a good idea. Although Melissa might not mind, it's a chance I'm not willing to take just yet. When I go back inside, Melissa's at the register with a customer. I stand at the edge of the counter and wait until she's finished with the transaction. I'm not looking forward to working with money, even though I know it's part of the job. I'd much rather stick to stocking the shoes out on the sales floor.

She briefly explains how to work the shoes into certain sections based on their style and type. It seems fairly easy and I do one side of an aisle while she does the other. Before long, we've both cleared off a complete row and the shelves look very striking. I haul the empty, broken down boxes to the back and leave them by the back door.

The remainder of the day passes by rather quickly and before I know it, it's nearing five o'clock. I look up and see an older gentleman walk through the store's entrance and make his way to the stockroom. I assume he's the other employee Melissa mentioned earlier. When he walks back to the front, formal introductions are made between the two of us.

Rodney instantly looks relieved, even more so when the three of us discuss the schedule I'll be working. I know they're both exhausted from working every day and can't wait to have a day off. I stick around for a little while longer before being released. Melissa tells me to be ready to learn the register tomorrow and I smile weakly. I'd prefer to do all the stocking, but I know there's more to the job than just that. For my first day, it hasn't been too bad.

Once I'm at my car, I pull out my phone and see I've had three missed calls. I hope Jennifer's not upset with me for not hearing my phone ring. I quickly call her back and listen for her to pick up.

"Hello?" The groggy voice on the other end hardly sounds like her, and I hope nothing's wrong. "Brian?"

"Baby, I'm so sorry. I'm headed home now."

"That's okay. I figured you were probably busy." She yawns, and it hits me she's been napping before having to go in tonight.

"I hate I woke you. Go on back to bed and I'll try to be quiet when I get home." I take pleasure in calling the apartment our home and wonder if she even noticed. "I'll make sure to wake you in time for you to get ready."

My stomach rumbles, and I realize I've not had anything to eat all day. My body is used to going long periods of time without food, so it's not unusual for me to go all day without something. I finally make it home and quietly walk inside. The television is playing, but the volume is turned down low. I close the blinds to the patio doors and take my shoes off before heading down the hallway towards the bedroom.

The door is cracked, and I gently push it open enough to see Jennifer sleeping in her bed. She reassured me earlier that she was up for going in tonight and I trust she knows her body well enough to make this decision. I'd much rather crawl into bed beside her, but I know how important rest is to her right now.

I go back to the kitchen and find a plate left on the stove for me. She must have fixed something earlier when she wasn't able to get ahold of me. Lifting the lid off the container, the smell of meatloaf meets my nostrils. It's been years since I've had this and I can't wait to dig in. She's also prepared mash potatoes with gravy and green beans. I feel bad for not being home in time to share dinner with her or to help her clean up.

I pull my plate from the microwave when I'm satisfied with the food's temperature and sit down to catch the latest scores on Sports Center. I don't realize just how tired I am until I'm done eating and start to stand up again to take my plate to the kitchen. My muscles have gotten sore and stiff, obviously from all the lifting I did earlier, so I set the plate down on the table across from me. I'll put it away later on.

I prop my feet up after taking off my shoes and close my eyes for just a moment. Before long, I've drifted off to sleep long before all the updates have scrolled across the bottom of the television screen.

Chapter 29

Jennifer

THE SOUND OF MY PHONE ringing jolts me from my sleep. I look over at the red glowing numbers on my alarm clock and instantly panic.

Crap. I was due at work thirty minutes ago.

I grab the phone from the nightstand before it shuts off and see Rebecca's name lit up on the screen.

It's been over a week now since we've spoken, even when our paths crossed at work. Talk about awkward. It's never been so painful between us in all the years we've been friends.

"Hello?" I talk into the phone at the same time I'm grabbing clothes from the closet.

"You were supposed to be at work half an hour ago. Are you not coming in tonight?" Her voice is sharp and I quickly detect the bitterness in her tone. I hate this animosity between us. It's almost more than I can stand.

"I'm on my way right now. I'm sorry, I overslept," I blurt into the phone. "I'll be there in a few minutes if you can cover for me 'til then." I miss my friend and would give anything to have her back in my life again, but there's still a part of me that's angry, hurt, and confused. Most of all, I feel betrayed. *Will I ever be able to work things out and forgive her?*

I walk to the kitchen to grab my things and find Brian sound asleep on the couch. I'm slightly disappointed he didn't wake me up as soon as he got home. I must've been deeply asleep and didn't hear him.

Poor thing, he never bothered to change from the clothes he put on this morning. I lean down and brush my lips lightly against his forehead, but he doesn't budge. I turn off the television and lock the door behind me. Maybe in the morning he can tell me all about his new job.

The entire ten-minute drive to the hotel, I think about Rebecca and how our conversation will go. I mentally try to prepare myself since it's almost inevitable she'll have something smart to say. My irresponsibility deserves whatever she throws my way.

I'm a little surprised she's not standing on the sidewalk waiting for me when I pull in. Instead, she's busy checking in a young couple. I'm not sure if I'm relieved she's distracted at the moment or if I'm just lucky to avoid the confrontation.

Either way, I take advantage of the couple being there and slide in behind her at the desk.

"Here, let me finish so you can leave." My tone comes across a little demanding, but not rude.

"I'll finish. It's not a problem," she says without looking at me.

So much for trying that plan.

As soon as the lobby clears, Rebecca turns to face me.

"Well?"

"Well, what?" I ask, uncertain where she's about to go with this conversation.

"I've seen you look better before." She gives me a onceover making me uncomfortable. "Is that boyfriend of yours keeping you out so late that you can't show up to work on time? You've never been one to be late for work, Jennifer. His bad habits rubbing off on you already?"

I don't appreciate her harsh tone nor her comments directed towards Brian.

"Wait a damn minute." I quickly jump to defend myself. "You know that is hateful and uncalled for. You have no right to make accusations against either of us."

Looks like now is as good a time as any to get everything out in the open. It had to happen eventually.

"Well, it's true. Since he's come into your life, you've changed. You're not the same person I thought I knew."

"I cannot believe you. I thought you were my friend." I'm practically spewing my words at her now. "We go out, and you get so drunk you hit on my boyfriend. How dare you. And you say *I've* changed. Maybe you're just jealous."

"Look, you have no room to talk about being drunk. You were so wasted you had no idea what was going on." *Is she insinuating something here?* "How do you know he wasn't hitting on me? Huh? Did you think about that?"

I don't give her a chance to say more. The thought did occur to me that maybe he had been the one to initiate something with her but she, being my best friend, should've never let it get to that point. She should have put him in his place and cut it off, if that'd been the case.

"A real friend would've never done what you did. And it didn't happen just once. First in the cab, then in my own apartment with me in the other room. How could you, Rebecca?"

I'm so angry, my body starts to tremble. Suddenly, I burst out in tears, and Rebecca blankly stares at me. She knows she's wrong and owes me an apology. Yes, we were all over our limits, but alcohol doesn't excuse our behaviors. I've dealt with Brian on my own, but can I give her another chance, too? Can I forgive her and continue to have them both a part of my life again? I'm not sure I could trust them in the same room together, but I also know the friendship she and I had was

232 · Amy Stephens

something I've missed deeply. And to know my best friend was not the first person to find out I'm pregnant—what's she going to think once she finds out?

"Jenn, look, I'm sorry. It's been eating me up inside ever since that night. I've wanted to talk to you, but I also knew how angry and upset you've been. I've hurt you deeply, and I don't know if I could forgive myself if I were you." Rebecca genuinely looks sorry for her mistakes. "You're the sister I never had, and we should've never let it come to this. We're both more responsible than what we've admitted and I'm sorry."

I want to remind her that my only mistake was that I drank too much. She, on the other hand, drank too much *and* lost her self-control. I would never have put the moves on Greg, no matter how drunk I was.

"Can you ever forgive me?" She opens her arms and while I hesitate at first, I give in and hug my best friend.

"I want you to know this whole thing made me so upset, I ended up in the hospital Friday night. I was so sick from worrying about everything." I stop for a moment, knowing that's only half the truth. I was also sick for another reason she's yet to find out about.

"Why didn't you call me?" Her face fills with concern. "I knew you'd called in, but I had no idea why."

"Brian took me." I look down at the floor, unsure why I suddenly feel funny about letting her know he's back in the picture. "I couldn't drive myself."

"Well, thank goodness he was able to. I mean, if you were that sick..."

"I had to call him." I can't explain why I chose to contact him over her—I just did. The way I was feeling, I was thankful just to make it to the ER regardless of how I got there. "He'd been gone all week, too," I threw in, just so she'd know. In the end, it was sort of reassuring having him there, especially with the news we'd found out.

"Are you doing better now?"

I nod my head knowing full well where this conversation is headed. "Now that I've gotten plenty of rest. The doctor gave me something for my nausea, and it's helped tremendously. I'm able to keep food down now." *Should I tell Rebecca now or give it some time with our friendship on the mend?*

"You poor thing. You look like you've lost weight, too. You *never* get sick," she stresses.

"Well, there is something else." I figure I might as well tell her. This secret will reveal itself before too long, anyway.

"What?" A look of concern spreads over her face. "Are you okay?"

I hesitate, then let it out. "I'm pregnant." I hold my hand up indicating I'm not finished yet. "Please, before you start lecturing me or blaming Brian, just let me say it's just as much my fault as it is his."

"You're what? Did you say pregnant? I'm going to be an aunt?" This is not the reaction I was expecting from her at all. I just knew I was in for a lecture.

"I've got to make a doctor's appointment this week, but yes, I'm having a baby." I try to smile through the tears that have now gathered in my eyes. "We found out while I was at the emergency room."

"What did your parents say? I bet your mom's thrilled knowing she's going to be a grandmother."

"Well …." I stop short and walk away from the counter. Rebecca notices my hesitation.

"You have told them, right?"

I look up, the expression on my face speaking for itself. "No, I haven't yet," I mumble, then shake my head sideways. "I'm still getting used to the idea of being pregnant and all. I know they'll be happy for me once they get over the shock. I'm sad it's probably not the way they would've wanted to find out, but there's no going back now. We're all going to have to make the most of it."

"How's Brian taking the news?" I know she still has her doubts where he's concerned.

"He's actually taking it better than me." I don't want to share my other news of Brian's proposal just yet. Too much at one time may be more than she can handle. Besides, I need time to think more about it myself. "He started a new job, so hopefully this one'll pay a little more and have some better opportunities for him."

"Oh, he's not down at that car place anymore?" Rebecca looks concerned at the news of his job change.

"No, there was a misunderstanding right before Christmas, and they had to let him go." *Why do I feel as though I'm about to start making excuses for him again?* "But he was fortunate to find this one rather quickly."

Rebecca and I continue to talk, catching up on everything we've missed out on while being upset with each other. She shares some of her plans for a summer wedding, and instead of getting excited, I actually frown, realizing I'm going to be big and fat come July.

Before we know it, several hours have passed. I've still got paperwork to do and I know she's got to be exhausted. It's been a relief getting everything out in the open and hopefully on the right path with our friendship again though.

****

I pull through the drive-thru and grab some breakfast for us before heading home. I can't wait to see Brian this morning since I had to run out quickly last night without even saying goodbye. I'm not sure how to break the news that Rebecca and I are back on speaking terms again, and I hope he'll be okay with it. I'm pretty sure neither of them will want to be around the other for some time, simply because of the awkwardness. And, actually, I think I prefer it that way.

Pulling into the parking lot, my heart drops when I see Brian's car is already gone. The least he could've done is texted or called to let me know he had to be at work early. I send him a text telling him I'm home and wait a few moments for a response. Nothing. *He is at work, right?*

I put my things away and sit down to eat at the kitchen table. The room is a complete mess. The plate I left for him to heat up is sitting next to the sink along with a couple other dishes and empty food packages. I'm not one for leaving messes at all, which he's well aware of, and it pisses me off knowing he left them for me to take care of. He better have a darn good excuse for not cleaning up.

I go ahead and pick up everything until I'm satisfied with the way the kitchen looks. I don't want to overwork myself, since I'm still getting all my strength back. He definitely owes me one.

Just after noon, when I've awakened from my nap, I check my phone again. Sure enough, I've missed a text from him. Along with an apology, he says he's not sure how late he'll be working, but he'll call as soon as he can.

An idea hits me, so I jump in the shower and get ready. Nothing like a surprise visit from his girlfriend to make his day. I hope he'll be able to take a break so maybe we can grab a bite to eat.

I'm familiar with the location of the shoe store inside the mall, so I park at the entrance closest to it. Funny, I don't recall ever shopping in that particular store before. I walk in and glance around. Even though I don't see any customers right now, I don't notice anyone on the sales floor working, either. *That's odd.* You'd think someone would at least be up front to greet potential customers.

I walk down one of the aisles, and I suddenly hear laughter coming from the back. At the end of the aisle, I see an opening that must lead to the back stock area. I peak around the door but still can't see anyone. A male and female are carrying on a conversation and I realize the male's voice as Brian's. By the sound of things, he's enjoying whoever he's talking to.

I'm not sure who manages the store, but surely they wouldn't approve of the sales floor being left unattended. I walk around a few minutes more checking out the different shoe styles, although these typically aren't the types of shoes I'd buy. While I really was hoping to surprise Brian, it looks like the surprise is on me since I'm going to have to call him just so he knows I'm here.

I dial his phone and listen for the sound of his ringtone. Sure enough, I hear it play from where I'm standing just outside the store's back room. All of a sudden, the ringing ceases indicating my call is declined. *No he didn't!* I still hear talking between Brian and the female, but what they're saying doesn't make much sense. I try his phone once more. This time he doesn't even bother to decline it. I listen as it rings and rings.

Now I'm pissed. I come all the way down here to see him when I could've been sleeping, and this is the way I get treated? Better yet, ignored. Maybe I'm not being fair, but from the sound of it, the conversation wasn't about business. Besides, who's running the store? If Brian is training to be an assistant manager, he's definitely going to have to work on his management skills or this job is doomed to fail just like the others.

Angry and hurt, I run out to my car. If he gets hungry, let him get his own damn food.

On the drive back home, my mind drifts back to the other day when Brian asked me to marry him. And to think, at that moment, I had seriously considered it. Now, I'm not so sure he's ready for that kind of commitment at all. He's still got a lot of growing up to do, including accepting some responsibility. Most of all, I think I'd be letting my parents down. I know it's my life and my choices to make, but they raised me better. They'd be disappointed to know I settled for someone I'm not completely sure about. It'll be bad enough telling them about the baby, but to tell them he proposed as well would only make it harder on me. There are no rules these days that say we have to get married to be parents to this baby. The more I continue to think about it, the more upset it makes me.

Later in the evening, I sit down to eat at the same time Brian walks in the door. He looks and acts like his normal self, but I find myself giving him the cold shoulder. I just can't help it.

"You okay, babe? You seem like something's bothering you." He acts concerned, surely picking up on my mood since I've not said anything to him yet.

"Yeah, I'm fine," I answer coldly.

"You don't sound fine. Are you upset about something?" I detect the worried tone in his voice.

"You think so, huh?" I spit out. "Let's just say I called you today, and you didn't even have the decency to answer. And don't tell me you didn't know I called because I heard it ringing myself. Just like I know you declined it the first time it rang." It's too late. I'm pissed now. I stand up, disgusted, and dump my food in the trash.

"Babe, calm down. What are you talking about? What's come over you?" He seriously acts like he doesn't have a clue. Is he that good of an actor?

"Yeah, well, I went down to the mall today and thought I'd surprise you. Only I ended up being the one surprised. You never even came out of the back room, Brian. I heard you laughing and carrying on with some girl. Neither of you had any idea what was even happening on the sales floor. I could have walked out the front door with my arms full of shoes and no one would have seen a thing."

"I had no idea…" He continues to play dumb, although the expression on his face shows differently.

I cut him off before he can say more. "Exactly. Had you bothered to answer your damn phone, you would've known I was there."

Coincidently, his phone beeps alerting a text message and he's quick to pick it up. Glancing at it quickly, he shuts it off and puts it in his back pocket rather than back down on the table.

"Who was it?" I ask sternly. Warning bells are going off and I'm not sure what to think. He couldn't take my call but he doesn't hesitate to see who the text is from? And directly in front of me at that. I feel the heat course through my body. This isn't the way I wanted the night to go.

"Just my boss letting me know I need to open up in the morning instead of coming in later," he says without looking me in the eyes.

"Oh. Since when did bosses resort to texting instead of calling?"

I give up. It's not worth the drama or the headache to argue or start a fight. Maybe it's hormones going crazy early on in my pregnancy but I'm just not up for it.

Brian walks over to me and wraps his arms around me, pulling me close. He starts kissing me behind my ear, and before I know it, we're both engaged in a kiss that leaves us both breathless once we pull apart. *How did we get to this point?* We were close to arguing just minutes ago. Why have I suddenly started giving in so easily instead of standing my ground 'til the end? Could Brian be wearing me down or am I starting to become weaker? I've always been strong and straightforward. What's happening to me?

"Jenn, I've missed you."

I lean my head towards his strong chest, and I am swallowed by his masculine scent. "*Mmm*. Just hold me," I beg him, yearning to feel love and compassion.

He walks me backwards towards the bedroom. Piece by piece, he removes each item of clothing I have on. I find myself rubbing my hand on the outside of his jeans. For the next half hour, Brian makes me forget all about being upset with him. I have no idea how he does it, but I'm a sucker when it comes to him. Once again, he knows the right things to say and do to win me over.

Chapter 30

Brian

I THOUGHT THE WEEKEND WOULD never get here. I've worked every day this week, putting in over fifty hours in five days. I'm looking forward to my first paycheck next Friday, although I know a portion of it needs to go to Rebecca for the bracelet she helped me purchase. Neither of us has made any attempt to contact one another, and while I do feel better that Jennifer knows of the loan arrangement, I know sooner or later I'll have to be in touch. She's not going to let me go forever without settling up.

I ended up spending the money that'd been in the envelope from Jennifer's parents. I had to have gas for my car and money to eat during the week. Funny, but Jennifer knew I'd been jobless and obviously broke, yet she'd never even bothered to ask if I needed any money until I got paid. Talk about being oblivious to things. Just makes me wonder what else I could do that she'd never catch. Not that I would try anything else, but you never know.

We decide to do as little as possible this weekend. Jennifer's nausea has returned, but she seems to be handling it better now with her prescribed medication and by munching on crackers and sipping on some carbonated water. She has her first doctor's appointment next Friday morning, and I've already requested the day off to accompany her. I think I'm almost as nervous about it as she is.

We both fall back into a routine on Monday with Jennifer's classes for the winter semester starting back. Instead of her classes being in the evenings like they were during the fall, she'll be going straight to school as soon as she gets off of work Monday through Thursday. And since I've mostly been working day shifts, this schedule should be better for both of us. I'm usually home in time for supper and we both work together cleaning the kitchen, making sure everything gets put away just the way she likes it. Lord knows I don't want to upset her again about a dirty kitchen. It's easier to go ahead and help out. Besides, I know the pregnancy has increased her tiredness and I should be stepping up to help more.

On Friday morning, Jennifer rushes home from work to take a quick shower for her appointment at nine. I tossed and turned all night, eager to hear what the doctor has to say about our baby. I even had the urge to call my mom last night to share the news with her, but I talked myself out of it. No, I'm not homesick at all, but it's been so long since I've heard from anyone in my family. When I left, I didn't bother to tell any of them goodbye. I just walked out and never looked back. Now, with the baby and all, I kind of hate that my mom has to miss out on something that should be exciting for her.

I grab Jennifer's coat from the closet and help her put it on. She, too, has a certain level of anxiety about it, and I suspect that's normal for any new mother going to the doctor for the first time. Her cheeks are glowing and she's got a permanent smile plastered on her face.

The waiting room is surprisingly quiet. Jennifer fills out several pages of paperwork, even asking questions about me and my family's medical history. A nurse sticks her head around the door and calls her to the back. I stand up to accompany her, but the nurse stops me and explains she'll come back for me once Jennifer is through with the initial examination. Then, together, we'll be able to ask the doctor questions relating to the pregnancy and the baby.

I fidget with my hands for a while, and even resort to pulling my phone out. I send Jennifer a text telling her how much I love her and how proud I am of her. I don't know if she's with the nurse still or if she's waiting in the examination room alone. I simply just feel like telling her.

After what seems like forever, the nurse comes back to get me. I follow her down a long hallway until she stops and knocks on one of the doors. Inside, Jennifer is up on the exam table wearing a paper gown. I take a seat next to her and reach up to hold her hand.

Moments later, the doctor walks in and introduces himself to me. I shake his hand as he tells me, "Congratulations, Mr. Davis." I look over at Jennifer as she, too, catches the doctor's mistake of assuming we're married. I know she's noted this on her paperwork but the doctor doesn't pay any attention to that. I don't bother correcting him with my last name, Collins. I'm sure we're not the only couple this has happened to.

He starts off by telling us a few things about the pregnancy, different things Jennifer should expect to feel and experience, and finally about the final stages just before the baby makes his or her arrival. It's a condensed version but so much to take in all at once. Just as the appointment is coming to a close, we're told the baby's due date is mid-August. According to her last period, we should expect to meet him or her around August thirteenth. The ultra-sound, which will be set up for later on, will provide us with a more accurate date.

I look at Jennifer, and her face is full of so much emotion. What I hope are happy tears slide over her cheeks, and I reach over to wipe them away. She squeezes my hand firmly. If you'd asked me a year ago where I expected to be in my life right now, I never would've guessed I was on my way to being a father.

A father. I hope and pray I turn out to be a better father than my own was to me.

Jennifer changes in the curtained area off to the side of the room. As we leave, I place my hand on the small of her back and guide her to the door. The nurses have loaded her down with information and freebies pertaining to the baby. She finishes up her paperwork with the front desk receptionist and makes her appointment for the next visit.

We both sit in her car for the next several minutes looking through some of the stuff. It's all so mind-boggling. A real life baby is growing and developing inside her. I have to admit, the cute little baby bag they gave her is adorable. How could you not fall in love with that thing? Who knew there was so much to know about having a baby!

"Well, what would you like to do now?" I look over at her in the front seat. She has this radiant look about her, which she should being that she's just had her first doctor's appointment, but I can't help thinking there's something else.

After what seems like an eternity, she finally speaks. "Let's do it."

"What?" I ask, a little confused about her response.

"Let's do it. Let's get married."

"What? Are you for real?" This time I'm the one in a state of shock. "You're kidding me, right?"

"No, I'm not. Let's go to the courthouse and do it. Let's do the right thing for our baby."

It's funny how when I first asked Jennifer to marry me, I was the confident one while she had her doubts. Now, I'm the one second-guessing if this is what *I* really want to do. What happened to make me change the way I feel?

"What?" she asks jokingly. "I see how you are. Now that I'm ready, you've had a change of heart. You don't love me anymore." Playfully, she drops my hand and turns to look out the window. Her arms are crossed over her belly and she pretends to pout.

"No, that's not it at all."

"Well, what is it then?"

"I just didn't think you were ready for that, especially with me. I know we've had our moments, and even though we seem to be doing okay now, I just didn't expect you to change your mind so suddenly."

"If you're sure you're up for it, then so am I." Jennifer sounds very confident in her decision. I have no other choice than to believe her.

"Since you put it that way, what are we waiting for?" I feel like it's now or never. If we don't do this now, she may never agree to marry me again.

First, we stop by the mall to pick up my paycheck. I make formal introductions between Jennifer and Melissa, and, judging by Jennifer's expression and sudden clinginess, I don't think she's too happy about my boss being young and attractive.

When I first met Jennifer, she came across as being very confident with herself. Now, I'm not sure if it's the pregnancy or if the past situation with Rebecca has affected her, but I see her struggling with her confidence these days. Don't get me wrong, there're times when she's very self-assured, then there's moments she's quick to drop a tear if someone looks at her wrong.

I'm not sure if Jennifer's parents held tight reins on her being the baby of the family, or if they were just uncertain about leaving her alone, but even now, they haven't given her a chance to grow and blossom, to make mistakes and learn from them. As long as they keep taking care of everything for her, they'll always have that bit of control over her. Jennifer's confidence needs to develop from within, and the only way that's going to happen is for her to do something on her own without their support. Let them get mad or whatever, but she needs to be her own person.

I get my check cashed at the bank inside the mall and, since we're already here, we grab lunch at the food court. I'm almost scared to bring up getting married again for fear that she may just as quickly change her mind again. Before we leave, I pull her towards the jewelry store where I purchased her bracelet.

"Where're we going?" she asks, knowing time is running out on getting it done today.

"I can't have my bride getting married without a ring, can I?"

I have no idea how I'm going to pull this off, but I hope by some miracle I can find an inexpensive ring that will suffice until I can afford to get her something better. Maybe being a repeat customer will give me some sort of discount, too.

She sounds so sincere when she says, "Brian, we can hold off on the rings. That's something we can get later."

"No, I want you to have some kind of token of my love."

Her eyes glaze over with happy tears again. *Dang.* Why can't she do a better job of controlling her emotions?

We walk inside and, lucky for me, the same service clerk waits on us. I explain to her we need just a simple, inexpensive ring, and she points us to a case in the back. Jennifer immediately starts to scan over the selection.

I don't expect to purchase one for myself now, but Jennifer starts talking to the salesperson about finance options and within minutes, she's filling out the credit application. I include my income, but I know with my job history and lack of stability, the paperwork is better off with just her information. I can't believe how willing she is to consider a credit account with me. But, if we're going to be married, maybe she's looking at things differently now.

The sales clerk enters the information into the system then walks back to us with a smile on her face. "Congratulations. We've got you approved. Let me show you some bridal sets that I think you both will like."

I'm completely taken by surprise. I know Jennifer has had her full-time job since she graduated from high school, but I had no idea she had enough credit to establish a jewelry account. Once again, she can probably thank her parents for always making sure she has plenty of money and all of her bills are taken care of in a timely manner. She's never had to worry about having enough change to buy a gallon of gas to get to work or if there's enough money to have something to eat every day. She's never had to walk a day in my shoes.

We glance at so many sets of rings that they all start to look alike. I have her pick out something she's happy with — after all, a ring is just a ring to me — while I settle for a simple gold band. She completes the transaction and regretfully, we're unable to take the rings with us since they need to be sized. I'm a little disappointed, but there's nothing that can be done about it now. I notice the same reaction from her as well.

I glance at the time on my phone and realize if we're really going to get this done today, we better head down to the courthouse soon. I open the passenger door for her as she climbs into the car. As I walk back to my side to get in, I hesitate for a moment. The day couldn't be any more perfect. The sun is shining brightly for a cool January day and there's not a cloud in the sky.

When we arrive at the courthouse, a security officer points us in the direction for the Justice of the Peace. There are a few other couples ahead of us filling out paperwork and handling the fees.

"Are you sure this is what you want to do?" I hate to question her again, but this is a very important decision for both of us.

"If you don't marry me today, Brian Collins, you may never get the chance to again."

I love the little smirk on her face as she teases me.

We each fill out our part of the paperwork and she returns everything back to the lady behind the desk. We're told it's going to be a short wait, so I grab ahold of her hand and rub my thumb over her soft skin.

I think back to everything over the last few years. I've never been this close to anyone. I've had girlfriends and, while I liked the idea of marriage one day, I never made it far enough into the relationship to feel anything like what I'm feeling for her. Funny thing is, she and I haven't had much time together either, but something tells me we're doing the right thing.

I'm shocked Jennifer hasn't mentioned anything about telling her parents. I'm not sure how they'll take the news, but now they're going to have two things to accept—me and the baby. Whether we get their blessing or not, we at least have each other.

I stand up and walk to the water fountain. My hands are sweaty, and I can't believe how nervous I've become. A side door opens and "Collins" is called from a lady holding our paperwork. We both stand at the same time, and I take her hand in mine.

I look over to her. "Here we go, babe. It's not too late to change your mind," I tell her, and she pulls me forward.

248 · Amy Stephens

Chapter 31

Jennifer

"I NOW PRONOUNCE YOU MR. and Mrs. Brian Collins." The Justice of the Peace looks over at Brian first, then me. "You may kiss your bride."

Talk about a quick, simple service. He takes my face in both his hands and pulls me into a very deep, passionate kiss. I'm almost embarrassed by this display of affection from him. It's a side of him I have never seen before, especially not publically. I'm literally waiting for the Justice of the Peace to tell us to get a room.

I take in a deep breath and relief washes over my body. *I am Mrs. Brian Collins.* Jennifer Davis is no more. I'm officially Jennifer Collins.

Suddenly, just like a lightning bolt, it hits me. *What the hell have I done?* I've just eloped. Brian and I have just made a lifelong commitment to each other without either of us notifying any of our family or friends. What are my parents going to say? It's bad enough I haven't taken the opportunity to share with them the news of the baby, but now I'm going to give them the double shock of their lives.

Brian takes my hand in his and escorts me to the back of the room while another couple steps forward to take our place. I can't help but notice the happiness Brian wears across his face. Just moments ago, I was so excited about the idea of being married, and now that it's done, I can't believe I actually went through with it. I almost want to pinch myself, making sure it's real. Is it possible I dreamed the whole thing up?

Brian and I make our way out to the car, and I place all the important paperwork in my purse. I want to be so happy to be with my new husband. I just hope I've made the right decision.

I place my hand in Brian's lap as he pulls from the parking lot heading back to our apartment.

"So, how does it feel, Mr. Collins, to officially be my husband?" I hope that hearing the words spoken out loud will take away the little bit of uncertainty I'm feeling at the moment. I suppose it's a natural reaction. At least, I hope it is.

"It's one of the best feelings in the world, Mrs. Collins." He grips my hand and it's the reassurance I need to make me feel better.

"There's just one thing."

"What?" He looks concerned all of a sudden.

"I hate we're not able to take a real honeymoon right now. And the worst part, I can't even spend my wedding night with my husband." I'm saddened knowing I've got to be at work in a few short hours. Had this been better planned and not so sudden, I could've taken the night off or swapped it with another co-worker.

When we get back to the apartment Brian stops short of opening the front door. He leans down and scoops me up in his arms while maneuvering the door open. He turns sideways, since the doorway seems too small to allow us in properly, and carries me inside. I laugh at his gesture and wrap my arms tightly around him.

"*Ohhhhh*, I don't want to go to work tonight," I whine as he sets me back on my feet, wishing we could spend our first night as husband and wife together.

"I know, baby." He reaches up to brush a stray strand of hair away from my face. "At least we've got tomorrow night together, and the next night, and the next. We've got forever."

"Why don't I make us something quick to eat?" I look over, noticing the clock on the stove. "Crap. If I don't get some sleep, I'll never be able to make it. Is there anything in particular you'd like?"

I close the refrigerator door and look behind me when Brian doesn't respond. It's no wonder, he's not even in the room with me anymore. I continue to search the cabinets coming up with a quick meal solution.

He returns to the kitchen wearing nothing but a pair of shorts. He wraps his arms around my belly, and I stop what I'm doing long enough to enjoy the security I feel being with him. I have a husband who's going to take care of me, not to mention, I just married my baby's father.

Dinner is ready in no time and he tells me not to worry, he'll get the kitchen cleaned up when we're done. He insists I need my rest, and I don't argue. I'll use this as a test to see if he's truly a man of his word.

I head back to the bedroom, exhaustion taking over quickly.

My alarm beeps at nine o'clock, allowing me just enough time to get ready for work. I desperately struggle to wake up. The day was so eventful, first with the doctor's visit then with getting married. I don't think my body was able to unwind before getting back up again.

I go into the bathroom and splash cold water on my face, hoping it will revive me. I brush my hair and pull it up in my usual ponytail. After brushing my teeth, I apply lip gloss and a little mascara to my tired, droopy eyes. I change into my red polo shirt and glance at myself in the mirror. I wonder what I'm going to look like once my belly starts to swell. I turn to the side, pulling the shirt tight against me. The only thing that comes to mind is *what are my parents going to think once they find out about everything?* I need to work on figuring out a way to approach the subject with them.

Out in the living room, Brian's sitting on the couch with his feet propped on the coffee table watching a game on TV. Just like a typical husband already.

"Hey, baby." I try to smile, but right now, I'd give almost anything for just a few more hours of sleep.

"You look tired. Are you sure you can't call in tonight?"

I can't believe he's really asking me this. He knows how I feel about calling out.

"You could stay here with your husband and keep him company," he teases.

"I wish I could. I'm sure once I get there, it won't be so bad." But I already know if it's a slow night, it's going to seem like forever, so who am I kidding?

I walk to the kitchen to grab a water bottle from the refrigerator. All of our dinner dishes stare back at me. *Damn it, Brian.*

He notices the expression on my face and immediately says, "I'm going to get to it, dear. Don't worry, I just got caught up in the game. I promise it'll be spotless when you get back in the morning."

I don't want to say anything to make him mad, so I don't bring it up again. The last thing I want to do is walk out of here upset with him on our first night as husband and wife. I pull on my jacket and grab my purse. Brian meets me by the door with his arms outstretched.

"I'm sure going to miss you tonight, Mrs. Collins."

I lay my head against his shoulder for a moment, savoring the feel of his arms wrapped around me. It doesn't get any better than this.

I pull back after a few moments and look into his eyes. "I love you, Brian."

"I love you, too." He grabs ahold of my hand where my ring would be and lifts it to his lips.

"You're making it hard to leave, baby," I tell him. "But if I don't get out of here, I'm definitely going to be late." I pull away then glance back. He winks just as I turn to walk out. I tell myself over and over not to worry about the kitchen. A dirty kitchen is not the end of the world. What is disturbing, though, is knowing I'll have to break my news to Rebecca. I've got roughly ten minutes to figure it out.

I walk into the office and Rebecca stands up from the chair. "You look like you've hardly slept. You feeling okay?"

I get the impression that just because I'm pregnant now, I'll start needing special treatment. That's not the case, I assure you.

"Gee, thanks for letting me know I look like shit," I tell her jokingly. Even though it hurts my feelings, I know it's true. My sensitivity is at an all-time high right now.

"Seriously, did you not get any rest today?"

"I got a couple hours. Not near enough though." I try to remain hopeful and quickly decide that now is really not a good time to share with her about my marriage. "I just had a busy day with lots of things I needed to get done."

"Look on the bright side. Once you're done in the morning, you've got the next few days off. Maybe you'll be able to rest then." She tries to offer some encouragement and for that I'm grateful.

"Don't worry. I'm already counting down the hours."

Rebecca gathers her things and leans over to give me a hug. She pats her hand to my belly before walking away. "Take care of my little niece or nephew."

"*Aww*, thanks. You know I will."

"Hey, you got plans for Sunday? Maybe you and I can spend some quality girl time together. Just me and you."

I think back over the last few months that Brian and I have been together. Before he came into the picture, she and I used to spend every weekend together, whether it was going out to the movies or clubbing, or just getting manicures and hanging out at the apartment. New Year's Eve was the last night we spent together. So much happened then, and I've tried to push it as far from my mind as possible. But the truth is, I've missed our fun times together, too.

"Let me check with Brian. With his new job, he's been working a lot of hours, too." I can see by the expression on her face she's not happy about me bringing up his name. Now I'm glad I held off from telling her our news. I know she's not crazy about him, but I'm willing to give them both time to fix the situation between them, for my sake.

"Sure, fine. Just let me know." Without giving me time to respond, she walks towards the door.

"Rebecca, wait," I call out to her. "That's not fair and you know it."

"What's not fair, Jennifer? You work things out with your boyfriend that you still barely know anything about, and you spend every waking moment with him. All I asked for was a couple hours with my best friend, and you can't even make that decision on your own without consulting with him first."

Why can't she just accept him? Why does she always have to question our relationship? I don't like being put in these situations where I'm forced to choose between the people I love most, especially now that Brian is my husband.

Chapter 32
Brian

I MOSTLY WORK DAYS NOW, going in at nine every morning and getting off in time to spend a few hours with Jennifer before she goes into work at night. Even though I've told her she doesn't have to fix us a meal every night and that I'm perfectly fine with picking up something to go, she still tries to prepare something, saying it's the proper thing for a wife to do.

It's been a month since we exchanged our vows, and I have to admit, it's been nice coming home to someone I get along so well with. I'm relieved we seem to have overcome our previous issues.

Friday finally arrives, and I plan on taking her out to eat for our one-month anniversary. It's kind of hard to keep it a secret from her when I drop the hint she needs to make sure she's gotten plenty of rest.

Works been...well, it's been work. There's nothing special about the job except the paycheck. I've accepted there's nothing exciting about selling shoes, especially those that are bargain priced. It's no wonder they had such a hard time keeping good help. It's probably the most boring job I've ever had.

I get off work a few minutes early and pull into the hotel. It's time for another payment to be made to Rebecca. I seriously think she believed I wouldn't come through on my agreement with her. I've proven her wrong, and I actually take pride in myself that I'm able do this without the help of anyone, especially Jennifer. Just the expression on Rebecca's face the first time I approached her with some money was priceless. Yes, it was rather awkward, but I did it without any confrontation. Let's just hope today's the same.

I walk to the counter where she's currently not waiting on anyone. My presence catches her by surprise.

"Hi, I needed to drop this off." I keep the conversation as minimal as possible while I hand over a couple of folded bills.

"Thank you, Brian. I must say, I never thought I'd actually get anything from you." Just hearing her say this stings a little. "You've definitely proven me wrong."

I notice the hint of sarcasm in her voice, and decide the best thing for me to do is ignore it. We've yet to bring up the incident from New Year's Eve and I'd like to keep it that way. I'm pretty sure, in her mind, she still holds me responsible, even though she was the one who made a move on me first. It didn't make it right for me to react but, in the end, she started it.

"Maybe one day you'll have a better opinion of me, Rebecca. I'm sorry you can't forget the past."

"Look, I love Jennifer and her well-being is my utmost concern, whether you are in her life or not. It's no lie. I'm not thrilled with some of her decisions that involve you, but I'll always respect my best friend."

I didn't come here to argue with her or to defend myself. "I should be able to make the final payment to you in a few weeks. Then you won't have to worry about seeing me." I start to walk to the door, ready to get the hell away from here.

Apparently, Rebecca doesn't feel the same way though. Just as I'm about to walk out, she calls out to me. "Brian, why have you never taken Jennifer to meet your parents, or introduced her to your friends back home? Is there something you don't want her to know?"

I stop immediately and turn to face her. How dare she bring up my former friends and family! "Why the hell should it matter to you if Jennifer ever meets my parents? Just because I left my past behind, doesn't mean I want to drag her down that path of shame. Some things are just better left alone." I try to keep my voice calm, but she's not making it easy. *What business is it of hers to say this to me?*

"Seems to me you'd want your family to meet her. She's a good girl, you know."

She just doesn't know when to shut her mouth.

"You don't get it do you? I've never taken Jennifer for granted. You think you know me, but you're wrong, Rebecca." The best thing for me to do is walk away, just leave things alone before they turn ugly, but I'm forced to take a stand and defend myself to the end. How dare this bitch put her nose in my business again!

"I don't know what she sees in you, but now you've trapped her. Her life will never be the same again, thanks to you getting her pregnant."

I've taken this shit long enough. I walk up to her and look her face to face. "I don't know what's wrong with you, but you should spend more time worrying about yourself instead of me and my wife."

She becomes deathly silent while her face is overcome with shock. If looks could kill, I'd certainly be dead right now.

"What did you just say?"

"I said, you need to concern yourself with something other than me and my wife." As soon as I say the last word, it hits me. Jennifer hasn't told her yet. I never even thought to ask if she'd told her or not. I know she was waiting for the right opportunity to tell her family, but I had no idea she'd kept the news from Rebecca, too. After all, it's been a month now.

Part of me wants to smile and rub it in Rebecca's face that her so-called best friend didn't feel it necessary to share this major life event with her, but I remain the better person. On the other hand, I wonder why Jennifer hasn't told anyone. Surely Rebecca would've discovered it on her own if Jennifer had updated her personal files.

The shock is clearly written all over her face and I love it. Serves her right.

I realize there's nothing more for me to say, so I turn to leave once again. Rebecca reaches up and grabs ahold of my shirt collar. I attempt to pull away just as another employee walks into the room. She jerks her hand back immediately, and I reach to straighten my wrinkled shirt collar.

"Is everything okay in here, Rebecca?" the co-worker asks.

Rebecca bites back her anger and attempts to pull herself together. "We're fine, Gail. This is Jennifer's...husband." She hesitates before saying the last word. It's as though the word husband burns her tongue. "He was just leaving."

This is my cue to run out. I'm tired of the questions and belittling from her.

I sit in the front seat of my car staring at nothing in particular. I'm furious and my heart is pounding in my chest. If the two of them were not best friends, I would've told that bitch off and put her in her place. I've had my fair dealings with girls like her, and I don't want to put myself in a situation I'll regret later. Funny thing is, Rebecca wasn't this way when we first met. I'm not sure what happened for her to resent me this much now unless she's still placing fault on me for that night. The only one she should be pointing fingers at, is herself.

I arrive back at the apartment later than I'd planned. Thanks to all the bullshit, I'm in a bad mood now. I don't want

Jennifer to detect anything, so I try to compose myself as best I can before going inside.

Standing in the hallway, I notice Jennifer has on a new outfit. While I don't think she's started to show much, she's convinced none of her old clothes fit anymore. I must say the oversized top and stretchy leggings look cute on her.

"Look at you, babe." I give her a small kiss on the cheek and pray she doesn't pick up on how overly nice I'm trying to be. "Don't you look cute." It's sad, I know, but it's hard keeping it all to myself. I want to burst the more I think about it.

"You don't think it's a little much?" she asks, and turns to look at her reflection in the hallway mirror.

I reach out to touch her belly that I still think is just as flat as it was prior to finding out about the pregnancy. She places her hand on top of mine. We stand in silence for a moment, and I must admit, thinking about our baby does take my mind off what happened earlier.

"Are you up for a nice dinner out tonight?" Earlier, I was starving, but now I seem to have lost my appetite. Maybe once we get to the restaurant, the smell of food will change my mind.

"Sure, what did you have in mind?"

"How about we go back to that really good seafood place you took me to when we first started dating? It's a perfect place to celebrate our one-month anniversary, don't you think?"

Her face lights up at the mention of seafood. "*Ooooh,* that sounds delicious." Jennifer's eating habits have definitely increased lately, aside from some of the weird cravings she's had, too.

"Let me change and we can go." I walk to the bedroom and take off my shirt, gripping it tightly in my hands. I still can't believe Rebecca had the nerve to grab me by the collar like a child. I wonder what she'd been about to do?

With it wadded up in my hands, I pitch it over to the corner. I turn around and see Jennifer standing behind me.

"Babe, you okay?" she asks, worry evident on her face.

"Yeah, I was just thinking about something that happened earlier today. I... I had my first irate customer." I hate lying to her but if I tell her about the incident between me and Rebecca, it'll surely affect our evening and that's the last thing I want to happen.

I slip on a shirt from the closet and walk over to meet her at the doorway, turning off the bedroom light as I follow her out.

I take Jennifer's jacket from the back of the kitchen chair and drape it over her shoulders. I shut the door behind us and walk to her car, hating that we're having to take hers yet again. It doesn't make me feel better, that's for sure.

The traffic is a little heavier than usual, so I don't reach out to hold her hand until we're out on the highway.

"Babe, I've been thinking." I hesitate for a moment to gauge her mood. "Since things are going pretty well for me at work now, what do you think about me getting a new car? Nothing brand new, but something in better shape than what I've got. I know I can't afford much, but I have managed to save a little bit these last few weeks with all the overtime I've worked. Sales have picked up, and Melissa says there's no reason why I can't continue to work a few extra hours each week. The bosses are proud of the progress we're making, too."

She's quiet for a second, as though she's processing what I've mentioned, then turns to look over at me. "I have to say, I am not that car's biggest fan." She snickers a little, as though there is more to the story than I know.

"Maybe this weekend we can start looking around."

"Sure, it's not going to hurt to see what's out there. Who knows, we might just run across a good deal." She grips my hand and we make the remainder of the drive in silence. *Well, at least she didn't say no.*

We arrive at the restaurant and manage to secure a table for two in the back corner. And, just as I'd hoped, the smell of fried food makes my mouth water. We glance at the menu and agree on an appetizer we both like.

After the waitress returns with our drinks, Jennifer excuses herself to go to the restroom. I pull out my phone to play around with one of my stupid games, and I notice I have a missed a text. I click to see who it's from. *Rebecca. Grrr. Seriously, what now?*

Rebecca: Our discussion is not over!

I simply want this crap with Rebecca to go away. Is that too much to ask? I'm okay with the fact she doesn't like me. Actually, the feeling's mutual. I'd tried to get along with her in the beginning, but now, I feel sorry for the guy that proposed to her. Did he really know what he was getting himself into? It still leads me to wonder why Jennifer held back from telling her we were married.

I don't' bother responding to the text and place the phone back in my pocket just as Jennifer walks back towards our table. Suddenly, she stops to speak with a couple at a table down from ours. It appears as though she knows them from the way she's smiling and chatting away with them. Before heading back, she reaches down to hug the woman while the man places his hand on her forearm.

"Who's that you were talking to?" I ask as she's barely had time to sit back down again.

"Oh, that's Rebecca's parents. I've not seen them in forever. They were asking about my parents and how I've been. If they're still here when we finish, I'll introduce you to them."

Great! Just fucking great! Can I not do anything without being reminded of that bitch? It's long overdue for her to go away from my life. Better yet, from *our* lives.

"Sure, I'd love to meet them," I manage to say between gritted teeth and a fake grin.

I quickly change the subject and make small talk until our meal arrives. I will not allow the evening to be ruined by her. Jennifer's face lights up as soon as the waitress returns. I'm pretty sure she'd have to agree—this place has quickly become one of my favorites. I've never tasted seafood so good.

We both stuff ourselves to the point that neither of us can eat another bite.

"I have something for you." I reach for her hand across the table and hold it in mine. She has no idea what I'm about to spring on her.

"Surprise huh?" She attempts to put a crazy look on her face, but all this does is make me laugh out loud at her failed attempt. We've had our fair share of surprises these last few weeks, that's for sure. This one is a good surprise though.

I reach into my jacket pocket and pull out the ring box from the jewelry store. I stopped by earlier to check on them, and the saleslady had a surprise of her own—they were ready for us. I reach for Jennifer's hand while she brings the other one up to cover her mouth.

"Awww, you remembered. I've been so busy lately, I completely forgot to call and check on them." She holds her hand up to admire them, then turns it for me to inspect. "They're so pretty."

I know it's not an extravagant set by a long shot, but the look on Jennifer's face is priceless. I think I could've given her a ring from a gumball machine and she'd be just as thrilled. One thing's for certain, she's unlike anyone I've ever been with. Sure, her family has always made sure she never went without, but she's always appreciative of everything, regardless of how big or small or how much or how little something costs.

I take care of our bill when we're finished and it feels good to handle something on my own for a change. For once, I didn't have to rely on her. I hold her hand as we walk through the restaurant towards the door. Without being too obvious, I managed to hold off long enough before leaving to avoid meeting Rebecca's parents. I'm not saying I purposely ate slowly, but I did feel better as I watched them stand and walk away from their table. Jennifer's back was to them so she never noticed.

Out at the car, I open the door for her. At times, I'm still not sure this is all real—I feel like I'm going to wake up in the front seat of my car and it's all going to be a dream. The idea of being married is also surreal. I can just hear my dad now. *"How'd you manage to talk someone into that? Surely they don't know the real you."*

I shake the thought from my head. I've changed. I'm not the same person I used to be. Yes, I've definitely changed, and it's all been for the better.

Back when I was still living at home, my dad was always such an ass—he literally hated me. Even when my mom would try to intervene, it was no use. My brothers could do no wrong and I could do no right.

I don't know if Rebecca mentioning my past has anything to do with it, but I'm curious to know if Jennifer would be up for a road trip. Oh how I would love to show my dad, firsthand, how I've changed. It's the first time I've actually considered going back to visit.

We don't say much on the drive back home, mostly because of what's going through my mind. I shut the car off then turn to look at her. "Jennifer, what would you say if I wanted to take a trip back home?"

For a moment, she doesn't answer and just stares straight ahead as though she's thinking about what she wants to say. Then, she shifts in the seat and turns to face me. "I wondered if you ever missed them. I think it's a great idea." She brings her hand up to rest on top of mine.

"I want you to come with me, of course."

For a moment, I think I've said the wrong thing. She looks down to her hand but I realize it's not a look of uncertainty. She's gazing at her rings, the light from the streetlamp beaming down on them. I can see their sparkle even from where I'm sitting.

"I want my mom to meet my wife and her future grandbaby. My dad, well, he'll probably not have anything nice to say, so you'll just have to overlook him. Funny thing, though, I kind of miss the fights and arguments with him. He was such a pushover when I was younger, but now, we stand eye to eye and I'm much stronger than him. I can hold my own." I hesitate for a moment, then continue. "I just hope I don't turn out to be like him with my own kid."

I look away, not wanting her to see the small tear that has formed in the corner of my eye. Embarrassed, I quickly pull myself together and open the car door. The last thing I want is to appear weak in front of her.

Hand in hand, we walk together to the front door. I wrap my arm around her and hold her, probably longer than I should. I don't want her to think anything more, so I pull away and lead the way inside.

Chapter 33

Jennifer

I PULL INTO MY USUAL spot at work tonight, and think back on the nights Rebecca and I used to joke about the mysterious silver Honda. Little did I know, I'd now be married to the owner of that car. And surprisingly, it's still running. Don't ask me how, but it is. We've always taken mine anytime we've gone somewhere and Brian's always been okay with it.

He's come a long way since then. In some ways, I feel as though we've known each other forever, then there's times I feel like I hardly know him at all. The more I think about his idea of going home to meet his family, the more I'm up for it. Whether they approve of me or not, they can't say we didn't try.

Putting all the pieces together, Brian's relationship with his father has been strained and far from normal. My father, on the other hand, is the complete opposite and would be ashamed to have that kind of relationship with me. I'm thankful our difficult times have been nothing like what Brian's had to endure.

I think about what Brian mentioned earlier, about looking for a car. What better way to boost Brian's confidence. I know we'll never be able to afford a brand new one, especially not now with so many things happening in our lives, but if we can find something that's slightly used, yet still in decent shape, it's bound to make him feel better. He's stuck with his new job, and seems to be content with it, so why not. His dad needs to see he's making progress and is a better person than what he was when he left.

Ever since I started working full-time right out of high school, I put back a little each week. My parents always stressed how important it was to have something to fall back on in an emergency situation and this, well, it kind of is one of those times. Some weeks I could put away a lot and other times, especially if I had expenses at school, it wouldn't be as much, but over time, I've been able to save a nice little chunk. With the baby on the way, I don't want to take too much from my savings, but I think I can spare a couple hundred dollars to put towards a car for Brian.

I gather up my purse and book bag and head inside before Rebecca thinks I got lost. I hadn't noticed the line of people waiting to check in when I first pulled in or I would've immediately gone on in. Our boss frowns on overtime, so I quickly step in and take over so she can get off the clock.

"Everything okay?" I ask as soon as the last guest has walked away.

"I guess I'm just a little tired. You know, trying to adjust to being back in school again." Rebecca tries to play it off, but I know when something's troubling her. Maybe she hasn't heard from Greg in a few days.

Our friendship still feels strained at times, despite the fact that we've made up and both claim to have put the past behind us, but I can't help feeling there's still a slight grudge. It's just one of those things I feel the less I bring it up, the better off we are. I don't know if she and Brian will ever come to a resolution, but for my sake, I sure hope they give it their best attempt. I know it's probably still embarrassing, but we can't dwell on the past.

"No need to rush off. Hang around for a little bit so we can talk," I tell her, hoping to get some answers for her odd behavior. "I ran into your parents tonight."

"Oh yeah? I wish I could stick around, but I'm actually meeting a few friends from school next door. They're already waiting for me."

I'm completely taken aback—she and I have always gone out together. Just me and her. Never has she ever wanted to go out alone or with anyone else but me. I'm hurt and not sure what to say.

"Okay, then." Rather than show the pained expression that I know must be obvious on my face, I turn away and pull some paperwork from the filing cabinet. I'm not in the mood for another dispute—if she prefers to go out with her other friends, so be it. I have my life now, too.

"Hey, about Sunday," she calls out when she reaches the front door. "I'm not going to be able to go shopping after all. My parents have something they need me to help them with, so maybe some other time, okay. Go ahead and enjoy your day with Brian."

Her words sting but I manage to fight back the tears. Talk about getting a slap to the face. I'm so heartbroken I don't have anything more to say.

I watch as she grabs a bag from her trunk and heads across the parking lot to the club. I miss my best friend, but I don't like the sudden change that's come over her.

Throughout the night, I steal glances outside just to see if her car's still in the parking lot. I miss our girl time, and I'm jealous that she'd want to go out without me. Then again, maybe she doesn't feel I can be fun anymore since announcing my pregnancy. I have to wonder if this is just a phase she's going through, maybe even jealousy. All I know, I'm not the one who's started acting strange.

Sometime in the early morning hours, her car disappears without my knowing it. I'm disappointed she never bothered to check in and say good night.

I manage to work on some schoolwork until I can't hold my head up any longer. I grab my phone and walk to the doorway figuring some fresh air will do me some good and hopefully give me an energy boost to make it through the rest of my shift.

I type in a text to Brian and send it. He's the one person I know I can count on right now.

Me: I miss you. Just wanted to tell you how much I love you.

I'm fairly certain at this time of the morning he's sound asleep, so finding my message when he wakes will hopefully put a smile on his face. I'm startled when my phone goes off, alerting me of an incoming text, and I quickly slide it open to read it.

Brian: Miss you too, baby <3

****

On Sunday, we both sleep in and are in no hurry to get out of bed. Our only plans are to browse a few car lots later in the day in hopes of spotting a good deal. Most are closed on Sunday anyway, but it doesn't hurt to look. Brian even started to look a few dealerships up online just to see what might be available for us. I don't want to jump on the first good deal we find since we can always go back later.

After breakfast in bed followed by a quick shower, we're all set to go.

Thank goodness we're not in any hurry, because the first two lots we visit have nothing to offer in our price range. I know the prices on the window are negotiable but they're not even anywhere close to what we can afford. I'm starting to think maybe we're in over our head and we should probably rethink this altogether.

The third one we come up on has lots of signs and balloons advertising a big sale. The selection is huge and Brian wastes no time checking out a few models. I'm not sure if there's a certain style he's looking for, but we should definitely consider a four-door car with our addition on the way.

Before long, I'm worn out from all the walking we've done. We decide to call it a day, even though the look of disappointment is evident on Brian's face. I know he's anxious, but there's just so much you can do in a day's time.

On Monday morning, as soon as my classes are over, we go back to the same lot again. Brian was able to swap shifts at work and doesn't have to go in until later in the evening. I have a feeling he's not going to give up so easily today.

Immediately, a salesman walks out to greet us. I sort of let Brian take over the process, since he knows more about how it all works than I do. I listen carefully to him tell the salesman a couple features he's interested in, and in just minutes, we're on our way to the back of the lot. It seems one that fits our needs has just been brought in.

I can see from the look on his face that this could be the one. It's newer than what I expected but the salesman assures us he can work out a reasonable deal—one we won't be able to refuse. I'm pretty sure it's all part of the sales pitch and he tells that to everyone. It's a good thing we drove separately today because the process of shopping for a car is almost more than I can stand. From Brian's endless questions and the salesman's insistent remarks, I'm ready to pull my hair out and leave him here to handle it all.

It doesn't take long before my head is pounding. Brian notices how quiet I've gotten and keeps glancing over at me. I honestly think a car salesman will tell you anything you want to hear. They want to put you behind the wheel of something, whether it's what you really wanted or not, and make it look like you just got the offer of the century.

In the end, Brian agrees on a deal he feels is worthy and with payments we can afford. To my surprise, Brian pulls out some money he'd put back from working overtime, and combined with what I have and his trade-in, I let out a sigh of relief. Yes, this might just work.

I leave him at the dealership finishing up some last-minute paperwork while his new car is being prepped to leave the lot. Who knew he'd own another car so similar to the one he's giving up. It may be the same make and model, but it looks so much better than that clunker.

****

The next morning, I hurry home to see Brian before he has to leave for work. Since he'd had to go in after leaving the dealership, he was late getting home last night and went straight to bed. All I want now is to feel his arms around me.

He greets me at the door, my arms loaded down with cups of coffee and a bag of assorted breakfast items I grabbed for us before leaving work. After setting everything down on the table, I make my way over to him.

"I missed you last night." I lay may head against his shoulder and breathe in his masculine scent. He's shaved and showered and his smell is exhilarating.

"I missed you, too," he manages to say at the same time his phone rings. Instead of taking the call in front of me, he walks back to the bedroom.

"Everything okay?" I ask when he returns moments later. Not wanting to sound like a nosy, insecure wife, but I dislike the fact he felt he had to walk away. I tell myself it's probably nothing and I'm just overreacting. Still, I find his reaction a little unusual.

"Yeah, just my boss." He picks up one of the coffees and takes a sip.

"Well…" I wait for him to say more. "What did she want?"

I blame it on pregnancy hormones and not uncertainty. We're better now than we've ever been, so there's no need for me to feel this way. And while I'm not fond that his boss is a pretty, young female who does happen to call and text him often, there's nothing I can do about it. I'm thankful he's got the job and for that, I owe her. Right now, though, there's no room for doubt or insecurities. That's the one sure way to dampen a relationship.

"Look, don't take this wrong way, okay. She just wanted to know if I'd like her to pick me up something for breakfast. We're both due in at the same time this morning. I told her I was already enjoying breakfast with my beautiful wife." He pulls me to him and holds me close against his chest. His reaction is reassuring, but I can't help but wonder how often she's done this in the past. Has he bought her breakfast as well?

"Care for another cup of coffee?" I ask quickly, needing to change the subject. "Maybe one for the ride into work?"

"Nah, I think I'll pass this time," he replies, still holding my hand in his. "I wouldn't want to accidentally spill anything in my new car." I love the smile that quickly forms across his face at the mention of his car. I'm happy that he's happy and that's all that matters.

We say our goodbyes, and I change into something a little more comfortable before leaving for class. I've been tossing around the idea of taking a few over the summer, since I'll be missing the fall term to have the baby. Part of me wants to enjoy the time off to prepare though, while the other half says I need to stay focused and on-track with school. If I fall behind, I might never get caught up again. Either way, the news isn't going to be exactly welcomed by my parents. There's no easy way to tell them, but if I have some concrete plans for the future, it might help to ease the news.

Towards the end of the week, Brian mentions the trip back home again. I'm nervous just talking about it, but I'm sure nothing compares to what he feels. He makes last minute arrangements with his boss, who's more than willing to let him have the time off. I wonder if he's told her much about his background or if she's genuinely just easy to work with. Ever since that day I showed up to surprise him and they were laughing and carrying on in the stock room, I've had mixed feelings about her. It's not like Brian talks about her when we're together, but the less I have to hear about her, the better off I am. I suppose I should be thankful they have a good working relationship since some people aren't so fortunate.

I pack our bags on Friday evening before heading out to work. Our plans are to leave first thing in the morning as soon as I get home. I hint around that he needs to call them, just to let them know to expect us, but he says he wants to surprise them. It's best that way. I don't question why, but I know the trip has weighed heavily on his mind all week.

The next morning, we load up our little bit of luggage and head out. It's a beautiful day, perfect for our nine-hour trip. A couple hours in, we stop for a bathroom break. I apologize, but he knows I can't help it—it just sort of goes with being pregnant.

When we're back on the highway again, I shift around in the front seat trying to get comfortable. Laying the seat back, I fluff the pillow I brought along and pull my jacket around me. Brian adjusts the volume on the radio even though I tell him it's not a distraction to me. When I'm tired, as is the case this morning, I can sleep in almost any kind of situation.

Hours later, I feel a light tapping on my arm and realize Brian is trying to wake me. I bring the seat back up and try to focus on the surroundings. He exits the interstate stating we needs to fill up with gas.

"You hungry?" he asks.

Although I packed a bag of snacks, I'm ready for some real food.

"Sure."

"As soon as we get done here, I'll pull over there." He motions towards a fast food place on the other side of the highway. "Will that be fine with you?"

I nod my head, still not entirely awake yet. I'm feeling groggy and I hope once I eat, I'll be able to get in a couple more hours of sleep. The two I've been asleep are nowhere near enough.

I really wanted something more than a burger, but I'm not going to complain. It's best we grab something quick and get back out on the road again. While waiting in the drive-up, Brian says we're making good time, and we're almost halfway. The anxiety returns but I'm sure it doesn't compare to what he's dealing with. I have to say, though, he appears to be fine on the outside.

I offer to drive, just to give him a break, but he refuses saying I need to rest. He's right, but now I'm not so sure I can go back to sleep. The car is silent except for the crinkling of our food wrappers. I'm extra careful not to drop any crumbs since Brian promised me he'd never let this car get in the same shape as the last one. He admitted just how embarrassed he was about it and I agree, I peeped through the window a few times—it was a definitely a site to behold.

We both startle when his phone beeps, alerting an incoming text. He informed me a while back that the mysterious texts he'd been receiving had come to a halt so I'm even more curious who it could be now. Surely that boss of his wouldn't interrupt him after he'd made arrangements to take off. He passes the phone over to me and asks me to see who it's from.

I glance down, expecting to see her name, but it's not hers that appears. Someone named Rodney –a name I've heard him mention before but can't place. *Rodney.* "Who's Rodney, babe?"

"Oh, he's the guy that closes at night. He's training to be a manager, just like me. What's the text say?"

Oh my God! I think to myself as I read the words silently. I look over at Brian while he tries to concentrate on the road, but the look on my face causes him to swerve. He quickly jerks the car back into the lane.

"What. What's it say?" he asks again, this time gruffly.

"Your boss…your boss just got fired."

"What?" His face instantly goes pale, but I'm more concerned about him paying attention to the road.

"Yeah, it says, 'Melissa got let go this morning. Got questioned about several deposits that are missing. You know anything?'"

The look on Brian's face causes my body to go numb. I don't like his reaction at all.

"Damn it. That can't be true."

"It's what it says."

"No. She'd never…" he yells out.

I turn the phone in the direction for him to see the text for himself. I was never much for Melissa, but I'm even more skeptical about her now. Fired? Missing deposits? It doesn't sound good.

On a brighter note, will this be Brian's opportunity to move up? Is he ready for a promotion?

Suddenly, I break out in a sweat. *No. Please God, no. Don't let Brian go down with her. Don't let him have anything to do with what Melissa was fired for.*

Chapter 34
Brian

DRIVE. I MUST CONCENTRATE ON driving—I can't deal with the text right now. I knew I shouldn't have taken the day off, but no, I just had to make the trip back home. Going back home was the wrong thing to do. If I'd been there, I know we could've come up with something. *There's a mistake somewhere--I know there is.* There's no way Melissa did anything with the deposits. She always had them ready for me each morning. I'd initial the slip indicating I verified everything, then she'd walk to the end of the mall and drop it in the bank deposit slot. It happened daily, we never missed one. *Shit!*

Then it occurs to me.

I run my fingers through my hair. *No, I can't deal with this right now.*

Jennifer looks over at me, sensing my sudden frustration. Her gaze penetrates deep into my soul. *Damn it, why does she have to stare at me like that?*

"Are you okay?" She places her hand on top my leg but I jerk it away. I don't want anyone touching me right now. Not even her.

"Fuck!" I say loudly, and regret it as soon as it comes out.

"Brian, slow down!" she yells.

I look down at the speedometer, my speed well over the limit. I lift my foot from the gas pedal and allow the car to slow. One text. One simple text made me lose my cool.

"I can't believe it. No." I grip the wheel even tighter, unaware of what's going on around me. I'm not thinking clearly.

"What are you talking about?" I hear her voice coming from somewhere beside me.

"Melissa, I hope to God this is some damn joke."

"Brian, I don't understand you. I'm not Melissa. What's going on? Why are you talking to me like I'm her?"

She reaches over to shake my arm and it's then I realize I've been completely zoned out from everything. It's like I was lost in another world. For a moment, I thought I was talking to Melissa.

"You're so worked up. You've got to settle down. Talk to me. Tell me why this has you so upset."

When I look over at her, aware now that it's my wife and not Melissa, I see tears in the corners of her eyes. She's scared out of her mind. I take a couple deep breaths and try to concentrate on the road.

"I few weeks ago," I begin, recalling the events that morning, "I was sort of having a bad day. Melissa asked if there was something wrong, if I needed to talk about anything. It wasn't any one particular thing. It's just some days I think about why I left and ended up here and everything that's happened up to now."

"I'm not sure I'm following you."

"The store was slow, and somehow I ended up telling her about my past jobs and the trouble that seemed to follow me. Everywhere I've worked, you know, something bad always happens and I'm let go. It's been this way for a while now and I guess I sort of expected it to happen again. I even told her about being wrongly accused over at Jared's.

"She said she understood my frustrations and that I shouldn't worry about anything. I was headed in the right direction and pretty soon, I'd have enough training that I could have my own store. She…she seemed to understand where I was coming from. Almost like…like she'd been in my shoes before."

Jennifer turns her head to look out the window and I see her wipe at a tear lingering on her cheek. I know it hurts, knowing I've discussed such personal situations with my boss and not her.

I continue on, putting myself under even more scrutiny. "Melissa told me she was proud of my job performance so far. Other than you, she's been the only person to really give me a chance. She actually commended me for doing so well. She's almost like a best friend, telling me things I need to hear."

"Brian, she's your fucking boss. Isn't that what bosses are supposed to do? Praise you for a job well done."

Her tone catches me completely off-guard and I realize she's reading more into what I'm saying. She's thinking something else, something completely way off. I'd never do that to her.

"Jenn, I know you've never been fond of her, but she's really been a cool person. I've never had a boss like her."

"So why are you getting so worked up over this? If she's such a good person, I'm sure your company will figure out there's been a mistake and everything will come clear in the end."

I hope what she's saying is true. Then it hits me…. right smack in the face. *No. Please tell me no. It can't be.*

"*Uhhh*, how could I be so stupid? I cannot believe this." I grip the steering wheel tighter and feel my blood pressure rising. One minute I'm commending Melissa, then the next, I'm ready to backhand her. I unconsciously accelerate my speed. I'm totally fucked!

Jennifer starts flailing her arms, panic setting in. "Brian, just stop the damn car and let me drive. You're so worked up over this, you're going to get us killed," she pleads. "You've got to tell me what's going on or you've got to pull over. Your driving...it's... it's scaring me!" she screams, her voice a loud shrill that I can barely understand.

The car veers slightly to the right, running over the reflectors lining the side of the highway. *Bump, bump, bump.* I jerk the car back into the lane, probably harder than I should. No one, and I mean *no one* is going to talk to me that way.

"Damn it, Jennifer. Don't fucking yell at me!" I turn to look at her, my body now fuming. Yes, I realize I'm driving way over the speed limit again, but who gives a fuck? It's bad enough the situation I'm dealing with, but now my wife wants to make it even worse by yelling at me. *Fuck her!*

I pull up too quickly on the car ahead of me and jerk the car over to avoid hitting the rear bumper.

"Brian, please stop. Slow down."

"Just please shut the fuck up! I know what I'm doing." I'm angry with Jennifer. I'm angry with Melissa. I'm angry with the world. Every. Last. Single. Person. "What part of that do you not understand? Just let me figure this out."

Without thinking, I bring my hand up. *Slap!* It grazes her cheek and she immediately brings her hand up to cover the sting of the blow. I can't believe I just slapped her!

She wouldn't shut up. She kept screaming at me about my driving, only making it worse.

Angry tears spill down her cheeks. Embarrassed, I can't bring myself to look at her. I've reacted just like my dad. I'm...I'm just like him.

As soon as I'm able to slow the car down, I pull off the side of the road, knowing she's right. I'm out of control. It's not safe to drive until I've calmed down and apologized for my outburst. When the car comes to a screeching halt, Jennifer grabs her purse and jacket and jumps out, leaving the car door wide open. Her hand still clenches her cheek as her pace increases. I've never seen her move so quickly, especially being pregnant. It's as though…as though she'd scared to death of me.

"Jennifer." I call out to her before she gets too far ahead. "Look, I'm sorry. Please, just let me explain. Please get back in the car." I slowly ease forward, coming as close to her as I can with her door still wide open and also avoiding any cars passing by. If anyone going by notices trouble, no one bothers to slow down.

It doesn't take me long to realize she's not going to stop. No amount of begging and pleading is going to change her mind.

It's not safe riding down the emergency lane—not for her, not for me, not for my car. Still, she keeps trudging along, never once looking back. I finally bring the car to a stop and get out on the passenger side to avoid any oncoming vehicles.

"Jennifer, please stop!" I yell to her again. The faster she walks, the angrier I get.

She turns to face me, a look of disgust on her face. The red mark from my hand is still clearly visible on her cheek. It's as if it sickens her to look at me, so she turns and keeps on walking.

"Jennifer, you've got to stop. This is crazy. You know I didn't mean to do it. Get back in the car." She's so far up ahead by now, I doubt she's able to hear me. And even if she can, it's not like she's listening. Her mind's made up.

What do I do now? *Shit!* I can't just leave her.

I pick up my phone and the text from Rodney is still on the screen when I slide my finger across to unlock it. How? How could this happen? I think back to all those damn deposits Melissa had ready for me. In the beginning, I'd count and verify the money just like I was supposed to, and every time, it was exactly right. Every. Single. Time. I felt it was a waste of my time just to check behind her. Then, okay, I slipped. I got careless and started initialing the deposit slips and reports even though I didn't always verify it all. Melissa always made comments about how she was such a perfectionist—the money was always right on the penny, it was always turned the same way, it was never wrong. But what went wrong? What happened to the deposits?

The bitch set me up! That's what happened. She knew I wasn't counting the money behind her. If I had of, I would've caught it. *How many times was the deposit wrong and I was too stupid to verify it?* I got lazy and comfortable, and she took advantage of me. It's no wonder she was so nice and friendly to me. She was using me.

I turn the car on and reach over to shut the passenger door. *Damn it, Jennifer. You might not stop now but you will eventually.* I pull back into traffic once it's clear, and drive slowly so I can see her, but she's not there. She's not on the road anymore. What the hell? She's disappeared. How? How can she just disappear like that? I start to worry, then see the exit sign up ahead. At the pace she was walking, it's bound to be where she is.

I pull off when I reach the exit, uncertain which direction to take. It's a fairly busy exit with several gas stations and restaurants so there's no telling where she might be. After driving through a couple places, glancing inside as best I can, nothing looks out of the ordinary.

Then, as soon as I pull across the street, I spot her. Just inside one of those pancake places sitting in a chair near the doorway. The huge front glass does nothing to hide her or the bright red jacket she's got on. She turns to look out just as I drive into a front parking spot. For a moment, our gazes lock.

I sit and stare at her, hoping she'll give in and walk outside. I think about how everything played out and all I want to do right now is kick myself. Just like those famous words spoken by my father, without a doubt, I was a stupid dumb ass. One thing's for certain, I'm not leaving without her.

As soon as I step out of the car and walk towards the door, she stands up and runs down the hallway. I try to catch her but she's too quick for me. I gain lots of attention throughout the restaurant, and everyone strains their heads to watch my performance as I beat and bang on the bathroom door, pleading with her to let me in.

The manager approaches me and asks if anything's wrong. I explain to him my wife's upset and we had a slight misunderstanding. From inside the bathroom, I hear her shout out to me. "Go away, Brian! I'm not leaving with you!"

"Jennifer, please let me explain. Talk to me. Please, I'm begging you to let me make things right."

Silence.

"I'm not going away without you, Jennifer." I pound a little harder on the door.

The manager comes over yet again, only this time he tells me I need to take my problems elsewhere. He claims I'm disrupting the business, and I'm not going to be allowed to harass her any further.

"I don't give a damn what you say, buddy. My wife is in there, and I need her to come out. I'm not leaving here without her." I try hard to remain calm, but I feel my blood pressure rising again. No damn man is going to tell me to leave without my wife coming with me.

The manager walks back to the counter and grabs the phone. "You've got less than thirty seconds to get the hell out of my restaurant before I call the cops to have you removed!"

This is the final straw. I don't like being threatened. I'm at my breaking point now, so I kick the bathroom door as hard as I can. Jennifer lets out a loud scream. And just for dramatics, I kick it a few more times.

A guy sitting at one of the tables close by stands up to intervene. He reaches to grab ahold of my arm, and I snatch it back just in time. "Don't touch me," I say through gritted teeth.

He's several inches taller than me, with an almost athletic build to him, but he doesn't intimidate me. "I'm going to ask you nicely to leave her alone. I don't know what the circumstances are, but she's told you she's not coming with you. Now back off and let her be."

"Why don't you stay out of our business!"

There's no doubt in my mind the cops are already on their way by now. Stupidly, I pick up a glass from the table where he's sitting with some old man and I fling it at him. The dark liquid hits him directly in the face and runs down. I know it wasn't the smartest thing to do, but he shouldn't have stuck his nose where it didn't belong. It is our problem, not his. The restaurant is deadly silent, everyone fearful what my next move will be.

"Fuck you all!" I belt out loudly and run out the front door.

Chapter 35

Jennifer

I SIT ON THE TOILET, wiping my tears with tissue. A shredded mess surrounds me on the floor. Each time Brian raised his voice or banged on the door, I felt my stomach tie up in knots. It wasn't long, though, before everything quieted down.

Suddenly, I hear a kind voice on the other side of the door. "Honey, it's safe to come out now. He's not here anymore."

I stand up and steady my balance, uncertain whether to believe whoever's on the other side or not. I walk to the sink and see what terrible shape my face is in. With trembling hands, I turn on the water and wait for it to heat up. I splash a bit onto my face but it doesn't help much. I'm a sight to behold.

I stand at the door, contemplating if I should turn the latch just yet. I muster as much courage as I can and crack the door open. I peer my head out just enough to glance around the hallway to see if it's all clear. Sure enough, I don't see or hear any sign of Brian.

Just outside the door, though, is a rather attractive young man, probably mid-twenties, looking at me with concern. I notice he's holding a handful of soiled napkins and his shirt is slightly stained. I wonder if he's the reason for the commotion I heard when Brian was still here.

He immediately grabs a chair and offers it to me. "Here, let me help you."

I hand my purse and jacket over to him and sit down at the closest table. I glance around, feeling the stares from the remaining customers. I know they can't help it, but I feel as though I've been the center of a freak show.

"Thank you," I mutter, and immediately drop my head down. It's the most embarrassing situation I think I've ever been a part of.

"Can I get you something? A Coke maybe?" he asks. His voice is soothing and kind. He nods towards one of the waitresses who immediately walks over with a glass.

"Thank you, ma'am," I mumble.

"Now, hun." She rests her hand on my shoulder. "You gave us all a pretty big scare earlier. You going to be okay now?" Her southern drawl is comforting, in an almost motherly sort of way.

I nod my head, unable to form any more words just yet.

"Take all the time you need, dear. There's no rush. My name's Nancy. If you need anything, just holler." She walks back behind the counter, leaving me here with the concerned young gentleman.

I take a sip of my drink and the cool, bubbly liquid feels good against my scratchy throat. I look over and see he's placed my things in the seat across from him.

"Thanks," I tell him. I take another quick glance around to assure myself that Brian is truly gone.

"You going to be alright now?" he asks in a concerned kind of way.

"I think so. Thank you for asking."

"I'm not sure who that guy was, but you don't deserve to be treated that way. It's none of my business, but he's a jackass."

"I'm so sorry to have caused such a scene in here. I hope he didn't do that to you," I say and point to the stain on his shirt.

"It's not a big deal. I just wanted to make sure he left you alone. It was obvious you were upset and he was the cause."

I'm unable to meet his eyes, humiliated by this whole mess.

I reach for my purse and pull my phone out. I forgot I'd silenced it earlier when I was trying to sleep. Now I see there're over a dozen missed calls and almost as many texts. No doubt, they're all from Brian.

I turn the phone back off and drop it down in my purse. I simply can't listen or read anything from him right now. My heart can't take any more from him at the moment. I'm…I'm much too weak for him to destroy the little bit of self-worth I still have. Never, in all my life, has anyone treated me the way he did. I…I didn't deserve it, no matter what he says.

I take another sip of my drink and notice the restaurant has emptied significantly. I'm pretty sure everyone was just waiting to see the outcome. The manager walks over and pulls a chair up beside me.

"Is there anything I can get you?" His voice expresses deep concern.

I reach up to wipe a strand of hair away from my face. I know I look a mess. "I'm good now, thank you."

"I don't recognize you. Are you from around here?"

"I'm from Morgantown. Do you know how far away I am from there?"

"I'm guessing maybe six or seven hours. Is there someone I can call to come get you?"

"I can just use my phone. Do you mind if I hang out here while I wait?" I hate asking, especially if Brian decides to come back, but I don't have much choice. If I try to leave, I'm not sure where a safe place to wait would be.

"Stay as long as you need. And don't worry. If that guy comes back, the cops will be on him in a flash."

"Thanks."

He stands, then pauses before returning to work back behind the counter. "My shift's over in thirty minutes. If there's someplace I can take you, just let me know. Oh, and you're welcome to have something to eat, too. On the house, of course." He points to a menu that's wedged in-between the napkin holder and a wire basket of condiments.

"I'll just call someone to come get me." I do my best to remain calm, but I know as soon as I make a phone call, the tears are going to flow once again. For the sake of my pregnancy, I need to take a deep breath and relax.

I'm left alone again with the gentleman and older man. They seem harmless and like they're genuinely good people. After all, how many people would stand up in another person's defense these days?

"I'm Todd, by the way, and this is my grandfather."

"It's nice to meet you." I acknowledge the older man then turn back towards him. "Thanks, Todd. I'm really sorry for—"

He cuts me off. "Please stop apologizing. That guy's behavior was uncalled for. I'm just glad you're okay." He offers me a smile and I make an attempt to return one as well. I admit, it feels good.

I pull out my phone again, contemplating who I should call. My heart tells me Rebecca, that we still have that bit of connection and she'd come to my rescue no matter the reason why. On the other hand, if I call my parents, I'm only setting myself up to have a lot of explaining to do.

I stare at Rebecca's name until my eyes blur. I know, without a doubt, she'll be there for me. She has to be.

I hold my finger above the button next to her name and hesitate before pressing it. Yes, I tell myself, this is what I need to do. I know I'm going to get a long lecture, but I should've listened to her all along. I stand up and walk over to look out the window. I still have that fear he's outside somewhere watching me—watching me from across the street, from down the road, from somewhere I can't see him. I shiver and walk away, listening to the phone ring and ring. Just when I'm about to give up, thinking that she's not going to answer, I finally hear her voice on the other end.

"Hello." She sounds groggy, as though I've awakened her.

I open my mouth to say something, but I can't make the words come out.

"Hello," I hear her say again. "Jennifer, is that you?" She knows from having my number programmed into her phone that it is.

I do everything I can to hold back the sobs, but suddenly they overtake my body and I'm a basket case. There's nothing I can do to stop them. I let out a hiccup as I struggle to catch my breath enough to speak into the phone. "Rebecca."

"Jenn, what's wrong? Are you hurt? Please talk to me!" she screams into the phone. "God, are you okay?"

"I'm fine," I manage to say between sobs. "I am now."

"Where are you? What's going on?"

I don't feel like replaying the entire story back to her right now, not over the phone. I just need to know she can come get me. I can explain everything later, in-between the long lecture I'm sure she's going to give me. I deserve it though. I should've listened—I should've seen the warnings. I give her the name and location of where I'm calling from and she tells me she's on her way out the door now.

"Thank you," I whisper so softly I wonder if she was able to hear me. "I love you, Rebecca. I knew I could count on you."

I put my phone away just as the manager approaches me again.

"So, were ya able to get ahold of anyone?" he asks.

"Yeah, I've got my best friend coming to get me." He passes me a handful of napkins to dry my face. "It'll be a couple hours before she can get here though."

"Well, you're welcome to hang out here as long as you need," he reminds me again.

I don't have much of a choice, so I'm thankful he doesn't mind. Especially since I was the reason for the commotion earlier.

"Thanks."

I sit back down at the table with Todd. Although he's a complete stranger, there's something comforting about him.

"So, were you able to get a ride?" he asks.

"My best friend is coming to get me," I tell him. I seem to have a better grasp of things now that I've calmed down. "But it's going to be several hours before she can get here. Didn't you say it's about six or seven hours?"

"Man, I hate you've got to wait that long. I don't think you have to worry about that guy coming back, but still, it'll seem like forever for her to get here."

"I'll be okay. The manager said it'd be fine. Besides, I've got my phone. I can call 9-1-1 if I need to, but I really don't think he'll mess with me again."

"Well, you just never know. Look, I know you don't know me and it's probably crazy for me to offer, but why don't you let me take you at least halfway to meet your friend? That way, it'll shorten the time you've got to wait."

I think about this for a moment as thoughts of Brian, once again, cloud my head. At one time, Brian was a stranger to me, too. We met under weird circumstances, completely different from this though, but look at me now. Look at the situation I'm in.

I know his intentions are good and I've already seen several people approach him and the gentleman with him. It's as though everyone here knows them. I think about it for a moment, then give in.

"Are you sure you wouldn't mind? I really don't want to be a burden to you." I'm thankful there's still good-hearted people in this world.

"I'm positive." He offers a smile, and right now, that smile fills my heart with the encouragement I need. I know I've got a rough battle ahead. "If it will make you feel any safer, I can get my grandfather to ride along. We were just out killing time anyway. My grandmother passed away last year, so I try to spend as much time with him as I can when school's out. I like to get him out of the house."

School? Surely he means college. If I had to guess, I'd say he's probably a year or two older than me.

"That's very generous of you, but it's not necessary for your grandfather to come along. You...you seem harmless." I can't hide the slight grin that's come across my face. There's just something about him that's real and genuine.

"I just thought I would suggest it even though I know he won't mind. You've been through enough already this afternoon."

"Really, I'm fine with it." I reach down to cover my belly as my stomach growls. To anyone else I look normal and not the couple months pregnant that I am. I realize it's been a while since I last ate. "Sorry about that," I tell him, slightly embarrassed.

"Tell you what," he says. "Why don't you grab a bite to eat, and I'll run my grandfather back home. He lives a couple

290 · Amy Stephens

minutes from here. That'll give you some time to eat before we head out. Sound okay?"

I nod my head, already feeling better about my decision to let him take me. Then he pulls out some money and sets it on the counter.

"Nancy," he calls out to the waitress. "Can you see that my friend here gets a bite to eat?" He rests his hand on my shoulder and I look up at him.

"You don't have to do that."

"But I want to. I'll be back soon."

I order a bowl of grits and a couple pieces of toast from the menu. My nerves are still on edge but I think this will help me settle down and relax before I have to leave. Nancy is quick with my order and I don't waste any time digging in.

The manager walks over, his coat draped over his arm. "Have you decided what you're going to do?" he asks. "For a moment I thought Todd was going to keep you company."

"Yeah, he seems like a pretty nice guy. He's offered to take me halfway to meet my friend. He just wanted to run his grandfather home, then he's coming back."

"Todd's a nice guy. I've known him and his family all my life. If he says he's going to take care of you, he definitely means it. You're in good hands."

"Thanks for reassuring me. I needed to hear that."

"Yes, ma'am. You both be careful out there tonight. If you're ever back this way again, stop in and say hello. I wish you well."

"I sure will."

When I'm done with my food, I visit the restroom again. It'll be a long time before we get to stop again so might as well take advantage of the facilities here. I check out my reflection in the mirror and I cringe at the sight. I look a total mess and I'm almost ashamed for Todd to see me this way.

I walk back out and see a white pick-up truck pull into the handicap spot. I walk out on the sidewalk to meet him. Todd quickly jumps out and runs around to open the door for me. He offers his hand as I step up on the side rails to climb inside. I don't think I've ever been inside a vehicle that sits so high off the ground.

It's a completely different view from up here. I look around wondering if Brian is sitting in his car nearby, watching for me. For our sake, I hope he's long gone. It doesn't mean it'll be any easier when I get home, but for now, it's probably best. The last thing I need is for him to cause any more trouble once we're out on the highway. But it does piss me off that he left me. Yeah, he may have called several times, but to leave me? It doesn't say much about him. I'm starting to see, more and more, what a huge mistake I've made in my life.

Before we pull out, I turn in the seat to face Todd and extend my hand to him. "I feel so stupid. Please accept my apology for not introducing myself earlier. My name is Jennifer. Jennifer Davis. I…I mean Collins."

He accepts my hand and I notice how firm his grip feels. "I'm sorry to meet under these circumstances, but it's still nice to meet you. So, are you Jennifer Davis or Collins?"

"Collins," I volunteer. "I'm still trying to get used to having a new last name."

"Oh, did you recently get married?"

"Do we even have to talk about it?" I try to make a joke of it, but I know it's not going to help.

"Uh oh. I'm sorry. You don't sound too happy about it."

"If you only knew." There's no way I'm going to share my roller coaster experience with Todd right now. The only thing that would prove is how weak I am on decision making.

Call me crazy, but I feel safe inside Todd's oversized truck. I buckle my seatbelt, and Todd pulls across the street to the gas station before getting out on the highway. I use the time while he's pumping gas to call Rebecca and update her. She tells me she's not fond of this hasty decision but it will save us both time in the long run. I'm to call or text her every hour with an update. Even though I'm still skeptical myself, I like this idea. "He's a good guy," I tell her.

"Yeah, isn't that what you tried to convince me of before?"

While I don't like what she has to say, I know she's right.

Todd climbs back inside at the same time I end my call. I offer him some money to help pay for gas but he kindly refuses and pushes my hand away. "No, you hang on to that, should you need it for later on."

We ride in silence for a while then I tell him about my call to Rebecca and her plan for keeping touch.

"I'm not sure what's going on with your situation, but you're very lucky to have a friend who's willing to drop everything at a moment's notice."

"We've had a rough go lately, but thank goodness she didn't give up on me. It's been tough, for sure."

I don't admit it to Todd, but I'm scared to death about going home. I don't know how to face what's going to happen next. Brian's not going to give up so easily.

"So, Jennifer, tell me. What's your story?" he asks, breaking the silence once we're several miles down the highway. "How did you end up here this afternoon, so far from home?"

At first, I don't say anything, careful about what information I want to share. I slowly begin to open up to him, relaying everything I've had to endure these last few months — everything but the part about my being pregnant. I don't feel it's best I share that just yet.

He doesn't say anything for a while and only stares straight ahead. I wonder if I've made a mistake in confiding in him. Does he think I'm crazy?

"It's sad some men have to be that way, but we're not all like that." He hesitates for a moment. "Don't take this the wrong way, but sounds like you've got your hands full—a real winner. We all make mistakes, some worse than others, but you can also learn from them, too. Just be careful with what you do."

"Thank you for not judging me. I don't know where I'll go from here, but tomorrow is a new day. I think after I get some rest, I'll be able to think more clearly." I glance down at my phone and send Rebecca a text. Todd tells me our exact location and I make sure to include it. Rather than read the texts that are still coming in from Brian, I delete them one by one. I really don't care what he has to say at this point. As far as I'm concerned, he can go to hell.

"Excuse me." I let out a yawn and quickly apologize while covering my mouth. "I've only had a few hours of sleep today and I guess it's finally catching up with me."

"Why don't you get some rest? You can leave your phone here on the console so when your friend texts you again, I can reply back for you." He taps the cup holder between us, indicating where to leave it. "If you reach behind the seat, I've got a jacket that you can use for a pillow."

"Thanks. I think I will close my eyes for a bit." I reach behind me and, sure enough, there's a jacket folded on the backseat. "Thank you, Todd. For everything." Before I know it, I've drifted off into a deep sleep.

Chapter 36
Brian

I'VE SENT JENNIFER SO MANY texts, I've lost count at this point. Either she's not getting them, or she's chosen to ignore them, which angers me even more. The same is true for calling. I've filled up her voicemail so I can't leave any more messages. By not returning my calls, what's she trying to prove? She can't stay here forever.

My battery is almost dead now and it pisses me off because it's all her fault. I toss the phone down to the floor on the passenger side of the car.

As I sit in the parking lot across the street from the restaurant, I wonder if she's still inside. Surely she couldn't have left the little bit of time I was drove away to cool off. I was a little hesitant at first, but figured it was what I needed to do before I came unglued on someone—someone who thought they could give me their two cents worth on how I needed to handle a situation with my wife.

Being in this unfamiliar location, I was hesitant to get too far away from the interstate, and I was only gone for maybe an hour at the most.

I look up and see a cop car riding through the parking lot. It's not a good sign, especially if someone's called them because of me. So I screwed up and lost my cool. Big deal—it's not like I killed anyone. We just had a fight and no one got hurt.

Maybe their feelings were hurt, but there wasn't really bodily harm. And that slap on her cheek? Well, I'm not going to say she deserved it, but she's got to learn when I'm upset about something, she doesn't need to talk to me that way.

Rather than give the cops a chance to spot me—if it is indeed the reason why they're here—I go ahead and pull out. *Let the bitch find her own way back home. It's her problem now, not mine.* The more I think about Jennifer and her mood swings lately, I'm probably doing the right thing by leaving her here. It'll teach her a lesson. Let someone else deal with her. Let them see what I've been putting up with. One minute things are great with her, then the next minute, it's just like all the others. According to her, I'm doing something wrong, yet again.

At the red light, I hesitate before turning north or south. If I turn to the right, it'll be towards my parent's house and since I've already come this far, I might as well go ahead and drive the rest of the way. Damn it, I'd almost be there by now if all that shit hadn't happened.

I completely push Melissa out of my head for the time being. I'll deal with that when I get back. That is, if I decide to go back. Who knows, I might decide just to move back home. To hell with everyone.

I set the cruise control to monitor my speed and turn the radio on. The music is loud, just the way I want it. The louder it plays, the less I hear the thoughts churning around in my mind. An hour later, I pull off to refuel. I grab something to drink then walk around to the passenger side to retrieve my phone from the floorboard.

Just as I expected, there's still nothing from her. *Stupid bitch. She's really trying my patience.*

For the sake of calling, I punch in her number one last time. It's the same thing—a full voicemail. Just to irritate her, I hang up and call right back. Again and again, over and over I call her phone until I get tired of hearing the sound of her voice on the pre-recorded message.

Finally, after a few more attempts to aggravate her, the phone clicks and I can tell someone's on the other end of the line. I push the phone closer to my ear to listen but no one says anything.

"Ah, you stupid bitch. You finally decide to pick up huh?" My tone is hateful, to say the least.

"Hello," a male voice speaks into the line.

I'm taken aback, not expecting to hear another voice, especially not one that belongs to a man.

I hang up and figure I must have misdialed. I laugh when I think about what they must've thought when I said that to them.

There's no sense in wasting any more time on her, so I toss the phone down on the seat and get in behind the wheel again. I'm done.

****

It's almost nine o'clock when I arrive at my parent's house. I shut the car off and stare at the front lawn. My mom has yet to start planting anything so the yard looks dull, lifeless.

As usual, the neighborhood is quiet, with little to no activity at all. I don't see any lights on inside so I wonder if they're asleep already. Back when I was still living at home, they'd always retire to their bedroom early. It was one of the reasons I found it so easy to sneak out.

Well, if they are asleep, the last thing I want to do is wake my dad. An argument with him this time of the night is not what I want to deal with at the moment. I let the seat back and close my eyes for a minute. I don't really want to sleep out here tonight but I also don't want to spend the money for a hotel room, either.

A couple hours later, I wake and shift around in the seat. One thing is certain: I haven't missed sleeping in my car although these seats are a little more comfortable than that piece of junk I had previously.

The time feels later than what it actually is, so I do my best to get situated again. I toss and turn, waking every couple minutes. This broken sleep has really made me irritable. The sun is close to coming up but I feel more tired now than when I first pulled in last night. I'm also chilled, the light jacket I brought along not doing much for keeping me warm. I crank the car and turn on the heater. I figure if I let it warm up, I'll be able to get in another hour or two before surprising my folks.

Tap, tap, tap. The sudden noise startles me and I roll over to see where it's coming from. Just outside my window, my dad stands, wearing a pair of sweats and a robe. It's the very same robe he's had for all these years. Just another sickly reminder of what I left behind.

I pull the seat up and look around. It's daylight out now and I'm sore and stiff.

I roll down the window and greet him. "Dad."

"What the hell are you doing out here? And why would you leave the car running like that?"

It's just as I suspected. His tone is just as harsh and brutal as it's always been. I should just back out now and leave before it gets worse, but I really want see my mom.

"Nice to see you, too," I sneer. "I had a couple days off from work and thought I'd come home for a visit. But judging by your reaction I'm still not welcome."

His gaze scans over my body—the little bit he can see of it inside the car—and stops on my arm that rests along the top of the door. He reaches over to grab hold of my hand, but I snatch it away just in time.

"What's that? You get married? Who'd be stupid enough to marry you?" he spats, noticing the ring on my finger.

I've had just about all I can take of his smart mouth. I don't need to be reminded who the *stupid* one in my relationship is because it damn sure isn't Jennifer, despite my dad's accusations. No matter how angry I am with her, she doesn't deserve to be called names from someone who doesn't even know her.

I look away from him and bite my tongue.

"Well, you got nothing to say?" He's insistent.

I step out of the car, ready to stand eye to eye with him.

"Brian, is that you?" The sound of my mom's voice halts me from doing something I could regret later.

"Mom." I ignore him and walk towards her, my arms already outstretched to pull her close. She holds me tight, and I'm reminded how much I've missed her.

She and I walk inside the house, Dad following behind with a sour expression across his face. He hates more than anything to be ignored.

Mom fixes breakfast and we all sit at the table in silence. It doesn't take long for her to notice my ring, too. I probably should've taken it off, but since Dad had already spotted it, I knew it was only a matter of time until he brought it up.

"Son, what's this? Is there something going on we don't know about?" Mom looks confused, but more than anything, she looks hurt. I feel bad for not being in touch sooner.

I take in a deep breath, careful to say the right words. "Yeah, well, it was kind of sudden. I'm sorry that Jennifer, that's her name, couldn't make it this time, but I promise to bring her next time. She's truly sorry she's not been able to meet you but she's been busy with…she's been…uh, busy with school and couldn't break away from her studies." The lies roll off my tongue, each one building upon the other. Well, it's not like they're really going to know the difference. Jennifer *is* in school, so at least that part is true.

"Oh, honey. I'm sorry, too. Tell me, where are you living now? Where are you working? Are you doing okay?" Mom goes on and on, asking a new question before I can even answer the previous one.

I need to just shut up before I completely screw everything up. I don't want to let it slip that we're in the middle of a huge fight right now.

Mom and Dad get ready for church, and I decide to take a nap while they're gone. When Mom's out of sight and safely in her room, Dad walks over to where I'm lying on the couch.

"Don't touch a damn thing while we're gone. You hear me? You're lucky I'm letting you stay here, *alone.*" His mouth is clenched so tightly, I wonder how the words are able to even leave his mouth.

"Just shut up, you son of a bitch." I don't understand why we can't have a normal conversation without something hurtful being said. It's beyond ridiculous.

Mom walks back in the room minutes later and leans down to kiss me on the cheek. "I'm so glad you're home, son. I'll call your brothers and see if we can all have lunch together after church."

"Sure, Mom. Sounds like a good idea to me." I fake a smile for her sake. I'm not thrilled about her idea of the perfect family get-together, but if it'll make her happy, that's all that matters.

I turn the television on, but I'm sound asleep in no time.

Chapter 37
Jennifer

I TWIST AND TURN TRYING to get comfortable. It's no use. I open my eyes and forget for a moment where I am. I look over to the driver's seat only to find it's empty and the truck is shut off. I get worried that something's happened and I'm not where I'm supposed to be. Then I notice, just outside the truck, Todd and Rebecca are talking. I'm not sure how long we've been here or even how long I've been asleep, but it's now fully dark.

They both turn to look in my direction at the same time. Todd walks over and opens the door, helping me step down since the truck sits so high off the ground. Rebecca immediately pulls me to her for a hug and rests her hand against my back.

"It's all going to be okay," she whispers, and I struggle to remain intact, especially in Todd's presence. "I'm not going to let anything bad happen to you again."

When she finally releases me, I turn to Todd and wipe at my cheeks. "I guess you both have met. I'm sorry I slept so long."

"Don't apologize. You were exhausted," Todd says.

"Todd, what can I do to repay you? Can I get you a room for the night?" I'm forever grateful for everything he's done.

"You don't owe me a thing. I'm just thankful I was able to help."

"Then at least let me give you something for gas, please," I insist and open up my wallet.

"No. Just promise me you'll stay safe." He reaches up to wipe away a single tear that manages to work its way down the side of my face. The moment catches me completely by surprise. His touch is so gentle and so soft.

"I will." Our gazes lock and I feel a warmness in my heart. Yes, there're still good people out there.

"Here, let me help you get your things from the truck." Todd steps up on the side and pulls out my purse and jacket from off the seat. I hate I don't have my overnight bag that I'd packed. It's in Brian's trunk and I wonder if I'll ever see it again. Todd stops for a moment before getting back down and opens up the glove box. I watch as he pulls out a piece of paper and something to write with.

In just a few moments, he hands over a folded slip of paper then places his hand on mine.

"Don't take this the wrong way. It's just my number. I don't expect you to call me or anything, but please, if you get into a situation like this again, you know how to reach me."

"Thank you again, Todd. You've been a blessing to me."

"Well, you know, if you're ever up my way, you could always look me up. Just to say hello," he adds before stepping down.

I casually tuck the folded paper in my back pocket and reach up to give him a hug. The boots he's wearing places him several inches above me.

By now, Rebecca's waiting for me in the car. She waves at him and he throws his hand up her way.

"Goodbye."

I climb inside and watch as his truck pulls away from the parking lot. I may never see him again, but I know he's one special man.

I don't know what to say or where to begin. The first few minutes are very awkward, and I know the silence can't continue much longer.

I decide to break the ice first. "I'm sorry, Rebecca." My voice quivers and I fight back tears. This long ride home may be just the therapy I need. I spend the next few hours pouring my heart and soul out to the one person who's always supported me. After sharing most of the details with her, we both cry and end up holding hands.

"It's all going to be okay," she says. "I'll kill that bastard if he hurts you again."

We arrive back in town shortly before daybreak, and I tell her I don't want to go to my apartment. Right now, I don't want to be alone. I have no idea where Brian is, if he's back in town, or if he continued on to his parents' house. I do know that I'm scared not knowing his whereabouts and that I'll have to deal with him when he decides to show back up again. And he will, eventually. He won't stay gone forever.

So instead of my place, we go to her parents' home and quietly head upstairs to her room. Growing up, I spent many nights here and it's comforting being in familiar surroundings. Her parents are good people and won't question why I'm staying over.

I slip on one of Rebecca's t-shirts and crawl into bed, pulling the covers up as high as I can get them without covering my face. Hiding under them doesn't make the pain go away, but for the moment, I'm able to settle down and fall into a much needed restful sleep. Right now, I need all the rest I can get — for myself and for the baby — because I'm not sure what tomorrow holds.

****

"Did you sleep well?" Rebecca asks when I wake several hours later.

I roll over, the sunlight beaming in through her bedroom window.

"I did. I feel so much better." I sit up and lean back against a stack of pillows. "Are your parents here?"

"They're out for the afternoon. Kind of figured we might need some time alone."

I lower my head, embarrassed her parents know about what happened. My stomach growls, a reminder that it's been awhile since I've eaten. The bowl of grits and toast I had back at the restaurant have long been gone.

As if Rebecca's a mind reader, she asks, "Are you hungry? We could grab a bite to eat."

I'm not much for going anywhere but the idea of ordering in a pizza sounds pretty good. She places our order over the phone while I head downstairs to fix us something to drink. My throat is parched from going so long without anything.

When the pizza arrives, we take it upstairs to her room. She tosses me the remote and we climb up on her bed. There's nothing better than a marathon of *Sex and the City* episodes. We're all set for some much needed girl time.

After a couple hours of laughing and giggling, she turns out the light. Nothing more is said about Brian or returning to my apartment, even though I know I can't stay here forever.

The next morning, I gather up my things and get ready to head home. I feel bad for missing my classes today, but I've got to deal with my current situation first. Rebecca drives me over to my apartment and it's reassuring pulling in and seeing my car, alone in the parking lot. It still doesn't mean Brian won't show up at some point, but for now I can breathe a little easier.

Inside, I carefully look around seeing if anyone's been here. Everything looks just as it did before we left. I gather up a fresh change of clothes and head to the bathroom. I need a hot shower and maybe even a soak in the tub. Rebecca assures me she'll be in the living room and won't leave until I'm completely okay with it. Just seeing Brian's things on the counter sends shivers throughout my body.

Before tossing my clothes over in the hamper, I reach inside the back pocket of my jeans and pull out the slip of paper. I unfold it and stare blankly at the writing.

Todd Williams
555-281-7787

Todd Williams. Such a nice person. I fold it back up and place it in the top drawer of the vanity. Sure enough, when I'm finished with my bath, Rebecca is hanging out in the living room. Even though I'm scared of being left alone, I know she can't stay with me forever.

At this point, I'm not sure where things stand with Brian. We are, after all, still married. Is it too soon to throw everything out the door? Is it worth salvaging what we have left or do I put myself at risk by staying with him? Can he seek help or do we check into marriage counseling? There's just so many questions I don't have the answers to.

Towards the middle of the afternoon, when I've finally relaxed, Rebecca glances at her watch and announces it's time for her to leave for work. I encourage her to go ahead and that I'll be fine, but I'd be lying if I said I was ready to be left alone so soon.

She gives me a hug before walking outside. "If you need me for anything, call me. I can be here in no time. Try to get some more rest and I'll see you later on tonight."

She's right, I need more rest, especially since I'm due in at work later on tonight. I gather up my blanket and curl up on the couch. I don't fall asleep for a while, but with the deadbolt locked, I'm fairly certain no one can get to me. Not even Brian.

****

Rebecca greets me with a smile when I walk into work. "You look well-rested."

"I feel better, thank you. I'm still a little edgy about everything though."

"Still nothing from him, huh?" she inquires.

"Nope, not a word."

"Have you tried calling him?"

"No, not at all. Thank goodness he finally gave up calling me Saturday night. He was supposed to work today, but I have no idea if he showed up or not. With everything going on with his boss getting fired, who's to say he didn't call in."

"If it'll make you feel any better, I'll be glad to hang around tonight with you."

"Rebecca, no, I can't let you do that. I'll be okay. If he shows up and tries to start trouble, I know how to call the cops."

"If you insist. Love you, girl. Take care."

I watch her walk out and I'm left alone. The night passes much too slow and I struggle to find things to help me pass the time. Before leaving home, I remembered to take Todd's phone number out of the bathroom drawer and I stuck it back in my pocket. I was leery leaving it at home, even tucked away in a drawer, for fear Brian might stumble across it should he show back up.

I know it's lame and a bit crazy, but I program the number into my phone. I'm not sure why, but it's comforting knowing he's now only a text or phone call away. I know I'm fidgeting, scrolling through my phone just killing time, but I click back on Todd's number again. The button used to send a text message stares straight at me. I start typing a short, friendly message thanking him again, but then quickly erase it. To be honest, I do this several more times, never having the guts to finish much less send it. I don't know why I feel the need to text him, especially since it's the middle of the night, but he's been on my mind. I still can't get over how generous he was to drive me.

I try it one more time.

Me: Wanted to thank u again for taking me to meet my friend. It was very kind of you.

This time, I don't erase it. Instead, I hit the send button. I immediately put the phone down on the desk, afraid to touch it. I can't believe I just sent Todd a message. *What was I thinking?*

Not wanting to know if he responds back, mostly because I feel it's probably one of the stupidest things I could've done, I toss the phone back in my purse and close the drawer.

Chapter 38
Brian

"IS THAT ALL YOU'VE DONE the whole time we've been gone?"

I hear my dad's dreaded voice, and I sit up on the couch. I rub my eyes, not realizing I've been asleep for so long.

"Dad, can you just cut me some slack for once?" I ask, not really caring to hear his response.

"No, son. I can't." His voice is stern. "I gave you so many chances. What makes you think you deserve another opportunity just so you can screw up again and hurt your mother and me?"

My mom hears our loud voices and runs into the room. I'm sorry she's had to deal with him all these years. The truth is, he'll never change.

"Just fuck you, old man. Fuck you!" I scream, ashamed to be using such language in front of her. "I regret ever coming back here. And to think, I really wanted to see you both."

I pull the keys from my pocket and storm out the front door. My mom tries to run after me, but my dad holds her back. "Let him go. He's a disgrace to this family."

I want to turn around and punch him, but his words burn my soul. I hate knowing this man is my father. I hate it because he's right. I am a disgrace—thanks to him.

I jump in the car and carelessly back out of the driveway, narrowly missing the bumper of his truck. Part of me wants to pull back in and repeatedly crash into it, but it's not worth damaging my own. I turn out of the neighborhood and head for the interstate. *I've spent long enough in this town.* It's time to head back home and make things right with Jennifer. My father's words echo in my mind. Hopefully, it's not too late.

I drive, stopping only for gas and a bathroom break. I don't even bother getting anything to eat. I try to relax, going through different scenarios in my head. For once, something's got to go my way.

I get back in town after ten o'clock. Surprisingly, I'm still very much awake. I pull through the apartment complex and notice Jennifer's car. I wonder if she made it back though. I get out and walk around to the outside of the apartment. Even though the blinds are closed to the patio doors, I can tell the room is dark and there's no one home.

Is it possible she's still back at the interstate somewhere? What if no one came for her?

I think back to the voice I heard on her phone. Was it that guy, the one who got up in my face? Is she with him? I'll kill him if he's with my wife.

I'm not sure what to do or where to go at this point. If I let myself into the apartment and carry on like nothing ever happened, she's bound to show up eventually. She's got work and school—she's got to come back for that.

I sit in my parking spot for a few moments, then decide I better leave. I'm starting to get really sleepy, and here is not the place I need to be found sound asleep in my car. Looks like I'm back to my old ways again.

The next morning, my phone ringing wakes me from a deep sleep. I unplug it from the charger, hoping to see Jennifer's name light up on the screen. Disappointed, it's a number I don't recognize. At first, I don't answer, figuring it must be a wrong number. Then, before the ringing stops, I take the chance and answer it, deciding it could be her using someone else's phone if hers is dead.

"Hello?"

"Yes, may I please speak with Brian Collins?" the person on the other end asks.

Fear suddenly overtakes me. "Speaking." What if something's happened to her?

"This is Charles Sullivan with asset protection. You're scheduled to be at work this morning at nine, but I was wondering if you could possibly be here at eight. There are a few things I'd like to talk to you about."

My body breaks out in a cold sweat despite the cool morning temperature outside. *Shit!* This is about Melissa. I know I'm about to be in trouble.

"Sure, Mr. Sullivan. Give me a few minutes to finish getting ready, and I'll be right on over."

I pull across the street to the gas station and check my trunk for a change of clothes. *So much for showering and cleaning up this morning.* I run my hand over my facial stubble and decide to leave it be. There's simply no time to shave and this isn't exactly the right place to do it, either.

I roll a set of clothes up and tuck them under my arm as I walk inside to the restroom. No one pays any attention to me. I use the handicap stall, once again thankful it has a sink. I brush my teeth and comb my hair before leaving. I roll everything back up inside my dirty clothes and walk back out to my car. My stomach rumbles from hunger, but it's going to have to wait until later. This mess at work comes first.

A quick glance down at my phone shows I have a couple minutes to get there.

I lock my car and take the mall entrance through the back way, since the main doors don't open until later. Everything's quiet, but I tell myself not to worry, it's all going to be okay. What's the worst they could do? I'm pretty sure they'll ask me some questions regarding the deposits since they did have my initials on them, but I'll probably just get verbally reprimanded or at least written up. I'll apologize and promise to be more careful next time. *Yeah, yeah, that's probably all they'll do.* Still, it doesn't stop me from getting nervous.

I walk up to the metal roll-up gate and glance inside. Someone I don't recognize is over at the counter. I know I should've called Rodney back to get the scoop on everything, but I was so wrapped up in my own mess with Jennifer, I never got around to it.

Surely that's not who's replacing Melissa. Wouldn't they at least consider me for it?

I insert my key into the lock, but for some reason, it doesn't work. The guy looks up and walks over.

"Your key's not going to work. The locks were changed a few days ago," he says with no inflection whatsoever.

I should've realized this since most places change locks when there's a change in management. I tell myself there's still no reason to be alarmed.

"Please, go on back to the office."

I do as I'm told and all of a sudden, I'm not getting a good feeling about this. The door to the back office is open but I'm not sure if I should walk in or knock first. My foot brushes against the side of a box that's left in the floor and I stumble, catching myself before I fall. *Klutz!*

An older, silver-haired man hears the noise and steps out of the office.

"Brian?" he asks. "Are you okay?"

"Yes, I'm fine. Just caught the edge there." I stick my hand out to greet him, but he motions for me to enter the room instead.

"Take a seat please."

If I felt uneasy earlier, I'm even more apprehensive now. The vibes I'm getting from this man aren't good.

"Brian, I'm Mr. Sullivan. We spoke on the phone earlier."

I sit up a little straighter in the chair. "Yes, sir." *Could this be about the position? Do I take a chance and let him know I'm interested?*

He clears his throat before he speaks. "Without going into any details, I know you've been made aware of the situation involving your former manager."

"I found out from a text message from another employee. Can you tell me a little more about what happened?" I try to sound professional.

"Actually, Brian, I need to make you aware that you're still under a probationary period with our company. Rather than drag the situation out further than it needs to be, we've decided to replace the entire staff with new employees in order to deter the possibility of this happing again."

"Do what, sir? I'm not sure I heard you correctly." I feel flushed suddenly and I'm sure my face shows just as much.

"Brian, we've already put the new managers in place. We'll no longer be needing you here," he says bluntly.

"There must be some mistake." I feel like I've just been slapped in the face. How can this be? "Sir, I didn't take the money. Melissa did this on her own."

"Brian, I'm going to have to ask you to leave now. Your final check will be mailed to you. If you've had a change of address other than what's on file, I'll need you to update that now. Otherwise, there's nothing more to say concerning the matter."

I stand from the chair, not sure how to react.

"Mr. Collins, I'll see you to the door," the other gentleman who was at the front counter says.

I wasn't even aware he was standing behind me.

He walks out first, and I follow. I stop just outside the office door and glance around. I really liked having my assistant manager position. I thought I was finally headed in the right direction. A burst of anger suddenly fills me, and I kick the box I tripped on earlier.

"God damn box," I mumble under my breath.

I don't stop there. I suddenly start kicking other boxes, even picking up a few smaller ones and tossing them across the room. My actions are just that—completely out of control.

"Mr. Collins." I hear my name called but I don't turn around.

My temper tantrum is at its peak. Aside from the curse words flying off my tongue, I flip over the table that we used to eat at during our breaks.

I'm hurt. I'm angry. I've been made a loser once again.

I run to the front of the store and grab onto the gate, shaking it like a madman. A mall security guard steps from around the corner. As soon as the gate is lifted, he steps up beside me. He doesn't have to say anything—I know he's here to escort me out. Acting like a fool doesn't do any good. Not for me or anyone else.

Out at my car, I lean against it and try to calm down enough to regain my composure. To sum up my morning, I'm jobless, quite possibly homeless, and nearly broke.

On a positive note, I've got a full tank of gas, but running isn't the solution, either. With nothing better to do, I ride around until I feel I've calmed down.

It's nearing lunchtime already and my stomach reminds me I haven't had anything to eat. I know I should be cautious with how much money I spend, since I'm not sure how long it's going to take to get my last paycheck, but I'm craving a beer. It's just the thing I need.

I pull into a sports bar and grill and grab a seat up at the bar. I feel funny ordering a pitcher of beer when I'm the only one in my party, but I don't feel I'll have any trouble getting rid of it. One pitcher and a sandwich and I should be good to go.

For the most part, the restaurant is quiet. The bartender keeps me company and we end up watching a replay of a basketball game from the day before. In addition to the pitcher, he's also slipped me few beers on the side. I'm a sight to see — giving him high-fives and leaping from the bar stool each time a game changing play is made. To say I'm loud is an understatement. Time gets away from me and before long, the shifts are changing out. He brings over my check and asks if I can settle my tab.

I pull my wallet from my pocket, hanging on to the side of the bar for stability. I'm definitely drunk as hell. I slap a couple bills down on the counter and hope it's enough to cover it.

"You good? Need any change?" the bartender asks, and I wave my hand over the tray.

"I'm good." I bring my hand up to cover the burp that escapes my mouth.

"Thanks, man. You going to be okay to leave? I can always call a cab for you."

"Ah, hell. I'm just now feeling *goooood.*" My words are so slurred, it's a wonder he was even able to understand them. I stumble to the door and find my car out in the parking lot. I sit for a moment, noticing other people walk by. *No, I can't do this. I cannot drive out of here.*

I certainly don't want to risk getting pulled over, so I close my eyes, hoping the spinning that's going on in my head subsides. Within seconds, I pass out.

When I come to, its dark out. I have a terrible taste in my mouth, and my tongue feels like it's wrapped in cotton. I desperately need something to drink to get rid of this taste and feeling. What I don't need, though, is another beer. I feel like shit!

Suddenly, I catch a whiff of something that nearly makes me puke. I lift the seat up and it's then I notice where the foul smell is coming from—the wet spot on the front of my jeans.

"Fuck!" I scream, hoping no one is nearby to hear me. I can't believe I pissed my pants while I was passed out. It's almost as bad as throwing up on myself, which I'm thankful didn't happen.

I crank the car and the clock on the dash illuminates after ten o'clock at night. I can't believe I've slept the whole evening. I shift in the seat, suddenly feeling disgusted now that I'm aware of my accident. I've never, in all my drunken days, had this happen before. It's awkward and uncomfortable, to say the least.

Uncertain where I'm going, I decide to pull through the hotel parking lot just to see if Jennifer's at work. Rather than risk being seen, I turn around quickly when I notice her car parked in her usual spot. *So she did make it back after all.*

I am relieved she's at work and hopefully she's okay, but what next. Where do we go from here?

Chapter 39
Jennifer

I PULL MY PHONE FROM my purse for the first time since sending the text message to Todd. Although there's been no reply, I frown, uncertain why it bothers me so much. *Oh well, it was a nice gesture on his part, regardless of if I ever hear from him again or not, and I shouldn't get my hopes up*

Something else that has been weighing heavily on me is school. This semester's been trying for me, and I'm afraid my grades are going to suffer, especially not knowing my future with Brian. I fear this may be just the beginning. After much thought, I emailed my advisor, explaining to her my situation — my pregnancy and my troubled marriage. I'm hoping by this afternoon, I'll have a reply with some words of encouragement as to what plan of action I should take.

By the time I reach the parking lot at my apartment, I'm sweating profusely. Will his car be there or not? I'm filled with relief to see both spots are empty. I'm not sure what I would've done had Brian's car been there.

As I walk inside, though, fear quickly returns. *Son of a bitch!* Just looking around, I sense someone's been here. Sure enough, the lid is up on the toilet and the towel hanging on the rack is damp. Beads of water are still evident on the shower wall.

He knew I'd be at work, and I shudder thinking he probably rode by just to make sure I was there. Just knowing he's back frightens me. I'm thankful he decided not to stick around, but what do I do now? I check the trash in the kitchen and discover an empty bag of chips. The least he could've done was do a better job of covering his tracks. *Or was that his whole point? Did he do it just to get at me?* At this point, I wonder if I should notify maintenance about getting the locks changed. It seems like a big request, considering we're married, but can I afford to take any chances?

My stomach grumbles but there's no way I can eat anything right now. I really shouldn't avoid eating since I'm not the only one who needs nourishment now, but how can I when he upsets me so? I think about how much this baby is going to change my life. I rub my small swell, and I'm saddened knowing I may have to do this alone.

It's just not right. I don't want to be a single parent. I don't want to go through this pregnancy alone. This coming Friday, we're supposed to find out if it's a boy or girl. It's hard for me to believe Brian would jeopardize our relationship now, knowing we're so close to finding out more about our baby.

****

The next few days get easier since I haven't seen any more signs of him. It doesn't mean he's gone forever, but he's not trying to bother me. I do wonder, though, where he's been staying and how work is going for him since his manger was fired. Did he get the promotion he was hoping for?

On Friday morning, I come home from work feeling distraught. I should be enthusiastic and excited knowing today's the day I learn what I'm going to have, but I'm far from it. I ran it by Rebecca, knowing she'd be thrilled to accompany me, but at the last minute, she had something important come up, something that couldn't be changed. I know if I'd pushed it a little more, she could've been persuaded but I decided not to. Now, I'm wishing I had.

I busy myself with little things to do around the apartment, but it only makes the time pass slower, not to mention, it causes crazy thoughts to enter my head. I pick up my phone and stare blankly at it. I pull up Brian's name with the message box beside it. I start typing a message and send it before I have a chance to talk myself out of it. I can't do this alone.

Me: Dr. apt today. Finding out what baby is going to be. Can you leave work?

I'm not sure I can handle seeing the hateful side of him that I had to experience on Saturday, but a part of me is sad for him, sad that he's doing this to himself. He needs some kind of professional help.

Almost immediately, he responds.

Brian: What time?
Me: One.
Brian: I'll be there. Thank you.

It's too late now. I may have gone against my better judgement, but my heart tells me I did the right thing. And the heart doesn't lie, does it?

I manage to eat a light lunch then drive downtown to the clinic. I find a parking spot close by, all the while glancing around for Brian's car. I don't bother to wait on him and go ahead inside. He knows where I'll be if he makes it. If...he hasn't changed his mind. I just pray he's settled down and doesn't cause any more trouble.

I've been in the waiting room for a few minutes when I see the door open. I take in a deep breath and watch as he walks in. He's dressed in jeans and a button-up shirt I'd forgotten all about. Surprisingly, he looks well. His hair's a little unkempt, but that's normal for him. Always in need of a cut.

My gaze locks on his as he takes the chair next to me. I tense up just from his proximity to me. It's the first time we've been in the same room together since the fight.

He finally breaks the silence. "Thanks for letting me come."

I pause for a few seconds before answering. "You're welcome. I know we haven't talked, but I figured you would want to be here."

The nurse calls my name and we both stand to go back to the examination room. I hop onto the table while the nurse explains everything that'll take place today. The exam with the doctor is very brief, and it's a relief to find out the pregnancy is going very well so far. Then we're escorted to another room down the hallway and greeted by the technician who's going to do the ultrasound. It actually hasn't been too difficult pretending Brian and I are here together and for the right reason.

He's very quiet and tuned in to everything the nurse says. I lie back on the table while she preps me with a cool, lubricating jelly. She slides the wand across my belly, and the sound of the baby's heartbeat soon echoes throughout the room. It's absolutely the most beautiful sound I've ever heard.

After a few swipes, she turns towards me and Brian, who is sitting as close as possible to the exam table, and asks, "So, would you like to know what you're having?"

I feel tears of happiness build in my eyes. I look over at him and his eyes, too, glisten with tears. He replies to the nurse before I can get in a word edgewise. "Oh, yes, ma'am."

"Let's see." She applies a little pressure on my abdomen then makes a few clicks to the computer beside her. "Look right here." She points to the screen, and we're able to see a clearer image of the baby.

It's a girl.

Brian grabs my hand and this time, I don't pull it away from his grip. "Baby, we're having a girl. It's a girl."

I see a side of him that makes me think there's...there's...that there's hope for us, after all.

I wipe at the tear that slips down my cheek. Is there a possibility we can make this work? Does he deserve another chance?

We finish with the appointment and leave the clinic with a few black and white snapshots. I can't take my eyes from the pictures of our baby girl. She's beautiful. I'm so overwhelmed with emotion.

I stand outside my car, not sure what more to say to Brian.

He breaks the silence first. "Would you like to grab a coffee?"

"I suppose that would be okay. Do you not have to go back to work?" I question.

"They'll manage fine without me."

I take it to mean his problems at work must be resolved now. I'm thankful he didn't get mixed up with the mess with Melissa.

We each take our own cars down the few blocks to the coffee shop. Brian opens my car door before I have a chance to on my own. He extends his hand to me and I take it. I want to be angry with him, but no matter how much of a wall I try to put up, I can't help but see the old Brian is back.

We grab a table over in the corner away from everyone else. Being in a public place never stopped him from losing control before, but I hope and pray today is different. I shouldn't be afraid to be with my own husband.

"Jennifer, I owe you a huge apology. I don't know what came over me this weekend."

I stare at him intently. "You scared me to death. I've never been yelled or hollered at before. And when you slapped me...I just didn't know what to do."

"I know I was abrupt with you. I was stupid. Can you please forgive me, Jennifer? I want to come home to you and...our daughter." He says those magic words that make me vulnerable—the words I give into every single time.

He pulls my hands from around my coffee cup and holds them in his. I look up and meet his gaze. I so desperately want to believe him. Call me weak or naïve, but I want to forgive him. I want to make this work. I want him to come back home and hold me. I want to feel his arms around me. I simply want him, my husband, to love me—the way a marriage is supposed to be.

"Brian, I..." I try to say something but he stops me.

He traces his fingers over the skin on my arm, and I feel tingles as his fingertips glide from one spot to the next. "Just say you'll give me another chance to prove to you that I can be a better man."

I've never been so torn.

"Can you give me some time to think about it?" I suggest. "Maybe do dinner tomorrow night?"

"Yes. That sounds wonderful, baby."

"Okay." I take a sip of my coffee that's now barely warm. "I'll see you then."

He stands to leave, then leans over and kisses me on the cheek. I reach up and touch the place where his lips caressed my skin. *What have I gotten myself into? Please tell me I'm not making a huge mistake.*

I toss my paper cup in the trash and walk to the car. Before I pull away from the curb, I check my phone and see I've had a text. A horn suddenly blows, another driver alerting me they'd like my spot. I drop the phone and quickly pull away, forgetting all about the missed message.

****

Rebecca's standing at the door waiting for me when I pull up for work.

"Well? Tell me, I'm dying to know. Are we having a boy or girl?" Her enthusiasm takes me by complete surprise.

I can't contain my excitement any longer. "It's a girl!"

"Yes, I'm going to have a niece!" It warms my heart knowing she still feels that connection to me, despite all we've been through. "I'm so happy for you."

"I..." I falter for a moment. "I didn't go to my appointment alone."

Her smile quickly fades. "Jenn, you're a very smart woman. I can't tell you what to do—it's your life and your decisions. I'll support you, either way, but just know I'm worried. I don't want to see you get hurt, physically or mentally, again. If he so much as lays a finger on you, I'll—"

I cut her off. I know she's right, and I'd feel the very same way if I were in her shoes.

We chat for another couple minutes before she leaves for the night. Somehow, I just couldn't muster the courage to tell her about our dinner plans.

While it's fresh in my mind, I jot down my next doctor's appointment on the desk calendar at work. Even though it won't affect my schedule, it's nice to see it written on there. Then, while I'm at it, I pull out my phone. I need to add it to my calendar there as well.

I'd completely forgotten all about the missed text from earlier, so I slide my finger across the screen to view it. Suddenly, the phone slips from my hand and lands on the desk. It's from him. It's from Todd.

Todd: Anytime you need me or just need a friend to listen, I'm here.

A friend. He called himself a friend. I'm overcome with emotion that the person I met not even a week ago thinks of me as a friend.

Although it's late, I decide to reply back.

Me: Thanks. Hope you have a good weekend.

Within minutes, my phone beeps.

Todd: Are you working tonight? You're up late.
Me: Yes. Here 'til seven a.m. Off next two nights, thank goodness.
Todd: Been busy myself. Studying. Had several important tests this week.
Me: How'd u do?
Todd: Not bad. Grades posted next week.
Me: How much more school?
Todd: One more semester after this term. Been going summers. Take state tests at end of year. If I pass, I'll be a licensed pharmacist.
Me: I had no idea. That's wonderful.
Todd: Yeah, follow my father's footsteps with the family practice.
Me: Sounds like a promising future ahead of you.
Todd: Thanks. Want to make my parents proud. Want me to take over one day.

We continue texting for most of the night. No doubt, he's a smart guy. I envy him, more than he knows. All my plans for college were going well, too, until…until Brian came along.

Chapter 40
Brian

THE DAY TICKS BY SLOWLY while I wait until it's time to go see my wife. *Yeah, I'm still having a hard time getting over the idea that I'm married.* It's funny how quickly the time flies when you're busy working, but in my case, now that I'm officially unemployed again, I can't make it speed up for anything in the world.

Around five o'clock, my phone rings.

"I'm awake now if you'd like to come over. That is, if you're still up for dinner tonight."

"Sure, I…I can be there… shortly." I'm careful with how readily available I am. I need to pull it off that I've been busy at work all day.

"Okay, I'll see you soon."

We hang up and I think about everything I need to pick up at the grocery store. Instead of eating out, I figured I surprise her by cooking. It'll be cheaper. I'm down to my last couple bucks until my final check comes in. I worry how I'm going to explain why it's come in the mail, but I'll figure something out between now and then. I could always make up some stupid excuse, like maybe the store is going through a banking change and needed to send them out until the new accounts are set up. Who knows, she may not even question it at all. I hate that I've spent so much of my life making excuses.

At the store, I end up grabbing some meat to make burgers. For the most part, it's inexpensive, plus it'll leave me with just enough money to purchase one of those express packages of fresh cut flowers. They just might be what I need to come back home for good.

When I arrive at the apartment, Jennifer's dressed in an oversized t-shirt and stretch pants. She's barely showing, at least not much from what I can tell, and the larger clothes make it even less obvious. The apartment is neat and organized, as it is the majority of the time. When she spots the flowers I'm holding behind my back, a smile forms across her face.

"Are these for me?" she asks. "They're so pretty."

And cheap! I think to myself. I just hope I remembered to peel off the price tag.

"I thought they might brighten your day." I pass them over to her and kiss her softly on the cheek.

She places them in some water and I take a seat over on the couch. I don't say much, and neither does she as she puts the bag of food away. It's as though we're strangers again, getting to know each other for the first time.

I'd like nothing more than a beer right now to settle my nerves, but I then I remember that I took the last ones with me when I'd stopped in for a shower the other day. I was expecting her to send me a nasty phone call or message when she realized I'd been here, but she never did. Nothing. Makes me wonder if she even knew.

After a few minutes, she joins me on the sofa. We sit at opposite ends and I'm good with that for now.

"Let me know when you're hungry so I can get the grill going," I add, trying to overcome the awkwardness.

"Okay. Maybe we shouldn't wait too late then. I slept most of the day and only had something light this morning."

"So did you sleep well?"

"Uh huh. Thanks for asking."

"And the baby? Everything okay with her?" I notice Jennifer puts her hands around her belly and I slide over next to her. "Mind if I feel?" It's a bold move on my part, but just what we need to break the ice.

"I started thinking about names," she tells me.

"Oh yeah?"

"It's so hard. You know, without seeing her first. I don't want to name her the wrong thing."

I let out a light chuckle. She's right. It would be awkward naming the baby one thing but having her *look* like she should be called something else.

"Well, we've got plenty of time to come up with a few. And even after she's born, we'll have time to decide then."

I like that she's talking about the future.

The rest of the evening actually goes quite well. The burgers were probably some of the best I'd ever made—and thank goodness for that.

"So, what are your plans for the evening?" she asks after I've helped her clean up the kitchen.

"Well, that depends."

"On what?" she questions.

"Well, what would you like them to be?" I step closer and wrap my arms around her. She doesn't pull away and eventually brings her hands up to rest against my back. As I look down into her eyes, I'm so close to kissing her sensuous lips.

I take the plunge, figuring it's now or never. We're married for crying out loud. I shouldn't have to ask for permission to kiss my wife. She welcomes my touch and before long, we're panting, trying to catch our breaths.

I guide us back towards the sofa then lift my shirt over my head. She eases her hands up to my exposed chest and her warm touch is soothing and inviting.

"Please don't make me leave again," I whisper. The coolness of my breath next to her ear sends a wave of chills over her body. I kiss the area just below her neck and push her shirt down so I'm able to do the same to her shoulder. Next, I gently cup her breasts through her top, tenderly massaging them, and she brings her body up close to mine. It's working; I'm getting to her.

I get down on my knees in front of her, and slowly lift her shirt. Her baby bump is so small, but it's there—along with a living, beautiful human being inside her that I helped create. I push down her stretch pants and take in the white, lacy thong she's got on.

Jennifer doesn't wear them often, so here's where I'm a little confused. Did she wear them with the intent of me seeing them?

Without any denial, I lift her shirt the rest of the way off then unfasten her bra. Her swollen breasts spring free and I immediately bring my mouth down to suck on one of her protruding nipples. She's sexy as hell lying here naked. Pregnancy definitely looks good on her.

Using the tip of my finger, I trace the skin around the band of her panties. The delicate lace allows me to slide it easily over, revealing a juicy mound that's calling my name. *Oh, how I've missed this.* Not to mention, she's so damn wet. I glide my fingers back and forth, listening to her soft moans. She brings her hips forward, making it easier to insert my fingers even deeper. I can take no more.

I stand and drop my pants to the floor. My erection is rock hard and desperate to feel the inside of her. She slides over on the couch, making room for me. I'm gentle, but firm with her as I slide my cock inside her with ease. I've been told how much better sex can be, for both parties, when the woman is pregnant, and right now, I believe it's true. It's definitely doing a number for me.

We move back and forth until I can feel her tightening around me. She begins to tremble and grabs ahold of my ass, pushing me deeper inside. Suddenly, I'm thrusting, faster and faster, until we come simultaneously.

"No, please just stay right here," I hear her say when I make an attempt to stand.

"Okay, baby. I'll hold you as long as you want me to."

****

The next morning, I lift myself from behind her on the couch. I'm stiff and can't wait to wipe the dried stickiness from our lovemaking that's splayed across me. I think back to only a few hours ago, and I start to feel that maybe we're going to be okay after all.

The phone rings, and Jennifer stirs. I make my way to the bathroom and listen to her carrying on a conversation with Rebecca. In a few moments, she sticks her head inside the door and asks if I mind her going out for a bit. Seems Rebecca would like to treat her to a pedicure.

"Sure, baby. That's fine with me. You need some pampering." I wonder how long it'll take for her to tell Rebecca I'm back. I'd like to see the expression on her face when she hears the news. The bitch despises me and, I hate to tell her, but the feeling's mutual.

I listen to Jennifer brushing her teeth at the sink, then shut the water off and slide back the shower door. I turn to face her so she can see me naked and fully erect. Honestly, I could do her again if she'd let me, but I don't want to take my chances.

"Are you going to stay here while I'm gone?" she asks.

"If that's okay with you."

And I leave it at that.

****

The next morning, I expect Jennifer to be up bright and early, getting ready for school, but she's still sleeping in. When I question her about it, she explains to me how tired she's been the last few weeks. It concerns me, but she assures me it's normal and goes along with being pregnant.

Then she tells me she contacted her advisor concerning everything that's happened lately. They both feel it's best, with everything going on, that she put her classes on hold. Since she doesn't feel she can give it her all, no doubt, it's the best option for her. It sucks for me, because I was hoping to hang out here at the apartment while she was in school. Instead, I realize I've got to come up with another option, and fast. Here I go again, having to pretend I'm going to work. At least this time I don't have to wear a stupid uniform; I can wear normal clothes. I hate lying to her again, but what other choice do I have?

She kisses me goodbye, and I walk out to my car. *Shit. What the hell am I supposed to do now?*

I drive around town killing time and gas. I drive over to the golf course I discovered awhile back and pull my car into a spot overlooking the lake that's in the middle of the course. I notice people out jogging around the track that surrounds it. It must be nice to afford membership to a golf course like this where you can play as often as you like. Several golf carts drive past, and I wonder what it'd be like to work here, chauffeuring rich men around all day, taking them from one hole to the next. Toting their clubs for them. Popping open a beer for them. Throwing them a towel. I bet there's some good tips to be made.

My mind flashes back to the present. I should definitely check to see if they're hiring. It'd be perfect for me.

I pull out my phone, taking note of the time. I drive back into town and stop at a fast food place. Rather than pull through the drive-thru, I figure going inside to eat will kill some time, plus I'll also be able to take advantage of free refills. I know it's risky being so far away from the mall, but really, who's going to see me here? It's not like too many people know me and will run back to tell Jennifer.

The thought has barely left my mind when I look up and see none other than the bitch herself. Rebecca. She turns around and nearly walks right into me.

"What are you doing here?" she asks. "Shouldn't you be working?"

I'm careful with what I say to her. "I'm, uh, just on a break. Thought I'd grab a quick bite." I try to carry my food to my table but she blocks me.

"Well, isn't that funny. You drove all the way over here just to eat this?" She points down to the tray. "That's a bit crazy, don't you think? You've got the whole food court, yet you come here."

I realize I need to come up with an explanation, quick.

"Yeah, but I needed to pay a bill over this way."

"Speaking of bills, when do you think you'll have your last payment for our arrangement?"

Just when I think I've got the situation under control, she goes and asks me a question like this. *I'm fucked!*

"As soon as I get my final check, I'll be able to settle up with you." *Oh shit. Did I really just let that slip?* I suddenly realize the gravity of what I've just said. Yep, my final check.

She heard the words too, loud and clear. "What do you mean, final check?"

I can't hide the truth forever. Rather than dig my hole deeper, I tell her about losing my job. "I'm already looking for something else," I toss in, hoping to sound optimistic. "So don't worry about it, alright. You're going to get your money."

"Brian, you are kidding me, right? Surely you didn't get fired again." Her words sting like venom from a snake bite, but the smirk on her face is even worse. *This bitch needs to be slapped!* "What does Jennifer think about it? I bet she's not too happy. Fired from two jobs in less than two months."

"I haven't told her yet." I might as well hold nothing back at this point. I'm doomed, for sure.

"You *what*? How could you not tell her! You idiot! You think not telling her is the right thing to do?" Rebecca's raised her voice so loud, other people have started to look at us.

"I've been waiting for the right opportunity."

"Oh, Jesus, Brian. You are an even bigger idiot than what I first thought. I can't believe my best friend still tolerates you." With that, she flips my tray up, causing all my food to land in my lap and on the floor. Then she storms from the restaurant, not looking back at me. I'm a sight to behold.

Just great! Here we go, all over again.

Chapter 41
Jennifer

I'VE ENJOYED A NICE, QUIET afternoon alone today. I was able to take a nap earlier and now I'm rested, refreshed. I even made a trip down to the grocery store to grab something for dinner. Okay, so I took the easy way out and got a frozen lasagna, but hey, they're still pretty darn good. It'd be nice to have a glass of wine to go with it, but alcohol is strictly off-limits for now. I settle for a bottle of the non-alcoholic stuff and hope it tastes okay.

Brian comes home a little earlier than expected, but I figure with the new management, things must be working out pretty well at the shoe store now. He hasn't said much at all about it, though, which seems rather odd. Yet, today, he looks troubled, almost like something's bothering him.

I check on the lasagna and pour us both something to drink. I meet him in the bedroom where he's changing and pass it to him, but not before giving him the warning that there's no alcohol in it.

"How was your day?" I ask as he takes the glass from my hand.

He takes a swallow, avoiding my question by asking one of his own. "Is there some special occasion?"

"Just a quiet evening alone with my husband."

"Well, it sure smells good. How much longer?"

I decide to try again. "Did everything go okay at work today? You haven't mentioned anything about your new manager."

I notice a strange expression come over his face. His eyes become cold and bitter, and I swear, I must have hit a nerve. He's not the same person he was moments ago.

"She called you, didn't she?" He turns to face me, his expression now full of rage.

"What are you talking about?"

All of a sudden, I'm scared. Something's not right. I back up to the corner of the room.

"Rebecca. She just couldn't wait to call you could she?"

I remember this look on his face as the same one he had during our last argument. I'm confused about what's going on. Have I missed something?

"I've not-" I'm unable to finish speaking before he slams the wine glass across the room and into the wall. It shatters, liquid and glass spraying everywhere.

My hands are trembling so badly, I drop my own glass to the floor and lift them to cover my face. My body is filled with panic. I ease towards the doorway, making my way to the kitchen. I want to get out of the apartment, away from this crazy person before it gets any worse, but I'm afraid I can't make it to the door quick enough.

"Brian, you're scaring me," I try to plead with him hoping to bide myself some time. Maybe even talk him down from the rage he's expressing.

"I guess now you know, huh? Your stupid bitch friend didn't waste any time telling you I got fired again, didn't she?"

I hope to God the neighbors above me are home and can hear our screaming down below. God, I hope they call for help.

"I've not talked to her. What are you talking about?" It suddenly comes to me—he's telling on himself. He's confessing something that he's apparently kept hidden.

"I got fired again! That's what! I lost my *fucking job*, again!"

I've never seen someone's face so red before. I'm afraid to say anything to him for fear it may be the wrong thing, sending him even further into his rage. All I can do is stare at him with tears streaming down my face.

Quickly, I decide to take the sympathetic approach instead of the accusatory tone with him. "I'm sorry, Brian. I had no idea."

"Sorry. That's all you can fuckin' say is you're sorry?"

Brian walks right up to my face, and I feel his hot breath on my wet cheeks. I want to leave, run, but I'm trapped. He corners me in the kitchen, and I have no choice but to listen to him. I say a prayer he settles down and comes to terms with himself before someone gets hurt.

This side of him explains why he's had issues with past relationships and with his family. It's no one's fault but his own.

"Can I do anything to help?" I ask with a shaky voice, my words barely above a whisper.

"You can tell your friend to mind her own damn business." He points his finger in my face. "She needs to stay out of our lives! Tell your friend to stay away from us."

"Brian, I swear to you, she didn't say anything." I'm not sure if defending Rebecca, even though she hasn't told me anything on the matter, is the right thing to do. The more her name is mentioned, the worse it makes him.

"Right! You think I believe that? You're fucking friend will do anything to point out my mistakes, and I've had enough of her shit." He reaches for the wine bottle I left out on the counter, and I cringe, thinking he's about to hit me with it. Suddenly, everything happens in slow motion. I drop down to my knees and cover my stomach. With every bit of strength within him, he hurls the bottle towards the kitchen sink.

334 · Amy Stephens

Pieces of broken glass shatter across the room. I turn my head to avoid any of it hitting me, but it's too late. I feel the stinging sensation instantaneously and reach to touch my face. Just below my eye, my fingers coat in my blood that now drips from my wound. I need a towel to keep from making a mess, but I'm too scared to move from my crouched position.

Noticing all the blood, Brian steps towards me. With one hand, I grab a large piece of glass off the floor and aim it at him. "NO! Don't you come near me!" I scream, waving it in the air.

"Babe, you're hurt."

"I said don't come near me, Brian!"

"Let me help you," he pleads as the blood continues to pool in my other hand.

I apply pressure to my cheek, knowing I need to stop the blood from flowing, but I'm not sure if it's doing any good or not. I'm almost too scared to see what it looks like. "Get away from me," I say between clenched teeth.

"Fine, bitch. But you better not tell anyone I did this to you. You hear me? You better keep this to yourself."

His tone changes so quickly again. I wonder if I had allowed him to help me would he have calmed down. Regardless, I just want him gone. I want him out of my life and this time, for good. I can't handle a 'next time.' Next time may be too late.

He starts to back away then turns to me. "You know I love you don't you?"

I simply stare at him, nothing to say. He is totally messed up. How can someone go from being angry and full of violent rage one minute, then telling me he loves me the next? He's toyed with my emotions for the last time.

"Get the hell away from me, Brian!"

He grabs his jacket from the chair and runs out the front door, leaving it wide open. The force he used to snatch it open causes the doorknob to leave a hole in the wall.

The cool breeze coming in only makes me tremble more. I gradually stand up from my spot in the corner, almost afraid to move for fear he's going to run back inside again. I'm glad he's gone, but for how long?

I quickly shut and lock the door. I know I should call Rebecca, but I can't bring myself to do it. This is so…it's so bad. I run my blood-covered hand over my belly just to make sure my baby is okay. That's right, *my* baby. That sorry you-know-what doesn't deserve to have a baby!

I walk to the bathroom and run the water in the sink until it's warm. Using a washcloth, I wipe at the blood, afraid to see what the gash looks like underneath. While the bleeding seems to have stopped, I'm careful not to reopen it. Getting a better look at it, even though it was an awful amount of blood, I think it's more of a surface cut than anything serious. At least that's what I'm thinking. Judging from the amount of blood on my shirt, though, you'd think it was much worse.

I rethink calling Rebecca then grab my phone, holding it tightly in my hand. I can't bring myself to do it—I simply can't. I stare blankly at it, unable to believe Brian did this to me yet again.

My phone lights up alerting an incoming text, but I can't bear to see who it's from. Not again—I can't handle him calling and texting me all night long. I'll…I'll throw my phone away before I deal with that again.

After what seems like forever, I finally click on the message and relief overcomes me. Todd. The message is from Todd.

Todd: Thinking about you earlier. Hope you are okay. Text me tonight if you can chat.

I drop to my knees, overcome with emotion. *Did he sense something was wrong?*

The timer on the oven beeps, and I manage to stand again. I'd completely forgotten all about the food. With wobbly knees, I stumble into the kitchen and almost drop the pan of lasagna as I take it from the stove. I drop it onto the counter, the aroma causing me to suddenly feel sick to my stomach.

I hear a sudden noise and jump. For a moment, I thought it was Brian coming back, but I realize it's only the neighbors above.

I can't keep living this way. What...what...what happens next time? He...he...could kill...me.

With every ounce of energy I have left within me, I go to the hall closet and pull out a small overnight bag. I start grabbing things from my closet and dresser drawers. I know I can't take everything, but I need a few things. Just to get me where I'm going, wherever that may be. I fill a smaller bag with toiletry items and set everything down on the floor, just inside the door. I fumble around in the kitchen, pulling out drawers, grabbing paperwork and a few other things I feel are important, and stuff them in my purse.

Standing at the doorway with my arms loaded down, I look back at my apartment one last time. I used to love this place. I felt safe. I felt happy here. It was my home. Now, I'm not sure what to feel anymore. *Used. Insecure. Stupid. Numb.*

I turn off the light and shut the door behind me, then walk to the car and drop my bags onto the backseat. As I back the car out, I don't turn back to look at my apartment. Just like Brian once did, I drive away into the night, in search of a better place.

Epilogue

I STARE DOWN AT THE gas gauge and breathe a sigh of relief—I'm so thankful I filled up with gas earlier. I can drive for several hours without needing to stop. Once again, I glance in my rearview mirror to see if I'm being followed. While I didn't notice anything out of the ordinary when I left the apartment, I'm terrified that he was watching me, that he's lurking around a corner or trailing several cars behind me. The closer I get to the interstate, the lighter traffic becomes. With more distance between the cars in front and behind me, it should make it easier to spot someone if they're following me.

I merge into the proper lane and catch myself driving slightly faster than a speed I'm truly comfortable with, but I feel every second, every mile, is valuable. The sooner I can get away from him, the better I'll be.

Uncertain the exact time I left, it feels as if I've been driving forever. Just when I start to settle down, I glance in my rearview mirror and notice a car lingering a safe distance behind. I tell myself it's just my imagination, that I'm safe now and no one knows my whereabouts. But the car continues to dawdle, keeping its distance the same. *No, he can't be behind me! I can't let him catch me!*

I drive up behind the truck in front of me and match my speed to his. He's a tad below the speed limit so the car behind me should catch up with us soon. If indeed it is Brian, I can always alert the truck driver I'm in trouble. I can flash my lights or honk my horn, anything to call attention to myself. I double check my phone over in the seat beside me.

The closer the vehicle gets, the tighter I feel my throat closing. I am sweating profusely. I keep telling myself to breathe, one deep breath at a time. The truck suddenly turns on its blinker so I do the same. This truck is my protection.

Not realizing how close we are to exiting, I suddenly slam on breaks to keep from rear ending the truck. My stomach clenches. Then the car behind me slides over to the other lane to avoid us both and I laugh when I notice it looks nothing like Brian's car at all. Kind of hard to mistake a big black SUV for Brian's white sedan.

Instead of getting off at the exit, I remain on the interstate. After driving for two hours, I spot a sign for a rest area up ahead. Some fresh air, as well as a bathroom break, is much needed. There are no other vehicles behind me now so I feel relatively safe pulling off. I park in a well-lit area as close to the restroom facilities as I can, and sit for a few minutes to regain my composure.

Inside, I stare at my reflection in the bathroom mirror and take in the horrific sight. My hair is in matted knots and I dread knowing I've eventually got to get a brush through it. But my face. It's...it's not easy to hide and a bandage will only call more attention to it. I lean forward to get a close-up view. I cleaned it as best I could but I use my fingernail to scrape away the little bit of blood I left behind.

Even though I'm wide awake, I stop at a vending machine for something to drink. Before going back out to my car, I pull my purse strap across my chest and clench it tightly. You never know who's around in the middle of the night. I hate living in fear.

I climb back in my car and press the lock button. I stare out and wonder where it is I think I'm headed. I never really thought about it until now. I just drove the only way I'd ever been before. My ultimate goal was to get away as quickly as possible.

I pick up the phone from the passenger seat and hold it between both hands. I haven't spoken to my parents lately and I can only imagine how they're going to feel when they discover I'm no longer at the apartment. I've left them clueless as to what's been going on in my life. A big mistake on my part, since they've always been so supportive, but this...this is different. I know a sudden phone call to them this late at night wouldn't do any of us any good.

On the other hand, I could call Rebecca, if for no other reason than to let her know I'm okay. But am I okay? At this point, I'm not even sure I know who I am anymore. Or, I could contact the one person I promised I'd call if I ever got into trouble again.

Todd.

I think back to just the other night when were we texting. He assured me if I ever needed anything, anything at all, no matter how big or small, he was only a phone call away. I honestly think Todd's one of those people who would give you the shirt off his back or give you his last dollar. People with his character are few and far between. They're truly a gift from God.

Not sure if it's because of the text from him before leaving the apartment tonight or if it's something else, but I have to wonder why I instinctively chose to take this direction on the interstate, the direction that leads straight to him.

I pull up his text again. Reading his words brings a calmness to my body. Once the screen fades to darkness, I feel the phone slip from my hands. It bumps the side of my leg as it lands on the floor, just between my feet.

I feel a sudden twitch in my belly and I immediately move my hands to cover the area. I feel it once more, only this time a bit more pressure. As the fluttering sensation continues, I realize I'm feeling the baby move for the first time. I can't believe my baby is moving around inside my body. And just as soon as the feelings start, they quickly fade away. I move my hands around, hoping to feel more movement, but everything is calm again. It's as if she was telling me that everything is going to be okay.

I run my hand along the floorboard of the car until I brush my fingers over my phone. I unlock the keypad and read Todd's text once again. Without thinking further, I hit the button and type out a reply.

Me: I need you. I'm in trouble.

In a matter of minutes, my phone rings.

"Hello?" I barely get the word out before I start sobbing uncontrollably.

"Jennifer, talk to me. Are you okay?" Todd's voice is calm, soothing, unlike the harsh bitterness I dealt with from Brian earlier.

In between the sobs, I manage to say a few words. "I…left him…tonight. I can't take this anymore."

"Where are you? I'm coming to get you. Just tell me where to find you."

To Be Continued…

Coming January 2016

Never Look Back

Book two in the Coming Home series

Also from Amy Stephens

Cooper: A Holiday Romance

Available now

Chapter One

KATE NORTH SHUT DOWN HER computer for the afternoon and inhaled deeply. She'd waited all day for five o'clock to arrive. Since the upcoming Monday was a holiday, the thought of having three days off from work excited her. Not that she had any specific plans for her extended time off, but knowing she could turn off her alarm and wake when she wanted was reason enough to be in a good mood. Just three days of pure bliss.

At home there was no one to answer to and no one expecting her to wait on them. Just peace and quiet all weekend long. With the weather already cooling off, she planned to sit out on her back porch in the new swing she'd bought for herself and read a good book. If she was lucky, she might even read a couple. The weather called for blue skies and pleasant temperatures. She couldn't ask for anything better. And if it got a little chilly, she'd just grab a blanket.

Moving back to her hometown of Orange Grove last year had been hard, but, so far, she'd not regretted it. In fact, it'd turned out to be a blessing.

Her father's partner at North Insurance Agency had recently retired, and he was beside himself wondering how he was going to make it on his own. With Kate coming back home again, it worked out perfectly. Her father needed help, and the job opportunity was just what she needed.

Since she'd never done that kind of work before, she'd spent the first few weeks getting acquainted with the day-to-day operations. Her father had been in the insurance profession for as long as she could remember, so she was somewhat familiar with the terminology. She caught on quickly and before long, her father suggested she take some classes and get her license as an agent, too. She was a natural with the clients. Being an insurance agent had never crossed her mind until the situation had presented itself. It'd been just what the agency needed. Since coming on board, the business had already shown a substantial increase and stood to get only better.

Like many little girls, growing up she'd wanted to be a teacher, but that had quickly changed after she'd started college. After a couple classes, she realized education might not be her calling after all. She loved kids, but she just didn't know if she'd have the patience to work with them on a daily basis. She was more the assertive and demanding type — characteristics about herself that might not go so well amongst students. It hadn't taken long before she'd swapped majors from elementary education over to pre-law.

It was then that she'd met Lance. They were both in their second semester of their sophomore years, and she'd fallen head over heels in love with him after they'd debated a controversial subject in one of their classes. She was so smitten. Of course she hadn't won, but he was outspoken, and she liked that about him.

Kate's roommate had invited her to attend a party several weeks later and, low and behold, guess who else was there? None other than Lance himself. They'd paired off and before the night was over, she'd managed to line up a date with him the following weekend. One date led to several more, and before long, she found herself staying over at his off-campus apartment more than her dorm room. They became inseparable for the next two years.

Upon graduation, they'd both been at a crossroads with their future. Lance still had more schooling, but she was at a loss with what she wanted to do as far as starting her career or continuing on with law school. He'd taken her by complete surprise when he'd proposed, and even more so when he'd suggested they make Manhattan their new home. After all, he'd been born and raised there and knew his way around with ease. It also helped that his father was ready to put him to work in the family's law firm.

He suggested she look for a job as a paralegal in one of New York's many fine law firms just to see if it was indeed what she wanted to do. She could always go back to school later on. Kate, though, was an emotional wreck. It was almost too much to process in such a short period of time. She was so unlike her normal self.

Looking back, she should've seen the warning signs. Their relationship had been too perfect. She should've known it was too good to be true.

The wedding was small and had consisted of a few close friends and family members. The honeymoon, on the other hand, was extravagant. Lance had given her a girl's dream honeymoon—a week-long trip overseas to Paris. She had been in heaven.

She'd briefly come back to Orange Grove, long enough to pack all the things she needed for the Big Apple. It was only normal she broke down before leaving out, giving her parents a teary goodbye before starting the new journey in her life. It had been hard enough leaving them when she went away to college, but now she would begin the next phase of her life.

She was uncertain being in a new city, a huge one nonetheless, and not knowing a single person. She'd always made friends easily, but she was thankful she had Lance to help her navigate her way around. He was only a phone call away.

Manhattan was nothing like her small hometown, but she did her best to adjust, all for the sake of her husband. Slowly, she began to like it, especially when he'd treat her to shopping sprees at some of the finest stores she'd ever had the pleasure of visiting. Clothes and shoes were—without a doubt—the way to a woman's heart.

Lance's family seemed to have an endless supply of money, and it hadn't taken long for her to realize that money *could* buy her happiness. His mother always made sure she was pampered in the most luxurious of ways, too, with trips to the spa and salon.

The job search, on the other hand, wasn't as easy as Lance had made it out to be. She was merely an unknown with no connections among some of the most elite candidates. She was a little disappointed Lance's family hadn't done more to help her get her foot in the door. She hated staying at home so much and felt she needed to contribute more to their household. Her husband didn't seem to mind though.

She tossed around the idea of returning to graduate school just to fill the empty void in her life, but she talked herself out of it. The thought of venturing into the city alone still frightened her.

It was only natural she befriended his secretary since she spent more time on the phone with her than she did her actual husband. She knew his hard work would pay off later on, but as it turned out, she got more than what she bargained for.

She'd never forget that cold, winter day.

Apparently, Lance had forgotten all about their lunch date. Although she thought it strange that his secretary wasn't at her desk when she arrived, she'd brushed it off and walked right on into his office. Never again would she barge into a room without knocking first. Ever.

She couldn't believe what she stumbled upon. With his pants down around his ankles, he was steadily pounding his secretary on top of his desk. She had her skirt hiked up around her waist while she belted out fake panting noises with each thrust. Kate stood there staring at them with her mouth hanging open. The worse part of it all was this woman, she'd...she'd considered her a friend. The only friend she'd made thus far. They'd gone shopping together, and she'd had her over to their apartment. She'd never once suspected a thing. She'd attributed his late nights at the office to his excessive workload. Now, she knew differently.

But it didn't end there. When she'd filed for divorce, he had the nerve to actually blame her, saying she just wasn't able to satisfy him in the bedroom. Funny how he seemed to enjoy the previous three years they'd spent together. Up until he'd been caught red-handed!

It wasn't uncommon for them to have sex four to five times a week. She even recalled a time not long ago that Lance demanded it on a daily basis—morning and at night. Even though they were still newlyweds, it wasn't worth bringing up their sex life to her attorney. She just wanted out of the relationship. She wanted it over. Yes, she'd made a terrible mistake in going there, and she couldn't wait to leave. How could a marriage go from being fairy-tale perfect one day to a horrific nightmare the next?

Kate immediately changed, and her heart had turned cold towards all men. Just like the old saying, it'd be a cold day in hell before she ever decided to give her heart away to another man. How dare he blame her for the failed marriage! Once the divorce was finalized, she'd ended up with a nice settlement. He'd needed to save his reputation as well as his family's, and yes, money talked.

Because she'd not wanted to move back in with her parents upon returning to Orange Grove, she temporarily got a one-bedroom furnished apartment. Just before her six-month lease was up for renewal, Kate decided to look into buying a place of her own. She knew coming back here was where she belonged.

She wasn't ready to be an actual homeowner yet, since it was just her, but the new townhomes being built just down from the insurance agency caught her attention. She knew the moment she walked in to tour the model unit, the split-level two-bedroom was perfect for her.

She even worked out a deal with the builder to refer new clients to the agency. It was a win for them both—she'd quote potential buyers a great rate, and he'd complete the sale. She moved into the first completed unit early that spring and watched her little neighborhood slowly develop all around her. Her settlement money had also come in handy for furnishing her new place.

All the yards were small, but it was ideal for her. Wooden privacy fences surrounded each lot giving her just enough room out back for her swing and several small flower gardens. During the hot summer months, she'd even gotten the courage to sunbathe out back. And since the homes on both sides of hers were still vacant, it hadn't bothered her to be out back lounging in her bikini. She missed her old self, the person she'd been prior to Lance. Her best friend, Dana, had joined her a few times, too.

She was thankful to reconnect with someone who knew her inside and out. Dana was sad to hear that Kate's marriage had turned sour, especially since she was planning one of her own. She'd even held off asking Kate to be her maid of honor until the last minute just because she knew the way Kate felt about the whole marriage thing. It was a sore subject, but she was relieved when she'd accepted.

Kate had even surprised her by planning a bachelorette party. It was only going to be a couple of their girlfriends from high school, but she wanted the night to be special. There were still a few more things to take care of, but in a few weeks, the ladies were going to have one kick-ass party.

Kate locked the office door behind her and walked out to her car. It was still early for a Friday night, but her comfy PJ's were calling her name. She'd done her grocery shopping the first part of the week, so she wasn't going to have to bother with getting dressed the entire weekend. Nope. Her pantry was fully stocked and there was no way she was going to let anyone talk her into leaving the house. She was going to stay cooped up inside, and she dared anyone to disturb her.

About the Author

Amy Stephens is a new adult/contemporary romance author. Originally from Greenville, Alabama, she now lives in Robertsdale, Alabama, just minutes from the beautiful Alabama Gulf Coast beaches, with her husband and son. She is a graduate of Troy University with a Master's in Human Resource Management. She works in retail management full-time during the day and pursues her passion for writing in her down time.

When she's not working or writing, you will find her reading, watching her favorite football team, the Auburn Tigers, her favorite baseball team, the Atlanta Braves, or watching NASCAR. She enjoys spending time with her family and friends.

She is the author of the Falcon Club series: Falling for Him (book one) and Falling for Her (book two). Both books are available now. Don't miss her first series, Coming Home, re-releasing later this year. Don't Turn Back (book one, available November 2015), Never Look Back (book two, coming soon), and Heart of the Matter (book three, coming soon). The Ride Home for Christmas (2014) is her first holiday romance story. A new stand-a-lone holiday novella, Cooper: A Holiday Romance will release November 2015.

For more information, please visit:

www.facebook.com/amystephensauthor

http://www.goodreads.com/amystephens

amystephensauthor@gmail.com

63539010R00211

Made in the USA
Lexington, KY
10 May 2017